Will handled the engine controls without ⎵ ⎵ ⎵
supply to prevent a rich cut as the engine revs rose. He sat back and reveled in this new machine, "Oh what a beauty!" he stroked the side of the cockpit. She was everything he hoped, and more. The controls felt alive, positive, but at the same time responded to the lightest pressure of hand or foot. The little airplane seemed to fly itself, eager to please, a true pilot's machine. He glanced over the side of his cockpit and gasped. He checked the altimeter, perhaps the gloom of the earth still shrouded by night made it look further away. No, he really was passing four thousand feet, in just a few minutes. This was an incredible performance. The little Sopwith Pup boasted a mere 80 hp, yet it climbed faster than many machines with twice the power.

As he climbed, he flew into the morning. The sun appeared above the horizon ahead, turning the tops of the clouds that still obscured much of the ground into soft shades of purple and cream. Leaning back, he could see the vast dome of the sky fading from a deep blue where a few stars still glinted, through pale lemon to an exquisite pink where the sun caressed the icy cirrus clouds flirting with the stratosphere. The light also sparkled off the sight of the Vickers heavy machine gun mounted in front of his face. It brought him back to reality. He had a job to do.

He checked the altimeter again. The Pup had whisked him to nine thousand feet in minutes. The Zeppelin must be ahead, he trusted McGuigan's judgment. Surely it must be some navigation error that would have been revealed by the daylight. They must have turned back to sea by now, but he could catch them with this little thoroughbred, even if it did mean flying out over the water. He pulled up his coat collar. The air at this height chilled despite the bright sunlight. He glanced down; Maldon lay below to his right, still in darkness. He could see for miles over the sea, the clouds only clung to the land. He quartered the sky, raising his gloved hand to peer between the fingers against the glare of the rising sun. Nothing.

He made a wide circle over the town, not even thinking about flying, the Pup seemingly responding to his thoughts. He made quick calculations. If the Zep had turned away to sea again a minute after passing over their watching station, it would still be only fifteen miles away. He should be able to see it, but it simply was not out there. It could only be over the land: but why? He frowned behind his goggles. It would be suicidal to be over land, in broad daylight. It made no sense, but many things in this war made no sense. He turned away from the sea and turned south. He would search inland. Five minutes later, he turned west, held that course for another ten minutes, and then turned northeast, still holding his altitude. His head swiveled all around and up into the sky. He rolled the Pup from side to side and nudged the nose to and fro to search the blind spots. Still no sign. Could McGuigan have been mistaken? Will shook his head angrily. It was a ridiculous notion, it was impossible that a trained man, and one of their best, could mistake a Zeppelin for anything else. No, it was here, lurking in the shadows. He reached the end of his beat, and stuck his head over the side to pick up a landmark as he rolled into a climbing turn to the right. He looked down and back through a break in the clouds for a significant feature: a road, a river, a familiar wood. Instead, he saw the stern of a Zeppelin still exposed as it slipped into the clouds, like the tail of a fish sliding into the reeds.

Turner's Defense

Chris Davey

To Andy
Happy Readings!
Chris Davey

LUCKY PRESS, LLC
ATHENS, OHIO

Published by:
Lucky Press, LLC
PO Box 754
Athens, OH 45701

SAN: 850-9697

Online at www.luckypress.com
Author's website: www.turnerlogs.com

ISBN-13: 978-0-9713318-8-4
ISBN-10: 0-9713318-8-X
LCCN: 2007021022

Book Design and illustrations within: Janice Phelps Williams
Cover painting: Robin Smith

Printed and bound in Great Britain by
CPI Antony Rowe, Chippenham and Eastbourne

Library of Congress Cataloging-in-Publication Data

Davey, Chris, 1952-
  Turner's defense / Chris Davey.
    p. cm.
  ISBN-13: 978-0-9713318-8-4 (trade pbk. : alk. paper)
  ISBN-10: 0-9713318-8-X (trade pbk. : alk. paper)
  1. Air pilots--Great Britain--Fiction. 2. Airships--Germany--
Fiction. 3. World War, 1914-1918--Military intelligence--Great
Britain--Fiction. 4. Espionage, British--Germany--Fiction. I. Title.
  PR6104.A84T86 2007
  823'.92--dc22

                                    2007021022

AUTHOR'S NOTE

Although many of the incidents in this story set during the Zeppelin campaign against England during the First World War are based on events drawn from contemporary reports and well researched histories of the period, this book is a work of fiction. Most of the people met are fictitious, though the places they visit are in the main real. My intention has been to create a fictional whole that gives the reader a perspective of how it might have been to live, fly and fight in this unique period of history.

CHAPTER 1

Essex, March 1916

P.C.122, Mick Horne, coasted to a stop and leaned his bicycle against the wall of the station booking office. He lifted his tall police helmet and mopped his brow with a blue spotted handkerchief. The effort as he pedaled up the gentle hill from the center of Chipping Ongar, to the railroad station entrance had raised beads of sweat on his broad forehead despite the chill night air. A big man with a round, friendly face, framed by a red beard now flecked with gray, Mick projected an easy confidence. He was a policeman old ladies waylaid for a chat, and thieves avoided if they could: the very model of an English constable.

He turned toward a wooden hut that sagged against the wall separating the passenger platform from the loading dock, where milk churns stood lined up for the early morning train to London; as he walked the few paces, he looked up. He was still staring at the sky when a thick china mug was thrust into his hand.

"Prithee, good constable, what evil sprite yonder comes?" The frown on the policeman's face dissolved into a broad grin as he turned to the night watchman who had stepped from inside the hut holding two mugs of steaming tea.

"Bloody Kaiser's men and their gasbags. Can't you hear them, Tom?" Mick asked.

The old man cupped his ear with his free hand. "Oh aye, I might be blind as a bat but there's nowt wrong with me ears." A deep, throbbing drone faded and swelled, audible above the cold breeze that snapped through new leaves and stung their faces. Tom peered into the sky through thick spectacles. A library of classics read by the poor light in his hut had left him with bad eyesight and a pretentious vocabulary.

Above them a full moon slipped through thin drifts of cloud. Two nights before, high over the town of Epping, Mick Horne had seen his first Zeppelin, held in the searchlights massed in the northeastern suburbs of London. The hair on the back of his neck had stood up as he watched it, eerily beautiful, a silver cigar shape hovering far overhead. Tonight, he saw nothing.

Over two miles above, and ten miles down the railroad line toward London, Captain William Turner, MC, had resigned himself to the fact that he would also see nothing. He shone a weak, red-shaded flashlight at the oil pressure gauge on the instrument board of his B.E.2 biplane. It only needed a glance to see that his engine had steady lubrication; he had no need to burn his night vision away gazing at flight instruments telling him what he already knew. His sensitive hands and feet on the stick and rudder bar told him the big biplane wallowed along holding the altitude gained in the last hour of his patrol. Height and speed had whipped the same cold wind that chilled the constable and night watchman on the ground below into a slashing slipstream that swirled around the windscreen of the open cockpit, plucking and tugging at his scarf and driving icy fingers into the exposed skin of his face.

Will eased the stick to the left, adding a touch to the rudder bar to balance the turn as he felt the machine slide under him like a car on ice. He moved automatically, unthinking, the airplane as much a part of him as if the wings grew from his shoulders. He peered over the side of his cockpit and then forward between the double wings. The moon spilled cold mercury on the cloud below, light enough to outline a ghostly horizon. It felt unreal, as if he were flying through one of his own dreams. Will shook his head, took his feet off the rudder bar, and stamped them against the floor of the cockpit until he felt pins and needles.

"Pull yourself together, William," he spoke out loud but only heard his voice inside his head. Looking down he could see the lights of London through gaps in the cloud. "Blackout my ass." Will wondered what people were doing far below that needed that much light at two in the morning.

At eighty miles an hour he held his course for one last sweep toward the city. He crouched behind the windscreen. Shielded from the worst of the slipstream he had no sense of speed. The engine roared but he felt rather than heard it, the vibration buzzing through the controls and the framework that supported him. The stink of hot oil and exhaust fumes sometimes caught in his nose and mouth, but it seemed to him that he floated, suspended over the city. At last the familiar horseshoe shape of the River Thames, as it curled around the Isle of Dogs, appeared from under his right wing: an ink black swirl in the surrounding pattern of scattered light. He wheeled into a turn, then straightened on course for his home field at Abbots Roding; just twenty-five miles from London, but a different world in the heart of the Essex countryside.

Will tugged the collar of his leather coat higher and squirmed down in his seat, searching for a more comfortable position as he coasted out over the fields and woods of Essex leaving the suburbs of the city behind. Two hours on patrol had numbed his backside. The wicker seat gave slightly and he groped with clumsy, gloved fingers to rearrange the cushion. Another false alarm, he thought. Two hours spent chasing shadows with an obsolete biplane masquerading as a night fighting machine. Two hours peering at the pale fingers of searchlights groping for the elusive German airships that had plagued England from the beginning of the war twenty months before. The "Zeps," as people called them, roamed almost with impunity above towns and cities, scattering bombs that killed, wounded, wrecked homes and spread fear and alarm.

He took deep breaths, trying to make up for the lack of oxygen. "Where are you, you miserable bastards?" he bellowed into the slipstream. He felt foolish but more alert; enough to realize that the moisture splattering against the windscreen did not come from his engine. A strong, evocative smell flooded the thin air around him. Will glanced up, uncomprehending for a moment as he watched the stars that pricked the black night wink out as if a cloud had slipped above him, cutting off his view of the sky. "Oh, bugger!" he swore. Even as he reached for the trigger on the Lewis machine gun fixed to fire over his top wing, a light exploded in his eyes.

Far below, the policeman pointed into the sky. "Did you see that? Over there toward London?" Mick asked.

Tom wiped the lens on his spectacles and stared up again, hoping to catch the spark they had seen. "Even with these old peepers, that looked like a light."

Mick pulled out his notebook, licked the end of his pencil and carefully wrote down the time. "Probably a signal from one of our boys in his airyplane, but no harm in noting it down. Now is there anymore tea in that pot?"

※ ⇥━━⇤ ※

The icy wind pouring into Will Turner's slack-jawed mouth, freezing his teeth, and jabbing an exposed nerve jerked him back to jumbled consciousness. He opened his eyes, but what he saw made no sense. Lights spun around his head. The wind swished through the wires and he could hear the airframe creaking, but the reassuring roar of the engine no longer pressed on his ears.

"Where am I?" He heard his own voice but no reply. Somebody seemed to be shaking him, his body flopping from side-to-side and back and forth. The movement roused him further. There was nobody in the airplane with him—no observer to answer him. So who had hold of him? The seatbelt hurt where it cut into his thigh.

"Good old airplane," he spoke aloud again. "What are you doing?" He grabbed the stick and scrabbled with his feet for the rudder bar. The controls flopped and jerked. He could make no sense of his situation, but experience and instinct saved him.

"Christ Almighty, a spin!" He reacted without thinking. He thrust the stick forward and peered ahead. He could barely see. Something covered his goggles. He tore them off. He tensed. The impact with the ground could come at any instant. He could be at ten thousand feet. He might be at ten. Hard opposite rudder would yank him straight, but trying to judge the direction of the spin in the dark: confused, concussed . . . impossible.

He pushed the rudder to the neutral position and prayed the elevators had forced the nose down enough to gain airspeed. He felt the controls come alive; heard the pitch of the wind in the wires rise to a howl. At last he saw something to give him his bearings. Railroad tracks lined up exactly on the nose, reflecting the thin light, framed between the wings, directly below. Not far enough below.

"Come on, sweetheart!" Will shut his eyes and hauled the stick back. The force of gravity smashed down on him like a giant's fist as the biplane screamed out of the dive, pushing his head into his chest, dragging his cheeks down, making his arms feel like lead. From the corner of his eye he saw treetops flashing past on his own level. The clamor of the engine bursting back into life made his heart leap.

The pressure on his body eased. He peered over the side of the cockpit and moved the stick forward. "Oh good God!" He slumped back in his seat. He had clawed his way to a safe height but realized that the only thing that had saved him from becoming a crumpled and charred lump of grisly wreckage, amongst the charred wreckage of the B.E.2., was a railroad cutting into which the big biplane had dipped at the bottom of the dive, giving him an extra fifty feet of space.

Will forced himself upright in his seat. He had to find the field. He had no idea why the engine had stopped or why it had started again. His machine might be fatally damaged, and he could not see out of his right eye.

His compass spun, upset by the gyrations of the spin, but the railroad track that had saved him once might save him again. He banked to follow the metallic thread; twisting in his seat he could see the scattered lights of London fading behind. The track had to be the branch of the Great Eastern Railway Company that served the people of Chipping Ongar and North Weald as their link to London, and the airmen of Abbots Roding as a solid, immovable signpost.

The confusion he felt a minute before gave way to a dull pain that now throbbed above his eye. He raised his hand to his face and probed gingerly. His vision cleared. He touched his tongue to his gloved finger and tasted blood.

The railroad terminated at Chipping Ongar station. He banked again to line up precisely on the track. When the silver thread disappeared, he eased the stick over and rolled into a left turn.

"One el–e–phant, two el–e–phant . . ." he counted off five seconds, thirty degrees around the compass at that rate of turn. He straightened the machine with a firm push on the controls and chopped the throttle, feeling a dropping sensation in the pit of his stomach as the airplane sank toward the ground. Gliding at exactly sixty miles an hour for a minute would bring him over a river, a broad ribbon reflecting the moonlight. The landmark appeared and he sighed with relief. Altitude? Too high. Will booted the rudder hard to the right and thrust the stick forward and to the left. He braced himself against the cockpit edge feeling a blast of air against his cheek as the airplane tipped up on one wing in a fierce slip. It dropped, with one wing pointing at the ground and the nose slewed sideways, giving him an unobstructed view of his landing point. He frowned as a line of flickering lights sprang from the surrounding darkness.

Arranged in an "L" with the short arm across the direction of the wind all he had to do was touch down following the long arm, but the lights marched across his line of flight at an angle. "Damnation!" He heaved his airplane out of the slip even as the lights flickered.

A mile away at the station Mick and Tom turned and looked at each other. The sudden roar of the biplane overhead had brought them from the hut to peer into the sky. They had seen the dim shape swoop past like a giant deformed bat against the luminous night sky, and they had listened to the diminishing roar of the engine until it stopped. A few seconds later they heard a low rumble. "That didn't sound too healthy, Tom."

The night watchman glanced up at the sky, "I'd like to say that was thunder, but 't wasn't."

The policeman frowned, "You're right. I think I'll take a ride by the flying field on my way home." He pitched the dregs in his mug into the bush. "Thanks for the tea." He mounted his bike and pedaled away with a wave of his hand.

"Godspeed, good steed," Tom called after him. "See you tomorrow."

CHAPTER 2

Home Defense Experimental Unit, Abbots Roding, England

"Oh bugger! Oh sod it! Oh sodding buggery!" Will unbuckled his safety belt and stood up on his seat. A wave of nausea swept over him, making him sit down on the edge of the cockpit. He dragged off his leather helmet and touched his forehead. "And bloody ouch!" he said to nobody in particular as his fingers found the oozing cut above his right eye.

"Now, now," a voice called from the darkness, "hardly language becoming an officer and a gentleman." A shadowy figure wobbled toward him on a bicycle. The cyclist dismounted and leaned his bike against the wing.

"Good evening, Boss. I did not expect to find you here." Will spoke slowly: not because he was dazed. He always sounded as if he used every word with care, and even after nearly two years in England, since his arrival from his home in the American South, he still pronounced "here" as if it had two syllables—he•ya—and his habit of pronouncing every word in full instead of contractions—*didn't, wouldn't* or *you'll*—gave his speech a rare clarity.

Major Ernie Simpson unclipped the light from his handlebars and shone it at Will. "I could say the same about you. What the hell have you done to your head?" He pointed the bicycle light upward. "And why isn't your gun loaded?"

Will took the light from him, as much to get it out of his eyes as to use it; he pointed it at the machine gun on its mounting. "Well, I be damned! So that is what hit me." The circular ammunition drum that clipped to the mechanism of the Lewis machine gun had disappeared. Simpson helped him down. Will leaned against the fuselage of the biplane. "My word, solid ground under my feet feels very good at this moment."

Simpson took the bicycle light back from him and examined the wound on his forehead. "Christ, Will, there's a cut the shape of the narrow edge of a Lewis drum on your noggin. I've never seen that before. We'd better have that looked at." People who came into contact with Major Ernie Simpson used many words to describe him: immaculate, little, efficient, devious . . . and often bastard. Some people used them in combination: "devious little bastard," seemed most popular. Despite the difference in their age and rank, Will counted him a close friend. Simpson took a canteen from the saddlebag on his bike and soaked his handkerchief. "Here, put that on your head. You know, the Lewis manual lists about a hundred ways for it to cock itself up; you just found another. Besides, losing an ammunition drum overboard is not a court martial offense, it's a ten-bob replacement fine. I'll put it on your slate."

"Gee thanks, sir." Will smiled despite the pain lancing through his head.

A Crossley tender, its headlights dimmed, clattered to a stop. A crowd of men piled out of the pick-up style wooden-sided body and swarmed around the stranded airplane. Their flashlights probed everywhere as they examined the damage.

"Strewth! Skip," a cheery voice flavored with a salty Australian tang, called out from under the wing. "I knew your landing had gone straight down the gurgler when I heard you hit the tree."

Will squatted down and peered under the wing where Lieutenant Jackson admired the buckled rim and shattered spokes of the wrecked wheel. "That surely is damned astute of you, Jacko."

Jackson grinned back at him. "Anytime you need some advice about your flying, sport, I'm your man." Will laughed. Jackson had just completed his pilot training and had a grand total of forty hours in the air to his credit. "That was a beaut! Who would have believed one aeroplane could make that much noise."

"Well, I will let on that if you fly through the top of a tree, you can expect a little disturbance."

"Bloody hell, sir!" An excited voice called from above. They could see a pair of boots standing on the decking in front of the cockpit but the top wing masked the body of their owner.

"What's up, Bowen?" Simpson called.

"Bullet holes, sir, in a line across the top wing." The rest of Corporal Bowen appeared in the pool of light from half a dozen flashlights as he turned away from the wing and examined the rest of the fuselage. "And there's more behind the seat." The beam from his light picked Will out in the group of men clustered beside the machine. "Blimey, Mister Turner, by all rights you should have copped it."

"Well, Corporal, I regret I cannot oblige, but as you can see, there are no perforations in my hide." Will held his leather coat away from his sides.

"Come on, come on! Stop fannying about and get this aeroplane ready to move. Mr. Lipman's still up, and we don't want him piling into Mr. Turner's aeroplane—or what's left of it—do we?" The man who spoke barely raised his voice, but his words galvanized the mechanics. They raced to act on his instructions. "Cut two-be-fours to brace up and wedge that undercarriage leg. I want that wheel off and the spare on in two minutes." He turned and pointed to the excited group of junior officers now poking fingers in the holes evident in the wings and fuselage. "And you, young gentlemen, hoik that wing up in the air so we can get a couple of horses* under the main spar. Come on, get your backs into it, if you would be so good!"

"Yes, Sergeant Major!" they chorused.

Simpson took Will by the elbow and led him away from the group. They watched as the commissioned officers crouched under the wing and adjusted their positions until the straight-backed NCO facing them indicated he was satisfied. He took his cane from under his arm and raised it like a conductor's baton, and with a hint of a smile, gave the order. "All together now, gentlemen, on a count of three. One—two—three, heave!"

With a creak of protesting timber the airplane lurched back level. Two mechanics jostled a padded sawhorse into place under the wing, and the lifting team pitched forward with a grateful groan onto the damp grass as the weight lifted from their backs. "Thank you, gentlemen. My blokes can take it from here."

Will turned to Simpson, "I see Technical Sergeant Major Cole has our young gentlemen whipped into shape already."

"Team spirit, laddie," Simpson replied. "All for one and one for all—and all that tommyrot. Are you feeling fit enough to walk back to the mess?"

"Oh yes, sir. I need to get the circulation going again."

Simpson raised his voice over the sound of sawing and hammering as temporary undercarriage legs were fashioned and driven into place. "Sergeant-Major, do you need anymore help?"

Cole faced him and whipped up a salute. "Thank you, sir, but begging your pardon, we can move faster with—"

"Without unskilled people getting under foot," Simpson said.

"Er yes, sir. We can put the tail up on the tender and pull Mr. Turner's machine back to the hangar for repairs, if you gentlemen don't mind the walk."

---

*horses = sawhorses

Simpson eyed the young officers now staggering to their feet. "It'll do them some good." He glared at his pilots. "Come on! Let these men get on with their work." He retrieved his bike, swung a leg over the saddle and pedaled into the night.

"So what happened?" Lieutenant Bill Ives demanded as Will led them toward dim lights showing on the far side of the field.

They walked on for a moment, the silence only broken by the swish of Will's sheepskin boots in the grass as they waited for his answer.

"When? Where?"

"Up there!" they chorused.

Will took the handkerchief away from his forehead, folded it and pressed it back against the gash. "I found a Zeppelin." In the light from the kerosene flares marking the landing run he saw the look of astonishment on their faces.

"How?" Jackson demanded.

"I sniffed it out," Will said.

"Oh come on, Skip, stop arsing about, what really happened?"

"I told you. I smelled it and followed my nose." They had reached the newly erected Nissen huts at the edge of the field. Will opened the door of the orderly office and winced in the sudden light. He stood on the step and turned back to his young comrades. "And just like Bill's dog chasing motorcycles, when I caught it I did not know what to do with it."

They stood in a semi-circle, hanging on his words. He smiled, "Now it is too late at night, I am tired, my head hurts, and you children should be in bed. I will talk to you in the morning."

"Oh come on, old chum, that's not fair," protested Lieutenant Johnny Gale, a tall, gangling young pilot, prematurely balding with a prominent Adam's apple that jumped when he spoke.

Will held up his finger. "To bed, you scallywags, there is nothing more to be done tonight." He stepped through the door and closed it behind him leaving his grumbling friends to disperse to their huts.

Sergeant Moore looked up from his desk as Will strode in. "Blimey, sir! What happened to you?"

"I have been scrapping with the Kaiser's Zeppelin fleet."

"Very commendable, Mister Turner." Moore turned to the first aid box screwed to the wall behind him. "May I suggest we don't try head butting them in future?"

❦ ⊹⊶⊷⊹ ❦

The skin of thin cloud that partly obscured the night sky had congealed into a thick grey overcast at dawn. By the time they gathered for a late breakfast, a steady drizzle draped itself over the countryside. Will stood at the window watching the moisture dripping from the trees in the thin, watery light. He turned back to the table where Johnny Gale sawed at a tough slice of bacon.

"Windy," Will used the nickname that inevitably followed Johnny Gale through life. "It is one of life's mysteries how you eat so much and stay so thin."

"Rapid metabolism, old boy. My body is like a finely-tuned racing car and needs plenty of fuel." He reached across and stabbed a sausage from Bill Ives' plate. "You're not wanting that, are you?"

Bill glared at him, "It doesn't look like it." Windy grinned and carried on chewing. Bill pushed his chair back and folded his arms. "Well, come on, Skipper, there's no need for a formal briefing, let us in on the big secret. How come you, on only your second attempt, came to grips with a Zep?" Bill Ives, like most of the men around the table, held the rank of second lieutenant, and was barely twenty years of age. Will Turner, his superior in rank and position within the unit was only a few years older, and the most informal of officers, but Bill could not bring himself to use his first name. He had too much respect for the tall American's experience and skill, if not for his rank. "Skipper" served as a good compromise.

The mess hut had been laid out, as far as Sergeant Ronnie Moore could arrange, in the manner of a gentleman's club. A polished wooden bar, complete with beer pump and shining optic glasses on the wall behind took up one corner of the long room. Will perched on one of the high stools and leaned back against the bar. He smiled. "Luck, pure blind luck. I had no idea it was there—"

"No i–de–ah, at all?" Lieutenant Dizzy Lipman interrupted, mimicking his accent.

"At all, *y'all*." Will laughed out loud. "Fritz, just in a manner, snuck up on me."

"How does something six hundred feet long cr–eep up on anybody?" Basil Jankowski flushed scarlet, "Begging your pardon." Basil's accent echoed his friend Jackson's: pure Australian. But he had an odd speech impediment that made him separate the starting consonant from the following vowel on some words. It gave his voice an air of refinement that suited his appearance. He wore the uniform of the Royal Flying Corps with its high collared, double-breasted jacket, and whipcord riding breeches. It fitted his slim figure to perfection. He ran his long fingers nervously through his dark curly hair.

Will grinned at him. "That is a perfectly fair question, Digger, and one I have been asking myself all night." Jankowski relaxed. He felt himself very much the new boy and worried that he had spoken out of turn. The former Sergeant Jankowski had made his name at ANZAC cove, during the Gallipoli campaign, with a furious single-handed assault on a Turkish position with rifle and bayonet. Many of his comrades said he should have won the Victoria Cross instead of the Military Medal; they also said he was lucky not to get his bloody silly head blown off. Perhaps more important than the medal, Basil had earned the nickname

"Digger." Will Turner, just like every other member of the newly formed Home Defense Experimental Unit regarded him with something approaching awe.

"Didn't mean to be rude, old boy," Jankowski added almost in a whisper.

"I know you did not. The fact is, for all that the damn thing was right on top of me, the only way I knew it was there was because it blocked my view of the stars. I looked up and it seemed to me that a wedge shape moved across the sky."

"What did you mean about sniffing it out?" Dizzy Lipman asked. "You were joking weren't you?"

"Not at all. The only reason I looked up when I did was the sudden shower of what I thought was rain pelting all around me. But the water stank to high heaven of . . . ?" He looked around the breakfast table to see if anybody would rise to the bait.

"Antifreeze!" Windy Gale shouted triumphantly.

"*Exactement, mon brave!* Give that man a cigar," Will laughed out loud. "The water in the ballast tanks must be subject to freezing at high altitude so they lace it with ethylene glycol."

"It's not something you expect at twelve thousand feet sitting behind an air-cooled engine, now is it? So you can hardly blame yerself." Captain James Smith ran his tongue along the gummed edge of a cigarette paper and winked at Will. His gruff voice with its London accent fitted his appearance. His square, shaven head emerged from broad shoulders seemingly without the benefit of a neck. The fingers that rolled his cigarette were as fat as breakfast sausages and when he grinned a gold tooth gleamed. His broken nose and the scars on his cheek and above his eye completed the picture of most people's idea of a retired prizefighter.

"Thank you, Prof, but I cannot make excuses," Will shrugged. "I messed up and no mistake." Smith alone in the unit had the distinction of an academic doctorate; inevitably he was "The Professor" to his comrades. "I guess we were on converging courses, with the Zep about a thousand feet above me," Will explained. "Some eagle-eyed crewman must have been able to see me against the cloud layer, it was near as dammit glowing in the moonlight, but of course I could not see them, even if I had looked up. A Zeppelin hull against a black sky does not give nary a clue it is there, 'cept you cannot see the stars through it. I sat there for a few seconds wondering what was going on. Then something caught me one hell of a lick on the head and the lights went out. I guess they dumped ballast to climb as soon as they saw me and one of the gunners in the gondola got a good burst off as they passed by." Will paused to sip his tea. "First they tried to drown me and then they tried to shoot me."

"Did you get a shot off yourself?" Dizzy Lipman asked.

Will rubbed his chin. "I cannot say. I recall reaching for the trigger, but I do not know if the Lewis fired."

"I doubt it." Every man in the room turned to look at the newcomer, the unit adjutant, Captain Dick Thomas. He slipped out of his raincoat and hung it on a hook by the door, then beat the raindrops off the peak of his cap before flipping it on to the hook. Nobody thought it odd that he did everything with one hand—because he had no left arm. The sleeve of his uniform jacket was pinned to the side. "Somebody dropped a full magazine through a greenhouse in Leytonstone. The Metropolitan Police have been in touch with the squadron at Hainault and they haven't lost one, so the finger of suspicion points at you, Will."

"Did it kill anybody or do much damage?" Will asked.

"The owner is putting in a compensation claim for his glass and tomato plants."

"I will deny everything."

Dick lifted the lid of the teapot on the bar and sniffed the contents. He spoke as he poured, "Very wise." He turned to Will and smiled. "Just think: if that bullet had not struck the magazine, it would have had an uninterrupted path straight through your head."

"Thank you for that cheerful thought, Dick. As it was, the drum must have hit me as it fell off. I went out like a light. I came round with the poor old B.E. in a full out spin. I managed to straighten it out, do not ask me how. As it was, when I pulled out of the dive that followed, the force of gravity made it hard to get my head up, let alone operate the controls."

"That's the damndest thing," Windy spoke up. "Whenever you read anything about flying where somebody is trying to describe the sensation, they never mention that gravity force. But when I cut it a bit fine coming out of a loop in an Avro I pulled so hard on the stick I felt like I was being crushed into the seat. I swear the blood started draining out of my head and I nearly fainted."

Will nodded in agreement, "I believe that is possible. I think it is rarely described because it is so hard to put into words."

"I can," Bill Ives laughed. "It's like being sat on by a horse. And believe me, I've felt both."

"Anyways," Will picked up the thread of the conversation, "for some reason the engine just started as I pulled up from the dive. The propeller could not have been turning but I am guessing something in the gyroscopic forces must have flicked it over. I have no idea why it stopped, perhaps when the drum hit me I must have pulled back on everything: stick, throttle, and stalled the airplane, which may have stopped the engine in turn. I picked up the railroad somewhere over Epping I guess, and followed it back here. I used the system we discussed: end of the track, turn thirty degrees left, time a minute to the river, throttle back, down to home and beauty."

"Well, you certainly pulled off a beauty of a landing, Skip. How did you balls it up?" Jackson asked.

"How, Jacko? Completely—that is how. I forgot to allow for any wind. I had drifted off to the right and when I saw the flares, instead of seeing a straight line in front of me, they went off to one side. They flickered because I could see them through the branches of the tree. Before I could do anything, I hit it." Will paused and looked around the eager faces at the table. "Anyways, y'all, the lesson is, *practice*. As soon as this weather lifts, we practice in daylight what we have to do at night." He gazed slowly around the room. "For the moment it is more important to learn how to find a way to a safe landing, because if every flight ends in a crash, we will not have anybody left to find the damn Zeps . . . are we agreed?"

They responded with solemn nods and a chorus, "Agreed."

Will slid off the barstool, "In the meantime, while this weather keeps us grounded, we have to work out an effective system of lights and signals that will make sure nobody makes the same blunder I just did. I want to see sensible proposals by the time the Boss and I arrive back from the War House* this evening." He finished his tea in one swallow, stepped across to the table and picked the remaining sausage from Bill Ives' plate. "You will not be wanting that, Bill, it will ruin your fine manly figure."

◈ ◁▷◁▷ ◈

Will slipped the Wolseley touring car into second gear and accelerated. It surged up the hill to the junction with the Newmarket Road, where he braked and paused for a second to check for other traffic before swinging left toward London.

"This is a very nice automobile, sir."

Major Simpson leaned back in the heavily upholstered passenger seat, unbuckled his Sam Browne belt, and stretched his legs. He put his hands behind his head and tipped his cap forward over his eyes. "Yes, William, it's a very nice car indeed."

War Office, the British Army HQ in London.

They drove on toward the market town of Epping in silence for a few moments before Will spoke again. "In fact it must be the nicest car in the Royal Flying Corps inventory."

A ghost of a smile twitched at the corner of Ernie Simpson's mouth. "Get to the point, laddie, you know damn well it's not on the corps inventory. You're not going to tell me you haven't noticed it doesn't have a military registration number."

"I cannot play like I had not noticed," Will confessed.

"So who do you think it belongs to?"

"We—ell, there seems to be some kind of family crest woven into the fabric here on the door panels, so I guess it must be from an anonymous titled benefactor?"

Simpson's face, that part of which Will could see under the peak of the cap, broke into a grin. "Not bad, Sherlock, and almost correct. It does belong to a benefactor who takes a special interest in our little unit, and it did come from a titled family, but the two are not the same."

Will knew he was being teased, and the possible answer came to him. "Heck sir, is it yours?"

"Oh my, I wish it was. No, it's Sergeant Moore's car."

"Ronnie's?"

Simpson sat up straight, took his cap off and tossed it into the backseat. His black hair, parted exactly down the middle, ran to grey where it had not been cropped to a stubble around his neck and above his ears. "Of course. You sound surprised."

"Well, sir, I know he is give up to be clever with money, but he did not buy this on a sergeant's wages."

"No, he won it in a card game."

"Good grief, sir, so he was in a card school with some nob?"

"With the nob's son to be precise. Daddy generously donated it to Sergeant Ronnie to avoid a scandal. Have you ever given any thought to why Moore is in the Flying Corps?"

"Because he is too old for the infantry?" Will ventured.

"Exactly, now think about what you just said. Remember he's not a regular."

"He is a volunteer? I never knew that. So in fact he need never have joined up because he is too old for people to accuse him of shirking, and definitely too old for this new conscription everybody is talking about. He must have smelt a profit," Will laughed as he spoke.

"Like as not," Simpson said. "I tell you what though, I would have loved to have been there when he took this car off that young buck. I can just see him there, with those bulging eyes fixed on his opponent, a black market scotch and soda at his elbow, a bevy of tarts gathered around, an unbeatable hand in his fist and an ace up his sleeve just in case . . ."

Will slowed to a stop. A herd of cows wandered along the highway, blocking their path. "Sounds like you admire his card playing skills, sir. But I heard tell you are quite a player yourself. In fact, some folk say you once won a brand new D.H.2 in a card game."

Simpson sat up. "You shouldn't listen to idle tittle tattle young man. Now come on, push past this lot." He slid his side window down and leaned out. "Oi, you!" The farmer, urging his herd on with soft calls and gentle prods with a long stick, turned around. "Yes, you. Get a move on. Don't you know there's a war on?" Simpson demanded.

"Bollocks!" the farmer shouted back.

Simpson tugged the leather strap that slid the window up. "Typical! On the field I'm God. Out here in the real world I'm just another prat in uniform." He turned to Will, "And you can wipe that bloody silly grin off your face."

The straggle of houses and shops lining the main road clustered into longer chains of property until they linked hands to form the suburbs of London. Will spoke, "I do not really see what I can add to this meeting, sir. Though I have to admit I am flattered to be called to it."

"Don't be," Simpson said. "I want you there, your Uncle Frank wants you there, Tom Armstrong and Sir Percy want you there, because you have the combat experience and your engineering degree doesn't do you any harm either. The chairman does not know you from Adam, and the rest—"

"Hate my guts."

"That about sums it up. Trust me, accepting that MC is about the shrewdest thing you ever did. You damn well earned it for blowing up that train,* and, if you did not have it, Hubert Matrett would be trying to label you a coward. He's probably still trying that tack anyway, but nobody will accept that after you have shaken hands with His Majesty and collected the tinware."

"I still cannot believe Hubert Matrett will be there. I thought under the terms of a prisoner exchange on medical grounds he is not allowed to take an active part in the war."

"Ha!" Simpson exploded with a sound halfway between a laugh and hoot of derision. "Couldn't a lawyer have fun with the definition of 'active'? The Matrett family doesn't see the pursuit of financial gain as active service, except as service to the family fortune of course."

"Whatever they say about him, Hubert is no coward. It was his experience and guts that found us the German cavalry on the Marne," Will pointed out.

"And his recklessness and glory hunting that nearly got both of you killed, and landed him in a prisoner of war camp for a year."

Will nodded, "he paid the price."

"Trust me, he's hellbent on getting his money back."

Will twisted in his seat to look behind before swinging out to overtake a horse-drawn brewery cart. He thrust the Wolseley back into top gear. "The way you say that makes me wonder if you mean it literally, sir."

"I do. Believe me. Hubert Matrett and his scheming father, Sir Norman, are up to something. Admiral Sir Percy Scott is privately con-

---

* See Turner's Flight

vinced of it and I agree with him. Mark my words, it spells trouble for honest soldiers . . ."

"And airmen?" Will suggested.

"Especially airmen," Simpson grunted.

Will stepped on the brake as they rounded the next corner. A wooden barricade fenced off one-half of the highway, forcing city bound traffic to stop. Will turned to Simpson. "What *is* that smell?"

"Damp dung and unwashed humanity." Simpson said.

"No, it is coal gas, and something else . . . brick dust."

Simpson opened his door and stood on the running board to see over the crowd gathered on the far side of the barricade. He dropped back into his seat and slammed the door shut. "Your sparring partner from last night left his mark. Direct hit."

A policeman beckoned them forward, at the same time bellowing at the mass of people to get out of the way. Will swung the car into the middle of the road and the crowd parted. Nobody turned to look at them. The grim gathering stared at the bomb-shattered remains of what had once been a greengrocer's business that had stood in the center of a parade of shops, with apartments built above them. Firemen wearing their shining brass helmets picked their way over the rubble. The capricious effect of blast had left the businesses on either side almost untouched. Even the window of the neighboring furniture store remained intact. It appeared as if a careless giant had strolled through the darkened streets and stepped on that one part of the terrace of shops and homes, and crushed it beneath his boot leaving the rest unharmed.

Simpson signaled Will to stop as they drew level with the constable. "When did this happen, Officer?"

The policeman glanced at the Flying Corps wings on their uniforms. "Sometime after one this morning, sir. We heard the Zep, but nobody saw it. Two bombs: one in the field behind did no damage, this one . . ." He shrugged and waved his hand at the shattered wreckage of what had once been a trim home and a thriving business.

"Casualties?"

The policeman straightened his back and tugged his tunic square. "Two dead. Mr. Robinson the greengrocer, and his wife. They dug their son out alive an hour ago." He glanced over his shoulder, then leaned close. "Would you mind moving on, gentlemen? I don't like the mood of this lot, and the Flying Corps is not the most popular outfit around here this morning."

Simpson nodded, "Understood." He pointed forward, "Drive on, put your foot down, let's find out what the brass hats have to say." Half an hour later they passed through a barrier into the inner courtyard of the War Office. The walls towered above them; whitewashed stones edged narrow strips of lawn, trimmed so tight that each blade of grass measured the same length. Even the rain that made so much of London look drab, only served to add polish to their surroundings.

They signed their names at a wide reception desk, an expanse of polished mahogany. The sergeant in charge gave directions in a respectful murmur. They set off along echoing, stone flagged corridors. Portraits of ancient soldiers glared down at them from the walls. Simpson paused at the foot of a wide, stone staircase and touched Will's arm. He pointed at the painting above them. "Do you know who that is?" A wild haired old man with a face etched with passion peered down at them. It was a brilliant but unnerving portrait. The artist had caught the fierce vitality of his subject. He wore a long white coat over a red jacket. In the background, elephants swayed incongruously through cannon smoke against a bloody sky.

"I do not have a clue, sir. I would guess it has to be in India, but the soldier is not somebody I recognize."

Simpson grunted, "He should be better known. That's Paddy Gough, hero of the Sikh Wars and the Indian Mutiny. Mad as a hatter so they say.

An Irishman you won't be surprised to hear. Once, when his outnumbered force was being shelled to bits by the Sikh Army, he rode clear of his command to draw the enemy fire, holding his famous white coat wide so they would see him. He told his adjutant"—Simpson switched to a fair imitation of an Irish accent—" *'I ain't nivver bin beat, and I won't be beat now.'* And you know what? He wasn't. He got away with it." Simpson turned and looked at Will, "Are we going to be *beat* by these bloody Zeps?"

"Hell no, sir." Will touched the peak of his cap in salute to the old general, and started up the stairs.

Another immaculate sergeant ushered them into a wood paneled room. "You are early, gentlemen, please make yourselves comfortable."

Will moved to the window. He looked out on the expanse of Horse Guards Parade. "What can you tell me about the chairman of the meeting?"

Simpson stepped quickly to his side. "Keep your voice down." He jerked his head toward the office door from where the sergeant had emerged. "Apart from being the chairman of this committee, Colonel Roger Lechelle is a member of one of the country's oldest and wealthiest families. He's a marquis, which means when his old dad pops his clogs, he inherits the seat in the House of Lords, and a large part of the Eastern Counties. On the military side he has the MC, and a DSO. He's reckoned to be a real wild one in action. The darling of the press, and an absolute menace to the men under his command."

"What do you mean?"

Simpson lowered his voice to a murmur, speaking from the corner of his mouth. "He's determined to make his name and general rank, and he seems to think his men share his enthusiasm for his own career advancement. It's true they would follow him anywhere, but only out of morbid curiosity. He went beyond his orders a couple of months ago and led his battalion, from the front it has to be said, in a stupid attempt to break the line in the Ypres salient. There were hundreds of casualties. The General Staff hailed it a great tactical success and booted him upstairs before he either did any more damage or his men shot him."

"Hell's bells, Boss, and *he* is in charge of evaluating anti-Zeppelin strategy?"

"Not entirely, but he has a lot of influence."

"But why, for God's sake? He is an infantry officer." Will lowered his voice, "And not a very good one by the sound of it."

Simpson raised his eyes to the ceiling. "Ah, the innocence of youth." He held up his left hand and pulled down the little finger with his right hand. "Number one: as I told you, he's a nob, as you quaintly put it." Simpson tugged at the next finger. "Number two: the brass hats need to show they are taking the Zeps seriously, so who better than a national hero with a reputation as a firebrand? Number three: the General Staff can't be seen to be demoting him by putting him in charge of the canteen facilities—"

"Because he's a nob and a hero, etcetera, etcetera."

"You're getting the idea. I'll make a staff officer of you yet."

"Or a politician?" Will suggested

"Same thing." Simpson straightened his back. "Hold up, we've company."

Voices on the other side of the door announced a newcomer. "Tea, please, Sergeant, and see if you can't find us some decent biscuits." The door swung open and Admiral Sir Percy Scott bustled into the room. Will had formed a mental picture of what an old sailor should look like. Percy Scott did sport a beard, almost white and neatly trimmed to a point, but that was as far as he went to match the picture in Will's imagination. If anything, he resembled one of Arthur Rackham's illustrations of a friendly gnome for a children's book. He stood not much over five feet tall, almost bald apart from a wispy fringe of white hair above his ears. Dark eyes, the skin around them deeply wrinkled, appraised Will. The Admiral stepped forward, hand outstretched, before the younger man had a chance to salute.

"Scott. You must be Turner." He paused to undo the chain that held an old-fashioned cloak in place around his shoulders and passed it to the sergeant who had followed him into the room like an obedient dog. He slapped his cap; a survivor of Queen Victoria's navy, small peaked with faded gold braid, against his knee to drive some of the rainwater off and gave that to the sergeant. "See if you can dry this off, but don't put it on the radiator, there's a good chap." He had uncovered a uniform thirty years out of date. A plain, double-breasted jacket with brass buttons, no epaulettes, only the thick gold rings on the sleeve revealing his senior rank. His shirt sported a high wing collar, with the tie neatly knotted.

"Good lord, Sir Percy," Simpson said. "Did you walk here? You're soaked."

"Most of the way from the station." The old man beamed. "Couldn't be arsed to barter with the cabbies. Thought a bus would come along. Jump on that. By the time one did, almost here. Bally well save the fare. Exercise good for us all." Will glanced at Simpson who tried not to smile. Sir Percy Scott was nothing like he expected.

"Glad to find you chaps early. Wanted a quick word before the others get here." Sir Percy turned to Will, "The modifications you made to the old B.E.2. Any good?" He saw the surprise on Will's face. "Lively now. You can give me an honest opinion."

"The extra horsepower we squeezed out of the engine can only be good. Covering the front cockpit helps as well, but it is still trying to make a silk purse out of a sow's ear," Will answered.

"Only slightly better than a standard machine then?"

"That is about it, I regret to say."

"Blast. Thought so. No expert, but my sailor's eye tells me it looks clumsy. What's the problem?"

"It cannot climb high enough or fast enough, and it is too slow."

Sir Percy pulled a small notebook from his pocket and licked a pencil. "So what are your priorities for a Zep chaser?"

"A good rate of climb, the ability to reach at least seventeen thousand feet, and a speed of one hundred miles an hour in level flight."

"Have we got anything that will do that?"

"The new FE promised for next month should come close, with the new engine. The new Sopwith two-seater shows promise, especially if we can operate it with just the pilot. The same goes for the FE. Sopwith also has a design for a neat little single-seat scout. That might do the job very well in skilled hands."

"No advantage in two pairs of eyes on board then?"

"I could not say at this stage, sir. We need operational experience to see if the advantage outweighs the loss in performance."

Sir Percy scribbled. "What about armament? Heavier gun? Pom-pom? Rockets? Bombs?"

"Lewis gun will do just fine," Will said.

The sailor's eyebrows shot up. "You sound confident."

"I am, sir. But we need more special ammunition. Explosive, incendiary, or both." The old man's rapid-fire questions encouraged Will to give rapid-fire answers.

"We have tracer, Pomeroy, Brock, and the new Buckingham bullets. Why haven't we brought one down, yet?"

"Nobody has come close enough," Will replied.

"Why can't we get close?"

Will returned the frank stare. "Because we cannot find the damn things in the dark."

Sir Percy pointed at the sticking plaster on Will's forehead. "You did."

"Goodness, sir. How did you know about that?"

"It's my job. Your report was on my desk at six this morning." He paused. "Well, how did you find it when nobody else can? Capital piece of work."

Will sighed. "I wish I could claim it was skill, but truth is, sir, it was pure blind luck, and I think it was more that they found me."

"Still. Proves it can be done. Now are you sure about the machine gun being the answer?"

"Yes," Will nodded, once. "Absolutely. Everything else is either too heavy, or causes too much drag. So even if we could find the Zeppelin, we would never reach it to use whatever damn fool idea some armchair warrior has come up with."

Sir Percy laughed. "Capital, capital. So, if we can work out a way of finding the damn things and showing you where they are, you could get up there and shoot them down, given a halfway decent machine."

"Yes, sir."

"Good, because I am going to hold you to that. My reputation on the line as well." The door opened again and the sergeant marched in with the tea tray and placed it on a side table. "Splendid!" Sir Percy rubbed his hands. "Huntley and Palmer's," he picked up the teapot. "Shall I be Mother?"

CHAPTER 3

The Western Front, France

T he weather front dragging the rain that soaked Percy Scott on his way to the War Office had stretched across the English Channel, and reached the Western Front. The thin layer of stratus cloud that preceded it made a perfect background to highlight the shape of a Morane Parasol monoplane, high above the trench line as it tracked the straight course needed for a photographic detail. The little airplane offered perfect target practice and the German gunners showed their gratitude by hurling high explosive shells at it. Ned Robson swore as the Morane bucked so hard beneath him his teeth slammed together. An "archie"* shell had exploded close enough under the nose to make the delicate machine leap like a frisky pony. He wrestled it back on to an even keel, cursing the poor leverage of the short control column. Ned twisted round and yelled at his observer, who knelt on his seat to operate the plate camera fixed to the side of the cockpit.

"For heaven's sake, Jimmy, they've ranged us," he shouted above the hum of the rotary engine and the battering of the ever-present slipstream. "How much longer?" A line of dirty brown smudges conjured by the exploding shells trailed behind them tracing their course for the last five minutes, grubby stains against the clean gray of the advancing weather system.

---

* *The British nickname for anti aircraft artillery in the First World War, said to come from British pilots weaving between the bursts singing a line from a risqué music hall song that went, "Archibald, certainly not!" The later word "Flak" derives from the German Flugabwehrkanone—aircraft defense cannon.*

Jimmy kept his eye fixed to the viewfinder but held up one finger. His other hand pushed the lever and then he looked up, a smile on his boyish face. He leaned close and cupped his hand around his pilot's ear. "We're done, I have two plates left over. Let's go down and see if we can get a close up of those block houses."

Ned raised his thumb in agreement and turned to look ahead. He relaxed his grip on the stick, allowing the nose to drop. Where most airplanes had a horizontal stabilizer at the tail with the elevator control mounted as a movable flap on the trailing edge, the Morane just had the elevator. With no stabilizer the slightest pressure on the stick would either stand the airplane on its nose or its tail. In contrast, the rudder was too small and even on this latest model, fitted with ailerons instead of the archaic wing warping, the roll control felt sluggish. The pilot could never relax as the Morane demanded constant attention. A tall, gangling young pilot, Cecil Lewis, who Ned met at the depot in St Omêr, had warned him that the Morane was, "as sensitive as a gold beater's balance." While most pilots hated it, experts like Lewis and Ned Robson came to love this natural instability; revelling in the maneuverability it gave them. They also appreciated the good qualities of the peculiar French design. As its name suggested, the single high wing was mounted above the tapering barrel-shaped fuselage like an umbrella. The crew sat together in a single long cockpit that enabled them to speak even if it was by shouting close to each other's ear. The downward view, unobstructed by a second wing, was superb. Best of all, from Ned's point of view, the Morane used the beautiful 80-horsepower Le Rhône rotary: smooth and reliable.

Ned pushed the stick hard to the left as he dived, curving away from the line. Jimmy glanced behind; a flash of light far above caught his eye, the sun reflecting from the wing of an airplane. He grabbed the field glasses and focused them before slapping Ned on the shoulder and jabbing his finger upward. "A Hun over our side. A Rumpler, I think. Shall we teach the cheeky monkey a lesson?" Ned grinned, his hand went to the air and fuel levers to coax the remaining revs from the whirling engine as he eased into a climb.

They knew all about the new Rumpler C-type biplane and its rumored ability to climb to nearly eighteen thousand feet on the power of a reliable Mercedes engine, but Ned calculated the solid biplane with its flared-tail surfaces must soon start to descend to its home field. He would climb, and somewhere over the German rear area they would meet. By positioning themselves directly underneath and slightly behind the Rumpler, they would exploit its blind spot and be invisible to the observer, at the same time Jimmy would be able to bring his Lewis gun to bear by shifting the movable mounting he had devised to its forward position. He could fire upward at an angle, but not direct to the front for fear of shooting off their own propeller.

Ned craned his neck backward to keep the Rumpler in sight. The wing blocked most of his view above, but a clear panel in the center section gave a view of a rectangle of sky directly overhead. He turned to follow his quarry, fixing the German airplane in the window made by the cut-out. Ned urged the Morane upward, making unconscious corrections for the changes in trim as Jimmy scrambled around in the space behind him, rigging and loading his gun. The Rumpler materialized above them, changing from an indistinct dot in the middle of the frame made by the wing cut-out, to a well-defined silhouette growing in size until the wing tips disappeared beyond the narrow field of view. Ned could make out the pale gray of its under-surfaces and the streaks of mud on the bottom of the wings thrown up by the spinning wheels when it had taken off.

Chris Davey

"I'll fall back a tad. Open fire when you like." Jimmy slapped him on the shoulder. Ned ducked at the trip hammer blast of the Lewis inches from his ear as Jimmy clattered through a full magazine in a single long burst. Ned glanced up. The Rumpler had gone. A split second later his windscreen shattered and a bullet whined off the engine cowling.

"You bloody idiot—" Ned broke off and stamped on the rudder pedal while lunging against the stick to send them twisting away from the Rumpler that had reappeared a few yards in front of them. Even as he bellowed his protest, he realized that Jimmy had not accidentally dropped his aim and shot past his ear. The Rumpler crew had reacted with lightning speed to the hail of bullets Jimmy had sent cracking round their ears, by diving straight down in front of the Morane to give the observer a straight shot back at them.

"Steady on!" Jimmy protested. "You nearly had me over the side." Ned held the turn and glanced back over his shoulder. The German biplane held its course; he could see it disappearing into the gathering murk, the gap between them opening fast as Ned made for the British side of the line and the German crew headed for home.

"Thank the Lord for that," Ned shouted into Jimmy's ear, as the observer leaned close. Ned throttled down to make it easier to communicate. "You do realize he has a synchronized gun firing through the propeller. If he had got really arsy and come after us, we would have looked a right pair of silly asses as he chased us home."

Jimmy just laughed, "You had a capital plan there, old boy. But remember the old saying, 'No plan survives contact with the enemy.'" A look of alarm chased across his face. "Oh, hell! Better check the plates for damage." He twisted round and examined the wooden box used to store the exposed photographic plates. He turned back to Ned and grinned. "Everything tickety boo. Come on, let's use those last two as we planned."

Ned's hand went to the engine control again, restoring the flow of air and fuel to the rotary engine. The Morane surged beneath them and Ned set course for a section of the line he had marked on his map. The ground, indistinct from ten thousand feet under a spreading blanket of cloud, began to give up its detail. Endless zig-zagging lines of trenches, a moonscape of overlapping craters from the continual shelling, and, as they sank lower, the debris of two years of war—overturned wagons, dead horses, and shattered artillery pieces.

Jimmy crouched over his camera as Ned took them below a thousand feet. Their stealthy approach from behind their own lines took the German machine gunners in the trenches by surprise, but they recovered the instant Ned opened up the engine, to send streams of bullets after them as they skipped over the lines back into the safety of the British rear area. The watery sun they had enjoyed disappeared as if they had flown into a tunnel. Swathes of rain, glinting silver, blocked their path. Ned held his breath as raindrops, stinging like pellets, scoured the film of oil and soot from the exposed skin of his face. He adjusted his goggles and cursed, ducking as low as he could in the cockpit, robbed of the shelter from his windscreen, now shattered by their enemy's bullets.

He flew to their field without thinking, the ground below as familiar as the streets of the small Wiltshire market town he grew up in. The lowering clouds pressed them against the earth, but Ned smiled as he followed the contours of the rich farmland below. He returned the waves of a platoon of Tommies trudging back from the line as he sped past barely fifty feet above them. A familiar crossroads appeared through the gloom ahead. He banked right and climbed to two hundred feet, reversed direction and followed the boundary of a large field. At the far edge he tipped into a slipping turn, cut the engine and drifted to the ground, riding the blustering wind and bringing the Morane to a neat landing, the main wheels and tail skid touching almost together. Before the airplane stopped rolling, a troupe of mechanics appeared. Two jumped up and grabbed the struts, where they joined the wings, and hung there like acrobats to prevent the gale picking up the fragile machine and tossing it on its back. Others put their weight against the fuselage and undercarriage struts to keep the Morane rolling toward a hangar entrance. One of the mechanics made a throat-cutting gesture at which Ned stopped the engine. Without pause, the Morane rolled into the welcoming gloom of the wood and canvas Bessoneau hangar, where wooden chocks were shoved against the wheels.

Ned dragged off his helmet, unbuckled his seatbelt and stood up. "That's frightfully good of you chaps. Couldn't ask for better service at the Ritz." A heavily built, barrel-chested man stepped forward and jabbed a finger through a hole in the engine cowling. He looked at Ned, said nothing, but raised his eyebrow and made his handlebar mustache twitch. "Ah, yes, Technical Sergeant Major Johnston. Sorry about that. You might find one or two other teensy little holes."

The Sergeant Major's face switched from mock severe to a wide smile. "Problems with mice, sir?"

"You might say that. I'll take the squadron cat with me next time. Do your best to sort her out before this afternoon, please."

"No need to worry about that, flying's washed out for the day." Ned jumped down from the cockpit and turned to the tall officer who had ducked into the hangar, shaking the rain from his cap. "In fact, young Robson, no flying for you for at least two weeks."

Ned stared at his Commanding Officer, Major Bingham, "Sorry, sir, I don't understand."

Bingham leaned forward, "Your time's up. It's home establishment for you."

"But, sir," Ned started to protest but the major held up his finger.

"But, sir, nothing. It was good of you to come to us to fly the Morane, nobody else would, but now you simply have to go. Cheer up, you've done a splendid job, and just think of all those excitable young things with trembling bosoms you will be able to impress with tales of derring do during your two-weeks leave."

Ned groaned, "That will be awfully jolly, sir—"

"I should hope so!" Bingham laughed. "There's the reputation of the Corps to keep up."

"Yes . . . but then it will be on to an instructor's post for six months. I would rather be killed by the Hun than by a student pilot."

"You? An instructor?" Bingham gasped.

As if on cue Jimmy and the mechanics chorused, "Oh no, that will never do."

Bingham turned to Johnston, "What do you think the first thing Mr. Robson would teach our neophytes, Sergeant Major?"

"H'irresponsible h'aerial h'acrobatics, I shouldn't wonder, sir."

"What do you think, Corporal Branson?"

"The beating up of staff cars and escaping before their numbers can be taken, I should think, sir."

Bingham turned back to Ned, "So you see, your sins *do* find you out, and so it proved impossible for me to recommend you as an instructor. Instead, you are to report to Major Simpson at the Home Defense Experimental Unit at Abbot's Roding. God above only knows why he asked for you, but there it is."

Ned stared at him for a few seconds and then stepped forward and warmly shook the major's hand. "Thank you, sir. That's wonderful."

"Don't thank me. Thank Simpson and Captain Turner. They are the ones eager to have you. Now, your bags are packed, there's a lorry leaving in half an hour and you should make tomorrow's leave boat. That will just give you time to enjoy this wonderful celebratory fruitcake conjured up by your chaps." Bingham slapped Ned on the back, turned, and ducked back out into the rain.

Ned turned and looked at Jimmy and the mechanics, standing in a semicircle round him. "I had no idea."

Johnston handed him a buff envelope, "No, sir. It's bad luck to fly with a leave pass in your pocket and home establishment to look forward to. Almost guaranteed to get you killed or made prisoner. Here's your papers."

The youngest mechanic stepped forward with mugs of tea on a tray. Branson opened his clasp knife and cut into the fruitcake taking pride of place on the workbench and handed the first slice to Ned who raised his tea in salute.

"To the most decent bunch of mechanics an aviator could ask for. . . Happy Landings!"

Jimmy winked, "I'll drink to that."

CHAPTER 4

Whitehall, London

A single long table, polished to a luster so deep Will could not tell where the surface began and reflection ended, ran the length of the room. High-backed chairs, with the same deep red leather upholstery as those in the anteroom, stood ranked with perfect precision down both sides, with one extra chair at each end. A blackboard supported by a wooden easel and covered with a red velvet cloth stood at one side. Lieutenant Colonel Roger Lechelle sat at the head of the table with the light from a single, high-arched window behind him. Will's long-time friend Tom Armstrong, joined Will's uncle Colonel Frank Penrose, along with Ernie Simpson and Will sitting together on one side of the table. The four men faced Sir Norman Matrett, his son Hubert, and a stranger wearing a dark business suit. Admiral Sir Percy Scott took the remaining seat at the end of the table.

Will studied Lechelle as he shuffled the papers on the table in front of him. He was younger than Will had expected, under forty. His hair was similar to Will's: blond running to red in his thick mustache. He had a straight perfectly proportioned nose, thick eyebrows and a strong, square jaw. Every feature arranged for the delectation of swooning females, as Frank Penrose had put it, with no sign of the infamous receding chin of inbred aristocracy. Simpson looked into Lechelle's cold gray eyes; he read much of the man in them. They told him of Lechelle's unswerving conviction that whatever he decided would be correct. They reflected a personality that assumed authority as a right, that brooked no argument, that had complete confidence in its judgment. After a long career in the British Army, Simpson's instincts told him this could be the stupidest man he would ever have to deal with.

Lechelle banged his papers on edge to straighten the stack. "Gentlemen, I think most of you know each other, but for everybody's benefit, may I introduce Sir Norman Matrett and his son Hubert—Royal Flying Corps, retired." Heads dipped around the table with mumbled greetings. Will smiled at Hubert Matrett who nodded curtly in response. "This gentleman, however . . ." he indicated the man sitting between the Matrett father and son, ". . . will only be known to you by reputation." The stranger was plump with curly brown hair and a snub nose. He looked pleased with himself. "May I introduce Mr. Pickering."

The name sounded familiar to Will. He glanced at Tom who mouthed the word, "Mowers." Will nodded and smiled.

Pickering beamed at them. "We do indeed build the finest range of agricultural and horticultural machinery available today, but we are now designers and manufacturers of a variety of aeroplanes that will soon be available to smite the Hun from the skies . . . ploughshares into swords, don't y'know . . . what?" He laughed, an odd snuffling sound.

"Oh, really?" Will raised his eyebrows, earning a disapproving look from his uncle and a grin from Tom Armstrong.

Without waiting for Lechelle to lay down an order for the meeting, Sir Norman Matrett launched into a speech he had repeated many times to anybody who would listen. Sir Norman was a man fond of the sound of his own voice. A rich baritone with a trace of his Yorkshire roots forcing their way through his carefully cultivated accent, it frequently boomed out over the House of Commons. At first, new Members of Parliament would listen attentively. They assumed that a man of such stature—he stood over six-feet tall and carried an impressive belly—with such a commanding voice, must have something important to say. But eventually they would all either doze off or sneak away to the terrace for tea as he boomed on and on.

Sir Norman fired his opening salvo, "Gentlemen, it gives me no pleasure to point out that the efforts of the Royal Flying Corps to destroy a Zeppelin raider over England have been, and are likely to remain," he paused for effect. "Futile. In short, they are an embarrassment to the war cabinet of which I am privileged to be a member." Matrett banged his fat fist on the table. "Radical measures are called for. The press is demanding something be done . . ."

Tom Armstrong threw his pencil on the notepad in front of him and leaned back with his arms folded. "Well, Sir Norman, perhaps we should have invited the editor of the *Daily Mail* to this meeting. He's so damn clever I'm sure he can tell us what we need to do. He seems to have the answer to everything."

Norman Matrett's head snapped back, unused to being interrupted. He looked carefully at the man facing him for the first time. He took in the row of campaign medals and the blue and red ribbon of the Distinguished Service Order, the RFC wings, the scar gouged from beneath his big walrus mustache to the cheekbone, the dark eyes and heavy eyebrows. Tom Armstrong had a hard face. Matrett replied in a soothing tone. "No need to take offense, Major Armstrong, I am not blaming the men of the Flying Corps, after all, my Hubert here is proud to have served with them. It's the equipment you work with."

"Aye, we know that," Tom said, his voice level. "What's your point?" He made no effort to suppress his own Lancashire accent.

"My point is, *Major* Armstrong, that there has been one success:

young Warneford blasted LZ37 from the sky in Belgium last year. We must learn from that and use that lesson to defeat the Zeppelin menace."

Sir Percy cut in, "Yes, Sir Norman, we know all about young Warneford. Brave lad. Reckless. Dead. Sad. But we are here to discuss progress."

Matrett thumped the table again, making the water jug jump. "There is no progress, Sir Percy, but a solution has been staring us in the face and has been proven to work, but nobody in the RFC is prepared to admit to what the problem really is."

Frank Penrose spoke, his voice mild, "Sir Norman, LZ37 was returning to its base at dawn, and flew at a height that Warneford estimated as less than three thousand feet when he released his bombs. In a nutshell, he had the luck of the devil and did not waste it. Now, if we could oblige the Zeppelin commanders to always fly at low altitude in daylight, we would not be sitting here now. We could pot them with a revolver. We know what the problem is—"

"But *do* you, Colonel Penrose? Do you know the real problem?"

Frank stroked his long chin. "If you think we have missed something, please enlighten us."

Norman Matrett leaned back in his chair and hooked his thumbs around his suspenders. His triumphant smile returned. "Gas, Colonel. Inert gas. You might as well shoot peas at an airship as fire a machine gun. The cunning devils are surrounding the hydrogen cells with inert gas."

Will exploded. "Oh for heaven's sake, not that old chestnut again. I thought that was dead and buried."

Matrett rounded on Will, "So what makes you an expert, Captain?"

Ernie Simpson stepped in before Will could reply. "Captain Turner earned his degree in engineering from the Massachusetts Institute of Technology, Sir Norman. His scientific credentials are impeccable."

"Oh, an *American* college," Matrett sniffed. "I'm a reasonable man, Captain Turner. Explain to us why the Germans are not using the spent gases from the engines to shield the gas bags, and I will explain why you are wrong."

Will glanced round the table. Frank Penrose nodded and Tom Armstrong smiled encouragement. In his slow, precise accent Will pointed out the flaws in the theory that had been accepted as gospel until a few months before. In a few short sentences he explained that the weight of the piping and ductwork required to channel spent exhaust gases from the engines to protect the gas cells carried inside the rigid frame of the airship, would be so great it would never leave the ground. He also explained, giving precise figures, that the volume of exhaust gases needed would be far more than the engines could produce even at maximum power. Tom listened, nodding. Will Turner did not waste words. He set out a model argument.

Norman Matrett sat for a moment, his mouth opened and closed. He sipped water from his glass, then wagged a finger at Will. "All very well in theory, Captain Turner. But that's all you've got—theory. We've got hard fact." He turned to his son, "Tell him, lad."

Hubert Matrett tugged at the end of his sleeves and cleared his throat. He was as tall as his father, without the weight. His broad face lacked his father's prominent nose but he shared the bulging eyes. He also had what looked like a boil on his cheek. Will remembered that from the time they had served together during the retreat from Mons. His style showed he was truly his father's son. He paused for dramatic effect, then leaned forward and looked at each man in turn.

"Gentlemen, what I am about to tell you must be considered confidential. In fact, top secret." He hoped for a reaction but found none. "When my exchange had been agreed and arranged through the Red Cross in Geneva, I traveled to Switzerland, as is the normal custom. As an officer, I was given the choice of accommodation while I waited for my final transfer back to England. I chose to stay in a small hotel on the shores of Lake Konstanz . . ." he looked round the table again. "You realize the significance of that decision, of course."

Sir Percy twisted the end of his mustache with a flourish. "Topping view, clean air, nice grub—just the ticket for a man recuperating." Hubert frowned, he had hoped for a gasp of admiration at least for his cleverness.

"No, Sir Percy, I chose that location because the Zeppelin Company has one of its main bases on the German side of the lake."

Percy touched his forehead and closed his eyes. "Silly me. Should have remembered. We bombed it in 'fourteen."

Hubert ploughed on. "I bought some good field glasses and on clear days could observe the Zeppelin sheds; but my real stroke of luck came after a week at the hotel. The dining room had an outside balcony, beneath which they had a terrace bar. Sitting quietly one day, I overheard two men talking below. One was clearly an engineer, the other a naval officer." He stopped again, and looked directly at Will. "I am prepared to swear on the Holy Bible that the engineer described, in detail, to the naval officer, how the new exhaust gas ducting system already in use on the latest Zeppelins, was to be fitted to those already in service. He claimed that it would make them all invulnerable. The naval officer agreed that results were excellent so far." Hubert, sat up and pushed his chair back from the table. "What do you think of *that*, Mr. Turner? You have to agree with the German officer, the results have been marvelous for them."

"*Verstehen Sie Deutsch, Herr Matrett?*" Will looked him straight in the eye.

"Eh, what?"

"I said, 'Do you understand German,' Mister Matrett?' "

"Of course I don't. They were speaking English."

Frank Penrose leaned back and folded his arms. "Mr. Matrett, please don't think I am pouring cold water on your story, but I find it hard to believe that a German engineer, and a German naval officer, would be drinking beer in a Swiss hotel, discussing state secrets in English."

Hubert's face broke into a broad smile. "I did not say they were *both* German, Colonel Penrose. The man I believe to be a naval officer certainly was, but the engineer was Dutch—I recognized his accent. They were using a language they both understood, the King's English."

"What makes you so sure the German was a naval officer, Mr. Matrett?" Percy Scott asked.

"Well, obviously he was not in uniform, that would not be allowed by the Swiss. It was the content of their conversation, and the fact that the Dutchman called him, 'Captain.' "

Sir Norman could not contain himself any longer. His son had had enough time in the spotlight. "Well, it's obvious who the Dutchman was, isn't it?" He waved a finger around the table, like a schoolmaster inviting an answer from his class, "It must have been that damned Fokker chap. Who else could it have been? He obviously slipped into neutral Switzerland for a meeting with a senior captain of the Zeppelin fleet. Perhaps even Strasser himself."

"Antony Fokker is an aeroplane designer, Sir Norman," Tom said. "Why would he have a sudden interest in airship construction? And why meet on neutral territory? He has a factory in Germany, and that's public knowledge."

Sir Norman looked down his nose at Tom. "Because he's a business-man, Major Armstrong, and since the Eindekker monoplane, he has failed to win any more major contracts. He hardly wants his rivals to know what he's up to so he is not going to discuss this in a Bier Keller in Berlin. And . . ." he leaned forward like a card player about to show his ace, "he employs a man called Reinhold Platz who is reckoned to be *the* expert on welding tubular steel structures."

Frank Penrose sat up, "How on earth did you find that out?"

"Yes, I thought that would make you take notice." Sir Norman smiled condescendingly. "Military intelligence is not the be all and end all, Colonel. Big business has its own ways of finding things out. If we relied on you for help, we would all be bankrupt by now, and the War Office would be going cap in hand to the Americans for our armaments."

Sir Percy smiled at him then turned to Hubert. "Mr. Matrett, your father said you had hard evidence. So far, all I have heard is a report of a conversation you overheard. You were not in a position to take notes, and you do not claim shorthand as a skill." The affable old sailor had disappeared. He gazed at Hubert, his dark eyes steady and unblinking. "Can you produce any hard evidence?"

Hubert looked at his father, who nodded. The younger man pulled a page from a newspaper out of his briefcase. He unfolded and flattened it before pushing it across the table to Lechelle.

"Doesn't mean much to me. But it looks damned impressive. I expect you technical chaps will make more of it." Lechelle slid it down the table to Tom Armstrong who studied it for a moment, then passed it to Will.

"Well, is it or isn't it, Captain?" Sir Norman demanded.

Will studied the page, turned it sideways, then held it up to the light. His first reaction had been shock. Clearly sketched in pencil, on a page from a regional German newspaper, he could see a cross section of a Zeppelin hull. It showed one of the main frames, a gas cell suspended inside it, with pipes entering the base of the frame to appear again close to the top with a trumpet-like device fixed to the end. An arrow pointed down from the lower pipe with the single word, *moteur*, written next to it.

"It is a doodle, Mr. Matrett, an idea somebody was playing with. Where did you get it?"

Hubert started to get to his feet, but his father pushed down on his shoulder so he could answer himself. "A doodle, Captain!" Sir Norman's face flushed. "That, sir, is the reason that firing machine gun bullets against a Zeppelin is like piddling in the wind. It is the answer to your spurious argument about weight. They are using the pipes and ducting as part of the structure so the extra weight of the system is cancelled out by the removal of a main frame." He turned to Pickering for support. "Isn't that right?"

"Oh yes, Sir Norman."

"And my son had the foresight, and the nerve to swipe that paper off their table when they left."

"Well done, lad!" Lechelle barked. "Should get a medal for that."

Hubert reached across the table and took the page back. "It was nothing, Colonel, the least I could do." Simpson shot a glance at Will, ready to intercept any rash response but Will just shrugged.

Percy Scott scribbled a note, put down his pen and looked at Lechelle. "This is all very interesting, but there could be other reasons why our weapons appear ineffective. I have asked Quartermaster Sergeant Chaney to prepare a report."

Lechelle scrabbled through his notes, and looked at Sir Percy. "A report? From a Quartermaster Sergeant?"

"Yes, man: in that folder with your notes. Chaney, instructor at the School of Musketry for eleven years, went up with Mansfield on the first anti-Zeppelin sortie: machine gun adviser to the corps. Forgotten more about machine guns than the rest of us will ever know. Bloody good man."

"Oh yes, here it is," Lechelle grunted.

Sir Percy nodded toward Tom Armstrong, "You have studied the report and I believe you know Chaney very well. What's your opinion?"

"His report is very detailed and backs up his theory with hard figures. Chaney believes that where our pilots have made contact and believe their tracer rounds are disappearing into the airship with no effect, they are, in fact, burning out hundreds of yards short of the target, giving the impression they have punctured the outer skin. Our gunfire is having no effect because it is falling short."

Lechelle stared at him. "Good grief man, is he saying that our officers can't hit a target six hundred feet long? Sounds like damned impertinence to me."

Tom looked him straight in the eye. "No, sir. He is saying that we are opening fire before we are in range for effective shooting. In my opinion a problem exacerbated by wishful thinking and a tendency to believe it's always worth taking a shot. He is also talking from personal experience having taken part in numerous anti-Zeppelin patrols."

"Why do you think this happens?" Frank asked before Matrett could speak.

"Our pilots know how big the German airships are reported to be, but Chaney states that their sheer size is a very hard concept to grasp."

Lechelle stared at Tom, "A hard concept to grasp?" It was not the statement that had made Lechelle gasp audibly: it was the expression itself. The colonel expected his NCOs to restrict their vocabulary to the commands in the drill book. Not for the first time Lechelle had the uncomfortable feeling that the Royal Flying Corps was collectively too clever by half.

Sir Percy Scott, as a naval man, expected his NCOs to be articulate. He scratched his beard. "So Chaney is saying that our chaps just can't believe how bloody big the Zeps are and think they are close enough to open fire?"

Tom nodded, "That about sums it up."

Frank Penrose leaned forward with his elbows on the table. "So if we could get an aeroplane close enough, load up with this new explosive ammunition from this Kiwi chap, Pomeroy, and incendiary rounds, then blaze away, you are confident that we could set fire to a Zeppelin?"

"Absolutely," Tom nodded

Lechelle closed his folder, "Impressive report," he muttered grudgingly, then turned to Matrett. "You do not appear to be interested in Sergeant Chaney's opinions on our gunnery efforts."

"Frankly, Colonel, we are not. As I stated before, the German gas shielding system renders them completely ineffective. The only way that we will destroy the Zeppelin fleet is the same way that Warneford did. With bombs from above, and—" he broke off. "Do you find something amusing Captain Turner?" He glared at Will who sat shaking his head, a weary smile on his face.

"The only thing I find funny is that you have missed the obvious. Why should the Hun bother sending his airships over if we are planning to bomb our own people?" A shadow of doubt crossed Matrett's florid face. Will looked between the father and son, before continuing "Gentlemen, if by some miracle of aeronautical science we obtain an aeroplane capable of carrying itself and a bomb load above a high flying German raider, and in the darkness our intrepid aviators miss the airship, I can assure you that, inaccurate as we can be, we won't miss England. I can just imagine what your pals at *The Mail* will say when British bombs start raining down!"

Matrett stared at him, for once lost for a reply. His son rescued him. "Of course, this would be the means of attack while the airship was over the sea, or remote country. Papa was about to go on to explain that heavy cannon fire will also be necessary."

Sir Norman looked at his son; the surprise on his face obvious. "Aye . . . I mean, yes, of course that's right son. Heavy cannon. Blast the buggers out of the sky."

Sir Percy steepled his fingers in front of his face, his elbows resting on the table. "Exactly what do you mean by 'heavy cannon'? I can't for the life of me see how you plan to get even a six-pounder in range. A gun like that weighs tons, far too much for any aeroplane to haul aloft. On top of that, the recoil would smash any machine carrying it."

Hubert's confidence had grown. "No, Sir Percy, we don't envisage anything *that* heavy. We are talking about the modified Vickers pom-pom, a fully automatic cannon firing high explosive projectiles, or the new recoilless Davis gun." He had recovered his father's position with his quick response to Will's point about the danger inherent in aerial bombing.

"Mr. Matrett, we know that engaging the Zeppelins with heavy weapons would give us a far better chance," Will looked at Hubert and paused, "but the simple fact is that the guns you describe are still too heavy for any aeroplane, present or planned, to carry to the altitude required. To be successful, first we would have to intercept every Zeppelin before it reached our shores, then climb to a height where we could tackle it, and then engage it with these weapons without the recoil knocking our machine to pieces, or the muzzle flash setting fire to it."

Sir Norman smiled and looked around the table. "So what would you gentlemen say if I told you we have the means to do exactly that?"

Will began to speak, "Why, I declare you would be talking out of—" he did not get the chance to finish the sentence.

"Optimism." Ernie Simpson cut across his young flight commander. "A great deal of optimism." He glared at Will while Frank Penrose raised his eyes to the ceiling and Tom Armstrong stifled another laugh.

Percy Scott smiled at Matrett. "Unless you can back that statement up with something solid, Sir Norman, I would have to agree with Captain Turner. You're talking out of your arse."

Hubert laughed. His father beamed and Pickering giggled. Percy's Scott's obvious provocation just seemed to fuel their excitement. Sir Norman heaved his bulk out of his seat. "Gentlemen, what I am about to show you must remain a closely guarded secret. The fate of the Empire depends on it."

Hubert adjusted the easel and took hold of the red velvet cloth. Sir Norman paused for effect again. To Will it appeared as if he visibly puffed himself up. "Gentlemen, I give you—" he nodded to his son who whipped the cloth away, "the *Pickering Destroyer*." Pickering clapped his hands together. Both Matretts looked ready to take a bow in response to a round of applause that never came.

"Holy cripes! What the Sam Houston is *that*?" For all that his accent rendered his voice soft, Will's voice sounded loud in the sudden silence.

CHAPTER 5

The War Office, London

F rank Penrose unscrewed the stopper from a quart bottle of India Pale Ale and poured into each glass in turn. He raised his own.

"Confusion to our enemies, wherever they may be."

"I'll drink to that," Sir Percy grunted. He pointed to the plate of sandwiches in front of them, "Get stuck in gentlemen." They sat at a plain wood table in a cluttered but airy office arrived at by a succession of increasingly narrow stairs. The ceiling sloped inward, revealing their position at the very top of the War Office. Light poured in through rain-streaked windows tilted at the angle of the roof. A typewriter clattered in the room next door.

Ernie Simpson put his glass down and reached for a sandwich. "Chaney's report rocked Lechelle back on his heels. He didn't expect that from a sergeant."

Frank Penrose smiled. "Henry Chaney is being commissioned. The Royal Flying Corps needs the best officers it can get, regardless of their family background. That report was just one of the reasons he deserves it."

Sir Percy Scott wiped his mustache with the back of his hand and swallowed a mouthful of bread and cheese. "Absolutely. Just like the navy. A meritocracy, not an aristocracy. Some of my best officers came up through the hawsehole."

"Couldn't agree more," Frank continued. "He will be gazetted second lieutenant, RFC as of today, the announcement will appear in the *Morning Gazette* tomorrow."

"This will come as a surprise," Tom said. "Nobody deserves it more, but how will he manage with the expense of new uniforms?"

Frank waved a hand, "No bother, he's rolling in money though he doesn't know it yet. It has been agreed that officers commissioned from the ranks have an account opened at Cox and Company, the corps' official bank. They get a month's pay in advance and sixty pounds for uniforms and everything else they may need."

Simpson held his glass up for a refill. "Well, his report is one good thing to come out of this morning's meeting. What about the rest?" A collective sigh went round the table.

Frank Penrose leaned back and regarded his nephew and Tom Armstrong. "What do you make of the Pickering Destroyer?" He had taken off his tunic and sat with arms folded across a pair of fire engine red suspenders.

Will looked around the table. "It may well fly. If you provide enough power I believe you could make a barn fly . . . but this won't fly as well as a barn—or be as useful."

Frank raised an eyebrow. "Can you say with complete honesty that your objections are not based on the fact it's not your stunt?" He looked from his nephew Will Turner, to Tom Armstrong. "No offense intended."

"None taken, sir," Tom said. "It's a fair question. At the moment we need fast scouts and a reliable two-seat reconnaissance and light-bombing machine. We simply cannot divert the resources in men and material to a giant aeroplane, for any purpose."

Frank turned to his nephew. "Can I take it you agree?"

"Absolutely, sir. What really chills my blood is that when I challenged Pickering about the need for a minimum of one thousand reliable horsepower from his four engines, he just looked so damn smug, as if he had it in the bag."

Sir Percy Scott tugged at his beard. "I'm sorry, Turner, I don't follow."

"At the moment about the best engine we have available in quantity is Frank Halford's one-sixty horsepower Beardmore, but the Rolls Royce company has just provided us with a brand new two-hundred-and-fifty-horse engine. It is superb from every account: smooth, and very reliable . . ."

Percy Scott smiled, "As you would expect."

"Indeed, sir," Will agreed. "And, needless to say, expensive, in great demand, and short supply. It has been tested in an F.E.2 and given terrific results. It is needed for the planned new Bristol two-seater, Geoffrey de Havilland's new design, and just about any aeroplane with a stationary engine."* Pickering thinks that Matrett's influence can secure them as many as they need."

"And how many have Rolls Royce built so far?" Sir Percy asked; his pencil poised over his notebook.

"Thirty-one," Tom Armstrong replied.

"Bugger." Sir Percy snapped his notebook shut, put it in his tunic pocket and extended his glass for a top up. "I understand your concern, gentlemen; they obviously think they can lay hands on these engines in sufficient quantities to power their aerial threshing machine if they can get the contract to build them." The old sailor peered into the bottom of his beer glass, and then looked at Frank Penrose. "Did my old ears deceive me? Are they trying to get the go-ahead to build fifty of these things?"

Frank nodded, "I'm afraid so, Sir Percy."

"Ye Gods! Two hundred engines. How long would it take Rolls Royce to supply them and the spares I assume they will need?

"At a guess . . ." Tom leaned back and screwed up his eyes. "To be realistic, the rest of this year, if everything went well." He let his chair settle back and started counting off on his fingers. "Let alone all the other materials and man hours to build the Destroyer," he said the name with a derisive snort. "The fitters and ground crews to support them in the field. The five-man crew to fly them, guns, bombs, petrol. The cost doesn't bear thinking about."

---

* A conventional engine as opposed to the rotary engines in common use at that time in which the cylinders revolved with the propeller.

Frank stood up and opened a filing cabinet, then extracted a thin folder. "I have been thinking about it, Tom. By my estimate, to set up these Home Defense Squadrons that Matrett is proposing to the House of Commons, it would cost the equivalent of thirty squadrons in France."

Sir Percy sat shaking his head. "It can't be allowed to go ahead." He turned back to Will and Tom. "Before I put my reputation on the line, can you assure me there is no merit in this design proposal from Matrett? From a layman's point of view, if the ability to climb is everything in the fight against the Zeps, then surely four wings have to be twice as good as the two on a conventional biplane."

Tom answered for them both. "Sir Percy, I will put *my* career and reputation on the line. For reasons that are becoming apparent from our wind tunnel experiments at Farnborough, a biplane set-up is no more effective in the climb than a well-designed monoplane. There's an element of interference between the two wings that reduces the efficiency of the lifting surfaces, and any gain from lower wing loading is outweighed by the drag from the necessary struts and bracing wires needed to hold the whole shebang together."

"So why do we build biplanes?"

"Because they are easy to build strong, sir," Will took up the argument. "A biplane wing structure is effectively a truss, just like a railroad bridge." A single-wing monoplane is harder to beef up to take the strain of combat, but if you can, you end up with a lighter, faster and more efficient airplane."

Tom nodded. "The deciding factor is power. Given a competent design and equal power, the monoplane will usually out-climb the biplane every time because it has to overcome far less drag."

"So what you are saying is that climbing in a biplane is like pedaling your bike up a long hill holding an umbrella open behind you?" Sir Percy looked at Will and Tom.

"You hit the nail square on the head, Sir Percy," Will said.

Sir Percy shrugged, "I picked up a thing or two about naval construction in my time, and as a general rule if a ship looks right, she'll sail right. If that thing were a ship I would never set foot in it: four wings, four engines, a gun position on top of the very top wing! For goodness sake, the poor blighter up there will have vertigo before it even gets off the ground—if it ever gets off the ground. Then there are the bomb racks, the searchlight battery, the triplane tail, the wind-driven generator."

"Well, we have to do something, and soon, because unless we stop it, Matrett's harebrained plan, daft as it is, could become fact," Frank said. "Our contacts tell us that Sir Norman's plans have reached committee stage already. He has very powerful support in the House and from the press. We know that the Zeppelins, certainly at the moment, are causing little damage and very few casualties, but the impact they are having on the public is out of all proportion to the military results achieved. In short, gentlemen, the great British public is demanding something be done. And when that happens—watch out!"

Ernie Simpson scratched his head. "But surely it must be obvious to anybody that Matrett's real plan is to make a bundle of boodle? If they give the go-ahead for fifty of these things he stands to make a fortune."

"That's where he's such a clever sod," Frank replied. "He financed the building of the prototype from his own pocket. It's a big gamble but he has never shied away from that. Instead of being seen as a profiteer, Mr. Average Englishman sees him as a savior. You can understand why Matrett is so determined to force this through. He has a lot of cash riding on it."

"Well, there are a lot of lives riding on this." Frank reached back from his chair and banged the drawer of the filing cabinet shut. "The poor bloody infantry are going to go without air support for months, and the Flying Corps is going to be ripped to bits in the air, if all our resources are tied up combating what amounts to a side show. We are going to have to be just as determined to stop him."

Simpson sat up, "Can you just go back a moment? Did you say he *has* financed the building of the prototype, meaning a Destroyer exists?"

Frank shrugged, "I'm afraid so."

"Hell's teeth! How *do* we stop this?" Simpson growled.

Sir Percy placed a pair of half-moon spectacles on the end of his nose and pulled out his notebook again. "There is only one way, gentlemen, and we all know what it is." He glanced over the top of his glasses. "We have to start bringing down German airships before Matrett's plan is put into action. Chaney will give us the weapons we need. Anything you need in terms of equipment or men: let me know. Just make sure that within a very short time we can find the damn things and get close enough to put Lieutenant Chaney's good work to use."

"It's going to be a struggle to put a spanner in Matrett's works," Tom Armstrong said. "It looks like Lechelle is behind his scheme."

Frank Penrose stroked his long chin, "I'm not so sure. Between ourselves we know that Lechelle is not terribly bright, but his one great quality is that he is one of the most honest men I have ever met. Some may be influenced by Matrett's wealth, but you can rest assured Roger Lechelle won't be swung by a box of cigars and a night out on the town with a couple of trollops."

Sir Percy pointed his pencil at Will and then Tom. "I know you two have some plans to improve signaling between observers on the ground and our airmen. I want you to look at a system devised by a chap called Ingram. For some reason it has sat on the shelf at the Admiralty since last year, but I want you to dust it off and see if it has potential. I'm working on extending the warning we get with a line of picket boats out into the North Sea. Between us we'll nail them." He pulled out his watch and flipped it open. "Blast! Time and tide and all that. Must get my skates on. Meeting at Chatham before dinner." He drained his glass. It acted as the signal for the informal meeting to break up.

Will picked up his cap and stood. "Can we give you a ride to the station, Sir Percy?"

"Thank you, my boy. That would be splendid."

Tom stood, "You can drop me off as well."

Will delivered his passengers to their respective railroad stations. Londoners bustled about their business through rain slick streets everywhere under the stern eye of Lord Kitchener, whose grim mustachioed face gazed out from hundreds of posters exhorting young men to enlist.

"I swear his eyes follow me everywhere," Will jerked his thumb toward one of the posters fixed to the wall outside Baker Street underground station.

"Don't worry," Ernie Simpson said. "With a little more effort you could say you are doing your bit for a country that isn't really yours."

"It is only half my country. Do you think His Lordship will accept that I only have to do half a bit?"

Ernie laughed, "Providing you keep doing the dirty half, and leave me with the half that's all glamour. Come on, put your foot down, let's get home before our ever-eager halfwits break something else."

CHAPTER 6

The Orderly Room, Abbots Roding

Lieutenants Bill Ives and Stan Jackson stood ramrod straight, heads up, eyes fixed on a point on the wall above Major Simpson's head. "Well?" Simpson demanded. His eyes narrowed and he leaned forward, palms against the edge of his desk with his fingers arched so the tips rested on the polished surface.

"They started it, sir." Jackson's voice was firm.

"Well, it looks like you bloody well finished it." Simpson snatched a sheet of paper off his desk and jumped to his feet. In three swift strides he stood in front of them. "Have you seen this?"

Ives gulped audibly, "Yes, sir. Very regrettable."

"Regrettable!" Simpson's voice snapped, not much louder than usual, but the menace in his tone made the younger men flinch. He thrust his face close to Jackson's and held the page to one side, forcing the Australian to swivel his eyes to focus on it.

"A decorated, serving officer who also happens to be the son of a peer of the realm, is in hospital with a broken arm. His friend, the son of a Member of Parliament, is looking at the world through eyes so thoroughly blacked he looks like a failed prizefighter, and the third member of their party is, at this moment, attending the surgery of a Harley Street dentist being measured for dentures after somebody knocked his front teeth out—and you stand there and call it 'regrettable.' " This time Simpson's voice rose to a parade ground bellow making Will, who stood leaning against the back wall of the squadron office, wince.

A fly buzzing across the room sounded loud in the silence that followed. Nobody spoke. Simpson stalked to the window and stood looking out, hands clasped behind his back, raising himself up and down on his toes. Will noticed the back of his commanding officer's neck glowed bright red. Simpson took a deep breath and turned back to the two lieutenants. "Before I reply to Colonel Standing's letter, delivered by motorcycle dispatch rider I might add, I am prepared to listen to your version of events . . . well?"

"There you have it, sir," Jackson had taken the role of spokesman.

"Have what, for God's sake, man?"

"There were three of them and only two of us."

Simpson turned and looked at Will who shrugged. He turned back to Jackson. "I am not talking about the odds. I am talking about conduct unbecoming an officer and a gentleman. I am talking about conduct prejudicial to good order and discipline. I am talking about having the pair of you busted to the ranks and sent to the trenches where your *penchant* for fisticuffs and violence could be put to good use against Fritz." He paced across in front of them to the far wall, and spun on his heel to confront them again. "In plain English, tell me how this started."

"Well, sir, Bill . . . I mean Lieutenant Ives, and myself had walked into the village and stopped off at the Mucky Duck . . ."

"The what?"

"Black Swan Pub, sir."

"I see, carry on."

"Well, I had just ordered us a pint each when this toffee-nosed bastard in the corner of the swank . . . sorry, saloon bar, pipes up, and well, it sort of progressed from there."

"So what did he say that was offensive enough for you to belt him?"

Ives coughed, "He said, sir, that he was not surprised to see a peasant and a bloody colonial, guzzling ale. What's more he was not surprised to find that the RFC had commissioned peasants and colonials because only peasants and colonials would want to serve as flying bus conductors . . . or words to that effect. His two friends found that very funny."

"Oh come on, Ives. Why would an officer start calling you a peasant?"

"Because he was already three sheets in the wind, and—" Ives stopped suddenly.

"Go on, man."

"And because I know him."

"Aha! Now we're getting somewhere. How long have you known him, and where from?" Simpson, folded his arms and perched his backside on the edge of the desk, but he kept his eyes fixed on Ives. The younger man still stood rigidly to attention.

"All my life, sir. Our families are neighbors in Cambridgeshire."

"Is there a history of animosity between you?"

"You might say that, sir. It goes back to the Civil War. We sided with Parliament, the Buleys with the King."

Will nudged himself away from the wall and stood straight, with his thumbs hooked in his belt. "Lord sakes, Bill. Isn't it time to bury the hatchet? That was two hundred and fifty years ago!"

"Oh, there's plenty more gone on since then. They keep trying to buy us out, and we won't sell."

"Yes, yes, all very interesting, Ives, but still no reason to start a riot in a public house. You can think yourself lucky that Constable Horne didn't heave you straight into the cells." Simpson said.

"Well, that's right, sir." Jackson spoke up again. "We did not allow ourselves to be provoked. In fact we ignored them and started chatting to the landlord."

"So why did it start?"

"Because his lordship took a swing at Bill. As I told you, sir, we didn't start it."

"That's as may be," Simpson's eyes: bright, glittering and unblinking, seemed to Jackson to bore straight through him. "But you finished it. What did you two do to provoke him?"

"Well, sir, as Bill said, he was already pretty drunk when we got there. After a few minutes he came up to the bar, all pompous and hoity-toity, and says to Bill— 'Why do they let a fat little ploughboy like you fly one of his majesty's aeroplanes?' And we still ignored him."

"And then?"

"He pokes Bill in the belly and says, 'Why are you so fat, Ives?'"

"And?"

"And Bill says, 'Because every time I make love to your sister she gives me a biscuit.' "

"Oh yes, that would do it every time."

Simpson spun around, "This is not funny, Captain Turner."

Will passed his hand over his face and composed himself. "No, sir, sorry sir."

"And then it started?" Simpson said.

"Yes, sir, his lordship takes a swing at Bill and misses, and Bill pops him a beaut on the snout. And then it sort of got out of hand . . . ." Jackson's voice trailed off as he lost confidence and looked plaintively at Will.

"Sorta, out of hand?" Will frowned. "We heard you fell out the door and ended up rolling around in the yard. Somebody caught this Buley fellow one hell of a lick." He turned to Simpson. "These fellows are my responsibility, sir. I regret we will have to discipline them."

Simpson picked up his cane from the desk and thwacked it across the palm of his hand. "We can consider ourselves lucky it is still in our hands. If Colonel Standing had wanted to press the issue we could be talking about a court martial. For whatever reason he wants to keep matters between us." He turned to face Ives and Jackson. "But don't think for a moment you have got away with this. The punishment we have agreed between us is worse than that. You are going to join Lord Buley and his pals at their regimental guest night—and you are going to kiss and make up."

"Strewth, sir! That's . . ." Jackson faltered under Simpson's baleful stare.

"And in the short term I have devised a particularly useful punishment. One that is menial and boring but still befitting a flying officer." Simpson glanced at Will who had now perched on the corner of the desk and sat with one leg swinging. "We are very pleased with this, aren't we, Captain Turner?"

Will grinned, "Oh yes, we like this. You will not." He looked from Jackson to Ives who eyed him warily.

"How many rounds of .303 ammunition do you think Lieutenant Long has stacked away in the armory?" Simpson paced across the floor and looked out of the window. "Come on, come on." He wheeled around and pointed his cane at Ives.

"Thousands, I expect, sir," Ives answered.

"You're lucky. Not counting the stock issued for immediate use, only five thousand, six hundred and forty." He twitched his cane to point at Jackson, and then back to Ives. "You two are going to examine every single cartridge in minute detail, using engineering callipers and micrometer if needs be, to ensure that we never suffer a stoppage due to faulty ammunition . . ."

"But, sir, that will take . . ." Jackson's voice trailed off.

"Exactly. And when you are not doing that you will take turn and turn-about as duty officer." Simpson switched his glare from one to the other and waited.

Ives took the bait. "For how long, sir?"

"Until I bloody well decide, hell freezes over, or you are killed in action: whichever comes first." Simpson pointed his cane at the door. "Now get out of my sight."

Ives and Jackson saluted, made a regulation right turn, and almost fell over each other in their eagerness to get through the door.

Will said nothing as the door closed and Simpson turned back to his desk. In the silence the creak of the door to the inner office opening sounded loud. Tom Armstrong put his head into the room. "Safe to come in?"

Simpson sighed, "Sorry you had to listen to that, Tom."

"No, not at all, Ernie: a truly masterful bollocking. I feel privileged to have heard it. And a clever punishment to boot."

Simpson walked to the filing cabinet and opened the top drawer. He took out a bottle and three glasses and set them on the desk. He twisted the stopper out of the whiskey bottle. "I need a drink." He poured a measure into each glass, and passed one each to Tom and Will. Simpson sniffed his scotch and closed his eyes in appreciation of the rich, peaty aroma. "Fighting spirit is one thing—" The telephone interrupted him; he picked it up. "Yes, are you sure? Oh Christ on a bike! Thanks, Ted." Simpson slammed the phone down. "Quick, knock that back. Red tab."

Tom stood back and watched in surprise as Will strode across the room and pressed a button on the wall. An alarm bell sounded in the distance. Simpson gathered up the glasses and the bottle and slipped them back in the filing cabinet. Ernie Simpson and Will moved toward the window and stood peering out. Simpson looked at his watch.

"Who's on today?"

"Bowen. There he goes." They watched a single airman in full uniform carrying a rifle with fixed bayonet sprint from the nearest hangar to the gate where he slammed down a striped pole, stood to attention and sloped arms. Even at a distance they could see his boots and brasses shone.

"What's all this in aid of?" Tom asked, tugging at his mustache.

Will turned to him and grinned. "Needs must when the devil drives."

"And the devil's a hard driver and usually wears the red tabs of a staff officer." Simpson continued staring at the gate as he explained. "The top brass really don't like this set-up one little bit. We're not a squadron as such, but we take up nearly the same resources. They don't like the fact we are not part of the usual chain of command but seem to take our orders from you, Admiral Scott, and a mysterious room at the top of the War Office. And they would like nothing better than to catch us out and accuse us of being an ill disciplined, scruffy rabble."

"So you feed them as much bull as necessary?"

"Exactly, Tom. And we have to do it more often than we would like. You can guarantee that at least once every week some stiff-necked staff officer finds an excuse to come poking around. That wouldn't normally be a problem. As you know I'm a stiff necked starchy bastard myself and I like nothing better than spit and polish, but my people are too busy to be farting about playing at guardsmen."

"So every day you have a duty dog who wears his best boots under wrapping, wears cotton gloves to keep his hands clean, and is primed to double over to the gate to give a good impression."

"Exactly." Simpson turned to Will. "How long from bell to gate, Will?"

"Under a minute thirty."

"Good."

"But how do you know when a staff officer is on his way?" Tom asked.

"The only way in here is over the level crossing. The signalman is primed to keep an eye on any motor coming our way. If he sees red tabs he calls us."

Tom stood behind Simpson and looked over his shoulder. "Ripping good system, Ernie. We need something like that for the Zeppelins."

"You can say that again," Simpson said. "Hold up, here he is. That's odd, only one person in it." A bull nose Morris had pulled up at the gate;

its brass radiator shell sparkling in the sun and setting off the pale blue coachwork. "Now what's going on? Bowen's standing easy, he's slung his rifle back on his shoulder, he's laughing and talking with the driver. He's raised the barrier and climbed on the running board."

Tom stood on tiptoe trying to see what was happening. Will turned to him with a broad grin. "It is Uncle George."

The Morris pulled up outside the office and seconds later Colonel George Brett, VC, DSO flung the door open and beamed. "I say, chaps, where's the bar?" He returned their salute, then shook hands with Simpson and Will. "How the devil are you, Ernie? Will?"

"Very well, sir," Will said. "You remember Tom Armstrong?"

Colonel Brett took Tom's hand and clasped it warmly. "The famous Tom Armstrong. How could I forget? Top class batsman and aviator of renown. How the devil are you?"

"Fine thank you, sir."

"Splendid, splendid." He paused and sniffed. "I wasn't far off the mark. Is that a nice single malt I smell?"

Simpson opened the filing cabinet and retrieved the glasses and bottle, poured an extra glass and passed it to the colonel. He raised his own, "Cheers!"

"Cheers!" George Brett swallowed the scotch in one, closed his eyes and sighed then studied his glass with a smile. "Wonderful." Simpson raised the bottle again. "No thank you, Ernie, You'll be getting me tiddly."

Will regarded the old soldier fondly. He never seemed to change. His uniform fitted his stocky figure like the proverbial glove. When he took his cap off he revealed thick white hair swept back from a high forehead. Laughter lines made deep impressions beside his bright blue eyes. A luxurious handlebar mustache under a hooked nose gave the impression of a face with a permanent smile.

"Official business, sir?" Simpson asked.

"Oh, good Lord no: *strictly* unofficial in fact. That's why I drove myself. I must say that's a topping piece of nonsense with the chap on the gate. Who tipped you the wink? The chap in the signal box or the old boy outside the pub?"

"Ted in the signal box. Is it that obvious?" Simpson asked while Will and Tom grinned.

"Not at all. A real staff officer would be completely taken in. Your Corporal Bowen really looked the part. So much so I gave him half a crown for his trouble. Hope you don't mind."

Simpson shrugged, "Not at all: so how did you rumble us?"

"Oh, come off it, Ernie. I can't imagine you ever wasting a man with those skills on guard duty all the time. He has more badges on his sleeve than a boy scout."

Simpson smiled, "Not much slips past you, sir. Would you care to join us for lunch?"

"Thought you would never ask, and while I have you and your chaps together I can ask a favor that will need a volunteer. I just need a private word with you beforehand to see if you agree."

Will and Tom took their cue to leave. "We will just pop over to the mess and gather the troops, sir," Will said as he ushered Tom through the door.

"What do you think this is all about, Will?" Tom asked as they strode across to the long wooden hut that served as the mess.

"Whatever it is, if George Brett is involved, it will be unofficial, unconventional and probably dangerous. Whoever volunteers might end up dead, in a German prisoner of war camp, a bar, or a sporting house."

"So you will be putting your name down?"

"Why, naturally!"

Some RFC squadrons called the area where briefings took place the operations room. But on entering the hut George Brett could see why Simpson referred to it as the map room. A huge chart showing the east of England from the Wash to the Isle of Wight, the North Sea and Channel with much of the coasts of France, Belgium, The Netherlands and part of Denmark, covered the back wall. A long wooden table had been modified to give its top surface a slight angle, so pilots studying the smaller charts pinned to it could view them at a comfortable angle while applying the various set squares and protractors scattered about. Simpson had taken a map showing the Western Front from the Belgian Coast to Verdun in the south, and pinned it to a board fixed to one of the free areas of wall.

Jackson followed them in carrying his flying kit. His name had been pulled out of the hat during lunch in the mess when everybody had volunteered for George Brett's unofficial mission. Tom Armstrong had excused himself; explaining to Will with a smile that the less he knew, the less chance he stood of being court martialled with the rest of them if the whole stunt went "tits up" as he bluntly put it.

"The first thing you have to know, Jackson, is that this does not get you out of your punishment detail. You are straight back on measuring bullets if you come back alive." Simpson said as Jackson dumped his kit on a chair.

"Understood, sir," Jackson grinned.

"Just as long as you do. The second thing you have to know is that this job is totally unofficial. If you crash anywhere between here and there, you are lost. If you are forced down by bad weather in France, you look surprised and ask the way to Colchester. If anything does not go according to plan and you land anywhere except our old field at Fertécourt where Major Power will be expecting you, then you will play the idiot. Is that clear?"

"As mud, sir."

"Good, it should be easy enough for you."

"Begging your pardon, sir, but it's all very well *me* playing the idiot," Jackson said, "but how do I explain the fact I have a colonel with me?"

Simpson and Will turned to George Brett who smiled and pointed to the red tabs on his collar. "I'm a staff officer. Anybody will know I'm an idiot without having to ask."

"Right you are, sir." The answer satisfied Jackson.

Simpson turned to Will, "Would you take care of the technicalities, Captain Turner."

"Yes, sir," Will tapped the map pinned to the board. "You should know the way to our old field from St.Omer blindfolded. You can find your way to Dover and across the Channel easily enough, you have done it before."

"Yes, sir. Are we doing this in one hop?"

"That is the plan," Will said. "You have thirty-three gallons in the gravity tank, and we just installed the new eighteen-gallon tank they sent us, under your seat. That will give you a safe margin unless you run into un-forecast headwinds or get lost, neither of which is likely."

"That's reassuring," Brett said.

"I should explain, sir," Simpson interjected, "that Lieutenant Jackson served for six months as an observer before training as a pilot. He is a very experienced man and can find his way anywhere in the foulest weather – God knows how."

Brett winked at Jackson, "Splendid, so you're not as daft as you look."

"No, sir. Nobody could be that daft."

Will continued, "You have enough daylight to make Fertécourt where you will spend the night as a guest of our old squadron. You will not, I repeat, *not* use that as an excuse to get plastered no matter how much temptation is put in your way."

"Yes, sir."

"Tomorrow morning, at dawn, you will fly Colonel Brett south to the Somme sector where he will complete his task. You will return to Fertécourt, refuel, and fly back here."

Simpson took the pointer from Will. He swept it over the battle line. "At any time you may come across enemy aircraft. You will avoid combat at all costs. Your task is to take Colonel Brett to the area he needs to go, and bring him back here safe and sound. You will not indulge in low flying, chasing staff cars, or high jinks of any kind. Do I make myself clear?"

"Yessir."

Brett coughed discreetly, "I expect young Jackson is busting with curiosity to find out why we are going on this jaunt."

"Does he need to know?" Simpson asked.

"It would help, and I think he has a right to know why he is risking his neck."

Simpson nodded, "As you wish, sir." Brett turned to the chair behind him, picked up a leather case and placed it on the table. He opened it carefully and took out a rectangular, leather covered box. He held it up and pressed a switch. A flap dropped down and the bellows of a camera slid out.

Brett handed it to Jackson. "What do you think of that, laddie?"

Jackson whistled softly, "What a beaut! A roll-film type, but so compact. Who made this?"

Brett took it back and turned it over to show the maker's name. "Bernie Feldmann. It's a one-off, you can't buy anything like this. Bernie made it for me. He's a jeweler in Hatton Garden, we've been pals for years. We belong to an astronomy society . . ." Brett turned to Simpson and Will. "Don't look so surprised. When you have spent as long as me sleeping under the stars you start to take an interest." He turned back to Jackson and pointed to the lens. "Bernie started out grinding this to fit into a telescope, but he gave it up for the war effort when I told him what I needed. He also built the rest of it. Pretty damn smooth, eh?"

Chris Davey

"I should say so."

"Your job, young man, is not so much to get me to the Somme and back, as this camera. It's worth more."

"So what are we going to snap, sir?"

"Trenches and dugouts. Trenches and dugouts and pill boxes and barbed wire and all the other frightfulness Fritz has waiting for us."

"Begging your pardon, sir, but I spent months photographing that sort of thing with a damn great plate camera. Don't we have enough pictures?"

Brett twisted the end of his mustache. "A fair question, but the answer is no. At least not of what we need to be photographing."

Jackson scratched his head, "I'm sorry, sir, but I don't follow."

"Don't worry lad, neither did we, but Colonel Brett will explain." Simpson almost sounded sympathetic.

Brett reached into his briefcase again and took out an envelope. He spread a clutch of photographs over the map on the table in front of them. They showed sections of the front line that to an untrained viewer could as easily have been the surface of the moon: a sea of shell craters, cut by irregular lines. Jackson recognized them at a glance.

"It's the line south of our old sector, sir. You can see this is all chalk like the downs in Kent. That river must be the Somme." He picked out one photograph and held it up. "Somebody got down low to take this one."

"Good lad. Now what do you see that is unusual?" Jackson studied the picture for a full minute. He turned it one way, then another to catch the light. "Can't say I see anything that . . ." he paused. "Hold on, can I borrow that magnifying glass, sir?" Brett passed him the glass with a smile.

"Well, bugger me backwards! The bastards have dug out a line of bunkers about four hundred yards back from the wire. Look, you can see how they all link up with each other and the first line trench. This shot must have been taken when the light was just right to show up the entrances. They all face away from the line so they won't get blown in so easy."

"Bloody well done, lad!" Brett clapped him on the back. He turned to Simpson and Will. "So here we have a junior officer, still wet behind the ears by campaign standards, who can see what is going on, and the bloody general staff are still claiming it's my imagination."

"But why, sir?" Will asked. "That photograph is pretty conclusive."

"Yes, it's a cracking piece of work by young Ned Robson and his observer, taken a couple of days ago, but the brass say it's a trick of the light. That our trenches always appear fuzzy compared to Fritzes' when photographed from above because the Germans have no imagination and cut theirs in straight lines. They say there is no other evidence, and that's a load of old toffee as well. Prisoners have been boasting about the depth of their defenses. Want to know the reason? I'll tell you. They don't want to believe it. They are committed to their 'big push' to relieve the pressure on the French at Verdun. They have sold the idea to the country, and they can't delay until we work out new tactics, re-train and develop new weapons." Brett paused. "Sorry, I'm starting to rant, but I think you can understand why I am desperate to drum some sense into those at the top."

"It won't be easy, sir," Simpson sighed. "I went to that demonstration on Salisbury Plain last month. They had everything laid out with neat white tapes representing trenches. Some idiot blew a whistle while another halfwit gave a running commentary. It appears that after a big bombardment, our chaps are just going to climb out of their trenches and start a route march to Berlin."

Brett raised his eyes to the roof and spread his hands. "And the press lap it up and spew it back up to the public. Hell's bells and that's another thing! Surprise? Nine-tenths of the battle? We might as well take out a full page advertisement in the *Berlin Bugle* and announce the time and date and who we expect to invite to the party. I'm telling you, gentlemen, if this attack goes ahead in this half-arsed fashion, it will be the biggest disaster ever to befall the British Army. I simply have to get photographs that are so damn conclusive they cannot ignore them. This is the camera that can do it."

The room fell silent, broken by Jackson. "Strewth! We better get our skates on. Come on, sir. We'll get those snaps."

CHAPTER 7

The Flightline

George Brett walked a full circle around the F.E.2. "By gum, it's a big bugger. Looks like it was built in a shipyard."

Will helped him into the stiff leather coat that would be his protection against the blast of freezing air he could expect exposed in the nose position. The big two-seat biplane used a "pusher" configuration. The crew sat in a pod called the *nacelle* fixed to the lower wing and protruding forward. This looked like a giant stepped bathtub with the pilot flying from the rear position and the observer in front and slightly lower in the forward cockpit. A Beardmore engine sat behind them that pushed them through the air rather than pulled, like a conventional airplane, with the engine mounted in front of the crew. The system worked because four long booms, each extending from points halfway along the upper and lower wings, carried the tail unit clear of the propeller revolving inside the lattice frame formed by them.

"Now, what the hell is this?" George examined the buckle of a heavy webbing belt Will had passed around his middle.

"That, sir, is Mr. Turner's patented gentleman's athletic supporter," Jackson spoke from his lofty perch in the rear cockpit. He reached forward and tugged a similar heavy strap with a clip attached to the end, out of the front cockpit. "You clip this on your belt and you can't fall out."

George looked up as another member of the squadron approached, "Ah ha! The ever-efficient Lieutenant Long. Have you done what I asked?"

"Yes, sir." Harry Long carried a Lewis machine gun over his shoulder and its circular ammunition drum under his other arm. "I refitted the stock," he passed the gun to Will and turned the magazine over to expose the brass cartridges, "and the twentieth-from-last and fifth-from-last rounds are tracer."

"Can I ask why, sir?" Will asked.

"Certainly, m'boy," George said as he placed the drum over its spigot mounting, and turned it until he felt the first round engage in the mechanism. "I don't hold much with tracer as a rule. It just tells you where the last shot, but one, went. But if you replace the twentieth-from-last round, and the fifth-from-last, with a tracer, it will tell you exactly how far you have gone through that magazine. Mr. Long has already done that for our spare drums. Now, come on, give me a leg up." They lifted him bodily until his left foot found the awkwardly placed step in the side of the nacelle and he swung himself into the front cockpit. "This'll do very well. Spiffing view from up here, and I see I even have a windscreen."

"Another Captain Turner patent, sir," Jackson said. "It folds out of the way if you need to use the gun."

"I see no point in discomfort for the sake of it, sir." Will passed the Lewis gun up to the colonel who fixed it to the pillar mounting at the front of his cockpit. The old soldier looked down and smiled.

"Then you'll never make senior rank in the army, or headmaster at a public school."

"Thank God for that, sir." Will stood back and raised his hand in farewell. "Have a nice journey, gentlemen, give my regards to *La Belle France.*"

Jackson grinned and gave him a thumbs up. "I'll do better than that, sir. I'll give your love to Giselle at the *Chapeau Rouge.*" He pulled down his goggles and called over his shoulder, "Ready to start."

"Fuel on? Throttle set?" The mechanic's familiar response came back.

"Fuel is on. Throttle is set . . . contact!" Jackson replied, his arm working furiously as he cranked the starter magneto.* Will nodded his approval as the engine, already warmed by the mechanics, started on the first pull of the big propeller. Simpson joined him as they watched Jackson going carefully through his pre-take-off checks. The control surfaces waggled as he checked for full and free movement. The easy rumble of the Beardmore engine rose to a full-throated bellow and the F.E.2 trembled against the chocks as Jackson ran the revs up to maximum then throttled back to idle. Satisfied, he raised his hands and then crossed them in front of his face to give the okay for the chocks to be taken away. The biplane waddled forward with a mechanic trotting at each wingtip. Once clear of the other parked aircraft, the man on the port wing dug his heels in and swung the machine into the wind. The engine noise swelled again, the propeller blast rippling the grass like wind driven water on a pond. The F.E.2 accelerated, slowly at first, and then the tail came up; she gathered her skirts and soared into the air. Jackson made a wide turn that brought him back over the field. He dipped his wings once in salute and curved away. They watched until the airplane was a distant speck silhouetted against a layer of high cloud.

---

* *By now many aero engines were fitted with a magneto capable of generating a boosted current to the spark plugs for starting. The pilot cranked a handle while a mechanic swung the propeller.*

Turner's Defense

"Do you think Jackson will be able to stay out of trouble in the air, sir?" Will asked.

Simpson grunted, "I doubt it, but there's one thing I can guarantee."

"What is that?"

"If there's any chance of getting into trouble on the ground, George Brett will get them into it. The silly old sod still thinks he's twenty years old, and he'd rather be chasing skirt with a youngster like Jackson, than swilling port with the old farts at the club." Ernie Simpson scratched his chin. "And bloody good luck to him."

❦ ⊷━⊶ ❦

Stan checked his compass and settled the F.E.2 on a southerly course. He eased the throttle to reduce the engine revolutions, giving enough power for a steady climb without straining the engine. The new 160-horsepower Beardmores had given trouble in service. He had helped Will and Sergeant Major Cole carefully strip down this engine, replace the pins that joined the pistons to the connecting rods with specially hardened items, and fit new bearings and shells to the crankshaft. It now thrummed happily behind him, the bass roar of the exhaust carried away in the slipstream. The weather front that had brought the dull damp conditions had blown through leaving crystal clear air as if the rain had washed the sky clean. Glancing down he noticed that new crops in the fields below still showed the soil between the rows like the scalp on a balding head. The trees in Epping Forest directly below almost glowed in their new spring foliage. London stood out framed between the two starboard wings, his keen eyes picked out the gothic spires of Tower Bridge: barely twenty years old, the fresh stonework sprouted over the masts of the ships crammed into the Port of London.

Stan smiled—if only his mates at home in Sydney could see him now. Passed over for promotion to deputy assistant to the under-manager of the

– 75

National and Empire Bank, King's Cross Branch, he had resigned in a fit of pique fueled by a beery evening the night before. "Never discuss your career with a hangover," his father had advised. Good advice perhaps, but Stan had packed his bags and sailed for the "Old Dart,"* determined to enlist in the Royal Flying Corps, fired by newspaper stories about the exploits of pioneer fliers like Louis Strange.

Strewth! he thought to himself, now he counted Strange as a friend. With his flying pay he earned more than the manager who had told him with a smug look on his pasty face that his moral terpitude—whatever that was—had been the reason for his missing out on a promotion. In fact, he decided, when he saw the manager again he would spit in his eye. Then again, he mused, that would be behavior unbecoming an officer and a gentleman, and he was in enough trouble for that already.

He planned to cross the River Thames well clear of the sprawling suburbs that now oozed their way into the countryside. He identified the small town of Dartford on the south bank, easy to recognize with its adjacent cement works, the river studded with the sails of barges waiting to load at the wharves as the works churned out the thousands of tons of Portland cement demanded by the military engineers. Stan leaned to one side and closed one eye to line up one of the tall chimneys against the leading edge of the wing. The relative sideways motion revealed by his simple check proved a quartering crosswind pushed them on to a more easterly track. The wind blew from different directions at different altitudes: find the right height and you could often use the wind to your advantage. Madcap, devil-may-care Stan Jackson, on the ground, transformed into a clever, methodical, and scientific pilot in the air. A gentle sideways pressure on the stick combined with a push on the left rudder pedal sent the F.E.2 curving on to a new course, now with the benefit of a stiff tail wind the biplane scooted above the rolling Kent countryside with a groundspeed of nearly one hundred miles an hour. He leaned forward and tapped his passenger on the shoulder.

*Australian slang for Great Britain

"Under two hours," Stan bellowed. He held up two fingers and crooked one down to indicate the fraction. The colonel smiled and gave him a thumbs-up signal in return. George Brett had flown five times before, eager to take advantage of the new perspective of the battlefield offered by the airplane. His previous flights had been in B.E.2s or Avro biplanes where his cockpit had been hemmed in by wings, struts and wires. The F.E.2 offered an unhindered view. So unhindered it felt alarming at first, suspended over thin air with nothing between him and the ground apart from the fabric covered sides of the nacelle. He forced himself to stand, the wind battering against him as he emerged from behind the shelter of the windscreen. If they did meet an enemy aircraft the observer had to stand to work his gun. The sides of his cockpit hardly extended to waist level. He felt a tug and turned. Stan gave a reassuring smile and held up the safety strap to show it was clipped on. George took a firm grip on the Lewis and settled the stock against his shoulder, then swung the gun from side-to-side and up and down. He sat down in the wicker seat the workshop had fitted to replace the usual narrow shelf provided for the observer and re-fastened his safety belt. He glanced over the side. *Safe as houses,* he thought to himself.

The English Channel lay ahead beyond the famous white cliffs that had their mirror image in the chalk cliffs near what had once been the pretty little French resort of Boulogne; before the war turned it into a vast military encampment. Below, the last of England unrolled like a moving map, and they coasted out en route for France. *Two hours from a field in Essex to a field in Flanders, George thought.* Perhaps three from London itself to Paris. When this bloody war is over, I'm going to buy shares in the first company to set up an aerial carriage service, he promised himself. There's definitely a future in air travel.

● ⊶⊷ ●

Will hitched a lift on one of the unit trucks to Chipping Ongar the next morning where he caught the ten-twenty to London. He managed to snare a cab to Whitehall and arrived at his uncle's office shortly after noon. Frank Penrose welcomed him with a handshake.

"Thanks awfully for coming up to town at short notice. I'm afraid this bloody business with Matrett's ridiculous aeroplane is gaining a life of its own. We have a meeting this afternoon with yet another committee, but I'm embarrassed to have to tell you it's been put back to fifteen hundred hours. Still, all's not lost; you can escort a young lady to lunch." Frank opened the door to one of the inner offices. A tall, thin, woman wearing a long grey skirt and matching jacket stood behind Joe Thorpe. She had one hand on his shoulder and was leaning over to look at a sheet of paper he had on the desk in front of him. They were laughing.

"Jacquieline, may I introduce my nephew, Captain William Turner? We call him Will." She turned and stepped through into the main office. "Will, I would like you to meet Madame Jacquieline Courroyer." She held out her hand and Will took it and bowed from the waist.

"*Enchanté Madame.*"

Before he could kiss her hand she gripped his and shook it firmly. "Never mind the fancy French introductions, Captain Turner, I'm a damn sight more English than you," her accent was Home Counties English; a faint smile played on her lips. He stood for a moment transfixed. Her gray eyes bored straight through him. Will felt a bizarre desire to confess.

"How did you know I am not British?" he stammered.

"Well, I watched you cross the street from this window, and just like every other foreigner, you looked the wrong way for traffic as you stepped into the road."

"Really?"

She shook her head and raised her eyes to the ceiling as Joe Thorpe and his uncle burst out laughing. "No, of course not, you ninny. That came from a Sherlock Holmes story. Your uncle and Joe have told me all about you. Come on, you're taking me out to lunch." She snatched her hat from the stand and took Will by the arm. "I'll look after him, sir," she called back over her shoulder.

"Just make sure he doesn't get knocked over by a bus," Frank Penrose said as they stepped into the corridor.

"Do you have a preference for lunch, Madame Courroyer?" Will asked as she propelled him along the corridor and down the first flight of stairs.

She nudged him in the ribs with her elbow. "First, drop the *Madame.* It makes it sound as if I run a knocking shop for a living." She laughed out loud as his jaw dropped in surprise. "Your uncle and Joe call me Jac. That'll do. And secondly, I do have a restaurant I like, and you will be relieved to hear it's a Lyon's teashop about a ten-minute walk away. They do hot meals from twelve 'til three."

Will nodded, "You read minds then?"

"Yes, I probably do, but I don't have to be a medium to know that you live on your pay alone, and that's not easy for a young army captain."

"Now how do you know that?" His irritation showed in his voice.

"Keep your hair on. Your sister told me."

"What? You know my sister?" They had reached the bottom of the series of stairs that ended in a small hallway at a back door of the War Office building. A corporal stood behind a desk. He spun a ledger and handed Jacquieline Courroyer a pen.

She signed her name. "Yes, Jim, we'll be back in an hour." She handed the pen to Will who signed himself out. They emerged at the back of the building and walked the short distance to a narrow portal guarded by a single soldier. He stiffened and slapped the stock of his sloped rifle in salute. Will had the feeling it was for the woman striding along at his side.

"So how long have you worked for my uncle?" She stopped in mid stride and touched his arm to make him face her. It was the first time in the few minutes since they met that he had a chance to look at her properly. Her gray eyes seemed to draw him in; it was impossible not to look at them. High cheekbones and a strong nose and jaw blocked any perception of Madame Courroyer as pretty, or even conventionally beautiful. Her firm jaw spoke of character, a strong character. Her wide mouth, now twisted in a wry grin, suggested that character might well be generous. Will had to admit it: Madame Jacquieline Courroyer was a damned handsome woman.

"Very good. Very good indeed. How did you know?" she asked.

"Well, I do not have to be a medium. You sign your name in the staff column in the register, I sign mine as a visitor."

"*Touché, mon brave capitaine,*" she laughed aloud and put her arm through his. "You're not as stupid as you look, which is lucky, really, under the circumstances."

"Are you always this direct?" Will asked, falling into step beside her.
"Yes."

"Well, I thank you for that, because you know I am really just a simple engineer. But I have learned a lot since I came to England. In fact before I joined the army I could not even spell engineer, but now I *are* one."

She jabbed him in the ribs again and chuckled. "Don't come your simple country boy routine with me, Will Turner. Vicky told me all about you."

They had arrived at the Lyons teashop with its imposing white and gold façade. "Really?" Will said as he opened the door and stepped back to usher her in. "Pray tell, I am sure this will be an education for me." Jac just smiled and brushed past him. She approached the counter and spoke to the manager, resplendent in his immaculate white apron.

"Anything special for your favorite office girl, Percy?"

He winked and turned to the dumbwaiter set in the wall behind him. "Just what you asked for, but only because you've got a real, live hero treating you to lunch." He set two steaming plates on a wooden tray.

She turned back to Will, "The last steak pie in Joe Lyon's empire, with mashed spuds and new beans, and how about lemonade to go with it. Will that do?"

"Why yes, thank you."

"Don't thank me, you're paying." She picked up the tray and set it down at an empty table by the window. Will pulled back her chair then sat down himself.

"So what, exactly, has my sister told you about me?"

"Oh, the usual," she replied. "How you're a complete rotter, teased her mercilessly."

Will smiled, "Oh yes, I was an utter pig."

"Actually, no," she said, looking serious. "In fact, your sister thinks the sun shines out of your backside. She tells me that you are exceedingly clever, well-educated, brave, talented in many different ways, a charmer, a flirt, sometimes forthright to the point of being outspoken when you think you're right."

"What! Vicky said all that?"

"Yes. She also said that you were not always right and you are, in fact, possessed of very poor judgment in some areas," she paused and smiled. "Especially where women are concerned. Something about 'looking a gift horse in the mouth,' I think she said."

Will sat back and shook his head. "I think I know what *that* is all about."

"I've met your Marie. She's very sweet and you have to admit she's gone to a lot of trouble to be with you."

Will frowned. "She is not *my* Marie, and I wish she had stayed safe at home. It's bad enough having to worry about my headstrong sister without adding our little friend." A few months earlier Will's sister, Victoria, accompanied by her friend Marie Julien, had sailed for England as Red Cross volunteers and narrowly escaped death when their ship had been torpedoed off the Irish coast.

"Is that how you see her, as a friend?"

"Yes." Will took up the challenge in Jac's eyes and looked straight back at her.

"That's not how she wants it to be."

"Oh, so how do you know what she thinks? That medium of yours again?"

Jac threw back her head and laughed, "No, she told me herself. I like her, she's straightforward."

"She is, and she is also used to getting her own way."

Jac wagged a finger, "Then you'd better watch out." She cut into her steak pie. "Come on, it'll get cold."

Will realized how hungry he was and set about his lunch. They sat back at the same time. He eased the strap on his Sam Browne belt. "Very nice, and good value."

"I could say the same about you," Jac smiled then looked down to delve in her bag on the seat next to them.

"I beg your pardon?"

She found the packet of cigarettes she had been looking for and looked up, "Good value."

"Begging your pardon, ma'am, but what on earth do you mean by that?"

She offered him the packet. He shook his head, but before she could light her cigarette he produced a match and struck it by flicking it with his thumbnail. She smiled at the trick and accepted the light, inhaling deeply then sitting back and blowing a smoke ring toward the ceiling. "You're good value—to the British Government."

"I am sorry, I still do not follow you."

"Think about it. You're a graduate engineer with a wealth of experience in aviation. You could sell yourself to the highest bidder: the Royal Aircraft Factory, Tom Sopwith, The Bristol Aeroplane Company. Any one of them would pay you five times what you are earning as an army captain." She pursed her lips and narrowed her eyes, "You could even take the same route as that other neutral aeroplane engineer, Anthony Fokker. I bet the Hun would pay you ten times as much."

"Oh, for heaven's sake! I am hardly likely to do that, am I?" Will struggled to keep his voice down as other diners glanced toward their table. "I cannot imagine that in the course of your snooping you did not discover that my mother is English."

She smiled, "That was what I was hoping you would say, and of course I know that your mother, Charlotte, is English. How else would Colonel Penrose be your uncle?"

Will held up his hands, palms toward her, "I do apologize, my language was intemperate."

"No apology necessary, I'm a nosey cow. So can I take it that you don't approve of the Germans?"

Will's brow furrowed, "Of course I do not approve. They got us into this mess by marching into Belgium and France. Whatever way you cut it, that was an unforgivable act of aggression."

"What do you think of them?"

"The Germans?"

"Yes, as people."

"Well, I never gave it much thought. I do not know many personally. I was held prisoner briefly, and I have to say I was treated very well. The one or two I have met as prisoners of war, including the one I captured myself, seemed like pretty decent fellows."

She fixed him with her stare, "Hmmmm, pretty decent fellows," she repeated his words slowly. "So you don't hate them?"

"No, I cannot say that I do."

She stubbed out her cigarette, grinding it into the ashtray. "I do. I loathe, hate and detest them." She glanced up to gauge the effect of her words. Will looked taken aback at the venom in her voice.

He chose his words carefully, "This is something personal."

"Yes," she paused and looked out of the window at the bustling street. When she turned back to him he could see tears in her eyes. He waited, unwilling to press her, but she went on anyway. "Do you believe the stories about Hun atrocities in Belgium and France?"

"I believe they were exaggerated, but I do know they were responsible for some unspeakable acts, not least the murder of Nurse Cavell last year."

"Let me tell you about an unexaggerated atrocity in the first days of the war," she sat back in her chair. "Have you heard of a town called Louvain? Or Leuven in the Flemish dialect?"

"Yes, it lies to the east of Brussels."

"That's the place. I used to live and work there; I taught English. I met and married a university lecturer. A wonderful, kind, generous, peaceable, romantic, handsome man." Jac's words sounded firm, but brittle. He could tell she did not tell this story easily. "The Germans arrived within a few days of the outbreak of war. Just to show us they meant business, they burned much of the town, including the university library – German 'kultur,' don't make me laugh." She spat the words.

Will nodded, "Yes, I did hear about that, and there were rumors that they shot several civilians." He had put two and two together.

"My husband, my dear Phillipe," her voice had softened. "Rushed down to the university when he heard that his students were massing for a demonstration. Fearing bloodshed, he went to stop them. But the fucking Germans," she leaned forward and lowered her voice to a whisper, allowing herself a smile at the look of shock on Will's face in reaction to her language, "they weren't afraid of a bit of bloodshed. Oh no. They grabbed my husband and four of his students, stood them up against a wall and shot them. Just like that. What do you think of that, Captain Turner?" She sat back, the look on her face oddly satisfied.

"Sweet Jesus. That is appalling."

"Yes, it is, isn't it? So now you see why I don't think they are decent fellows." Her voice sounded almost bright, as if she felt relieved of a burden.

Will took a deep breath, "Yes, I understand. So I am guessing you made your way back to England, and you are doing what you can to fight them."

"Yes, but it's not much. What I would really like to do is for you to fly me over to Hunland in one of your aeroplanes so that I can machine gun them like the vermin they are. Don't suppose you could arrange that?" she said, smiling at him.

Will shook his head, "Regrettably, I do not think it would be allowed."

She studied him, then her face softened, "Will, I know that's impossible, but what are the chances of you taking me up?"

"What, just for the fun of it?"

"Yes, we are still allowed some fun, the government hasn't rationed it yet you know."

"Of course I can. It will be unofficial of course, but I will be delighted." The mood had changed. "So, you are not one of the, 'If God had meant us to fly he would have given us wings, brigade?' "

"Goodness no!" Jac laughed. "If God had meant us to drive he would have given us wheels and an engine, but that never stopped me. I know it's not supposed to be ladylike, but I just love motors of any type. I raced motorbikes before the war, you know."

"Really?"

"Oh yes, and I could drive Pa's Daracq touring car before he could. But an aeroplane has to be the most thrilling."

"So you have never been up?"

"No, but I have sat in one. Last summer your people brought an aeroplane to Horse Guards and set it up. For sixpence you could sit in it and a dashing young birdman explained the controls, they did it for the troop comforts drive. I went back again and had a bob's* worth. It was perfect. One of those late summer days when the big cauliflower clouds build up

* *Slang for a shilling. There were twenty shillings to a pound in the pre decimal British Currency*

– 85

like castles in the sky." She closed her eyes at the memory, "I could just imagine climbing and swooping through the valleys between them, soaring over the countryside, seeing the world from above, the wind rushing by, just like the birds have since the beginning of time. Is it an experience as fine as I imagine?"

"Better than you could ever imagine."

"My word, if they had just left me alone, I reckon I could have got that thing started and I would have been off! Away over Hyde Park and on my way to adventure, chasing the far horizon."

"Trust me, you will not be disappointed when I carry you up among the clouds."

She grinned, a wicked glint in her eye, "The chap at Horse Guards said it was as much fun as you could ever have with your clothes on."

Will's jaw dropped, "My goodness! What a nerve, someone should break him of that ungentlemanly behavior."

Jac roared with laughter, "I told him that too. I was so offended, in fact, that I accepted his offer of dinner that evening." She stood up, "Anyway, I'm going to hold you to that. Oh well, back to work, come on."

They left the restaurant and stepped out in the bright sunshine. She took his arm again and smiled back at the people who passed by. "They think we make a very handsome couple, you know?"

"Ah, regrettably it would never work out," Will sighed. "You are so much my intellectual superior, being a teacher and such, society would never allow it."

Jac smiled, "Your sister is right, you are a bloody charmer. What you mean is that I am ten years older than you and you can take your pick of all the young things who throw themselves at you."

"Never!"

"Ah, such gallantry."

Will changed the subject, "So what do you do exactly for Uncle Frank's department?"

"I work with Joe, he's my direct boss."

"Oh, so you are a—"

She put her finger on his lips, "Not so loud, Will. Yes, I help break the German codes. I speak German fluently. Rather ironic don't you think?"

They made their way back to the office where Will's uncle waited for him. The meeting that was the purpose of the journey to London took place in a committee room at the Palace of Westminster, the Houses of Parliament. Will repeated his argument to the committee members who listened with attitudes that ranged from polite but bored: to intense interest. The meeting wound up in the early evening. Will and Frank Penrose climbed into their official car with relief and ordered the driver to head for Frank's club. Joe Thorpe, dressed in a smart civilian suit waited for them in reception. He looked like a suburban bank manager. They sat down in a private room to a dinner of roast beef.

"So what do you think of our Jac then?" Joe asked.

Will leaned over the table and refilled Joe's wine glass. "An interesting lady. She told me that she helps you in decoding German signals, but if that is all she does, then I declare I must be a monkey's uncle."

Frank looked at him, a half-smile on his face, "What makes you say that?"

"Because an assistant, not even an assistant in a special department in the War House, does not need to carry an automatic pistol in her bag." Will sat back and looked from Joe to his uncle.

The two older men looked at each other. Frank nodded, "Joe, you're her boss, tell her to be more careful in future." He turned to Will, "Full marks for observation. You didn't say anything to her?"

"Of course not. I was brought up never to embarrass a lady by asking why she might be carrying a piece. It is usually a gal who works in a certain kind of establishment, and then it is usually a derringer. Unless of course she robs banks, then it is a Colt by tradition."

Frank sighed, "We better tell him, Joe, before his imagination runs riot and her reputation is ruined in his eyes." Joe nodded. "Did she tell you about her husband?"

"Yes."

"Did she tell you what happened after that?"

"No."

Frank loosened his tie, "Briefly, she came back to England, repatriated with many others from Belgium. She came straight from the station to the War Office and demanded to be given a job, and made it obvious she was going to be a damn nuisance unless she got one. She was a godsend to us: fluent in French, German and Vlaamse, the Flemish dialect of Dutch. We sent her straight back to Belgium as an agent. We gave her a new background, as a Belgian, and sent her to Brussels where she did a magnificent job for nearly a year. The information she sent back to us proved priceless. What we didn't know was that she was arranging her own little stunt at the same time."

Will scratched his chin, "Let me guess, could it have involved a town called Louvain?"

Frank nodded, "Very perceptive. She found out which German officer ordered the shootings. To her delight he had been promoted to brigadier general and posted to Brussels. She found out all she could about him: he turned out to be minor Prussian royalty related to the Kaiser himself. The only word for it is that she stalked him. When the time was right she made her move—she set about seducing him."

"I can see how she could do that easily."

"Yes, she's a bloody good-looking woman. You should see her when she's done up to the nines in evening dress," Frank said with obvious admiration. "Anyway, the rest was easy. She flirted with him over dinner at the Hotel Imperial, invited him to her room for a 'little nightcap,' got him half-plastered and down to his underwear, and then lured him out to the balcony of her seventh-floor suite."

Will gulped, "She didn't?"

"Oh yes she did. She heaved him over the railings. She said he squealed all the way down and made the most satisfying noise when he hit the cobbles. She told me she even managed to keep him teetering on the brink for a second or two so he would know what it must have felt like to experience the gap between 'ready' and 'fire.' "

Will swallowed the rest of his wine and shuddered, "Good grief!"

Joe took up the story, "Then of course she was away on her toes; straight down the back stairs and into the night. Two days later she shows up at our consulate in Holland. It was a masterful assassination in more ways than one."

"How so?"

"If she had just walked up to him and shot him there would have been reprisals against the civilian population – that's their way. But this way he was the guilty party. Everybody had seen him flirting with the mystery woman for days. Hotel staff had seen him go to her room, and then he's found dead, half-naked. The Germans had to cover it up themselves. There would have been a terrible scandal, and in all decency I suspect they wanted to shield his wife and family from the fact he was a randy old goat. It was presented as a terrible accident."

"Hell's teeth," Will said quietly. "Remind me not to cross her."

"Of course, I was bloody furious," Frank said with a sigh. "This war is dragging the whole world in, and my best agent is waging her own private battle. She well and truly blotted her copybook."

"Well, yes," Will said. "But you can understand why she did it."

Frank nodded, "Yes, I can. But we can never send her over again. There's a price on her head. They may have presented it as an accident, but their military intelligence department soon worked out the 'why,' and came up with the 'who.' It's quite possible that one of their agents here has revenge as part of his orders. That's why she carries the pistol."

Joe nodded, his face grim, "Between ourselves, she would just love them to try it. It would give her the excuse to top another one of the blighters."

Frank twisted the stopper from a bottle of scotch and poured them all a generous measure, "Gentlemen, we have cigarettes, we have whiskey, and by heavens we've got ourselves some wild, wild, women. God bless 'em!" He raised his glass in a toast.

CHAPTER 8

Fertécourt, France

George Brett and Stan Jackson stood outside the photographic hut on the airfield at Fertécourt. They both puffed on the noxious black cheroots that George always carried.

"Saints preserve us! Will you just look at yourselves, gentlemen," Major Liam Power approached carrying a tea tray. "You look like a pair of expectant fathers."

"I can't speak from experience, but giving birth can't be this painful," George Brett grunted.

"Well here's a nice cup of tea to steady your nerves, but you really don't have to worry. Tisdale is a genius, he'll make the most of your holiday snaps."

As if on cue, Corporal Tisdale opened the door. To their intense relief his face wore a broad smile. "I think you'll like the result, gentlemen. Please step inside." They crowded into the tiny room.

"Bloody well done, Corporal!" George Brett clapped him on the back. They gazed at the twelve prints now clipped on a line to dry. To an untrained eye they could have been a selection of photographs of ancient monoliths and archaeological diggings. For a soldier experienced in the hell of trench warfare they represented his worst nightmare.

Liam Power pointed to one photograph, "Jesus, Joseph and Mary, how many are there like that?" The picture showed a concrete blockhouse with steps disappearing many feet below the level of the surrounding trench. It appeared as if the photographer had stood at the entrance to get his shot.

"Dozens," George said, his voice grim. "All connected by deep trenches, traverses, barbed wire, machine gun positions, you name it, they've put it in there."

"Well, they can't argue with these pictures," Power said. "How many do you need?"

"We'll take a set back with us, and then if Tisdale can run us off some extras I will give you a list of recipients."

"I'll mark the envelopes, 'Top Secret,' sir." Tisdale said.

George laughed and shook his head, "No, don't. Mark them, 'Have a look at these.' The more people who see them the better the chance of them doing some good." They stepped back into the sunshine and breathed the fresh air, grateful to be away from the sweet, metallic stink of photographic processing. Liam pulled a leather-covered flask from his pocket, removed the stopper and held it over the mugs of tea he had set down on an oil drum outside the hut. He looked at them and raised a questioning eyebrow.

"Oh, yes please!" George rubbed his hands. "I think we earned it, or should I say young Jackson here earned it." Stan muttered something, his face flushed with embarrassment. "Don't be modest, lad. That was a masterful piece of flying." He turned to Liam. "He took us down so low and held the machine so steady, all I had to do was stand there, point the camera and press the shutter. We were so low I leaned over and shook hands with one chap whose picture I took."

Liam laughed, "Ah, you've something of the Irish in you, sir."

George Brett knew that Stan Jackson had pulled off what the airmen at Fertécourt described as a "brilliant stunt." Stan could hardly believe how well the plan had come together. He had to admit that when these

Poms had to do something depending on split-second timing, they made sure it worked.

The original intention had been for them to sneak out on their own, and make one pass down a particular part of the line in the Somme sector that George had earmarked. The camera they carried produced spectacular results, if near enough to the subject. Stan decided that the lower he flew, the safer they must be, as gunners on the ground would have just seconds to react before they disappeared from view.

Liam Power declared a lone flight too dangerous when they explained their mission on arrival. In the morning, with dawn brushing the horizon of a perfect spring morning, they set out as one of a flight of four F.E.2s led by Liam Power himself. They climbed to a height of ten thousand feet as they flew south to the Somme sector of the British front. Stan scanned the flawless blue sky with mixed feelings. On the one hand not a ripple of turbulence disturbed the cold, crystal clear air, making it easy to hold formation: the four airplanes seemed locked in a stationary tableau. On the other hand, Stan calculated that they must be clearly visible for fifty miles around. A salvo of archie bursting below confirmed his suspicions.

Their plan depended on the German observers on the ground being blinded by the sun rising behind their own line, if they made their approach from the east, and timed their arrival to the minute. The clear sky almost guaranteed that. The section of line that George had indicated on the map appeared ahead. Liam Power turned and led them straight over the trenches. Anybody watching from either side would assume they flew on a routine bombing mission of the German rear areas.

A few miles behind the lines, on a pre-arranged signal, Stan dropped out of the formation and turned back. He chopped the throttle and shoved the nose down, sending them plunging down through the icy air. As the speed increased, their machine tried to follow its instinct to pull out of the dive, but Stan used both hands and soon all his strength on the controls to keep them plummeting toward the German trenches. Behind them, the rest of the flight turned to follow and now hurtled in pursuit.

Stan forced himself to ignore the din of the wind through the wires. As the speed increased, the pitch changed from a dull roar to a demonic shriek, chasing them down the sky. He concentrated on the shattered landscape growing in his windshield. He had to make a ninety-degree turn to align them with the German trenches to allow George Brett to take his photographs as they ran parallel; and he had to make the turn exact.

Stan forced himself to wait, and wait. He gritted his teeth. They screamed through the air faster than he had ever known. A vibration started that ran through the frame of the airplane and right through his body. Crouching behind the windscreen to escape the torrent of wind, he prayed the wings would stay on. The ground rose up to meet them, to smash them. Stan counted to three, leveled out then heaved the stick over to his right. The horizon rotated to stand on end, then he sucked the stick back into his stomach.

"Ooooomph!" Stan gasped as the G forces smashed him down as the biplane howled through the turn. He flung his weight into the controls again to straighten out. He saw George stagger to his feet, the camera aimed at the trench line now just feet under their left wing. As the speed decayed, Stan moved his hand to the throttle to add power, but he forced himself to wait, fearing that vibration might ruin the photographs, and he knew the slower they passed over the target, the better the pictures had to be. The controls sagged in his hands. He fed power in to keep them in the air—just. George raised one hand, thumb extended, and slumped down in his seat.

"Thank God for that!" Stan jammed the throttle wide open and pushed forward on the stick. Their wing tip brushed over the barbed wire as he banked left to take them over their own trenches to safety.

Behind them, the German line collapsed in chaos. Alerted by the banshee wail of the diving airplanes the men in the trench lines dived for cover or grabbed weapons to defend themselves, but the rising sun blinded them. They ignored the first machine overhead as it swept along. That danger had passed. But they fought to drag machine guns and rifles to bear as the three pursuing F.E.s tore down on them; then threw themselves flat as the gunners in the front cockpits sprayed bullets from their Lewis guns into dugouts and trenches. The plan worked. Not a single shot came near the photographers.

They rendezvoused behind the British lines and climbed away, waving across the space between the four machines. Less than an hour later, they floated back to earth at Fertécourt. As they rolled to a stop, Stan unbuckled his seatbelt and leaned over the front cockpit.

"Are you alright, sir?"

George Brett pushed up his goggles and blew out his cheeks. "Never better, my boy." Stan clambered to the ground and helped the colonel down. For a second he appeared to stumble, but he checked himself as Stan grabbed his arm. "No, I'm fine, but by gum, I'm glad you warned me what would happen when you made that turn! I thought I'd been flattened. Never felt anything like it—better than any fairground ride. We'll make a fortune after the war, taking people up." He squeezed Stan's arm, "You do the flying, and I'll count the money."

"Did you get the pictures, sir?" Stan had asked, as the other fliers gathered around them, faces flushed with excitement.

George had held up the camera and kissed it. "Worked a treat, the whole roll fed through perfectly. Now let's see what's on it."

Now they had their answer, they slurped down the brandy-reinforced tea—triumph mixed with relief at being alive.

"You'll stay for an early lunch?" Liam Power suggested. "The riggers are going over your machine now to see if you did any damage in that dive. There will still be plenty of daylight; you'll be home in time for tea. And nobody will be any the wiser."

Two hours later, they soared into the air, with the good wishes of Stan's old comrades in their ears, and two bottles of contraband brandy secured under his seat. The promise of the clear sunrise had been fulfilled.

A scattering of brilliant soft white puffball clouds decorated a sky blessed with bright spring sunshine. Stan followed the battle line for a few miles as they steadied on course for the English Channel, visible as a gray line to their left.

George Brett raised himself and twisted around in his seat. Stan cut the throttle and leaned forward to hear. "Wipers!" George pointed forward. Stan nodded and changed course, taking them closer to the front. The old soldier had his camera out again. Stan felt just as curious to see what state the beautiful old Belgian town of Ypres must be in by now. The pivot of the infamous salient, it had been battered continuously by shellfire, but he had heard that civilians still clung on to a semblance of their old lives in the ruins.

They gazed down. Stan groaned. Only the cathedral maintained any of its shape. Perhaps the German artillerymen held some standards, but the glorious Cloth Hall, the pride of the once thriving community, had been reduced to a shot-blasted shell, its tower now the biggest pile of rubble in a churning sea of rubble. Ever the professional, Stan scanned the sky around them while George shot off another role of film then stowed the camera.

Only a solitary B.E.2 shared this patch of sky. Two thousand feet below it plodded along a fixed line while the pilot exposed another rack of photographic plates and the observer anxiously watched for enemy airplanes.

Stan jumped. A burst of white smoke materialized a few yards ahead. A British shell. German anti-aircraft artillery exploded black or brown. This one came close enough to hear the crack as it exploded. He flinched expecting another, closer. Instead, a line of bursts bloomed away to their right. A common trick, this salvo had been fired not to kill, but to warn and direct. Stan followed the line the British gunners had drawn across the sky. Three dots, like swarming insects, plunged down towards the B.E.2

from the German side of the line. Fokker Eindekker monoplanes:* once the terror of the skies and now obsolete, but still deadly to a lone observation airplane.

George Brett had seen them too. He leaped to his feet, swung his windscreen clear, and cocked the Lewis. Stan Jackson's orders had been clear. He was to avoid combat at all costs. He pushed the stick forward and over. For the second time that day, they heard the howl of the slipstream as the F.E.2 stooped like an ungainly hawk on the three German airplanes. "Orders my arse," Stan said aloud through gritted teeth, his words swept away by the wind.

A single wing fighter aircraft designed by the Dutchman Antony Fokker. The first mass produced airplane to be fitted with a machine gun that could be fired through the propeller.

CHAPTER 9

Office of Colonel Frank Penrose, London

Jacquieline Courroyer glared at Frank Penrose across the table in his office. "Hopeless, bloody hopeless. He'll be found out and shot."

Frank smiled, "I agree. I hoped you would say that."

Ambrose Spencer frowned, "Now what do you base that rather snap judgment on?"

She turned her gun-sight stare on Spencer. "Because Ambrose . . . Will Turner obviously belongs to the George Washington school of subterfuge. 'It was I, with my little axe, that chopped down the tree.' " Spencer looked puzzled. Jac continued, "He couldn't fool anyone, he's too bloody honest! Not only that, I just don't think Will Turner is cut-out for this type of work. He's too . . ." she turned to Frank Penrose for support but he just shrugged ". . . nice! He's too bloody nice."

Spencer frowned again, "Nice?"

"Yes, *nice*," Jac ploughed on, searching for the words to support her argument. "I don't know—he just doesn't seem to have that ruthless streak we need to fight the Hun."

Joe Thorpe's eyebrows shot up, then he laughed. "Oh yes, I'm sure the crews of the dozen or so aeroplanes he has sent down in bits or in flames, and the Hun soldiers he has machine-gunned and blown up are all agreed they couldn't have been slaughtered by a nicer bloke."

Spencer smiled at her, "You are also talking about the man who had me discreetly covered with a bloody great pistol that would have done justice to Jesse James the first time we met, in case I was an impostor."

"Okay, you've made your point. Perhaps he is sharper than he looks. But I still say that he will give himself away. I don't think he has the capacity for lying his way out of trouble."

"That's my point. He won't need to lie. He won't need to pretend to be somebody else," Spencer spoke quietly.

Jac studied him. He could have passed for a well-heeled businessman or senior government official in his expensively tailored blue suit. The diamond and gold tiepin he wore the only clue that he might be anything other than conservative in his habits. It irritated her that when some people met Spencer they would remark there was something "foreign" about him, as if that made him somehow inferior, but she had to admit he did have something about him that suggested a more exotic background. His thinning hair, brushed back from a high forehead, grew dark and wavy with a hint of gray in the temples that showed up against his dark skin. But his cultured tones were British, without a trace of any other accent. And when he spoke, people listened. "Explain." Jac said.

"He won't have to lie. He will have to forget."

"Forget what?" Admiral Percy Scott spoke for the first time.

"Everything from August 1914. Everything about Captain Turner, MC, RFC. He will have to become William Turner, Aviation Correspondent for *Modern Mechanics* magazine. He will have to return to the United States and come back to Europe as a new man, a man reinvented."

Frank sighed, "But there it is, he will have to lie from the outset."

Spencer smiled, "No, he won't, he really will be the aviation correspondent of *Modern Mechanics*." He opened his briefcase and extracted a copy of the magazine. He passed it to Frank. "Page twelve, his third article, published a week ago, an excellent piece on why the monoplane will eventually replace the biplane in military service."

Frank pulled his reading glasses from his pocket and wrestled them on one-handed in his impatience. The room fell silent. He read for a minute and then looked at Spencer over his specs. "He wrote this. I recognize his style. How the hell did you engineer this?"

Spencer looked uncomfortable under Frank's steady gaze. He shrugged. "Contacts in New York. Will submitted four articles to this magazine before he left for England, but they were not published. We thought it might be useful if they were. Just in case."

"In case of what?" Frank demanded.

Spencer stiffened. "In case we needed a neutral expert to go to Germany." He met the older man's gaze without flinching.

"Bloody Guy Gaunt, I'll throttle the bastard when I lay hands on him," Frank muttered, then flipped the magazine shut and slid it back to Spencer who allowed himself a smile as he caught Jac grinning at him across the table.

"Well, the only thing to do is ask him," Percy Scott spoke briskly. "If he's prepared to volunteer, all well and good. If he tells us to take a running jump, and I wouldn't blame him if he did, then we forget about it . . . Agreed?" He looked around the table. Heads nodded. "Good—wheel him in."

Jac stood and left the room. She returned a few minutes later with Will, who held the door open for her before following her inside. His eyes swept around the gathering as he pulled back her chair. "Good afternoon, gentlemen, can I guess from your faces this is not a discussion about my pension arrangements?"

The tension eased. "I see you haven't brought your Colt along to shoot me this time, Mr. Turner." Spencer smiled and held out his hand.

Will shook it, "No, sir. Mrs. Courroyer will shoot you if needs be, as she is the only one amongst us packing a pistol."

"Will! Behave yourself." Jac glared at him from under a fierce frown, but the others laughed as he pulled up another chair and sat down.

"Turner," Percy Scott fixed him with his intense dark eyes. "We need somebody to go to the German airship base at Tondern and get proof positive that the Boche are not employing this ducting system that Matrett is using to push his scheme ahead. Commander Spencer has a plan that he thinks should guarantee your safety. He will explain."

Spencer cleared his throat, "Captain Turner, I believe we have devised a perfect disguise for you and your potential activities. It's as near a foolproof plan as you can get."

Will smiled, "A foolproof plan? That will be something to see."

Spencer shifted in his seat, "As near as can be. It's a simple plan. You will return to the United States as Canadian, Captain Will Turner of the Royal Flying Corps and will embark on a speaking tour about the war. You will return as American, William Turner, aviation reporter for *Modern Mechanics* as the guest of the German Imperial Navy at their airship base at Tondern. While there you will gather as much information as you can about current Zeppelin operations, including photographs, hopefully destroying once and for all this exhaust gas theory. You will then leave again for the United States, but will be discreetly picked up by launch as your ship passes through the Channel."

Will said nothing for a moment, then held up his forefinger. "Great plan, but I see a flaw. How can I embark on a speaking tour if I am coming back?"

"You will enter the United States, in uniform, on your Canadian passport."

"I do not have a Canadian passport."

"You do now."

"Oh, I see."

"You will then change into civilian clothes and an actor, similar in appearance to yourself, will proceed on the speaking tour using your name and identity."

Will frowned, "How will the neutral United States authorities react to this fellow parading around in a British uniform spouting propaganda?"

"Sympathetically. The German American Alliance has already had a Boche aviator strutting around giving talks in Pennsylvania. A precedent has been set."

"I see. The idea is presumably that Captain Turner cannot be spying in Germany while he is highly visible in the United States."

"Exactly. Call it extra insurance against your being exposed as a British agent."

"And if I am exposed?"

"Then it's highly likely you will be put up against a wall and shot." All heads turned toward Jac, who spoke the words through a cloud of exhaled cigarette smoke. She shook the match out she had just used and flicked it into the ashtray. She looked around, "What?"

Spencer shrugged, "I had planned to go into the possible hazards later."

Jac drew on her cigarette then blew a stream of blue smoke at the windows in the ceiling. She winked at Will, "Yes, when you're safely back in Blighty." Spencer looked as if he might protest but Jac nailed him with her stare again. "There's no point trying to make this sound like a stroll in the park. Will is not stupid and I expect he would prefer it if you're straight with him." She turned and looked at Will. "Am I right?"

"You are."

Spencer nodded, "Fair enough. Yes, Captain, there is always the possibility that you might be exposed but I think it is unlikely. Your cover story is good, excellent even. Take a look at this." He slid the copy of *Modern Mechanics* across the table. "Page twelve."

Will's eyes opened wide as he scanned the article, then a smile spread across his face. "Fame at last. I just wish I had been published on my own merits, instead of as part of your plot."

Spencer winced, "Ouch. We prefer the word 'operation,' but if it is of any comfort, your essays have been very well-received and the editor wants more. You can speak to him while you're in New York."

"So what if by some mischance I am discovered?"

Jac looked at him sideways, "Lie, lie as if your life depends on it, because it does. Be indignant; threaten them with the might of Uncle Sam."

Spencer nodded, "That's your ace in the hole. Germany is desperate to keep America out of the war. They came within a hair's breadth after the *Lusitania* went down, and there is huge support for intervention on our side. My guess is that you will be bundled out of Germany and declared *persona non grata* if the worst happened."

Will looked around the familiar room; the same room where he usually met his uncle and Joe Thorpe and where he had been party to the discussions after the meeting in the plush conference room three floors below. He had come to think of it as his own office in town, with its never ending supply of tea, friendly secretaries and clean shirt collars. But where on previous visits he had been on familiar ground discussing technical matters, now he felt out of his depth.

He looked at his uncle, "Sir, what is your opinion?"

Frank Penrose stroked his chin, "I think it's an unnecessary risk. We might well bring a Zeppelin down at any time and disprove Matrett's theory by examining the wreck. The whole thing could be a fool's errand. And. . ."

"My ma will kill you if anything goes wrong?" Will smiled at his uncle.

Frank raised his eyes to the ceiling and sighed, "Yes, and my sister will kill me if something goes wrong. I admit it: I am allowing personal considerations to cloud my thinking. But when I take that thought out of the pot, I still don't think it's worth the risk. We can't afford to lose you for a month or more."

"There is one other factor that might influence your decision, Captain Turner," Spencer spoke slowly, measuring his words and their effect. "The party from the German American Alliance does not leave for over three weeks. There will be time for you to fit in a quick visit to your home. You are . . . ," Spencer consulted notes on the table in front of him, ". . . two months overdue for extended home leave."

Will sat bolt upright, "Are you serious, sir? Might this not compromise the disguise you have constructed?"

Spencer shook his head, "I don't see why it should. William Turner the technical writer is the same William Turner that hails from Tallahassee in Florida. You arriving in New York fresh off Mr. Flagler's Florida express service will add even more credibility to your story."

Will turned to his uncle, "That is a powerful attraction."

Frank shrugged and smiled, "I don't doubt your mother will be delighted to see you."

Will turned back to Spencer, Jac noticed his face had hardened. For the first time she noticed the scar over his eye and the muscle that twitched under his jaw.

"Mr. Spencer, before I commit myself to this . . ." he paused ". . . operation. I need answers to a few more questions."

"Fire away."

"You speak as if I have actually been invited to join a party from the United States on a visit to a German Naval Airship Station."

"That is correct."

"How was this invitation wangled?"

Spencer snatched a glance at his notes, "Mr. Vokes, the editor of *Modern Mechanics* received a very tart letter from a young lady from Philadelphia, a leading light in the German American Alliance, in response to an editorial in the magazine condemning the use of airships to bomb civilian targets. He responded just as sharply saying she had accepted German propaganda without question."

"Good for him," Will nodded.

"A couple of days later she turned up at his office and they had what might be described as a lively discussion, during which she revealed that the society had received an invitation to visit an airship base as part of a tour they were undertaking as guests of the German government—"

Will interrupted, "Let me guess. Vokes suggested that if she was so sure that the Zeppelin crews did not attack civilian targets, then perhaps his aviation correspondent could tag along in an expert capacity to find out the truth?"

Spencer inclined his head, almost a slight bow of acknowledgement. "Very good, Captain. Spot on."

"How long has Mr. Vokes worked for the British Government?" Will asked.

"Ever since his sister went down with the *Lusitania*," Spencer spoke softly.

"Then we can trust him."

"Absolutely."

Will nodded, "And would this provocative piece have appeared shortly after one of my articles first appeared?"

"Yes. It was a long shot but on this occasion we really did hit the jackpot. The young lady contacted the German consulate to see if it might be possible. To our surprise they are positively eager for you to visit their base. Obviously they see your visit as a wonderful propaganda opportunity. The only fly in the ointment is that they wanted to meet you. Vokes had to quickly invent an assignment for you in California."

Will tugged at the buckle on the cross strap of his Sam Browne belt and cinched it tighter by one hole. It gave him a moment to think. "Mr. Spencer, you arrange to have my articles published. Vokes writes his piece. German American lady responds and takes the bait, German government then cooperate. I may be subject to a suspicious nature but it all seems too easy." Jac and Joe Thorpe exchanged an approving glance.

Spencer leaned forward, his elbows on the table. "What you have to realize is that for every plan like this that comes together, another ten fall by the wayside. This one worked."

Will leaned back and laughed, "Just my damn luck!" He leaned forward again. "One final question, why Tondern? It is in the far north of Germany. I believe that up to fifty years ago it was actually in Denmark."

"Very good," Percy Scott glanced at Spencer as he took over. "I have a theory about that. The department arranging this Cooks tour for the Boche sympathizers want to give the impression they are being open, but in fact the last thing they want to do is have this group anywhere near anything vital. The base at Tondern is relatively small and we understand from our agents that it functions to a large extent as a training base using older airships. Most activity is concerned with operations with the German High Seas Fleet. The Senior airship captain, a chap named Martin Friedmann, is a naval reservist and a passionate advocate for the use of Zeppelins in a commercial role."

"Yes!" Will snapped his fingers. "*Modern Mechanics* again. They published a piece by him just before the war started, where he argued that the Zeppelin might one day replace the ocean liner for luxury travel."

"This is your chance to argue it out with him," Spencer suggested with a sly smile.

Will sat back in his chair again. He said nothing as he looked at each person around the table. Spencer clearly wanted him to go. His uncle just as obviously did not want him to undertake the mission. Mrs. Courreyer did not think he was up to it, and Joe Thorpe shared her reservations and those of his uncle. Admiral Sir Percy Scott tended toward Spencer's view point."

He made his decision, "Okay, I will go, but on one condition."

"And that would be?" Spencer asked.

"That this actor sticks to a script that I will write for him. I will not have him swanning around my country spouting hot air."

"Agreed."

Will jumped to his feet, "If that is all, I must get back to my unit."

Frank Penrose stayed him with a pointing finger. "Will, you don't have to do this. Nobody will think badly of you if you decide to back out."

"I would, sir."

Frank slumped in his chair, defeated. "I know, Will. I know." The meeting broke up with a scraping of chairs.

"You will need to get your skates on, *Mr.* Turner," Percy Scott shook Will's hand as he spoke, emphasising the civilian honorific. "You have a meeting with the German Consul in New York in three weeks."

"That is cutting it a little fine, sir."

The old admiral winked and put his finger against his nose. "Leave it to the lovely Caroline. You will be there."

Will knew better than to ask for an explanation. He turned to Spencer and offered his hand. "Well, Mr. Spencer, nobody can say that our enemy does not have a talent for irony."

"Why do you say that?"

"Because their senior captain, Martin Friedmann, has a name that translates literally, as 'Peacemaker.' "

CHAPTER 10

The Repair Shop, Abbots, Roding

Major Ernie Simpson poked a finger through the hole in the wing: slightly larger in diameter than a pencil, and singed around the edges. He eyed Jackson for a moment, then held up his finger for a moment before stabbing it through a second hole. "Woodworm?"

Jackson shifted from one foot to the other, "Bullet holes, sir."

"Good, at least you're not trying to flannel me," Simpson said, poking Jackson in the chest. "What was the last thing I said to you before take-off?"

"Avoid combat at all costs, sir."

"You disobeyed orders." It was a fact, not a question.

"Yes, sir."

"I should have you court-martialled."

"Yes, sir."

"But if I do that I will end up in the dock with you because your flight was completely unofficial . . . and you know that, don't you Jackson?"

"Yes, sir."

Colonel George Brett strode into the hangar. "And me, don't forget me, I will have to be court-martialled as well." They both turned to look at him. A night's sleep following their return from France and the chance of a bath and shave had restored George Brett to his usual immaculate appearance.

Simpson shrugged and leaned back against the lower wing. "So what happened? Wing headquarters for that sector are busily looking for the heroes who shot down one Eindekker and chased off two more."

"They can look as long as they bloody like. We chased off home before anymore trouble found us." Jackson sounded grim.

George Brett stroked his mustache. "That's pretty much what happened. Young Jackson followed my orders to advance, put us in position behind the Boche aeroplane at the end of the line of diving machines, and I let fly with the Lewis. Couldn't miss. He just kept going straight down. The other two turned about to face us and I gave the leading one a good squirt, at which point I daresay they remembered an urgent lunch appointment and buggered off, leaving the B.E.2 in peace."

Simpson nodded, "The only problem was that you sent the Eindekker crashing down behind our lines in full view of several thousand bored soldiers who are now clamoring for you to be awarded the VC, at the very least."

"Ah, well, perhaps Major Power could select a deserving crew and claim they did it. Providing nobody suspects us, all well and good." Brett turned to Jackson and extended his hand. "Sorry about that, laddie. You do deserve a medal for the whole stunt, but I'm afraid we have to keep our heads down."

Jackson shook his hand warmly, "Don't worry about that, sir. Glad to be of service."

"That's the spirit. Well, thanks again gentlemen, I must be on my way." Jackson and Simpson stiffened and saluted formally. George returned the salute and winked at Stan as he turned away.

They stood in the entrance to the hangar and watched the colonel drive away in his Morris touring car. Jackson took off his cap and scratched his head. "Funny thing is, sir, Colonel Brett's version of events is not quite right."

Simpson looked up at the tall Australian, his head cocked to one side, "How so?"

"Well, to be honest, he didn't exactly order me to attack. We sort of acted together."

"Oh, you do surprise me."

Jackson ignored the sarcasm in his commanding officer's voice. "No, it wasn't that. It was his description of the fight. I had to cut across the angle as I dived, so he had to make a tricky deflection shot from long range. And he hit the Eindekker, bang to rights. I saw bits fly off before the Hun fell away. The other two came steaming back at us. The leader got off a few shots, did some good shooting on us and put those holes in the wing, but Colonel Brett put a burst into him as he went past. Another deflection shot, and blow me if he didn't fix him up as well. I swear he was going down even if it was under control. The other one just buzzed off." Stan sighed in admiration. "Strewth, that was bonzer shooting. Two of the bastards skittled, and he didn't even fire off a whole drum."

"Well, I'm not surprised. All those years he must have spent on the moors and fields after grouse and pheasant teaches a bit about deflection shooting." Simpson paused, then tapped Jackson on the shoulder with his swagger stick. "You did well, Jackson, don't think it hasn't been noted." He allowed himself a smile, "Now get back with Ives checking ammunition."

Jackson saluted, "Yes, sir."

Chapter 11

Knightsbridge, London

Marie Julien had raised teasing to an art form. Will looked into her eyes trying to decide if he was the victim of one of her pranks. The urgent pressure of her hand on his arm convinced him she told the truth. They sat side by side on an overstuffed sofa in the drawing room of a Knightsbridge apartment, situated on the second floor of a grand mansion. She shared the rooms with his sister, Victoria. Their Aunt Constance had arranged the lease for the two girls soon after their eventful arrival in England from the United States. Just a few years before the thought of two young women living without a chaperone in London would have been unacceptable. The war had changed attitudes, and the Zeppelin raids had precipitated a rush to the country, flooding the rental agent's books with high quality, affordable accommodation, as the wealthy abandoned London for their weekend retreats. The poor had no choice; they stuck it out.

The two friends had done their best to lighten the atmosphere of their new home with feminine touches in the décor, but Will felt that Sherlock Holmes and Doctor Watson would have been perfectly at home among the wing-backed leather chairs and heavy, overly ornate oak desk and bookcases.

"So are you saying my sister goes out nearly every night and does not return until the early hours?"

"Yes she does. But Will, you must not jump to conclusions." Marie tossed back her blonde curls and fixed him with her gaze. Not much more than five feet tall, with a personality that his mother described as a "firecracker spirit," Will tried to resist her.

"But how can a body not arrive at the same conclusion that I am sure you have? You say she is collected and delivered home in an expensive limousine, and you have seen an older gentleman in the car. You have to be realistic, Marie, folk are subject to believing the most scandalous explanation. It is not what I think that is the problem, it is what other people think and say. My sister's reputation will be ruined."

Marie jumped to her feet, "Oh, damn what other people think!"

Will stared at her, "Marie!"

"Oh, do not try to get by with that outraged gentleman routine. You hear a damn sight worse than that every day."

Will scratched his head and grinned, "From cavalry troopers yes. Not usually from refined southern belles." She glared at him then flounced across to the drinks cabinet.

"I am standing in need of a snifter." She held up a decanter. "Scotch acceptable for you, Captain Turner?" Marie had been, in turn, irritating and charming him from childhood. He could never maintain his annoyance with her for more than a few moments.

Will sighed, "Yes, that will suit very well. And you can drop the outraged friend routine. We both want to know what is going on, and I am inclined to believe there is an explanation other than that my sister is having an affair with a married man."

Marie handed him his drink and sat down next to him, very close. "There, you have said it. Well thank you for saying out loud what we have both been dancing around for the past half hour." She touched her glass to his, "Cheers!" Marie sipped the scotch then puckered her lips, "Mmm, very nice." She placed her hand over his and linked her fingers with him. "William . . ."

"Oh my! Am I in that much trouble?"

"You will be if you do not listen," she snatched his hand up and kissed his fingers. "I hope you will not be offended if I point out that you are bad to impetuous decisions."

Will nodded. The thought crossed his mind that when he spoke with Marie or his sister they lapsed into the vernacular of their southern home. "I am beholden to you for that information, Marie Julien, I am *bad off* for your advice."

She frowned, "Are you making fun of me, Will?"

"Yes," he leaned toward her and kissed her forehead. "I must break myself of that."

Marie squeezed his hand, "Do that every time and I will not complain." She paused. "Now where was I? You made me all swimmy-headed."

"You had just let on that I might be a little impetuous on occasion."

"Yes, that is correct. And on this occasion I believe you have, once again, jumped to the wrong conclusion."

"Apart from good, old wishful thinking, what conclusion do you think I should reach?"

"I believe Victoria is engaged on secret work of national importance," Marie nodded emphatically.

"Why do you believe that?"

"Because she told me."

Will drew his head back and looked at her, one eyebrow arched. "She told you?"

"Yes, but she said that was all she could say."

"And you believe her?"

"Of course! But I did a little checking of my own."

Will raised his eyes to the ceiling. "You believed your friend, but you spied up on her as well? Marie, you are a little minx."

She grinned, "Yes, I am. What I did was hide down the steps of the house on the corner when the car arrived to pick her up. I was like to die when I saw the gentleman who opened the door for her and handed her up."

"Why?" Will's voice registered alarm.

"Because he was so handsome, of course. He is a naval officer, quite senior I think. I love men in uniform." She winked. "Especially Flying Corps, so dashing!" she picked an imaginary speck of fluff from the front of his tunic.

Will frowned and pretended to ignore her. "So you think she might be taken to some secret establishment every evening?"

Marie shrugged, "Well, most evenings. It makes sense though."

He nodded, "Yes, it is an explanation, and it is the one I prefer. Let us leave it at that." He stood and pulled Marie to her feet, "Anyway, I have some important news that is not of national importance. I am being sent home on leave."

"Home? You mean all the way home to Tallahassee?" Her voice squeaked with excitement.

"Do not sound so surprised. It is normal procedure for officers from the dominions to be given home leave at intervals. I have served nearly two years."

Marie put her hand to her mouth, "Oh, Will, how long will you be away?"

"Only a month or so."

She relaxed, "Oh, I suppose we can manage without you for that long," she leaned back, still holding his hands. "Officers from the dominions? Since when has our beloved United States been a dominion?"

"Never, my dear. You forget I am a Canadian for the duration of this unpleasantness."

She opened her eyes wide, "Ooooh, a rugged frontiersman, in uniform. Even better . . ."

"Be serious for a moment," Will said. Marie composed herself and lowered her eyes. "That is better. Now, I must be on my way, but first I wanted to tell you that Aunt Constance has arranged dinner at the Ritz tomorrow evening. I would be obliged, honored in fact, if you would be my guest."

Marie stared at him for a moment, "The Ritz? Will I be your guest? How very formal." She looked at him for a moment, coy from under her long lashes. He was taken completely off guard when she then flung herself into his arms and kissed him hard, full on the lips. She pulled her head back and beamed at him, breathless, "pompous ass! Damn right I will be your guest. And do not imagine for a moment that you are going anywhere soon." Marie slipped one foot behind him and shoved him in the chest, unbalancing him and dumping him straight back on the sofa. She fell on top of him, laughing.

◈ ◂━━▸ ◈

Two miles away from the apartment, Commander Ambrose Spencer RN, pushed open the door of a small room in the Admiralty building with his foot. He carried a cup and saucer in each hand.

"Tea up, Miss Turner."

Victoria Turner turned to him and smiled. Despite the severe hairstyle, and the headphones clamped to her ears, the rogue thought crossed Spencer's mind that if only he were ten years younger he might be tempted to ask her out. She was a beauty: jet black hair, blue-gray eyes a man could fall into and finely sculpted features highlighted by high cheekbones and a firm jaw line: a face that showed intelligence and determination. He sat down beside her as she turned back to the notepad in front of her and reached up to adjust a knob on the apparatus she faced. In profile, with her head bent and fierce concentration furrowing her brow, he thought she looked like a hawk ready to pounce. She scribbled on the pad, paused and wrote again.

She turned to him, a look of triumph on her face, "There it is again, *Nur HVB,* they are on their way."

Spencer nodded and turned to a telephone, he pressed a button on the set and paused, when he spoke his voice sounded calm, "Raid developing, put all stations on alert," he picked up the notepad and counted. "Code intercepted four times, assume a minimum of four airships, thank you."

Vicky sat back and slipped the headphones off, allowing them to fall round her neck. She sipped her tea and smiled at him over the rim of the cup. "In uniform tonight, sir—going on parade?"

Spencer laughed, "It does make life easier when I'm out and about. The cab drivers are more inclined to stop. Now, talking about being out and about, I want you safe home by midnight. You must promise me that if the Zeps do make London, you and your little friend take shelter in the cellar of your house, and don't do what you did last time." He frowned at her, trying to look severe.

Vicky put her cup down, "Yes, sir. It is just that having heard them so often, I want to see what one looks like. Aunt Constance gave us a pair of field glasses."

"Yes, but the roof of your house, albeit with a bottle of port and some nice stilton to fortify you, is not the safest place to be in an air raid, even if it does give the best view." Spencer reached forward and disconnected her headphones for her. "Come on, I will have the car brought round. You have done a splendid job yet again. Fluent German speakers who know Morse code and shorthand are not two-a-penny. I intend to take care of you."

She stood up and he helped her into her coat, "I wish I could work out what *HVB* stands for, sir. I have a feeling it is something quite ordinary, and they have overlooked its significance to us."

"Well, whatever it refers to, thank goodness they carelessly transmit it every time they set off on a raid."

The car pulled up outside the house a little after midnight. Spencer walked her to the bottom of the steps leading up to the heavy entrance door. He glanced up at the sky. Stars appeared through a gap in thickening clouds. He sniffed the air, "I do believe it's going to rain, that will make it harder for them."

Vicky laughed, "Is that your sailor's instinct, sir?"

His teeth showed in his dark face, "No, it's a westerly breeze, and I telephoned my mother in Wiltshire earlier, apparently it's bucketing down in Devizes." He snapped a salute, "Goodnight, Miss Turner. Do *please* take care."

"Goodnight, Commander Spencer, I will." Inside the apartment, she found Marie pretending not to have been looking out of the window.

"Nice evening?" Marie asked, an innocent look on her face.

Victoria clasped her hands in front of her chest and gazed at the ceiling. "Wonderful! The naval officer you saw, when you peeped from behind the curtain, took me back to his submarine where we drank champagne and danced on the deck. Then I made love to the entire crew."

Marie glared, "And where is his submarine anchored?"

"Oh, in the Serpentine of course." The famous boating lake in nearby Hyde Park was three-feet deep at the most.

Marie giggled, "The entire crew?"

"Every man jack of them."

"You greedy pig, you could have left one for me." She closed the book she was pretending to read and stood up. "I am going to retire. We still have to be at Red Cross headquarters by ten o'clock, whatever you do in the evenings."

Vicky nodded, "Good idea, we might have a . . ." she stopped mid sentence. She had been about to reveal the possibility of an air raid, but realized that Marie would pounce on that information and ask how she knew.

"We might have a . . . ?" Marie prompted.

"A lot of work to do."

Marie grimaced, "We usually do." They both worked as volunteer interpreters at the Red Cross headquarters. Vicky's fluency in German matched by Marie's ability in French.

The apartment was big enough that they both had their own bedroom. Vicky felt glad of that. She could not sleep and picked up a book as she slipped into bed. She had found it in a secondhand bookstore, a German-language account of an explorer's adventures in West Africa in the years immediately before the war. She had bought the book as it was her practice to read anything in German she could to improve her knowledge of the language. Despite her distaste for all things German, she found herself absorbed in a well-written account of an explorer's attempts to chart the notorious "Skeleton Coast," where the deserts of Namibia meet the Atlantic. She read how he had chartered a fishing vessel with a local crew, and despite their knowledge of the coast, they found themselves aground on a sand bar. Luckily, as a naval reservist, he was authorized to carry a copy of the codebook for communications between German merchant, and naval vessels, and he was soon in contact with a German cruiser to arrange a rescue. The *Handelsschiffsverkehrsbuch* had saved them. Vicky turned the page, looked up, and then flipped the page back. She read the passage again, gasped, then let out a whoop of delight.

"My goodness, Victoria, did you bring one of those sailor boys home with you?" Marie's voice came faintly through the wall.

Vicky leaped out of bed and slipped her robe on, "No, darling, you just go back to sleep." She padded out into the hall where the telephone stood on a stand. She picked up the receiver and dialed a number, looking over her shoulder to make sure Marie was not eavesdropping on the conversation. The line came alive, "Commander Spencer, please." She stood tapping her foot until he came to the phone.

"Miss Turner, what are you doing up at this hour?"

"I could not sleep, sir. Now, what does this mean to you? *Handelsschiff—Verkehrs—Buch*" she separated out the words of the typical German compound noun and emphasized the starting letter.

She heard nothing for a moment, then a groan followed by a delighted chuckle. "Oh, my God! How much more obvious could it be? *The Merchant Ship's Communication Book*. It's been compromised for years, so they know there is no problem if it falls into our hands; so they carry it in case they need to transmit a distress call to a German merchantman. They are signaling that they have conformed to orders and are not carrying the naval codebook that they cannot allow to be captured. How on earth did you work that out?"

"I will tell you tomorrow, sir. Is it likely we will have to take to the cellar tonight?"

"No, my dear, the Zeps have been wandering around over the east coast, dropped a few bombs on the moors in Yorkshire, and now seem to be heading home. The weather has beaten them yet again."

Vicky pulled her robe tighter. The wind lashed rain against the window. "That is excellent news. Goodnight, sir." She replaced the phone and tiptoed back to bed, a satisfied smile on her face.

❧ ◆━━◆ ❧

Will narrowed his eyes against the salt breeze and glare to peer into the distance. Sam Gordon stepped through the narrow doorway to join him on the wing of the bridge. He handed his binoculars to Will.

"Try these, you can make out land clear enough."

Will made a fractional adjustment to the focus. A thin band of gray sprang into view. It appeared to hover above the waves, separated by a thin layer of haze. He handed the glasses back to Sam and smiled, "Home sweet home."

"How long have you been away?"

"About two years."

Sam nodded, "Long enough even by sailor standards."

Will smiled, "Too long. It was only meant to be for a few weeks while a personal problem blew over."

"Really? Don't suppose you would like to tell me the salacious details so I can spread them around the ship? I do hope there was a floozy involved."

Will hesitated, "God knows it seems such a long time ago and unbelievably trivial. A fellow thought I was studying his fiancée and tried to shoot me."

"Good Lord! That hardly sounds trivial. But I suppose if you actually were studying his girl closely then I can see why he might take umbrage."

Will laughed, "I am sorry, that is a colloquial expression, where I come from 'studying' a girl means taking an interest."

"And were you?"

"Actually, she was taking more of an interest in me."

Sam sighed and slapped Will on the shoulder, "Ah, such modesty in one so young."

Will grinned, "Yes, that did sound a tad arrogant, but the fact is, she has since followed me to England. In fact, she was on my arm for a farewell party my aunt arranged at the Ritz. I have to say, she is a real sport. We had a wonderful evening."

"Then she's more than interested. If she gets too keen, I would suggest enlistment in the Foreign Legion. What about this would-be assassin? Did he do it sportin' and challenge you to a duel?"

"No, he got roaring drunk and let fly with his granddaddies old cap n' ball revolver. He then sobered up and spent the next six months chasing me around England and France with a view to apologizing. In the process, he nearly got himself shot by the Germans, and I rescued him from a British firing squad about to shoot him as a spy. We have since become the best of friends, but he is a trial, as he seems hellbent on enlisting in whatever is the most dangerous arm of the allied cause. I have promised his brother I will try to keep him out of trouble."

"Good grief! You do lead a complicated life."

Will sighed and shook his head, "Certainly not by choice. I am just a simple engineer. Events just seem to catch a hold of me."

Sam put his hand on the hatch handle, "Events will catch hold of me in a minute. I better get back to work before the Skipper realizes I am missing. You need to pack. Try not to get underfoot while we're docking." He stepped over the coaming.

"Aye, aye, Number one."

Sam laughed, it almost sounded like a bark, "We'll make a matelot of you yet."

Will grabbed the rails at the top of the stairway leading down from the bridge, raised his feet and slid down, his feet thumping on the deck as he arrived.

A bearded sailor kneeling by the rail glanced up from his work adjusting a cable and grinned, "Very good, sir. Properly nautical."

Will smiled, "Another few days on here and I will find a taste for rum." He ducked inside and made his way to his cramped quarters where he spent a half-hour finishing a letter to his Aunt Constance in England, thanking her for arranging his farewell party at the Ritz. As usual she had thought of everything, including bouquets for his sister, Marie, and his cousin Kate. As many of his comrades from the experimental unit as could be spared from duty joined him, and Aunt Constance had somehow arranged a similar number of young single ladies to attend. When he asked her how she achieved this she pointed out that the Royal Flying Corps had gained, in her opinion, a totally undeserved reputation as a glamorous organization and the girls clamored to be invited. This, despite the fact the RFC pilots could not "hit a cow's arse with a banjo." Will had already seen the bottom of too many glasses of champagne when his aunt came out with this gem, and he slid under the table laughing.

Will had arrived at Portsmouth dockyard the following morning with a thumping hangover. According to the cheerful coxswain of the launch sent to collect him, this was a grand naval tradition and he should feel proud of himself. The old sailor pointed out a long lean warship moored in the outer harbor. As they came close, Will smiled in spite of his headache. He read the name picked out in relief on her stern: HMS *Caroline*. It was the lovely Caroline that Sir Percy had referred to. The coxswain had pointed out the quarterdeck as they bumped up against a wooden platform fixed to the bottom of a ladder leading to the deck. Will thanked him. He knew he was supposed to salute as he came aboard in honor of the spot where the great British hero, Nelson, had fallen in his moment of triumph at the Battle of Trafalgar, but he had not a clue as to where that part of a modern warship might be found.

Lieutenant Sam Gordon greeted him at the top of the ladder and escorted him to the cramped cabin he shared with a civilian, introduced as Mr. Webster. He proved an easy travelling companion but offered no information as to his business in the United States. Will knew better than to ask.

He soon realized the crew loved their ship. Almost brand new, she was designated a North Sea Cruiser, a fact that delighted Sam Gordon as she had now completed two dashes across the Atlantic and back. Sam had taken the time to brief Will on naval traditions, with special reference to the wardroom. Instead of finding these customs irksome, Will discovered that every quirky practice had an interesting story behind it. He particularly enjoyed the loyal toast, given seated for the eminently practical reason that the deck space available in the old wooden ships of the line was so low, that any attempt to stand would result in the ships officers being concussed.

Caroline had slipped her moorings and surged down the English Channel before night had fallen. The following morning he had been given a thick sweater, a heavy blue jacket in a coarse cloth and a pair of sea boots, and told that comfort was the order of the day while at sea. It seemed typical of the atmosphere on the ship. Military discipline based on pride, tradition and respect rather than the written orders and petty procedures that dominated army life. It soon became obvious that few orders were given or expected, everybody on board knew their job and got on with it. The officers and men knew their ship inside out.

The young engineering officer who had showed him around the gleaming engine room had explained the unusual disposition of *Caroline's* armament. She mounted six-inch guns to fire aft, but lighter four-inch weapons to fire forward. The theory was that her class of light cruiser would engage smaller, fast warships of the type the British classified as destroyers, while any pursuing ships would be deterred by the heavier guns. The engineer had pointed out proudly that he felt the flaw in this theory was that the six-inch guns would rarely be used. *Caroline* had the speed, thanks to his engines, to simply walk away from anything the Germans could muster.

Will smiled at the memory, the pounding machinery a delight to any engineer. He was going to miss the ship and its crew. A few minutes work had his valise packed and he stepped back on deck. He found a spot underneath the bridge and clear of the side to avoid the working parties now assembling.

Land that had been a faint line marking the horizon now crowded in on both sides. Beyond Coney Island he could see the Verrazano Narrows with the bulk of Fort Hamilton dominating the Brooklyn side and Fort Wadsworth facing it from Staten Island.

"The famous New York skyline: has it changed much?" Webster spoke close to Will's ear, making him start.

"I do believe it has sprouted higher still in two years."

"Very impressive, even from this distance."

Will stuck his hands in the pockets of his British warm.* The tip of Manhattan Island lay ten miles distant yet the tops of the towering new skyscrapers could be clearly seen, the late afternoon sun blazing off windows like the facets of a diamond.

"You have a point. It is damned impressive."

"Considering it was built by Yankees," Webster chuckled.

"I will give them credit," Will drawled.

A bell clanged above them and the urgent tremor felt through their feet changed to a purposeful throb as *Caroline's* engines slowed, her sharp bow nibbling at the waves as she slipped discreetly into American waters, with just the courtesy Stars and Stripes flying from the masthead. They both stood, lost in their own thoughts as they slid through the Narrows and into the Upper New York Bay.

Webster pointed, "Look, there she is—Lady Liberty."

Will gazed at the famous statue. It took his breath away. He had seen it as he left for England nearly two years before, when he would have admitted it made no strong emotional impact on him. Now she showed him the way home. He felt glad that Webster said nothing more as he found a lump in his throat.

Will coughed. "Quite a sight." His voice sounded strained.

Webster took out a hip flask and uncapped it. He offered it to Will. "A toast to liberty!" Will raised the flask in salute. Webster took it back and drank in turn, then laughed. "Except, of course, in many states liberty doesn't extend to drinking *to* anything." He paused and looked at Will with a smile, "I trust you have made the necessary arrangements?"

Will thought of the bottle of single malt and the fine brandy in his case for his father. "Oh yes, all taken care of."

Webster nodded toward the statue again. "Of course that's really meant to symbolize the friendship between the American and French nations. How do you think the French feel about American neutrality?"

---

* *Short thick overcoat usually made by the Crombie Company.*

Will shrugged, "Subject to being a mite sore, I would think."

"And you?"

"Mixed feelings. This war is a mess and no mistake. If I thought America could wade in and finish it in a few weeks, then I would be all for it. But I fear my friends being dragged into this stalemate, and then we would have good Americans being sacrificed to the vanity of stupid American generals."

"In the same way that good British, French, and German soldiers are sacrificed to the vanity of stupid British, French and German generals?"

"I guess," Will paused. "Good German soldiers?"

It was Webster's turn to shrug, "I'm too old to swallow the propaganda that every German is a monster. We're all some mother's son."

Will sighed, "Yes, you are correct there, Mr. Webster. Does that bother you? Do you find your sense of duty conflicts with your personal morals?"

"My word, Captain Turner, moral philosophy from an army officer." Webster grinned. He took another pull from the flask and handed it back to Will. "In answer to your question, no. My duty is to work to finish this war as quickly as possible. The quicker we win it, the sooner the killing stops."

Will drank again, "That is one way of looking at it." He handed the flask back to Webster who capped it.

"I need to pack," he slapped Will on the back. "The cruise is over, back to work." He winked and hurried away. Will leaned back against the bulkhead, then stepped forward as he heard his name called. He looked up to see Sam Gordon leaning over the wing of the bridge.

"Skipper is wondering where you are. Come on up." Will hurried up the ladder to be greeted by Captain Allen.

"Good afternoon, Captain Turner. Thought it might be handy to have a native with us to show the way."

Will grinned and peered ahead, "Squeeze between the lady with the torch and Governor's Island, under the bridge then a sharp right. Should take us there directly."

Allen turned to the man at the wheel, "Got that Bosun?"

"Aye aye, sir. Under the bridge and sharp right it is."

The towers of the Brooklyn Bridge loomed ahead. "My God!" Sam breathed. "It's bloody magnificent." Every head craned backward as *Caroline* passed beneath the bridge that many thought the crowning glory of New York's architecture. Will squeezed himself against the bulkhead at the rear of the ship's bridge and watched. Nobody seemed to hurry, or to be concerned about the swarms of small boats that scurried around them. Orders were issued and carried out with the minimum of fuss. The ship knifed through the harbor waters, seeming reluctant to give up her speed, but a shudder ran through the deck as the engines went astern to bring her to a full stop. Will realized a small launch had come alongside and a minute later a young United States naval officer stepped on to the bridge.

"Lieutenant Montclair, sir. I am to act as pilot to your berth."

Captain Allen returned his salute, "Welcome aboard, Montclair, appreciate the guidance." He motioned toward Sam, "My First Officer, and this is Captain Turner of the Royal Flying Corps. He's a Canadian." Montclair saluted them both.

"Glad to have you aboard, Lieutenant," Sam said as they shook hands.

"Pleased to make your acquaintance, I am sure," Will smiled.

Montclair stared at him. "I come from a part of Canada where we have a different accent."

Montclair could not contain himself, he grinned. "Indeed, Captain? Maybe a part of Canada where a few confederates fled after the War?"

"Something like that," Will laughed.

The ship came to life again. Montclair knew his business and within minutes, aided by a few gentle nudges from a tug, *Caroline* settled against her berth in the Brooklyn Navy Yard, inconspicuous in the ranks of gray-painted ships. A sailor had Will's valise and suitcase waiting for him at the head of the gangway. He made his farewells, Sam joining him at the rail.

For a moment he hesitated. The ship, cramped and uncomfortable as she was, had been a friendly and familiar part of his life for the last few days. The routine on board, though outside his limited military experience, reminded him that he was part of what had become another family in his life. From now on, for this job, he felt he would be alone.

He shook hands with Sam, "Thanks for the lift, Sam. One day I might be able to return the favor."

Sam smiled, "Across the Atlantic by aeroplane? That will be one helluva trip. I'll look forward to it."

Will trotted down the gangway then turned back to look at the ship. Captain Allen appeared on the bridge. He raised his cap. "Good luck, Will, you take care."

Will waved back, "I will, you can count on it." He turned and walked quickly toward the black Packard waiting at the end of the berth. He had been told he would be collected. A tall man wearing a gray business suit, but no hat, stood waiting by the car.

"Captain Turner?"

"Yes."

"Welcome to New York." He opened the door and took Will's bags to stow them in the trunk. Will stepped up and then hesitated, a figure lounged in the heavily upholstered seat at the back of the passenger compartment. He had his straw boater tipped over his eyes obscuring his face.

"Well, you took your time getting here."

Will stared, the voice sounded very familiar. The man sat forward, raised his hat and beamed at Will's reaction. "Roscoe Vandersand! You son of a gun." Will seized his friend's hand and in the confines of the car they managed to embrace. "Well I be!" He shook his head in wonder then slapped Roscoe on the back. "You don't know how good it is to see you. I thought you would have sailed for France by now and gotten yourself killed in the Legion."

Roscoe pulled Will down in the seat next to him. "Change of plans, Will. Big change of plans." He paused and motioned to the big man who had now climbed into the driver's seat. "Sorry, I'm forgetting my manners. Will, this is my friend Frank Nelms." Frank twisted in his seat and offered a big, bony hand.

"Pleased to make your acquaintance, Captain."

Will shook his hand, "Just plain old Will Turner here at home, Frank." He turned to Roscoe. "So, what is going on here? I do not believe you two just happened to be driving past the Naval Dockyard and saw me."

Roscoe laughed, "No. Captain Gaunt sent us to make sure you didn't get lost or into mischief."

"Gaunt sent you?" The look of surprise on Will's face matched the incredulity in his voice. "You mean you two are working for. . ." He stopped, suddenly aware he may be about to make his first security gaffe.

It was Frank Nelms turn to laugh, a deep rumble. "That's right, Will. The Allied cause: strictly on a casual volunteer basis, of course." He started the engine and with a snick of gears sent the big car weaving through the dockyard detritus. At the gate a uniformed sentry stepped forward and glanced inside. Without saying a word he stepped back, raised the barrier and saluted.

Will smiled at Roscoe, "Do all casual volunteers get the VIP treatment?"

Roscoe shrugged, "When they work for Guy Gaunt they do."

Will leaned back in the seat and stretched his legs. "Roscoe, I would enjoy hearing exactly what you have been up to. I know you squired my sister and Marie to their big farewell dinner, and I am guessing Frank here must be the businessman who made such an impression on Vicky, but how come I find you still here in New York?"

Roscoe leaned forward and patted Frank on the shoulder, "Feel free to blush old man," He sat back to see Will looking at him with an eyebrow raised and a wry smile on his face. "No big mystery, Will, I am . . ." he corrected himself, "I should say Frank and I are waiting in line to learn to fly with the Stinson sisters down in San Antonio."

"Wow! Marjorie Stinson, the flying schoolmarm. How did you swing that? I thought they were on contract to train Canadian pilots for the RFC, and there is some talk of shipping British recruits over to take advantage of the weather, but you two are all-American boys."

Roscoe laughed again, "We did a deal with your uncle of course. Vicky suggested I contact him. He set it up for us, though we still have to wait in line and pay for the tuition, in return we help out Captain Gaunt in his various . . ." Roscoe stopped, searching for the correct diplomatic term.

Frank filled in for him. ". . . enterprises."

"Yeah, good word for it, Frank."

Will leaned forward to look out as the Packard swung onto the entry ramp for the Brooklyn Bridge. He pointed forward. "Will you look at that!" Seen from the bridge span Manhattan seemed to rise up and stretch out, like a living forest of marble, concrete and glass. A brand new building, its height enhanced by two towers, dominated the view. The setting sun gilded the copper decoration surrounding the base of each tower.

"The new Municipal building, City Hall. Quite something, don't you think?"

Will sat back and nodded, "Indeed, quite something, even if it was built by Yankees . . . No offense gentlemen." Roscoe and Frank laughed. Will felt he was in the company of young men enjoying an adventure. "So tell me, without divulging any secrets of course, what exactly do Captain Gaunt's enterprises involve?"

"Should I tell him about Festner, Frank? That's our best yet."

"Hell, why not? The more people who know, the better."

Roscoe turned in his seat to look at Will. "How much do you know about Captain Gaunt, Will?"

"Only that my uncle often calls him, *Bloody* Guy Gaunt. I gather his methods tend to the unconventional. Apart from that, and the fact he was British Naval Attaché in Washington when the war broke out, not a great deal. I was just told that he would look after me in New York."

Roscoe nodded, "He looks after British interests here, especially naval interests but also countering Hun propaganda, that kind of thing. He is officially your liaison officer here in New York."

"Sounds harmless enough."

Frank hooted with laughter then spoke over his shoulder, "He deals with more than propaganda. Tell Will about Festner, Roscoe."

Roscoe leaned toward Will as the car dived into the canyon formed by the towering skyscrapers as they left the bridge and entered Manhattan. "What your uncle didn't tell you, Will, is that Guy Gaunt has style, real style. A few weeks ago he discovered through his contacts on the piers, that a German agent had successfully planted explosives with long time-delay fuses on two British ships. They both sank within a day of leaving harbor, and it was assumed they had both been torpedoed. But Gaunt knew otherwise. The agent had gotten himself a place as a foreman on the wharves, probably through a German sympathizer. Something had to be done, and he asked us to join him."

Will sat up, "Gollee gee! You did not bump this character off, did you?"

Roscoe and Frank roared with glee like two schoolboys recounting a successful prank.

"Lord no, Will," Roscoe said. "The German agent, Festner, might have deserved it, but Gaunt had a much more fitting way of disposing of him. We went to Gaunt's office and all three of us dressed up like stevedores. I have to tell you that Frank here really looks the part of a tough. We hung around near the pier entrance and Gaunt soon spotted Festner, God above only knows how he knew who the agent was, Gaunt only tells us what we need to know. We followed him to a bar where we watched him for an hour, then Gaunt slipped out to wait for him. Frank brought the car round and parked it in the alley, and I followed Festner as he left the bar." Roscoe shook his head slowly in admiration. "Gaunt was so quick I swear I hardly saw him move. He laid a blackjack up the side of Festner's head so neat he just grunted and fell back in my arms. In five seconds we had him bundled in the back of this car and we were on our way."

"So then you handed him over to the cops?"

"No—much better than that. He would have cried diplomatic immunity, and they'd have had to let him go. No, we drove back to the water and parked, then Gaunt told Frank to flash the lights. A real character came out of the shadows—looked like a pirate—a monster of a man. He greets the captain like his long-lost brother. They chatted away in Spanish for a few moments, then the pirate hands Gaunt a roll of notes, hoists Festner on his shoulder, and strolls away, whistling."

Will stared at Roscoe, "Good grief, what was that in aid of?"

Roscoe grinned, "We had sold Festner to the captain of an old four-masted Argentinian meat hauler as his new deck hand. By the time he woke up he must have been fifty miles out to sea on his way to Rio de Janeiro."

Will eyes opened wide, then a smile crept over his face. "My oh my, poetic justice."

"You bet, Will. Then we went back to his office, changed into our evening clothes and joined Mrs. Gaunt at the new Café des Artistes on West Sixty-seventh. for dinner, paid for by the captain's bounty money."

"I see what you mean—Captain Gaunt has style, that is for sure," Will said. He glanced out again as Frank negotiated a steam shovel working on one of the numerous construction projects and then swung north. "My orders said that Captain Gaunt would be arranging lodgings."

"All taken care of, Will," Roscoe said as he lowered his window and pointed at the façade of the Waldorf Astoria as the car pulled up to the entrance.

Will nodded, "This will do just fine." A porter appeared and whisked his bags away. Frank pulled off to park the car saying he would be joining them directly. Will and Roscoe strode across the marbled foyer deep in conversation, oblivious to the sideways looks from the group of well-dressed women waiting to enter the restaurant. The two young men made a striking pair. Roscoe Vandersand had been described by Will's sister as "extravagantly handsome," with his blue eyes, black hair, even features and dimpled chin. Will Turner, while never completely comfortable in uniform, nevertheless wore the double-breasted, high-collared RFC tunic with the Glengarry cap and highly polished riding boots with style—helped by his athletic six-foot build and sandy blond hair. Their indifference to admiring female glances just made them all the more appealing.

"An Englishman! And an aviator to boot. How very intriguing," a willowy girl of indeterminate years noted to her friend.

"A Canadian actually," her friend replied.

"However do you know that?"

"Oh, I have my sources here in the hotel."

"Strumpet." They giggled and stepped through the door to be greeted by the maitre 'd.

Roscoe led Will to the elevator that took them to the top floor. He tapped on a door at the end of the corridor. A moment later a white-jacketed steward ushered them in. Will glanced around. They had stepped into the main part of an extensive suite, furnished with heavy leather armchairs, a low table and a large partner's desk by the high window. A tiffany lamp provided extra light for the user.

"Ah, Captain Turner, welcome, allow me to show you to your room." The white-haired old man spoke with a marked Scots accent and walked ramrod straight as he led Will to a door leading off from the main room. "I hope this will be comfortable."

Will nodded, "I have just spent a week at sea on a light cruiser. I would be happy to sleep in the bath if you promise it will not roll or pitch me out of bed."

"Och yes, HMS *Caroline*, a fine speedy class of ship, sir."

Will looked at him with surprise, "You know your ships then?"

The old man's eyes lit up, "I like to keep abreast of latest developments, sir. Ye can take the sailor out of the sea, but ye cannae take the sea out of the sailor. Now, can I get you gentlemen a nice cup of tea?"

Roscoe answered for them both, "That would be wonderful, Robert. I expect Captain Turner must be gasping for refreshment by now." They sat down in the armchairs on either side of the table. Seconds later Guy Gaunt bounced into the suite. He strode across to greet Will as he scrambled to his feet. Gaunt had authority in his grip and mischief in his eyes.

"Turner, old boy, so glad you could come. Once we've had tea I would love you to join us on a little stunt before dinner."

For the second time in a few weeks, Will found the sailor before him carried no resemblance to the picture his imagination had supplied. Slim, of average height, dark hair brushed back from a receding hairline and immaculately dressed in a conservative blue suit, Guy Gaunt could have passed for a successful young businessman in any city in the world. But an hour later, Will found that his imagination had not led him astray when it came to his one secret fear. He had imagined he might be terrified in a particular situation. He was right.

CHAPTER 12

The Parade Ground, Abbots Roding

The Prof, Captain James Smith, gazed over the attentive faces standing clustered around the back of the Leyland subsidy truck* he had adopted as his lecture platform in front of the hangars. The complete personnel of the Home Defense Experimental Unit: mechanics, pilots, observers, and assorted ground crew had been joined by half a dozen sailors, all signalers. "Now, you all understand how to use the Ingram signaling scheme?" All heads nodded as one. The system of symbols laid out using white cloth, conveying search directions according to the relative position of various geometrical shapes, appeared straightforward.

"Good." He pointed over their heads to four lighter trucks, each with a contraption resembling a multiple-hearing trumpet mounted on the open back. "As for the sound detection device, the only way we will know if it really works is to try it in practice." He looked around. "Any questions?" He heard the usual shuffling of feet as everybody looked to the next man. "Oh come on, lads. Somebody must have a question of some sort." More shuffling and an embarrassed silence until at last a hand shot up. "Yes, McGuigan?"

"I was wondering, sir. Why do dogs all seem to have black lips?"

The Prof looked as if he might be pondering the question for a moment. "McGuigan."

---

* *The British Government subsidised the purchase of new trucks to hauling companies on condition they would be available for war work if the need arose: these were usually built by the British Leyland Company, now a division of the Paccar Corporation.*

"Yes, sir?"

"Shut up."

"Right you are, sir."

The Prof's grin betrayed him, "Okay, you 'orrible lot. On yer way!"

The meeting broke up, teams of men dispersing to the four detector trucks, the mechanics heading back to the hangars and the pilots and observers to their aircraft to carry out final checks of their equipment in daylight. Simpson and Prof Smith had plotted a rough position for each of the four teams in an arc covering the approaches to London from the north and northeast, at a distance of forty miles from their field. The men at the most easterly point would be a few miles from the Essex coast, the next two teams in Suffolk, with the most westerly unit in Cambridgeshire on the edge of the flat fen country. The plan allowed each team five hours to reach their area and find a suitable site with a clear view of the night sky. They had to be near a telephone wire to tap into it to communicate with Simpson and a plotting team at the field, via a priority line kept open by the post office, responsible for the telephone system. With each team twenty miles from their neighbor, even if the sound detectors proved useless, it seemed likely that one team or the other would hear any Zeppelin that came through the gap and at least give some clue as to its position and course.

Searchlights had been set up at strategic points, with the light situated at Kelvedon in Essex, well inside the arc, having already established a reputation for success in seeking out the giant airships even at great height. An effective detection and tracking system had begun to take shape. With Sir Percy Scott's line of picket boats stationed a few miles out in the North Sea, the Zeppelin captains would have great difficulty approaching London undetected. With the nights growing shorter, the British planners felt sure the German Imperial Navy would be bound to make a determined effort to bring terror to the capital during the month of April.

On the night of March thirty-first, a few days before Smith sent his men on their mission, the British defenders had had their biggest success to date. Captain Breithaupt in Zeppelin L15 had reached London and dropped his bombs on the suburb of Rainham at twenty minutes before ten in the evening. Five minutes later the sweating, cursing soldiers blazing away with the Purfleet gun punched a hole straight into the side of the giant airship, ripping two of the gas cells to shreds and damaging several others. Breithaupt jettisoned everything he could in an attempt to reach home, but L15 sagged, grew nose heavy and broke its back, crash landing in the sea fifteen miles north of Margate in the Thames Estuary. A British destroyer saved all but one of the crew, but attempts to tow the wreck to land failed.

Colonel Frank Penrose heard the news with a mixture of elation and frustration. His delight at hearing a Zeppelin had been destroyed by gunfire from the ground tempered by the news it had not burned. He had no wish to condemn anybody to being roasted alive, but the lack of fire added weight to Matrett's argument that the Germans had to be using inert gas to shield the gas cells. How, Matrett had argued, could a high-explosive artillery shell have failed to ignite the highly flammable hydrogen? Frank could not come up with a credible answer for the committee he had been called before, and he had no wreck to show that the Germans did not use a gas-shielding system.

Tom Armstrong and Simpson stood on the step of the orderly office watching the trucks roll out of the gate.

"The Guv'nor is none too pleased that L15 didn't burn," Tom remarked.

"Any ideas why it didn't?" Simpson asked.

Tom shrugged, "Schoolboy chemistry lesson that the committee conveniently forgot. Hydrogen doesn't burn, it has to combine with the oxygen in the atmosphere to produce an explosive mixture. My guess is that the split-second delay between the contact fuse on the shell being activated by the skin of the Zep, and it firing the explosive charge, was enough for the shell to penetrate into the heart of a gas cell, where it exploded in an atmosphere of pure hydrogen."

Simpson nodded, "So the ignition source was not in place long enough to fire the explosive gas mix when the leaking hydrogen combined with the air."

"Aye, right enough. If a second shell had arrived two seconds later it would have been fireworks night, or even if a piece of red-hot shrapnel had ignited something else, that would have done it."

Simpson sucked on his unlit pipe for a moment, "Lucky buggers. Still, I'm not going to begrudge them getting away with it." He turned to go back into the office. "Come on, let's see if we can think of anything we might have forgotten."

Out on the highway, Able Seaman Chalky White lounged on the hard bench seat of the requisitioned Commer truck, watching First Class Air Mechanic McGuigan expertly progress through the crash gearbox. Air Mechanic Bert Hickman slept peacefully behind them amongst the tools and supplies they carried for their three-night mission.

"Eee, by 'eck! You took a chance with that officer back then, Mac. I've seen chaps on a charge for less than that," White spoke with a heavy northern accent.

Mac laughed, "The Prof can take a joke so long as you do your job well."

"Even so, he's a reet tough-looking bugger. He doesn't look or sound like an officer. What's his tale?"

"Field commission during the South African War, retired from the army, worked in a foundry as a manager where he met aviation people from Hendon. While he was doing that he was taking a degree in political science with the Worker's Educational Association, and setting up a branch of the Labor Party in the East End. He was called back to the colours when the war started."

White sat up and stared at McGuigan, not sure he had understood the Irishman's accent above the clattering of the truck. "Did you say he founded a branch of the Labor Party?"

"Aye, he did, right enough."

"By gum! That takes the biscuit. So Captain Smith's a Red?"

McGuigan glanced at him and frowned. "Now did I say that? He's a member of the Labor Party and so am I. That doesn't make me a Red either. We believe in social justice."

"Yes, but even so—"

"Even so nothing. And don't go thinking he's a soft touch. He can take a joke but he won't take sloppiness or cheek. Fail to do your job, and he'll nail your bollocks to the nearest tree." McGuigan grinned and held up two silver coins, "But do your job well and he'll look after you."

White stared, "For us?"

"It is. Prof Smith wangled five bob out of the comforts fund for every team, but we're not to drink it all at once."

White's teeth gleamed through his massive black beard. "Eee, champion! I reckon I should put in for a transfer."

They found their ideal site before night fell. A few miles from the estuary of the River Blackwater on a slight rise that passed for a hill in that flat country. A telephone line ran along the field boundary and the low hedge did not obstruct their view. A comfortable pub sat at the crossroads nearby, near enough to be a convenient walk, but not so near as to be too obvious.

Mac swung the Commer into the field entrance and dragged on the handbrake. "Right lads, let's get on with it." Within half an hour they had set up their camp. The canvas cover over the cargo area of the truck was hauled off and used to create a lean-to shelter by leaving it fixed to the vehicle at one side. Chalky had shinned up the nearest telephone pole and attached his apparatus to the line using crocodile clips, and contacted the local exchange. He had soothed the flustered operator and made sure she knew that he had priority over every other caller on that line. The fabric panels for the Ingram signaling system had been sorted and placed ready for use in their wooden cabinet, and the light to illuminate them tested.

Mac climbed up into the seat that rotated with the sound detection device. He swung it through a full circle and then checked that he could elevate and depress the apparatus to point it at any part of the sky, at the same time using a pocket compass to orientate the graduated scale on the base of the device with magnetic north.

Chalky looked down from his perch on the telephone pole. "It looks like somebody's welded half a dozen gramophone horns together. Do you think it'll work?"

Mac clamped the headphones over his ears and switched the current on. He glanced up, "Say something."

"What?"

"Anything, a poem or something,"

Chalky burst into song, "*She was only a bird in a gilded cage, such a beautiful sight to seeeee . . .*"

"That's enough!" Mac snatched the headphones off and passed them to Hickman. "What do ye think, Bert?"

"*. . . but she fell for the lure of a rich man's goooold.*"

Hickman took the headphones off and glared up at the sailor. "Awful, absolutely soddin' awful. You'll never make a living on the stage."

"What do you think of the sound detector man, not Chalky's singing?"

Bert shrugged, "I reckon it's working. Think about it. The principle is the same as a gramophone horn but backwards. Sound vibrations in the air are magnified by that little electric thingummyjig, but instead of pushing the sound out, we're sucking it in."

Mac swung the device so the horns pointed toward the sea. "Well, the only way we'll know for sure is when Major Simpson sends somebody up to let us have a try at a live target."

"Or a Zep comes sailing past?" Chalky suggested from his perch above.

Mac nodded, "Whichever comes first."

"What do we do until then?" Bert asked.

"We wait m'boy, we wait," Mac patted him on the head. "And we get the kettle on and brew up."

❧ ⊷⊶ ❧

The Prof stowed the signaling lamp in its holder on the side of his cockpit and turned back to his pilot in the seat behind him, who was checking his instruments before starting the engine. "Good to be flying with you again, Ned," Captain Smith said.

"It's good to be back with the old team, sir."

"Lay off the 'sir,' when we're not in front of the men—there's a good lad. Jim or Prof will do. Besides, the rate you're going you'll have overtaken me soon." Ned Robson grinned; he had just been made up to First Lieutenant. The Prof locked a drum onto his Lewis and turned to face Ned again, his arm draped over the gun. "Have you done much night flying?"

"Not much to be honest, maybe five hours."

"That's more than most—you'll do fine." He glanced over the side of the cockpit, "Oi! Barney, bugger off." Simpson's chocolate brown Labrador retriever had cocked his leg against the wheel before scampering away with Buster, the armorer's scruffy mongrel. The Prof beckoned to the mechanic waiting by the wing. "Davis, round those bloody dogs up and tie them where they can't get run over."

Ned watched as the mechanic tried to grab Barney's collar, and failed. "The pups will think that's a great game. I don't think I've ever seen a Labrador that color before."

"You won't have. Most breeders think they're inferior and drown the pups. The boss caught some halfwit chucking Barney in the river and gave him sixpence for him. He seems like a fine dog to me." Davis had managed to grab the playful pup and the Prof beckoned him over, then fished in his pocket, found a piece of biscuit and tossed it to the dog. "There you go, lad." He turned back to Ned. "Did you see that?" The pilot nodded.

Half an hour later their F.E.2 biplane roared down the path marked by the kerosene flares and soared up into the night sky. The Prof and Simpson were convinced that with skillful navigation—using map, compass and stopwatch—it was possible for a crew to construct a scientific search pattern instead of blundering around in the dark. Ned's skill in holding a tight compass course, light winds and a luminous night sky under a near full moon enabled them to fly straight to the team posted near Cambridge. After an exchange of identifying signals, they set off for Suffolk on the course calculated before take-off, ticking off the landmarks they had selected as being possible to see at night. Any body of water, a river, lake, or even a stream, could be seen by the reflected light from the air. They found railroad tracks another useful pointer where they passed over open ground, but harder to see when they ran through cuttings or through woodland. Ned and Smith had the advantage of an intimate knowledge of the area they patrolled.

Kapitaenleutnant von Buttlar did not have the luxury of familiarity with the land over which he now hovered in Zeppelin L11. In fact, he was lost—not something he would admit to the crew gathered around him in the control cabin of his airship. In many ways, the gondola, as it was known, resembled the bridge of a ship. A helmsman stood at a large spoked wheel facing forward, looking through glass that sloped inward from top to bottom where it joined the side of the gondola at waist level. The engine room telegraphs manned by an engineer standing next to him, and the chart tables ranged along the side added to the nautical impression. A sailor standing at a second wheel at right angles to his comrade indicated that this ship was something unusual. He controlled the vast elevators at the tail of the Zeppelin. Where a ship's bridge featured reassuringly solid brass fittings, and oak planked floors, everything on this ship had been crafted from lightweight aluminum, icy cold to the touch.

Oberleutnant–zur-See Georg Klaas peered over the side of the gondola. A window hinged outward giving an undistorted view below. He found it difficult to distinguish between low lying banks of cloud, the coastline, and the maze of creeks and islands beneath him. The sea shone luminous and comforting in the moonlight, but ahead England lay in unwelcoming darkness.

"Well, navigator, where are we?" Klaas heard the impatience in his captain's tone but felt glad to be able to hear anything. At cruise power the huge Maybach engines, each carried in a pod on a framework hanging from the main hull of the ship, transmitted a harmonic vibration through the structure setting up an incessant, mind-numbing drone that seemed to saturate the thin air and drill into a man's skull.

Klaas closed the window and turned to the chart table. He adjusted the shaded lamp and jabbed a pencil at the map. "We are here. That is Mersea Island off the starboard bow, and this is the Blackwater Estuary."

"Are you sure?"

"Yes, Captain."

Von Buttlar studied the map, "I think we are farther north."

"I do not agree. You asked to avoid the naval forces at Harwich, so I have brought us in twenty kilometers to the south." He met the captain's eye. Klaas respected von Buttlar for his rank, but he had been guiding four masted sailing ships across the Atlantic when his captain still wore short trousers.

Von Buttlar glanced at the map and stepped to the far side of the gondola and raised his binoculars. He turned back to Klaas and slapped him on the shoulder. "Good work, navigator." He turned to the rest of the crew. "Gentlemen, I shall try a new tactic, taking advantage of this easterly wind. We shall proceed on minimum power maintaining this altitude. The only way the Englanders can detect us is by hearing us or by searchlight. They are at their most alert near the coast, so we shall go past them on tiptoe. At this height, it will be easier to find our way, and the wind is exactly in our favor to carry us inland."

The men in the gondola smiled in agreement. The prospect of at least part of the mission being accomplished at a mere two thousand meters appealed. They had crossed the North Sea at five thousand meters where the cold had, as always, sapped their strength and their will. Their lips were dry and cracked where they had sucked on the rubber pipes fixed to oxygen bottles. The gas they breathed in tasted foul, contaminated by oil and rubber. For the last hour they had drifted down to this lower altitude, feeling their frozen extremities come back to life in the warmer air.

The signal officer, Dieter Schildt, rubbed his hands and turned to Klaas, "Good, they will never hear us with the engines at idle. We shall slip past them like a ghost in the night."

Schildt's optimism was understandable, but he did not reckon with the new technology at McGuigan's disposal. Eight miles away he had the earphones clamped firmly to his ears and the sound detector pointing at the Zeppelin. "There it is again. I'm bloody sure there's something out there."

Hickman lowered the binoculars he was using to search the night sky. "I can't see anything."

"You won't, they paint the bloody things black I expect, but I'm telling you I can hear something."

"Well, what does it sound like—engines?" Chalky called down from the telegraph pole.

McGuigan shook his head. "Not exactly, more like a rumbly, swishing noise."

Chalky leaned back against the strap he had fixed around the pole. "You don't think it might be picking up a big ship at sea? Engines and propellers in water could make that noise."

"Or could it be some kind of sound reflection?" Hickman suggested. "Try lining it up on the reciprocal to see if it's the Prof you can hear coming up from the landward side."

McGuigan swung the apparatus round and elevated it. "Bloody hell, you're right! I can hear them clear as a bell." He snatched the earphones off and listened for a moment. "Can you hear them now?"

Bert Hickman cocked his head to one side, "Just, but only just." He took the earphones and put them on, listened for a second, then slapped Mac on the shoulder. "It works! This bloody contraption bloody well works."

Mac slipped out of the seat and moved to the signaling lamp mounted on the headboard of the truck. "Watch for their signal and I'll reply." By now the hum of the F.E.2 biplane could be heard filling the sky.

In the airplane above, Prof Smith leaned back and pointed down. "They must be about here. What's their code?"

Ned cupped his hand around the Prof's ear and bellowed, "M-A-C."

"That's original." He leaned over the side, pointed his signal lamp at a random point ahead and flashed, "R-S, R-S, R-S." A second later the response beamed up from the darkness. Smith turned around in the narrow cockpit and shouted in his pilot's ear. "Splendid piece of work, Ned. You've taken us to within yards of all four stations. Let's see how good McGuigan's morse skills are—take me around them."

Ned banked around the point where he judged the ground crew to be. Smith leaned over the side and beamed a longer morse message at the ground. He could never have guessed the effect it had on another group of watchers.

At Smith's first signal, von Buttlar's crew had frozen. Nobody breathed. The lamp flashing from the night barely a kilometer distant could only mean a British plane at their level. The signal from the ground confirmed their worst fears. They had blundered over an observation station. A low murmur passed around the gondola as the longer message flashed out.

"Quiet." Von Buttlar's voice snapped. "They cannot see us. Proceed on this course. Stand to your positions." The light had disappeared. He turned to Schildt. "Flags, what was that signal?"

Schildt frowned and looked again at the pad in his hand. "The first two are just combinations of letters, R-S, R-S, R-S, reply M-A-C. Then the longer signal in plain English, but it makes no sense."

Von Buttlar snatched the signal pad and read, "B-A-R-N-E-Y H-A-S P-I-N-K L-I-P-S." His cheek twitched then he grabbed the mouthpiece of the voice pipe connecting to the belly of the ship. "Bosun, jettison all bombs, dump forward ballast." He spun round, "Engineer, full ahead all engines, emergency power. Helmsman bring her round one-eighty degrees. Elevators up." He clutched the chart table to steady himself as the deck tilted, and glared at Schildt. "You damn fool. It's code. The verdammte Englanders are springing a trap."

Directly below Chalky and Bert Hickman's laughter at Mac's reaction to Prof Smith's message was interrupted by a shrill whistle, growing louder by the second. Hickman looked up, "WHAT *the* F—?" His oath disappeared, smothered by the roar of an explosion, by the time the second bomb exploded he and Mac were trying to worm their way into the dirt while Chalky had tried to trim his bulk by clamping his knees together and drawing in his elbows in an effort to hide behind the telegraph pole, twenty feet off the ground.

Clods of earth rained down as a series of explosions marched away from them across the field, the brilliant flashes imprinting the silhouette of the hedgerow on the retina of their eyes. It could only have been seconds, but it felt like minutes before they raised their heads. In the field and the wood beyond, pinpricks of light showed where smaller incendiary bombs burned themselves out. As their hearing came back, they could hear the heavy roar of engines receding in the night.

McGuigan rolled on to his back and then sat up, "Mary Mother of Jesus! What happened?" Hickman pulled him to his feet. They both stood dusting themselves down. "Chalky, are you alright?"

A nervous giggle came from above them, "Aye, I reckon so. Got a bloody good view from up here. You army types must get used to diving in t'holes."

Mac staggered over to the truck and retrieved a flashlight. He ran it over the vehicle and their equipment. "No harm done, just a bit of dust to clean up."

Chalky had slid down from his perch and joined them. "You can hear the Zep clear enough now. I wonder why we didn't hear it before?" The hum of the big Maybach motors still sounded clear as the airship headed back out to sea. Chalky reached inside his kit bag and pulled out a bottle of rum. He splashed it into tin mugs and handed one each to his friends. "Bottoms up, lads. Nobody will grudge us this to calm our nerves."

Bert gasped as the fiery spirit slid down. He wiped his eyes with his sleeve. "I think the buggers were coasting in on the wind with their engines shut down to idle. What you heard was the props swishing round and the background noise of the engines."

Mac nodded, "I think you're right there," he paused and held up his hand. "Hold up, are they coming back?" The sharp sound of an aero engine coming from the sea carried across the field. As they stared up an urgent signal light flashed the familiar "R-S." Mac jumped up on the truck bed and seized their lamp. Relieved to find it still working, he replied. The F.E.2 snarled overhead, its shape just visible. "Our gentlemen checking to see we are okay."

Bert peered after them, "I suppose they went after it, but not much chance of catching it judging by the way it seemed to climb. What do we do now?"

Mac eased himself back into the seat and swung the sound detector to point out to sea. "See if we can catch another one. Put the kettle on, Bert, there's a good lad."

❖ ◆─▭─◆ ❖

Ned Robson stepped on the brakes to bring the unit's unofficial Wolseley car to a halt. He pumped the bulb horn and the crowd clustered around the field gate parted to let them through. He stopped next to the Commer truck and stepped down, followed by Prof Smith, Major Simpson and Admiral Sir Percy Scott. Barney the Labrador jumped down from the car and followed Simpson, nose to the ground, tail wagging.

Chalky White glanced at the car, turned back to the cable he was splicing and then froze. "Fookin' 'ell!" He nudged Bert in the ribs before springing to his feet and slamming to attention.

Percy Scott waved his hand, "Stand easy, men," he pointed at Mac. "Tell us what happened."

"We thought we heard something, sir, out towards the sea, but then Captain Smith and Mr. Robson came up in the F.E.2. We heard that with the detector before we heard it with our own ears, sir."

"So you would say the equipment works?"

"Yes, sir. You can hear an aeroplane engine at least a minute earlier, but where it really helps is you can get a better idea of where it is. It kind of focuses the sound."

"Splendid, splendid. So you tracked our aeroplane, and then what happened?"

"We saw the identifier signal from our machine, and replied with our signal. Then Captain Smith flashed a practice message, and a few seconds later, all hell let loose. I think the Zep must have dumped all his bombs, sir, and he was right over the top of us."

Sir Percy beckoned them forward and they followed him to the edge of the first bomb crater. "You had a lucky escape."

"Yes, sir."

A crowd from the surrounding villages had gathered in the field to view the bomb damage. A short man wearing a flat cap and plus fours pushed his way forward. "Arthur Walsh, *Colchester Herald*, can you give me a statement, Sir Percy?"

Percy Scott frowned, "About what?"

"About what's hidden under that tarpaulin on that lorry for one thing. Is it a secret weapon?"

The Admiral thought for a moment, then nodded. "Yes, but it's a secret no longer. The British people are entitled to know that we now have a device that can detect a Zeppelin while it is still miles out to sea, and then track it. Before long, no enemy airship will be able to cross our coasts without being found, and soon after without being destroyed."

The reporter gave a sly smile, "Can I quote you on that, Sir Percy?"

"Yes." He turned back to the ground crew. "Come on men, we've work to do." They walked back to the gate. Simpson, Ned, and the Admiral climbed back into the car but Prof Smith lingered a moment with his men, Barney at his heel.

"You're a good man, McGuigan, no need to say what my practice signal was, I appreciate that."

"Ah, you're welcome, sir," he reached down and patted the Labrador. "And you know, sir, you're right. He does have pink lips."

Smith grinned and handed McGuigan another five shillings, "You earned it." He shooed the dog back into the car and climbed in after him.

Ned turned the car round, but before he drove out of the field gate, Sir Percy lowered his window and called the team over. "You're doing a bloody good job. This is real progress. Keep your eyes open, use that detector properly, and I know that no Hun will slip by you. Good luck." They stepped back and saluted as the car rolled out into the lane.

Simpson took off his cap and smoothed his hair, "You stuck your neck out with that reporter, if you don't mind me saying, Sir Percy."

Scott smiled, "In what way?"

"Promising that we would soon be able to destroy every Zeppelin that crosses the coast."

Scott grinned at him, "No, I stuck *your* neck out."

Simpson grunted, "You have a point, sir. But I am surprised you told him about the sound detector. I thought that was to remain a secret."

"No, we agreed at a meeting last night that the great British public need a boost. The detector has moved from top secret status to propaganda. The only effect it will have on the Hun is to make them more nervous, and if they are nervous they will be more cautious, and it will be boldness that makes their raids effective. The civilians now know that we are making progress and that might quieten things down."

Smith turned round from his seat in the front of the car and passed the admiral a folded newspaper. "For once the press are making things easier for us, sir. The postmaster just gave me this."

Sir Percy smoothed the page, and read the headline aloud, "*Cowardly Huns flee from lone British defender,*" he began to chortle as he read the opening lines. "*Late last night, observers at one of our watching posts detected a giant Zeppelin coming in from the sea heading towards London. Illuminating it with their powerful searchlight they called one of our patrolling defenders to the scene. Instead of staying to fight, the Hun baby killers turned tail and ran, dropping their bombs harmlessly in the fields below to climb out of harm's way.*" He turned the paper over, "Oh, you'll like this bit, chaps . . . *Our bold Flying Corps aviator expressed his disgust to our reporter – 'The spineless raiders would not stay and mix it with us, even though we were alone. We pursued them back almost to Belgium but were forced to give up the chase due to low fuel.'*"

Simpson snorted, "Bold aviator, eh? Have we had any of those issued? What a load of old tosh."

Sir Percy handed the paper back to Smith, "Actually, if you ignore the searchlight business and the imaginary interview, that's a fair stab at what happened. The Zep did turn tail and run as soon as it saw you. That's very encouraging."

The Prof scratched his chin, "I suppose it did. We chased it out to sea but it was gaining on us all the time. It went up like the proverbial lift after it dumped its bombs and ballast. We didn't stand a snowball's chance in hell of catching it. That is a worry in itself, but my main concern is that we failed to see it, even though we could not have been more than half a mile away."

"More searchlights, that's what we need. I'll see to it. But keep in mind that if we can bring an aeroplane close enough for the Zep to see it, and they always turn tail and run, then we have achieved our objective. Sending one down in flames will be a bonus, but our job is to stop them, and last night you did just that." Sir Percy leaned over and patted Smith on the arm. "Good work, the pair of you. You deserve a drink. Robson, stop at the next pub you see."

❦ ◆━━◆ ❦

Far away in the officer's mess at their base in Belgium, Georg Klaas and Dieter Schildt agreed that a second pre-lunch drink was in order. The white-coated waiter padded across the room and placed two brandies on the low oak table in front of them. They were alone in the room, sitting in high, wing-backed chairs. An oil painting of a clipper ship racing across a stormy sea on the wall above them faced a portrait of the Kaiser on the far side of the mess.

Klaas raised his glass in salute to the Emperor, "Bottoms up, your majesty!"

Schildt glanced up from his paper and smiled. "It would be nice if the old fool would drop in and stand us a schnapps in person."

Klaas put his glass down and raised his fingers to his lips with a theatrical flourish. "Now, now, Dieter. Don't be ungrateful. He is paying our salary after all."

Schildt shook the paper out and held it up, "And if our brave captain is correct in his report, then we really earned it last night."

"Really? What did we destroy with our precisely aimed salvo of bombs?"

"Most of Harwich according to this: port facilities, a large warship in flames, another run aground by the crew, and fires started amongst warehouses."

Klaas raised an eyebrow, "I'll be damned. I could have sworn we dumped the lot harmlessly in a field thirty kilometers away. Oh well, just goes to show how bad my eyesight is."

"Hmmm. It never ceases to amaze me how quickly they can report these stories and get them into the following day's paper. Why! It's almost as if the reporters had some gift of foretelling the future."

Klaas laughed out loud, "Dieter, this war has turned you into a cynic."

CHAPTER 13

New York City, USA

Will shut his eyes and breathed deeply. He tried to fix his fingertips to the rough surface of the wall. With infinite care he moved his right foot sideways.

"I say, old boy, are you alright?"

Will opened his eyes and turned his head sideways to find Guy Gaunt looking at him with concern. "I will be fine, sir. I have to let on that I do not feel comfortable with heights." They stood on a wide ledge, fifteen stories above the streets of Manhattan, on the west face of the Grand Imperial Hotel. The sounds of the street carried up to them, diminished by the height.

Gaunt's eyes opened wide, "I beg your pardon! But you're an aviator."

Will fought to control a tremor in his left knee. "I know, sir, it does sound ridiculous, but half the men in my unit are nervous of heights, 'ceptin when they are in an aeroplane," he gulped. "Could you pass me that screwdriver?" He extended his right arm and Gaunt placed the tool in his hand.

"My God, Will! You should have said. I would never have asked you to do this if I had known. I could have done it, and you could shout instructions from the window."

"No, sir. The job has to be done, and I am give up to be a fair hand wiring a junction box." He stood staring fixedly at a small metal box that he had just attached to the wall. Making the required hole in the masonry would have been easy if he could have brought himself to stand back from the wall and put his weight against the drill. As it was, he had managed to complete the task with his elbows against the wall. A single wire entered the box from one side, while two exited the other. On the ground Will could have completed the work in two minutes; hampered by shaking fingers, sweat creeping into his eyes and the hammering of his heart, the job was taking much longer.

As he raised the screwdriver to make the final connections he felt a firm hand grip his collar and hold him steady.

"Mr. Turner, sir, I've got you. You cannae fall off. Just imagine you are on a path three feet wide on the ground, and forget about the drop below." Robert's voice sounded all the more reassuring for his musical Scots accent.

"Thanks, Robert, I am almost finished." Will secured the last screw, paused, breathed deep and then checked all the rest. He turned his head slowly and saw Guy Gaunt smiling. "Rather not have to come out and do them again, sir."

Gaunt laughed out loud, and clipped the cover in place over the box. "Come on, Will, take my hand." With Robert's hand firm on his shoulder, and Gaunt leading, Will managed the few paces to the window where Roscoe and Frank waited anxiously. Gaunt stood back as Will threw himself into the room and rolled on to his back on the floor. He lay there, panting for a moment, and then sat up as Gaunt and Robert stepped through the window.

"Robert, I am standing in need of a drink, a large one." His request broke the tension. They gathered round and helped him to his feet, laughing and slapping him on the back.

Robert, pressed a tumbler into his hand and splashed brandy into it. "Och, sir, if you dinnae mind me saying, that's one of the bravest things I have ever seen. You should get the VC for that."

Will gulped the brandy down and gasped, "Robert, that is very kind of you, but I was the one whose knees turned to jelly. You and Captain Gaunt were strolling along out there as if you were walking down Princes Street* on the way to the pub."

"Aye, that's true, sir. But you were terrified, and we're not, and it takes a damn brave man to carry on when he's scared to death. I'm proud to drink with you . . . cheers!" Robert had poured for everybody including himself.

Roscoe raised his glass, "To Will and a job well done."

Will drank again, "I hope so. Frank, would you oblige me by going next door and saying something on the far side of the room from the cabinet?"

Frank put down his glass, "On my way." Gaunt clamped the headphones over his ears. A few moments later he turned to the others and winked, raising his thumb."

"Sounds like he's here in this room with us."

Frank put his head around the door, "Does it work?"

Gaunt nodded, "Splendidly. Would you mind going downstairs and checking that room?" Frank disappeared and again Gaunt smiled with pleasure. He had reason to be satisfied. The microphone installed in the hotel suite next to the one in which they now gathered had to be hidden from view, but still pick up the conversation of the German diplomats entertaining Mexican officials there the following day. The Bell telephone company had built a modified version of their standard telephone microphone to Gaunt's specification. They had kept it small: only eighteen inches from the top of the conical trumpet to the wooden base. It had been concealed behind a locked door in a drinks cabinet. The back and base of the compartment had been perforated with dozens of holes, out of sight of anybody in the room unless they dragged the cabinet away from the wall. Gaunt had absolute confidence the hotel staff serving that suite

---

* Famous street in the heart of Edinburgh

would deny any knowledge of a key if asked. They were all refugee nationalists from the Balkan states, and they all worked for him.

The cable had been the problem. They could not run it out of the suite by the door and along the corridor into the next room; it would be too obvious. Instead Roscoe and Frank had posed as carpenters and drilled a hole in the window frame and passed the cable behind the drapes and through the hole. But the need to have a second listening post on the floor below (Gaunt left nothing to chance) required a junction box to split the cable. The obvious place to hide it was on the wall outside, and Will seemed the obvious choice to fix it and make the connections.

Gaunt stood up as Frank reappeared, and slipped his dinner jacket back on. Robert produced a brush and dusted Will down. His borrowed evening clothes hung loose on his trim frame, but he looked presentable.

"Gentlemen, Mrs. Gaunt awaits our presence at the restaurant. We mustn't keep her waiting." Twenty minutes later Robert pulled the Packard to the curb and deposited Gaunt and his young assistants at the Café des Artistes.

Will paused as he followed Gaunt into the dining area, "My word, this is a little risqué."

Roscoe laughed, "You're not in the conservative South now, Will. This is New York in the twentieth century."

Will stood for a moment admiring the murals showing nymphs frolicking in forest glades. "Oh, I cannot say I disapprove. Why, I believe the artist must have been studying the woods around my hometown."

Frank laughed, "I must visit sometime."

Will slapped him on the back, "Mr. Nelms, you must."

Margaret Gaunt and her friend Naomi sat next to each other enjoying cocktails as the men arrived, a situation unheard of even a few years before when no woman would have entered a restaurant unescorted. Gaunt made the introductions. Will had the uncomfortable feeling that Naomi Lockwood, a solid woman with jet black hair cut in a modish short bob, was sizing him up in the way an experienced rider might look at a promising race horse. Frank Nelms and Roscoe knew both ladies well. With introductions complete and drinks ordered, Naomi lost no time before quizzing Will on his life in England. She handled her menu with the deft skill of a geisha with her fan. She knew her eyes, deep blue and surrounded by laughter lines, were her strong suit, and she made sure that Will noticed, using the card to cover and uncover the lower part of her face.

Margaret Gaunt, taller and slimmer than her American friend, leaned her upper body away from her and pursed her lips in mock disapproval. "Naomi, my dear," she said in her cut glass English accent. "I do believe you are flirting outrageously with Captain Turner."

Naomi fluttered her eyelashes at Will, "But of course, my dear," she leaned across the table and patted his hand. "I have never been introduced to a real live aviator before, let alone one so handsome." It was such an obvious remark, and coming from a lady old enough to be his mother, it provoked roars of laughter from everybody at the table, sparing Will's blushes.

Will smiled, "Well, ma'am, you will have to get used to it because my two friends here will soon be qualified as flyers." He grinned, "And you have to admit they are both more handsome than me."

Naomi sat back and roared with laughter, "Touché, Captain." She leaned forward again, "But seriously, I think you young men are so brave. You would never get me up in one of those things."

"Why-ever not, ma'am? They are perfectly safe—providing nobody is shooting at you—and that is not a problem here at home."

Naomi shuddered, "Oh no, I am terrified of heights, I feel faint just looking down the stairwell in a tall building." She paused and looked at Gaunt, Roscoe, and Frank, who had all turned to look at Will. "Is there something I am missing?"

Will had a half-smile on his face. "I have just enjoyed a little adventure with these gentlemen in which I demonstrated that I, too, hate being in, or should I say on, high places."

Naomi's expression had changed from artful to plain interest. Her eyebrows shot up, "Are you serious? You're not making fun of me?"

"Cross my heart and hope to die, ma'am, I am scared of heights, and I am by no means the only aviator who will admit to the same thing. Why, I declare that over half my present unit would stand back and let somebody else climb a ladder before they would. One of my friends is give up to be nervous if he wears two pairs of socks."

"But that is bizarre. You climb your airplanes thousands of feet into the sky. How can you not be nervous then?"

Will shrugged, "It is a scientific mystery, Mrs. Lockwood. I have heard that people who study these things believe it may be something to do with the fact you are not connected with the ground when you are flying, but whatever the reason is, I am glad that it works that way."

Margaret patted Naomi on the hand, "There you are, my dear, now you can pursue these handsome young devils into the sky."

Naomi fanned her menu card in front of her face, "Oh my! Who is going to be first to take me up?"

Gaunt laughed, "I think whoever qualifies first between Frank and Roscoe. Will has only a few days leave, and he sets off tomorrow to visit his family in Florida."

The Café des Artistes had opened only a few weeks before, but the chef had already established a reputation for fine cuisine. Naomi closed her eyes as she finished her dessert, the spoon still in her mouth, then slowly licked it and winked at Will, making him smile.

"Mrs. Lockwood . . ."

"Please, call me Naomi," she stretched the *o*.

"Naomi. Have you ever visited France?"

"No, I regret I have not, but as soon as this unpleasantness is finished I will be the first to step ashore. I adore their food. Of course, I imagine you are bored with it, having served there."

"Oh, I wish I could say that, but the French are nothing if not expert at adapting to the preferences of their guests, and the preference of the British Tommy is for egg and chips."

"Chips?"

"Yes, ma'am: cut and sliced potatoes deep fried and served with fried eggs. Then we wash it down with the cheap wine that we call 'plonk.' That is about all you will find anywhere near the front."

Naomi giggled, "Plonk?"

"Indeed. Wine so rough that we use it to clean the windscreens on our machines, but we must drink gallons of the stuff as well."

Naomi shuddered, "It doesn't sound very appetizing."

"It is a welcome treat for the men when they are on rest from the trenches. The diet there is made up of 'bully' beef, hard tack and plum and apple jam. Even the tea tastes foul because the water has to be disinfected. By the time they come out of the line, the poor devils are bad off for anything cooked fresh."

Naomi's eyes opened wide, "What, even the officers?"

Will nodded, "In the line certainly. Good officers share the hardships with their men. I know that sometimes they might receive a hamper from home, probably from Fortnum and Mason's, but like as not they will share it with their soldiers."

"But surely there are opportunities to get away from the front line?"

"Yes, there are. Many people take a leave in Paris, but even in Amiens you can still find a reasonable restaurant. Why, a member of my old squadron went to a big party for officers who had been to Eton, the famous English school. He brought the menu back to show us, it was plain magnificent, but the strangest thing was that he told us that the evening degenerated into a mass food fight," Will shook his head in wonderment. "Can you imagine that? A famous general pushed my friend's head into a trifle, but that was after my friend had thrown a cheesecake at him."

Margaret sighed, "Men! I have heard about beanos like those. They revert back to their childhood."

Gaunt raised his unlit cigar in front of him and looked at his wife. She nodded permission, and he struck a match and puffed for a moment. Satisfied that it was burning he turned to Will, "The English public school traditions are a mystery to me, but it seems to keep them happy."

It was Will's turn to be surprised, "Really, sir? I just assumed in a manner that you had attended somewhere like Eton or Rugby."

"Nooo! You can't blame me for English eccentricity. I'm Australian."

"Well, sir, I declare I am surprised. I thought I could hear you had an accent but I never put two and two together."

Gaunt smiled and blew smoke at the ceiling. He winked, "That's me, man of mystery."

Robert had the Packard standing outside the restaurant as they emerged. He delivered Will, Frank, and Roscoe to the Waldorf. As they climbed out, Will felt Naomi press something into his hand. She held it for a moment, "Do come and visit when you are next in New York."

"It will be my pleasure, ma'am." The car drew away to take her and the Gaunts to their respective suburban homes. He opened his hand and found her card. Roscoe and Frank stood grinning.

"So, Will, what do they call it in the front line when the infantry attack?" Frank asked, an innocent smile on his rugged face.

"It is known as 'going over the top,' and you can wipe those smug smiles off your ugly mugs. I will not be going over the top with Mrs. Lockwood, I will be safe back at headquarters. It is you two who get to compete for the honor of taking her flying." He nudged Frank in the ribs, "Come on, there is still time to take a little nightcap at the bar."

Roscoe and Frank had made their excuses and disappeared before Robert
served breakfast in the suite. Guy Gaunt joined him.

"Will, I need to run through a few details with you about this end of
the operation. Your namesake is already on his speaking tour. I have to say
he's a decent sort of johnny and he has been briefed not to go out there
and strafe his audiences with a load of rot, but at the same time he has to
mention certain times, dates and places that coincide with your service.
He also looks very much like you." Gaunt paused to pour some more coffee, then looked up and grinned, "Of course he's better looking, but then
he is an actor." Gaunt passed Will a slip of paper, "This is the address you
have to report to when you get back to New York. It is the office of the
German American Alliance. They will take you to meet their consul. Your
contact is this young lady, Matilda Ellerkamm. She answers to 'Matty' and
seems like the perfect little American lady, but scratch the surface and she
is a proper little *fraulein*. She is the little madam who had the stand up
row with Artie Vokes at *Modern Mechanics.*"

"Hmmm, not exactly my type, I have to say."

"Don't worry, unless a chap wears jack boots and goosesteps around
the house I doubt she would be interested."

Will poured more coffee for them both. "Just how effective is this
German American Alliance?"

Gaunt thought for a moment, "Not as effective as they were at one
time. German propaganda loves to lecture, and assumes that its audience
can't think for itself. They have failed to grasp the fact that the average
American can spot a fake a mile away and hates to be lectured to, or
thought of as stupid. I think they shoot themselves in the foot more often
than not."

"How about their actual intelligence services?"

Gaunt allowed himself a chuckle, "Up to all sorts of surprisingly
imaginative mischief here in the U.S., hence our little mission last night.

I have a theory that may sound bizarre, but I think they are trying to stir the Mexicans up against us.* I will grant that they are clever, but as my boss, Admiral 'Blinker' Hall, has said—'clever, but that fatal inch short of being clever enough to recognize that we are just as good.'"

He glanced at his watch, "Time to pack you off for your well-deserved leave. Roscoe and Frank are coming to the station with you, Robert is loading your things on the Packard now." He stood and they shook hands. "Will, I believe you are actually cut-out for this kind of work. I believe you will give a good account of yourself. There is very little advice I can give you apart from keep your mouth shut, and your eyes and ears open. You will be quite on your own, but I have no doubt you will bring this mission to a good conclusion." He slapped Will on the back as he turned to go, "And the best of luck."

Frank and Roscoe both believed he was simply passing through on his way to a well-earned leave. They bombarded him with questions about flying and the war as Robert weaved through the morning traffic. They stood talking on the platform as they waited for the train to depart. At last the cry of "all aboard" rang out. Will gripped each of their hands in farewell, then swung up onto the step to the car where his first class compartment awaited him.

"Will?" Roscoe had one last question and Will stood poised on the step with one hand gripping the rail as he looked down at them expectantly. "If there is one piece of advice you would give to us aspiring aviators about flying, what would it be?"

Will smiled down at them, "Never, ever try to turn back if your engine fails when you are taking off. Just crash straight ahead under control. If you try to get back to the field, you will spin in and most likely die. Will you promise me that you will never do that?"

They both nodded vigorously and replied in chorus, "You bet!"

Will struggled with a feeling of unreality as the train rolled on its journey south. It had not really sunk in that he would be seeing his par-

---

* *Gaunt was right. It was as a direct result of this that the U.S. entered the war the following year.*

ents and all his old friends again the following day. In some ways his life as an officer in the Royal Flying Corps seemed to belong to a different man, or at the least a different time, but the uniform packed in his case, and, more immediate, the scar over his eye that now itched in the growing heat created an unbreakable link to that other Will Turner.

He was glad to be alone in his sleeping compartment with his thoughts, but as the afternoon shadows lengthened and turned suddenly to dusk as they chugged through Virginia, he was pleased when the conductor discreetly mentioned that he would find some "sport" in the club car. Settling at the table with a group of middle-aged and elderly card players he surprised himself when they politely enquired as to his occupation.

"I am an engineering journalist. I write for *Modern Mechanics* magazine." The lie slipped out without snagging on his conscience, and as he sat there in his linen suit, with the collar of his shirt comfortably free of a necktie in the heat, he found himself enjoying his new role.

A few hours later, and a few dollars lighter, he retired to his compartment where the gentle rocking of the train soon lulled him to sleep. Thanks to the efforts of Henry Flagler he could have travelled on to Key West if the mood had taken him the next morning, but he had to change at Jacksonville for the last stretch across northern Florida to Tallahassee, the state capital and his hometown. This train stopped at small towns along the route, extending the 170-mile journey to nearly five hours. Will felt a quiet satisfaction that the car was almost full; his father owned most of the shares in the railroad company. By now it was early May, but already the heat of approaching summer made the passengers grateful for the breeze ducted through the cleverly made ventilators above the windows. He appreciated that with a quiet smile too, he had designed them. It would be easy to slip back into his old life, but just as his thoughts drifted into a nostalgic reverie, a commotion outside at the last stop before Tallahassee tugged him back to the present. Loud voices and laughter made the passengers sit up, just as a young conductor, immaculate in white and maroon uniform, appeared in the door connecting to the vestibule at the end of the car where the passengers climbed aboard.

His black face split in a wide grin, as he pointed at Will, "Are you Mr. Captain Turner?"

Will stared at the conductor, as all eyes turned toward him, "No . . . I mean yes, I am Will Turner."

"Sakes, are you in trouble!"

A second figure appeared behind the conductor. Taller, much wider: just as black. "Child, get out of my way." The boy ducked away giggling.

Will's jaw dropped, "Cordelia!" He stumbled out of his seat and into the arms of his childhood nurse, and lifetime friend. It felt like being crushed by a bear. She hugged him fiercely, then seized his shoulders and kissed him. Before he could say anything she pushed him away and looked him up and down.

"Good Lawd, Young William! What do you think you are wearin'?"

He felt twelve again, "My best summer suit, Cordelia. Won't it do?"

She exploded, "No, you damn fool, it won't do. Do not dare tell me you do not have your uniform with you."

"Well, yes I do, it is in the baggage car in my suitcase, but I cannot—"

His words were cut off as she seized him by the collar, "Come on, you can change in the baggage car, Jeremiah won't worry—"

"But, but—"

"But nuthin! You damn fool. If you think your mother is going to be deprived of her moment of glory after all you have put her through, you better think again. Come on." The passengers had been watching the exchange with amazement. Cordelia turned to them. "This is our town's own home-grown hero, Captain William Turner, of His Majesty's Royal Flying Corps," she rolled the words for effect. "And he is planning to meet his English mother, out of uniform. Have you ever heard of anything so thoughtless?"

A tiny woman, eighty years old at least, waved her umbrella at him. "Shame on you, son. Do what she says and smarten yourself up."

His protests had no effect. He was beaten before he had started. His carefully constructed cover ruined for love. He meekly followed Cordelia to the baggage car.

CHAPTER 14

Martlesham Heath, Suffolk, England

Colonel Roger Lechelle stalked forward, craning his neck backward and gazing up at the airplane towering above him. He glanced round as he sensed somebody at his side.

"Very interesting," Colonel Frank Penrose squinted up at the nose of the giant machine fifteen feet above his head. "But I doubt it will replace the aeroplane."

Lechelle grunted, "Where's Matrett? This demonstration was supposed to start half an hour ago. I can't abide tardiness, can't abide it."

Frank glanced back to the sheds on the edge of the heath land near Ipswich in the county of Suffolk. "Sergeant Thorpe is back, perhaps he can shed some light." He beckoned to Joe Thorpe who had just climbed out of the sidecar of a motorcycle pulled up on the tarmac in front of the sheds. Joe marched up and crashed to an exaggerated drill book halt. His right knee came up to slam a perfectly polished boot to the ground as his right hand sizzled up to the peak of his cap.

"Sah!"

Lechelle looked him up and down. He could not stop himself giving an approving nod. He loved nothing more than parade ground "bull," and Joe Thorpe knew how to serve it up by the bucket load. "Sergeant, what news of the two officers?"

"Proper poorly I'm afraid, sir. The doctor has seen them at the hotel and he reckons they've gone down with food poisoning. Could be a hospital job he says."

"Damn!" Lechelle slapped his cane against the palm of his gloved hand. "That means we'll have to postpone this bloody demonstration yet again."

"Begging your pardon, sir. Permission to speak?" Joe still stood rigidly to attention.

Lechelle raised an eyebrow, "Of course, Sergeant, stand easy, man."

Joe allowed his shoulders to relax and moved his feet apart, "I hope I'm not speaking out of turn, sir, but young Mr. Ives says he has been up on a twin engine machine, and Mr. Jackson is a very skilled pilot. They reckon they could handle it easily."

"Are you saying they want to give it a try?"

"Keen as mustard, sir."

"Then why don't they say so themselves?" Lechelle addressed the question as much to Frank Penrose as Joe.

Joe coughed, "Professional etiquette I think, sir. These flyers have their own code of honor. They don't want to be seen to be stealing another man's glory."

"Glory be buggered!" A fleck of spittle shot out of Lechelle's mouth. He waved his cane in the air. "You men!" Bill Ives and Stan Jackson stood beside the motorbike and sidecar, fussing with the tripod of a plate camera and the timing apparatus that Frank had arranged to be at the field for the maiden flight of the Destroyer. Ostensibly it was the operation of the recording apparatus that had brought them to the airfield. Bill Ives looked up and pointed to his chest. "Yes, you. Both of you." They went through the same routine as Joe, marching up, saluting and standing to attention.

Lechelle eyed them, tapping his cane against his leg. "Stand easy, chaps." They relaxed. What do you think of this machine?" He pointed his cane at Bill Ives.

"Magnificent, sir. Never seen anything this big before."

Lechelle twitched his cane to one side. "Jackson, ain't it? What about you?"

Stan stroked his chin as he craned his neck backwards. "It's a beaut, sir." Joe glanced down and saw that Stan had his fingers crossed behind his back.

Lechelle fixed them with a stare, his gray eyes gazing from under his luxuriant eyebrows. "How would you like a chance to fly it?"

"Oh yes, sir!"

"Have you got your flying kit with you?"

"Yes, sir."

"Good, that's settled. You're doing the test flight. Off you go and get togged up." The two young flying officers and Joe Thorpe came to attention, saluted and marched off. Lechelle turned to Frank Penrose as soon as they were out of earshot. "I'm going to enjoy telling Matrett about our little change of plans. I would never be surprised if his chosen pilots might have been offered a little incentive to give a good report." He touched his cane to the side of his nose, "If you catch my drift, dontcha know."

Frank's eyes opened wide, "Surely not!"

Lechelle nodded, his head jerking, "I know it sounds despicable, but I've had to deal with people like Matrett all my life. Underneath the title and the money, they're just 'trade.' They're not gentleman and never will be. You mark my words, if he thought he could get away with it, he wouldn't be above offering me a night out on the town with a couple of tarts if he thought it would influence me."

"Good grief!" Frank turned away pretending to examine the Destroyer while he suppressed the urge to laugh out loud. When he turned back to Lechelle his face again wore his usual expression, a faint smile and an almost vacant look as if his thoughts were elsewhere. It was a wonderful disguise, many people had made the serious error of underestimating Colonel Frank Penrose. "I'll just toddle along and brief these chaps. I'll leave you the pleasure of dealing with Matrett. Here he is now." A long, royal blue Rolls Royce limousine pulled up in front of the sheds.

"Splendid," Lechelle growled and strode toward it.

Frank turned and hurried to the hangar where his team had disappeared. He found them inside the door where Joe helped them into their flying gear. Frank smiled, "No need to overdo it with praise for the Destroyer, chaps. Colonel Lechelle may be brighter than we think. He's certainly got Matrett's number."

He cocked his head to one side, "Hark." The sound of voices raised in anger floated across the tarmac. "I do believe Sir Norman is expressing his pleasure at having his pet pilots replaced by a pair of hardbitten cynics."

"Cynics?" Stan's voice sounded muffled as he pulled a sweater over his head. His boyish face with its prominent nose and twinkling blue eyes popped through the neck opening, slightly flushed. "Us, sir?"

Frank laughed aloud, "Yes, you two. Now, listen. No heroics. If it comes off the ground, do one gentle circuit and land immediately."

"And if it doesn't come off the ground, sir?" Bill tugged his gloves on.

"Bring it to a stop in plenty of time, long before you hit the hedge. Remember, no risks."

Bill and Stan saluted Frank as they walked out of the hangar. Frank and Joe Thorpe stood side by side watching them striding across the tarmac toward the giant airplane squatting like a prehistoric flying dinosaur at the edge of the field. Frank looked around, peering into the dark recesses of the hangar to make sure nobody would overhear them.

"How did it go last night, Joe? Pretty well by the sound of it."

Joe repeated the careful look around then twiddled the end of his mustache as he stood raising and lowering himself by flexing his toes. "Like a dream, sir. Mrs. Courroyer and myself went into the pub posing as brother and sister. That way she could use her feminine wiles, if you catch my drift, sir."

"It's my day for catching drifts. You mean so she could flirt with the poor saps."

"Exactly. She laid it on with a trowel. Telling them how brave they must be and how handsome they looked in their uniforms; and what was this medal ribbon for and so on and so forth."

Frank nodded, "And meanwhile you plied them with booze?"

"Naturally as a well-heeled, local businessman I had to treat our bold aviators to a few rounds. The youngster was three sheets in the wind after a couple of whiskies, but the one I took to be senior had hollow legs. I've seen some drinkers in my time but the way he put away the scotch beat them all."

Frank winced. "I'm not surprised, I examined his records: shot down twice, once in flames, two observers killed, crashed twice on take-off, three times on landing, and that was just on his last time out. The poor bugger's nerves must be in shreds."

"His liver must be in tatters as well. In the end, Jac slipped something into his drink and he went out like a light."

"Good grief. What was it?"

"No idea, sir, and I would rather not know."

Frank sucked his teeth, "Yes, I know what you mean. Anyway, it worked like a charm. Lechelle never ceases to amaze me. If I had suggested using the terrible twins he would never have agreed, but a starchy parade ground sergeant marches up and passes on some griff and he laps it up."

Joe looked over his shoulder as if checking again for eavesdroppers, "Experience probably taught him to rely on his NCOs. We do our best."

Frank laughed out loud and slapped Joe on the shoulder, "Come on, let's see what the farmer and the wild colonial boy can do with Mr. Pickering's patent aerial locomotive." They hurried across to the edge of the tarmac where Stan and Bill Ives stood interrogating Pickering, the builder of the Destroyer.

Bill had his hands on his hips leaning toward Pickering. "What do you mean by a 'bit underpowered'?"

Pickering pulled a handkerchief from the sleeve of his expensive suit jacket and mopped his brow. "Well, um, you see I was let down by Rolls-Royce."

"Let down by bloody Rolls-Royce?" Stan's Australian twang pitched 'Royce' so high he did not need to add anything to underline his disbelief.

"That's a first," Bill sounded grim. "So what have you hung on there?" He jabbed his thumb at the four engines suspended on struts between the bottom and next set of wings.

"The very next best thing, Beardmores."

"Bloody oath! I thought you said this machine needed a thousand horsepower. Four Beardmores will give us barely six hundred!" Stan said.

"Ah, yes," Pickering held up his hands. "But the Destroyer is not carrying its war load. No guns, bombs—only you two on board instead of the six-man crew, and just enough petrol for a short flight. You'll have power to spare."

The two pilots exchanged a look then turned toward the airplane. They marched around it, waggling the control surfaces, kicking all four tires on the massive undercarriage until they reached the door cut in the box like fuselage behind the wings. They scrambled aboard, a mechanic shutting the door behind them.

Bill pointed, "Head for the light."

"Ow!" Stan ducked back down again, rubbing his head where he had banged it on a stout crossbeam, part of the fuselage structure. "I expected it to be made out of string and brown paper, but they've gone the other way. This thing's put together like a brick-built dunny."

Bill paused in his climb up to the open cockpit and stared down at his Australian friend. Stan grinned and translated, "A brick-built privy, mate."

"You're not wrong there," Bill slid into the pilot's seat behind a sturdy control wheel. A panel in front of the seat next to him sported an array of levers, knobs and dials instead of flight controls. Bill twisted the wheel and pushed it back and forward. He turned to Stan. "Shall we toss for who does what?"

"No, sport, if you're happy to be the helmsman, I'll be chief mechanic and look after the engine controls."

"Okay, but you might have to give me a hand here. These controls are stiff as a board. Come on, let's get on with it." They buckled their safety belts and Bill leaned over the rim of the cockpit and shouted to the foreman in charge of the team of mechanics. "Ready to start!"

"Which one?"

Bill looked out along the starboard wing, "Start at that end, and we'll work our way across." Each engine drove a four-bladed propeller large enough in diameter that one blade could always be reached easily from the ground. To start each engine, one mechanic took a firm grip on the bottom blade and three of his colleagues linked hands with him and each other. On a given signal the lead mechanic ran sideways dragging the blade with him while the rest of the team gave extra impetus and pulled him away from the propeller, that invariably spun into life on the first attempt if the man in the cockpit had primed the carburetor and spun the booster magneto with enough vigor. Stan Jackson knew his job, and they soon had all four engines clattering away.

Stan leaned across the cockpit and bellowed above the din, "I reckon we got the rough end of the pineapple, mate."

Bill pulled down his goggles and grinned, "The pair of us must be as silly as a two-bob watch." He looked over the cockpit edge at the mechanics that stood gazing up at them, concern obvious in their expressions. He crossed his hands in front of his face to wave the chocks away from the wheels and turned to Stan. "Give me half-ahead all engines, chiefy." The noise level rose as the machine began to shake. Bill gripped the wheel and pulled it back to hold the tail down and waited for the wheels to roll. Nothing happened.

"Shovel more coal on?" Stan asked. Bill nodded. The vibration grew as Stan advanced the four throttle levers. The Destroyer lurched and began to roll forward. The field was a wide expanse of grass giving the option to always take off into wind. A light breeze stirred the windsock showing Bill that he needed to turn and head back down the field to position for a take-off parallel to the sheds, and the watching audience. He jammed his foot against the rudder bar, pushed, and pushed harder.

"Christ! I've got the rudder hard over and nothing's happening."

Stan twisted in his seat to confirm that the rudders confined in the complex triple-tail unit had moved. "They're right over. Hang on, I'll try this." He pushed the throttle for the outside engine on the starboard wing to full power and pulled back on the corresponding throttle on the port wing. The airplane started to swing to the left as it stumbled forward, and continued to swing, despite Bill jamming full opposite rudder against the turn. He felt sweat trickling down inside his goggles despite the chill of the day.

"Whoa, you beauty!" Stan reversed the power inputs to straighten up. With deft adjustments of the throttles he achieved something like a straight line. Bill's desperate stamping on the rudder pedals made little difference. At last they reached the edge of the field. Stan repeated the trick using the thrust from the outside engines to turn, and lined them up for an attempted take-off run. He throttled all the engines back to idling revs to make himself heard.

"Bill, this thing's too bloody heavy to fly. Let's just make a fast run down the field. If we can show some daylight under the wheels that'll be enough. Then we can put in an honest report and shoot through like a Bondi tram* before somebody comes up with another war winner."

Bill took one hand off the wheel and raised his thumb in agreement. "Full ahead all engines. Let her rip!"

Stan adjusted his goggles, extended his hands above the engine controls and flexed his fingers like a concert pianist. Taking care to bring the

---

* "*Get out of here fast.*" *The streetcar that ran from Sydney, Australia to the seaside suburb of Bondi was famous for its speed.*

power up on all engines together, he opened up and held all four levers hard against the stops. The Destroyer stood quivering and bellowing for a moment, then rolled, at walking pace for a hundred yards, then at a trot, then a canter and finally a full-blooded gallop as Bill's pressure on the control wheel raised the tail at last.

He tried to focus on the airspeed indicator but he could hardly see the needle. The vibration from the straining engines not only shook the delicate instrument, it blurred his vision. To his surprise he felt the wings starting to take the weight. For a second he sensed the wheels leaving the ground, but then the machine seemed to check in the air and the wheels crashed down again. Then again: up, check, slam to the ground with a tooth-jarring crash. The Destroyer bounded across the field in a series of leaps. Bill snatched a glance at the gaggle of spectators, and as he did caught sight of something flailing in the air behind the starboard outer engine. He watched with detached fascination. A bracing wire had snapped; the first event in a sequence that he was powerless to prevent. The *Pickering Destroyer* had been massively over-built in places where it did not matter, and was pitifully weak where it needed to be strong. The engines depended on bracing wires to restrain them in the cradles constructed within the wing struts. Freed from the constraints of a crucial wire, the howling engine ripped itself from the mounting, shattering the propeller against the lower wing and sending splinters ripping through the fabric.

Instinct took over. Bill jammed the rudder hard to the left in a desperate attempt to counteract the violent lurch to starboard as the port engines dragged the machine round. He screamed a warning to Stan and hauled back on the controls, hoping that the drag on the tail-skid against the mud of the field might slow them. He watched, a fascinated but helpless passenger, as the Destroyer, hellbent on living up to its name, swerved toward the sheds and the knot of watchers. He sensed Stan furiously jerking the engine controls but could only watch as the indistinct group grew in his windscreen. The mechanics looked to be in the clear, they had scattered. He recognized Colonel Penrose and had to admire his amazing turn of speed, almost as fast as Joe Thorpe: for two old soldiers they could sprint when danger threatened. Pickering and Matrett had flung themselves flat in the mud but it was Lechelle he had to admire most. Even as the rampaging quadriplane bore down on him, he stood upright, unmoving, fearless and ultimately stupid as he looked death in the face.

For a moment Bill thought that implacable stare had done the trick and the Destroyer had turned aside rather than face it, but it was Stan's lightening quick reactions that saved them. His hands swept across the controls, cutting the ignition switches for the port engines and the renegade engine on the starboard wing, and holding the throttle for the remaining starboard engine wide open. The turning moment it generated was less because of its place next to the fuselage, but it was enough coupled with the extreme rudder input.

At this point, as their unruly mount changed course again and swung away from danger, Bill Ives did the strangest thing of his military career. As the wing swept harmlessly over Lechelle's head, the colonel still standing rigidly upright as if reviewing a parade, Bill saluted him. It seemed the right thing to do.

The emergency for those on the ground had passed. Their troubles had just begun for the crew of Mr. Pickering's airplane. The final burst of power from the engine that saved the spectators had helped maintain momentum as the quadriplane swung back across the field. With the three other motors now silent it only remained for Stan to kill that one too, and decisively turn off the fuel. He then sat with arms folded watching the boundary fence rush toward them at a surprising high speed.

It was a bright morning, but the air still had enough of a chill that the giant, warm, pile of farmyard manure on the other side of the fence steamed gently in the cheery rays of the sun. The Destroyer hit the fence at not much more than twenty miles an hour, just enough to trip it so the tail came up—and the nose came down, with a sound somewhere between a squelch and a thud in the softest part of the pile. The world disappeared in a fine brown spray. The two young airmen sat leaning against their straps for a moment, surprised to be unhurt, stunned by the sudden silence.

Stan turned to his pilot, then wiped his goggles with a gloved finger to clear his vision. "Shit!"

Bill wrinkled his nose, "No question about that, chum. And we're in it."

Frank Penrose and Joe Thorpe arrived at the wreck first. They had leaped aboard the motorcycle and roared across the field in pursuit.

"Ives, Jackson, are you all right?" Frank's anxious voice floated across the fence from beneath the upturned tail that now pointed at the sky.

Bill unbuckled his seatbelt, knelt on the edge of the cockpit and called back, "Yes thank you, sir. Just a bit bruised. I would stay there if I were you, it's a bit messy this side of the fence." The mechanics arrived within seconds, with everything on their truck needed to deal with any emergency. They set a ladder against the side of the Destroyer, and Bill and Stan crawled out of the door and down to solid ground. By this time Matrett, Pickering, and Lechelle had arrived at the scene. The two airmen pulled themselves to attention and saluted Frank and Lechelle.

"Regret to report test flight not successful, sir," Bill spoke in a clipped military tone.

Matrett exploded. His eyes bulged, foam appeared at his lips, "Not successful! Not bloody successful! You blundering idiots, you nincompoops, you just wrecked a year's work, you—"

"Matrett. Shut up." Frank Penrose spoke, his voice hardly raised, his authority absolute. Matrett paused, his mouth open, staring in disbelief at the man who dared to challenge him. Before he could take breath to protest, Lechelle cut in.

"Yes, Matrett, put a sock in it and stop abusing these officers. This is a military establishment and this is an army matter. What's more they have nothing to apologize for. They did a splendid job. I saw exactly what happened through my field glasses." He turned to Pickering who had stayed quiet. "The bloody engine fell off, did it not, Mr. Pickering?"

Pickering looked to Matrett for support, but his patron seemed to be suffering some temporary seizure with his mouth opening and closing with no sound coming out. "Well, as a result of mishandling, I think it may have moved out of alignment."

Stan's self-control had held to this point, but he had reached his limit. "You little bastard! You stand there putting on the jam dressed like a pox doctor's clerk and try to tell me that I mishandled the engines! It went bung because you hadn't nailed the flamin' thing on." He stepped toward Pickering with one hand outstretched. For a moment it looked as if his verbal assault might turn physical.

"Jackson!" Frank's voice cracked like a whip.

Stan stepped back, "Sorry, sir, crash must have shaken me up."

"Yes, I imagine it did. You and Lieutenant Ives report to the medical officer at once for a check up." They saluted and allowed themselves to be led away by Joe Thorpe. Frank turned to Pickering and Matrett. "Gentlemen. It is very obvious there are serious shortcomings with your aeroplane. It's only thanks to the swift actions of those young men that it is not a complete write-off and we don't have serious casualties to account for. I suggest you recover it to the hangars and consider a radical re-design before asking Corp officers to test it. As it stands at the moment, it's a death trap." Frank turned on his heel before Matrett or Pickering could reply.

Lechelle fell in step beside him. "I was going to let Jackson thump the little twit."

Frank looked at him, an eyebrow raised, "Really? Not very regimental."

Lechelle laughed out loud, "No, but thoroughly deserved."

Frank allowed himself a smile, "True, but too many witnesses." He glanced back at the up-ended Destroyer. "Now, what are we going to do about Matrett's pet project?"

Lechelle tapped his cane against his leg as he walked, "I will report back to the committee that the Destroyer needs more development work before we can allow our pilots to fly it. I will recommend that the War Office does not contribute to the costs. If Matrett is still confident enough in the machine to put more of his own money up, that is his decision."

"And your private opinion?"

Lechelle walked on for a few paces, then stopped and looked Frank in the eye. "Strictly between you and me, I think Pickering should have stuck to making garden mowers and cricket pitch rollers. That bloody aeroplane is as clumsy as a duck in a ploughed paddock, even I can see that." They had reached the tarmac where Lechelle's driver stood with the door of his car open. He turned to Frank and they shook hands. "Good day to you, Penrose."

Frank watched Lechelle's Daimler drive away and then walked across to the hangar entrance. He found the two pilots sitting on upturned packing crates being tended by Joe Thorpe and Jacquieline Courroyer, who had driven Frank to the field and watched the test flight from the comparative safety of the car. She was cleaning a cut above Bill's eye with cotton wool and undiluted iodine.

"Ow!"

"Stop whining, you big baby, it's only a little scratch, but with the microbes you two have picked up it needs cleaning."

Bill winced and looked up at her through his open eye, "For a secretary, you're a dab hand with the first aid kit."

"Bollocks, I'm no more a secretary than you." Jac fixed a sticking plaster over the wound and stepped back to admire her work. "There, you'll live."

Frank laughed at the shock on Bill's battered face, "Lieutenant Ives, I see you've made the acquaintance of Mrs. Courroyer. You will find she can be quite direct."

Bill studied her warily, "Yes, sir."

"So, I see you've been to see the medical officer," Frank picked up the bottle of rum sitting among the tea mugs on the table in front of them.

"Yes, sir," Stan checked in the teapot. "Doctor Lamb* gave us his patent medicine. Guaranteed to set you up after a shock. Tea, sir?" Frank held out a clean mug and Stan poured for him. "Sir, I must apologize for . . ."

Frank waved his free hand, "Think nothing more of it, Jackson. No harm done." He added a measure of rum to his tea and raised it in salute, "Cheers, chaps." He drank, then placed his mug back on the table. "I think I owe you an apology. If I had any idea that machine could be as dangerous as that without leaving the ground, I would never have asked you to get involved in this little stunt."

Stan shrugged, "Well, as you said, sir. No harm done."

Jac picked up Bill's manure-stained uniform tunic and held it up, "Except to their uniforms, sir." She wrinkled her nose, "Phew!"

Frank smiled, "I'll pay for cleaning. That's the least I can do. Come on, we can borrow some clean overalls for you to wear for now, and I will run you back to your field in the car."

"How will we get the bike back, sir?"

Frank turned to Jac, who grinned, "What an awfully jolly idea, sir! Do try to keep up."

---

* *Lamb's Navy Rum, a popular brand.*

CHAPTER 15

Tallahassee, Florida

The three days with his family and friends in Tallahassee proved a bittersweet experience. Will planned to slip in and out of town without fuss. He reflected on the old saying about the road to hell being paved with good intentions as the train wheezed into the station. The size of the crowd gave him hope that it might be for some visiting dignitary. But the mixture of waving union flags, United States and British, and the band parping out *Hearts of Oak,* and *Rule Brittania*, told him the press of people crowding into the station yard gathered there for him alone. Will Turner could imagine few things worse than fame. At this time it was the last thing he wanted or needed, but he was stuck with it. His people adored him.

Settlement in the area in the previous century had been mainly from the British Isles, France and even Belgium. No wonder the town was for the Allied cause with a vengeance, any representative from the German American Alliance showing up there would have been lucky to escape with tarring and feathering. Will's visit gave the townsfolk the opportunity to vent their passion.

He had tried to keep his arrival a secret. Somebody had blabbed, that much was obvious. A cable must have been sent. The culprit came into his head without bidding, "Marie Julien," he muttered out loud, "you are in deep, deep trouble if ever I get back to England." But in his heart he could not blame her. He could not tell her why it was of the utmost importance to keep his visit home discreet. As far as she was concerned he was just home on leave, his insistence on a minimum of fuss she would have put down to modesty.

He stood in the door of the railroad car with Cordelia at his shoulder, she leaned forward, "You are their hero, William, try to look and act like one. Shoulders back, head up, and straighten your tunic."

He tugged at his uniform jacket and straightened his cap, "Yes ma'am. You know we have a drill sergeant who reminds me of you?"

"An' mind you don't forget it," she hissed in his ear.

The train jerked to a stop. The young porter jumped to the ground to set his steps for Will to descend. His feet never touched them. A crowd of young men, black and white, surged around the door and lifted him shoulder high. They carried him around the station yard behind the band now thumping out *The British Grenadier* before setting him down on the open back of Nathan Walker's brand new Mack stake truck.

"Speech! Speech!" The crowd demanded something from him. Two years service as an officer in the British Army had taught him how to stand up and speak in front of an audience without freezing. He held out his hands palm down and lowered them, motioning for quiet.

"Ladies and gentlemen, I am obliged to you for this overwhelming greeting. I really do not know what I have done to deserve this—"

"Tell us about those medals, Will." A voice interrupted from the back.

He pointed to the medal ribbons on his tunic, "This one is for shiniest boots, and this one is for good conduct—they have not caught me yet." The people roared their approval. He motioned for quiet again, "I would just like to say that if my comrades at the front could see you all now, it would give them heart for the struggle ahead. Knowing that we have the support of the American people, if not the American government. . ." he had to pause to let the roar from the crowd subside ". . . makes all the difference. Now, I have kept you standing in the hot sun long enough, and my mother, who I have not seen for two years, is waiting patiently." He vaulted from the truck to resounding cheers, and ran the few yards to where his parents sat smiling in the trusty old Model T.

Charlotte Turner's British stiff upper lip had held to that point, but she fell on her son, kissed him and hugged him fiercely. He managed to disengage long enough to seize his father's hand.

"My God! It is good to see you, Son."

Will could only grin as his mother hugged him again while the cheering crowd surged around the car. "Mother, I declare you look younger than ever."

She uttered a choking noise between a laugh and a sob, "No thanks to you and your sister. Between the pair of you I think you have aged me a hundred years." She took a grip on his shoulders and pushed him to arms' length. "What have you done to your head?" The falling Lewis gun magazine had left a faint scar once the swelling subsided: insignificant to anybody but a mother.

"Oh, some idiot dropped a metal drum on my head."

"I hope you chastised him severely."

"I will when I lay hands on him," he turned, the car sagged with the weight of another body on the running board. "Henry! You son of a gun." Will seized his friend's hand in both of his own. "Damn! It is a fine thing to see your ugly mug." Henry Walker's grin split his face. All he could do was nod in delight. Will pushed him into the seat next to his father and dropped down beside his mother in the back of the open car.

"Father, can you get us out of here?"

John Turner twisted around in the seat and smiled, "Yes, but not in a hurry," he pointed to the band scrambling into the back of Nathan's truck. "You are the star turn in a parade, Will. You better get used to it." He pressed the pedal that engaged the gears and the Tin Lizzie moved into line behind the truck. The procession rolled out of the railroad yard and through the tree-lined streets. Most of the town had turned out to see their hero. Every corner had a knot of well-wishers and John obliged them by slowing enough for them to shake Will's hand, or if they were female, in many cases to smother him in kisses.

Will sat back, breathless, after being waylaid by friends of Marie and his sister on the corner of Monroe and Jefferson. "Goodness, whatever happened to old-fashioned decorum?"

"Swept away by this modern age and dissolved by your looks and charm, my darling boy," his mother gazed at him. Will flushed scarlet, not entirely sure if she was joking.

At last they reached the Turner family home, magnificent in all its eccentric glory and just as he remembered it. The central tower, balcony, and the wide steps to the front porch and entrance gleamed. "The old homestead looks magnificent, Father. Did you spruce it up for me?"

John slapped him on the back, "Lord sakes no, son. We did not know you were coming until three days ago," he paused, a frown on his face. "I will tell you why I had all this work done later. Come on, let us get you inside. You need to freshen up before you face your adoring crowd again." At least a hundred people had followed the impromptu parade all the way to the house. Good manners required that some acknowledgment be made of their enthusiastic welcome.

Charlotte stood up in the back of the car and made a quick head count, and winced. "Cordelia, darling!"

Cordelia Walker gathered her skirts and extended her hand to allow her husband Nathan to hand her down from the cab of the truck; a dainty and elegant gesture from a woman of stature. "I know, hon. Leave it to me." She turned to the crowd of young men who had invaded the front yard. "You, you, you an' you, come with me," she stormed up the steps to the front door, "Violet, Jim, get yo' selves movin', I am standin' in need of a mess of fishes and loaves."

Nathan mopped his brow and approached Will, his shake nearly crushing Will's hand as he thumped him on the shoulder, "Good to see you, William. I hope you do not mind Mrs. Walker ambushing you on the train. As you can see, she has not mellowed one tiny part."

"And we would not want her any other way." Will retreated into the cool interior of his family home. A flustered Violet and grinning Jim had just enough time to greet him as Cordelia bellowed instructions at them. He took the stairs two at a time and rushed to his old room. He gasped, it was just as he left it, complete with model airplanes hanging from the ceiling and engineering magazines piled high on every free surface. He threw off his cap and jacket. The Royal Flying Corps "maternity smock" with its double-breasted style and high collar had to be the most uncomfortable rig for a hot Florida afternoon. At least it allowed him to wear a shirt with the removable collar detached and no tie. He splashed water on his face from the bowl on the stand. As he emerged from the towel, Cordelia appeared in the door holding a collar, studs and his tie.

"You can go without the tunic, but the collar and tie have to go back on, and don't think you can go outside with your suspenders dangling like that, hook 'em up."

Will grinned, "Yes, Sergeant Major."

She frowned and jabbed him in the ribs, "Why are you so thin, child? Don't they feed you over there? I am goin' to see that you pick up* some before this weekend is out. Come on, we start now."

Will followed her downstairs and out on to the front porch. He stopped and stared. Even though he remembered Cordelia's formidable powers as an organizer, he was still amazed at what she had achieved in the half-hour since he arrived. Long tables had been arranged across the lawn. Jugs of lemonade had already been half-emptied, and food was appearing as relays of people shuttled back and forth across the grass. He recognized neighbors and their staff carrying plates of cold meats, fruit, pickles and bread.

---

*gain weight

He joined his mother standing on the steps where she stood giving directions. "Crikey, Ma! Are you laying on an impromptu feast for the whole town?"

She turned to him and beamed, "'Crikey?' Well, I never! They are making a proper little Englishman out of you." She turned back to the tables, "Yes, please Dorothy, on there if you would." Charlie took Will's hand, "Yes, we are going to feed the five thousand. I did not expect a turn out like this for you, but as they have been so good as to turn up, the least we can do is offer a little light refreshment. Our delightful friends and neighbors are pitching in with extra rations to help." She gave him a gentle push in the back. "And the least you can do is go out there and mingle. Go on, shoo!"

Will stumbled down the steps to be greeted by a back slapping crowd of his old friends. To an outsider they would have appeared an odd mix as black faces equalled white. Will Turner had earned his degree at the Massachusetts Institute of Technology, but he had served his apprenticeship and earned his engineering spurs working for Nathan Walker, one of the most successful black businessmen in the United States to that date. These were not just his old childhood friends, many were trusted workmates from his days working in the often dangerous environment of the foundry and the machine shop. And of course, amongst this enthusiastic gang he found Henry Walker, Nathan's son and Will's boon companion since they were old enough to get into scrapes. Cordelia would tell anybody that was from about the age of three.

The exploits that had, at the time, earned frowns and disapproval were now garnished and repeated in the drawing rooms and meeting places of town as items of civic pride as, unbeknown to Will, his fame had grown. They talked of the ice cream maker that had exploded and covered several worthy citizens in the makings, the steam-powered tricycle that went up the hill to the capitol building faster than most things went down it and then could not be stopped, and the self-designed and -built airplane that had led to his self-enforced exile in England.* The incident involving that creation had grown with the telling to include several more flights that citizens claimed to have seen that involved climbs thousands of feet into the air above Leon County and looping the loop.

The subject came up on the Saturday evening at a more formal dinner where the Turners entertained Marie's parents, Walter and Emily, the Walkers and the new editor of the *Democrat* newspaper, Stephen Forrest and his wife.

"So you regard the *Flyer* as a success?" Forrest prompted.

Will looked to Henry for support, "*We* do. On its short flight it proved stable and strong. It is standing in need of a decent engine, but it will fly well. Henry and I agree it will make a great little sporting airplane." He turned to Nathan Walker who sat concentrating on peeling an apple in one curling length. "Perhaps Walker Engineering could knock them out by the hundred as a sideline."

Nathan looked up, hearing his name and realizing what Will had proposed. He looked at John Turner who burst into laughter. Nathan turned back to Will with his shoulders heaving, "Do the words, 'not until hell freezes over' mean anything to you, William?" he sat back chortling.

Will smiled and shrugged, "As you can see, the elder statesmen do not share our enthusiasm for aviation."

Forrest nodded, but his keen eye for detail had picked out the photograph on the sideboard that showed John Turner and Nathan Walker proudly posed before the airplane built by their sons. The family dining room was small and intimate, crowded with pictures and ornaments. John Turner pushed his chair back.

"Ladies and gentlemen, I propose we adjourn to the library where we can spread out and Jim will serve coffee and liqueurs."

"Oh, you men," Charlie said. "I suppose you want to get rid of us ladies and smoke your smelly cigars and tell risqué stories."

---

* *See* The Aviator's Apprentice

John shook his head, "No, my dear, I am a thoroughly modern husband. I hope you ladies will join us, and if you would like a cigar I am sure nobody will tell. And of course, if you have any risqué stories to share, we are all ears!"

"Oooh!" Emily Julien squeaked. "What fun!"

As they stepped into the library, Will filled Forrest's glass then indicated the French windows with a tilt of his head, "Mr. Forrest, could I have a private word with you?"

"Of course." He followed Will into the garden. A half-moon reflected from the ornamental pond and cast a soft light over the lawns and flowerbeds.

Will glanced over his shoulder to ensure they were out of earshot of the increasingly loud party in the library, "Mr. Forrest, I imagine you have a piece planned about my visit home."

"Why, naturally—an extensive piece. I hoped you might be able to give me some details about your service with the British."

Will's cigar glowed, lighting his face for a second, "What would you say to a deal?"

"What kind of a deal do you have in mind?"

"Let me explain. As you know, the United States remains neutral in this conflict to date."

"Only thanks to that fool Wilson. If the people had their way, Uncle Sam would have been in and finished it by now."

Will sighed, "Might prove a little tougher than you think. Anyway, the problem is that I am an embarrassment to the State Department as it stands. In fact, I have been officially warned that I stand to lose my citizenship by serving with the armed forces of a foreign power."

"That is outrageous!"

"Maybe, but it is the law. However, I have been told unofficially that while I maintain the pretense of being a Canadian citizen there should be no problem, providing," Will held up a hand, "as we say in the trenches, I keep my fool head down."

"I think I know where this is heading."

Will nodded, "If you will restrain your piece, and avoid any mention of my military service, the instant the United States declares war on Germany and her allies, I will send you an in-depth piece on the war in the air, and the ground, that will scoop anything your rivals can produce. You have my word."

"What about the column I have planned for the next edition?"

"Fill it with family detail, your readers will want that anyway, and maybe some guff about my success hotting up airplanes for racing. You do not have to say where."

"Hmmmm, so you are saying if I make do with bread today, you will spread it with honey at some time in the future?"

"A bucket full."

Forrest grinned around his cigar, "You have a deal."

Will gripped his hand, "Thank you."

They walked back into the library in time to hear Walter Julien expounding on his theory that all the Allies needed to do was make one big push and put the cavalry through. It was a line Will had heard many times. He smiled when his mother asked hopefully if it was true that this would happen in a few weeks.

"Indeed I believe that is the plan, Ma. If we can wrap this up, then the girls will be safe home by the end of summer. In the meantime, I do not want them crossing the Atlantic Ocean again until it is safe."

"But you crossed, Will." Cordelia pointed out.

"Officers traveling without their unit are often found space on a warship. The ship I sailed on sinks U-boats, not the other way round."

"But what about these frightful Zeppelins?" For the first time Emily Julien sounded concerned.

Will drew on his cigar, then puffed a cloud of smoke slowly at the ceiling for effect, "Ma'am they could not hit a barn if they were in it. Very soon, I guarantee we will start to shoot them down. The girls are quite safe. They have a deep cellar under their apartment and if there is a raid, they simply sleep down there until it passes. Even if by some chance a bomb fell on the house, they would simply walk out through the coal chute, no doubt complaining about the noise. You know how they are."

Walter gave a whoop of delight, "That's my girl! Full of spirit." He raised his glass. "A toast to our little ladies!"

Will winked at Emily as he raised his glass, "To the girls."

※ ⊹⊱⊰⊹ ※

A balcony ran round three sides of the Turner home at second-floor level. Will took the tray he found Violet, the maid, carrying to his father where he sat facing the dawn and enjoying the cool of the morning.

"I will bring an extra cup, Mr. William." She bobbed a curtsey and turned to go back down to the kitchen. Will watched her go, surprised by the gesture.

He placed the tray in front of his father, "Since when did I deserve that?"

John smiled up at him from his chair, "Since you grew up." Will shrugged and sat down next to him. He looked around at the fresh paint-work on the railing and window frames, then stood up to study the new lightning conductor disappearing toward the cupola that crowned the top of their home.

"You were going to explain why you have had all this work done." Will said. John opened his mouth to speak, then paused as Violet reappeared with a second tray.

"Your cup, Mr. William, and some fresh cinnamon rolls," she looked at him from lowered eyes with a shy grin.

"Why, thank you, Violet. That is most kind of you, I am much obliged." She bobbed again and disappeared through the door.

John looked at him, an eyebrow raised, "Do I get one?"

Will passed the plate, "I am favored."

"Trust me, son, the whole household basks in your reflection. When Violet goes down to French Town to the coffee shop where she meets her friends, I am told she is treated with deference on the strength of your medals."

Will poured his coffee and snorted, "I have two. Have you seen what our young naval ensigns at Pensacola have decorating their chests? Makes mine look downright paltry."

John patted his son's arm, "You will not get by with that line, son. One of your medals is what I believe is known as the Mons Star, because you went to war with the first wave of British soldiers."

"Will grinned, "Yes, it makes me a 'contemptible,' an 'old' con-temptible no less."*

John regarded him steadily, "And the other is the Military Cross. As my brother-in-law Frank put it so well, 'they do not come up with the rations.' Your story about receiving it for organizing the repair of damaged machines only washed with your mother for as long as it took us to obtain the official citation."

Will frowned, "Oh, I hoped not to worry Mother."

"You scared her half to death, but she is pleased as can be. Do not forget she is British through and through, and proud of it." John sipped his coffee, then looked his son straight in the eye. "Will, this business about the big push, is it likely to win the war for the Allies?"

Will looked down at his feet, grimaced, then looked up at his father. "If courage and determination could do it, then our boys would be in Berlin by the end of the week. As it is, courage and determination do not stop machine gun bullets. From where I stand this war has been one dis-aster after another, for both sides."

"Both sides?"

---

* *The German Kaiser described the British Expeditionary Force sent against his army to oppose their advance into France in 1914 as, "that contemptible little army." The British veterans of that force proudly described themselves as "The Contemptibles" ever after.*

"Yes, sir. I have an Australian officer in my unit, a survivor of the Gallipolli Campaign. I believe he is so shocked with what he saw he cannot even speak about it. Men died in the thousands through outright military blundering and disease. On the Western Front in France and Belgium the British high command seem to have no other plan than hurling men against the German wire in the hope something will give, and since the beginning of this year the Germans have been pouring men into some hellhole called Verdun." Will shook his head sadly, "Everybody is pinning such high hopes on this big push, but the soldier I most respect, Colonel Brett, has grave misgivings."

"Why is that?"

"He believes the Germans have engineered defensive positions that will not be easily broken by the fiercest artillery bombardment."

"What do you think?"

"I will not play like I understand military tactics, but I draw up from the prospect of throwing good men into a battle with no new idea other than to try again what has never worked before." He looked up at the rising sun and sighed, "Anyway, Father, enough of Europe's loss, you were going to tell me why you have spent so much on the house."

John sensed that his son wanted to change the subject, and it was one he himself cared about deeply. "William, there is trouble afoot. A pestilence stalks the land, or rather crawls over it."

Will stared at his father over the rim of his coffee cup, "I declare you are starting to sound like Preacher Flint."

"This pestilence is real, not a prophesy. Boll weevils," John spat the words. "Damn things are wiping out the cotton crop, just as the big freeze back in the Nineties wiped out the orange farms."

"I knew they had been found, but had no idea they had become such a problem," Will said.

John smiled, "You had other things on your mind apart from the rural economy. Well, there are folk out there destitute and Nathan and I are trying to do something about it. So are some of the other businessmen in town. It is no use offering charity, these are proud men, so we offer work where we can."

Will sat back, a frown on his face, "That is bad. Awful bad. Is there nothing can be done about these damn weevils?"

"Unless you can think of a way of spraying insecticide over thousands of acres, no."

Will sat for a moment, then shrugged, "I will work on it."

John drained his coffee and stood, "Come on, Son. Time for a good fortifying breakfast before church."

The day passed in a whirl of handshaking, back slapping and advice to "give 'em hell." It was a relief when they motored through town in the evening to the Walker home for an outdoor supper laid on for Will and his old workmates and their families. He admired the improvements to the workshops and ate his fill of Cordelia's home cooking.

He had one official duty to perform. He presented a check for a hundred dollars to Richard Harris, a serious young man who had graduated from Doctor Bethune's college in Daytona. Frank Penrose had arranged the award, along with a personally signed letter from General Trenchard, for his brilliant suggestion for the solution to Will's requirement for an effective interrupter gear, enabling him to fire through the propeller arc of his modified B.E.2.* Richard mumbled his thanks as Will made the presentation accompanied by the cheers of his colleagues. Later in the evening, Will spent half an hour chatting to the young engineer.

He confided as much to Nathan and Henry over a glass of Cordelia's orange wine as they sat under the live oaks, in front of the house after the employees had left. "We will be hearing more of Mr. Harris, I will warrant."

"Yes, we will. He is going to stir up a storm with his ideas on civil rights."

* See Turner's Flight

Cordelia had appeared at his shoulder and leaned across her husband to refill their glasses, "An' maybe we need a storm to clear the air."

Nathan grunted, "That's as may be, but I am getting too old for fussing and fighting. I will leave that to you young folk." He turned to Will, a mischievous grin on his face. "Can we count on your help when the trouble comes, William?"

Will sighed, "Nathan, do I have a choice? You may have noticed trouble seems to find me."

"Better carry a brick in case old Mr. Trouble comes looking for you, Will." Henry advised, slapping his friend on the back.

The next morning, Will left town before the sun rose.

CHAPTER 16

Abbots Roding, England

Ernie Simpson looked out of his office window and gasped. He beckoned Sergeant Moore to join him.

"Bleedin' 'ell. What's that?" Moore breathed, his voice quiet. The reason for their surprise bumped across the field and disappeared behind the armorer's workshop.

Simpson picked up his cap, "Come on, Sergeant. It's only polite to greet visitors, even when they turn up in a winged perambulator." By the time they turned the corner the strange machine had pulled up in front of the sheds where a crowd had already gathered. On first seeing the new airplane everybody formed the same impression. The designers appeared to have taken a giant baby carriage, jammed an engine on the back driving a pusher propeller, stuck on enormous wings, and, as an afterthought, built booms to carry an over-tall tail fin. The layout followed the same plan as the F.E.2 series, but whereas that looked ugly, Simpson decided this new machine seemed to have been designed as either a joke, or a piece of outlandish modern sculpture.

The pilot, a short man, clambered down from the cockpit, picked out Simpson in the crowd and marched up to him. His accent confirmed what the reversed colors on the bright cockades on the wings told them. Their visitor was French.

"Major Simpson? I am Capitaine Louis Calmette, at your service."
The second crew member had been helped to the ground by the mechanics. The pilot gestured toward him, "Lieutenant Jean Duchenois, also a pilot but today my gunner."

Simpson returned the salute then offered his hand, "Pleased to meet you. To what do we owe the pleasure?" Calmette wore an old-fashioned leather crash helmet and a scarf wrapped several times around his neck. His dark eyes twinkled above an enormous mustache as he handed Simpson a letter. He tore it open and read, as he did his eyes widened.

"Good Lord! This is from the French Minister of War, no less."

"Indeed, Major Simpson, copies are already with your own HQ." He unwound his scarf. "Great Britain has sent a million men to France to fight the Boche, and France has sent Jean Duchenois, myself, and the new Voisin, to fight your Germans." He shrugged in apology, "It is, I think, a poor exchange, but we will do our best."

Simpson handed the letter to Dick Thomas and took Calmette by the arm. "I am sure you will, Captain. Now show me your aeroplane. It's a little—"

"Unconventional?" Calmette suggested.

"Ye-es, a good description," Simpson agreed as he peered up at two tear drop shaped fuel tanks fixed under the top wings.

"It is an example of our peculiar national engineering philosophy. Anything you can do, we can do different. I know it is hard to believe, but it is a much better machine than it looks." Calmette pronounced every *i* sound as an *ee* and *th* came out as a *z*. He exuded charm and his accent fitted his looks to perfection. People said he resembled a young Louis Blériot, the first man to fly the English Channel, but while he had the same build and huge walrus mustache, his lively smile made sure he was never mistaken for Blériot with his permanent hangdog expression.

"How high will it climb?"

Calmette smiled, "That is the, how you say, strong suit? She will go to almost five thousand meters."

Smith had joined them and he let out a low whistle, "Fifteen thousand feet. That *is* useful. How about speed?"

Calmette shrugged—a gesture that the British Tommy had come to realize conveyed more meaning than a hundred words in the French language. This shrug was an apology. "I regret, only 130 kilometers."

Simpson closed his eyes and made a quick calculation, "That is not a problem, Captain Calmette. Eighty miles an hour or so is fast enough to catch a Zeppelin. It's more important that you can get up there and stay up there. What's your endurance?"

Calmette looked puzzled for a moment, fishing for the word in his head. He brightened, "Ah! Duration! *Oui, quatre heures.* Four hours."

Simpson smiled and slapped him on the back, "Jolly *bon* old chap. Your strange looking aeroplane could be very useful. What weapons do you carry?"

Calmette touched the side of his nose, "Today, just a Hotchkiss *mitrailleuse,* a machine gun. But tomorrow, we have a surprise."

Dick Thomas had finished reading the letter and put it in a folder he carried. "Well, Captain, today we have lunch. Will you and Lieutenant Duchenois join us while Sergeant Moore arranges your accommodation?"

"Our pleasure!"

The reason why Duchenois struggled to reach the ground soon became apparent. His arms were loaded with bottles and packages. "I have wine, brandy, and cheese, gentlemen," he explained as the flying officers gathered around. He wore an enormous fur coat over his uniform. He had replaced his leather flying helmet with his kepi, the rigid-sided, small-peaked cap familiar as the headgear of the French gendarme. Duchenois had deep, brown, soulful eyes, a small mustache and a slight build. Even by the youthful standards of most British pilots, he looked young. It soon became apparent that his English did not match that of his comrade, as Calmette had to translate for him when the discussion in the mess soon switched to technicalities. Most of the young flyers had at least a smattering of French, and lunch became a lively affair.

Windy Gale slapped his hand on the table and pointed to Calmette as they sampled the brandy the Frenchmen had brought with them. "I have just realized, I *know* you!"

The Frenchman looked at him for a moment, then a smile broke out from under the mustache. "I think I know you, also, Monsieur Windy."

Gale sat back and roared, "Hendon. You were one of the examiners there just before the war. You turned a blind eye when I rolled over the line on my last landing."

Calmette laughed with him, "You are correct—but you were only this much over the line, " he held up two fingers half-an-inch apart. "Not a problem among friends."

The two aviators had been sent as a gesture by the French government. They had chosen the right men for the job. Calmette and Duchenois had enormous experience flying at night in pursuit of German raiders. Their enemy had always been flying airplanes, and they had achieved some success. If they thought that finding and shooting down a machine a hundred times bigger than the Rumpler biplanes they usually pursued should be easy by comparison, they had the tact not to say it.

In the afternoon the mechanics familiarized themselves with the unusual aircraft and then Calmette took Simpson, followed by Smith, for a flight. Both the British airmen expressed surprise at how well the ungainly machine climbed. The Voisin fitted well with the ethos of the experimental flight, as it was a prototype itself, employing a new and powerful Renault engine. Smith took the Frenchmen to the map room and explained the system of warning posts, searchlights and the Ingram signaling system.

"This is excellent, Capitaine," Calmette said. "We will start tonight."

Smith's jaw dropped, "Tonight? But surely you want to get to know the area in daylight?"

Calmette lit a pungent Gauloise* and waved away Smith's protest with the smoke, *"Pas de problème, Capitaine.* I flew many hours over London and the east of England when I worked here before the war." He patted Smith on the shoulder, "Come, let us take tea before we fly."

The nights were growing shorter as summer approached. They stepped out of the map room into a perfect English spring evening. The setting sun brushed a few high clouds pink and gold. A flight of ducks sped across the sky homeward bound for the river, riding a light wind that promised to keep mists away. Smith felt a chill—a perfect night for a Zeppelin raid. They must put everything into the air they could to oppose them, but he wished their French guests were a little less bold, and he still had doubts that Gale and Jankowski had sufficient experience flying at night.

Smith's misgivings about the night's operations grew when they entered the squadron office to find Dizzy Lipman helping Sergeant Ronnie Moore adjust a flying helmet.

"Hold still, Sergeant. Well, that's it. You don't want it too tight." Dizzy stood back and surveyed his handiwork. "There, I don't know if you will frighten the enemy, but by God, you frighten me – with apologies to the Iron Duke."

Moore grinned, "Thank you, sir."

"What's going on here?" Smith demanded.

Before Moore could answer, Simpson stepped through the door. He was dressed for flight as well. "Sergeant Moore and I are going to do a little hunting. We need everything in the air tonight, and for once we have more serviceable aircraft than we have pilots to fly them. We are taking one of the B.E.2s."

"But, sir!" Smith started to protest.

Simpson's jaw jutted, "But what, Captain Smith?"

---

* *A strong, unfiltered, popular brand of French cigarette.*

"You know the standing orders. Squadron commanders are not expected to fly on operations. In fact it's discouraged."

Simpson snorted in disgust, "For one thing, we don't have the status of a squadron, and for another, if I don't put in some hours soon, I will lose my flying pay."

Smith ploughed on, "Okay, sir, if you don't care about your own skin, what about Sergeant Moore?"

"He volunteered."

"I did, sir," Moore jumped in. "I really want to go up after a Zep."

Smith turned to him, "Whatever for, Sergeant? You are more valuable to us on the ground."

Moore sighed, "Call me a silly old sod if you like, sir, but I have two little lads at home in Peckham. When this is all over and they ask me, 'What did you do in the war, Dad?' What am I going to tell them? That I spent the war on my backside in an office?"

Smith shook his head, "That won't wash, Sergeant. You have done time in the trenches and been over the top."

"Ah, yes, but so have thousands of other blokes. Being an airman is something special. And don't forget—I won the Eastern Command shooting competition twice in a row. I can keep my end up in a fight."

"But what happens if you go west?* How do we go about getting all those extras you seem to find through your network of connections? For heaven's sake, we had one of the new Rolls Royce engines delivered this afternoon. How the hell did you wangle that?"

Moore looked at Simpson who shrugged, "He has a point, Sergeant. Should we reveal one of your secrets just in case? It's up to you."

Moore frowned, "Okay, sir, but this has to stay strictly among those of us here now, are we agreed?"

Calmette translated for Duchenois and the two Frenchmen nodded. Lipman looked at Prof Smith, "Intriguing. Of course my lips are sealed." Moore opened a desk drawer and extracted a key. He squatted in front of the safe, unlocked it and took out a fat brown envelope and brought it back

---

* *To be killed in action.*

to the desk. The officers gathered around as he pulled out what appeared to be a bundle of postcards and fanned some of them out on the desk.

Only the sound of heavy breathing broke the silence until Dizzy spoke, "Good grief! That girl is wearing absolutely nothing."

"And what *is* she doing to that young chap?" Smith picked up the photograph and turned it on one side. "Oh, yes, now I see." His eyebrows shot up.

Calmette picked up another and held it up to the light, "Ah yes, I recognize this studio," he spoke with the air of a connoisseur.

Duchenois took it from him, "And I know the model. She is a waitress, *trés jolie,* even wiz clothes on, but like this . . . *formidable!*"

Moore took the picture from him and thrust it with the others back into the envelope, "Yes, well gentlemen, now you can see how we sometimes manage a little extra."

Smith stared at him, "A *little* extra! Good God man, a brand new prototype engine is not a little extra. I know full well that all manner of fiddles go on, I've done a few myself over the years, but do you mean to tell me that the army's supply system now involves the use of pornography as a means of exchange?"

Moore smiled, "Oh goodness, not just pornography, sir. There's whiskey, fags, motor parts, it all helps—"

Simpson cut in, "Well, that's all we need to know, Sergeant," he turned to Smith. "So there you have it. If we don't make it back safe and sound, and you need something special, you have the means at your disposal to obtain it."

Smith held up his hands, palms raised, "Alright, I know when I'm beaten," he turned to the door then stopped with his hand on the knob. "Er, Sergeant, just in case, how many dirty postcards does a Rolls Royce engine cost?"

Moore grinned, "Two dozen, sir."

"Is that all?"

"There's great demand, sir. It's as if they were printed on gold leaf."

Smith grunted, "I can well imagine. Come on, we've Huns to chase."

They stepped outside and joined the rest of the crews in front of the hangars. Prof Smith took Dizzy by the arm, "You're my driver tonight, Dizzy. Let's just watch everybody else get off."

"Worried about the boss, Prof?"

"Yes."

"I wouldn't be, he's been getting in some practice lately, putting up good flights on the old B.E.2."

Dizzy carried out a careful check around the machine before they climbed aboard. Smith checked the gun and their signaling equipment then strapped into the narrow seat in the front cockpit. They watched the others roar down the flare path and disappear into the night as their engine warmed. Simpson and Moore led off in a B.E.2, followed by Stan Jackson and Windy Gale in another F.E.2. The two Frenchmen galloped past in their ungainly Voisin with Jankowski and Bill Ives hot on their heels. David Highams, a pilot just posted to the unit, and Ned Robson had both volunteered to fly alone in the two Avro 504s used by the experimental flight. Smith had more misgivings about using rotary-engined machines at night, but recognized the skill and experience of the two men now flying them. With Will away, Smith had slipped into the role of flight leader, effectively doing Will Turner's worrying for him. Despite his tough appearance, Captain James Smith, the Prof, was an expert worrier.

Dizzy slapped him on the shoulder as the silhouette of Ned's Avro against the last gleam of evening light faded to a shadow, "Hold on, we're off." Smith leaned against the back of the cockpit and relaxed. There was nothing he could do except trust his pilot as the biplane lurched into line with the flare path. The muted cackle of the idling engine rose to a full throated bellow behind him as Dizzy pushed the throttle lever forward. The F.E.2 jerked and rumbled as the big wheels rolled over the uneven grass. The ride smoothed as the tail came up with the first of the kerosene flares passing beneath the wing. Then, a second later, the motor disintegrated with a metallic crash, and a flare of vivid orange flame.

Dizzy wrestled with the controls as the F.E.2 sagged back on the ground and bounced and racketed through the darkness toward the boundary hedge, invisible in the dark. Without the din of the engine Smith could hear the squeal of the wheels, and the creak of the undercarriage as he hung on to the sides of the swaying cockpit as the F.E.2 slowed. They rolled to a stop, with a last apologetic squeak from the axle.

"Damnation!" Dizzy threw off his seatbelt, stood up and turned round to survey the damage. Smith grabbed the flashlight and swung over the rim of the cockpit and dropped to the ground. He played the beam over the engine.

"Bloody hell! It's a good job that didn't let go a few seconds later when we were in the air." Oil had spewed over the engine and propeller like blood from a severed artery. It dripped from the tail booms and the wing root. One cylinder had gone leaving a shattered piston hanging out of the block with the broken connecting rod sticking out of the crankcase.

Dizzy joined him on the ground looking up at the stricken machine. He grimaced, "That conrod reminds me of a compound leg fracture."

A Crossley tender pulled up. Sergeant Major Cole stepped down and stalked up to the stricken machine. "That's well and truly cattle trucked,* sir. How did you manage that?"

Dizzy's voice rose in protest, "It's not my fault. It's the soft bearings in these rotten old Beardmores."

"I know, sir, I'm sure you didn't over-rev it—this time." Cole's voice was soothing, but his authority on matters of engineering was such that Dizzy felt obliged to justify himself to an NCO, in a way that would have been unheard of elsewhere in the army. Cole rubbed his hands together, "Well, Mr. Lipman, it looks like you're going to get the new Rolls Royce to try out."

"Really?"

---

*rhyming slang

"Yes, sir. It's an ill wind that blows no good as they say."

"Oh that is splendid, Sergeant Major. How long will it take to fit?"

"No more than a day I would expect, sir."

"Is there anything else left to fly tonight?"

Cole shook his head, "Sorry, sir. Looks like you have the night off."

Smith took Dizzy by the arm, "Come on, we'll make ourselves useful in the office." They set off across the field guided by the flares while Cole and his men towed the damaged airplane back to the hangars. "We were flaming lucky there and no mistake."

"What—you mean getting the new Roller?"

"No, I mean not having to crash land in total darkness with a dud engine."

"Oh, that would have been no problem. I would have just pancaked us into the field over the hedge." Dizzy smiled, his teeth white in the dark.

"Yes, but can I point out that, being in front, I would have arrived at the crash first?"

"You have a point. I shall make you a nice cup of tea to steady your nerves." They arrived at the squadron office and stepped inside, blinking in the sudden light. Corporal Bowen looked up from the desk usually occupied by Moore.

"There's a lady to see you, Captain."

Smith dragged his flying helmet off and turned round to see Jacquieline Courroyer sitting on the edge of a table swinging her long legs.

"Hello, Prof. It's good to see you." She pushed herself off the table as Smith dragged off his gauntlets and shook her hand warmly.

"Likewise, Jac," he said, grinning. They were old friends. "But lucky. If Dizzy hadn't buggered up our engine, we would have been up on the Zeppelin hunt for the next two hours."

"I would have waited," she winked and tilted her head toward the door. "Can I have a private word?" She turned to Dizzy. "Do you mind if I borrow your boss for a while?"

Dizzy smiled and nodded, "I'll just make everybody tea and wreck the kettle."

Jac and the Prof stepped back into the darkness and paced toward the hangar. "What's all this about, Jac? You didn't motor down here to try Dizzy Lipman's tea."

"No, although I am interested to see how you are doing. The guv'nor sends his regards and says could you please shoot down a Zep for him as soon as possible."

The Prof gave a grim laugh, "Tell Colonel Penrose he'll know when we do. I imagine it will light up the sky all over London when we finally torch one of the bastards."

"I look forward to that." Jac fell silent for a moment, then took Smith's arm and turned him to reverse the direction of their slow stroll. "This is more of a private matter. You know Will Turner has an American friend who came over with his sister to work with the Red Cross."

"Yes, Marie, a flighty little piece, but I like her, bags of spirit."

"That's her, and you're not the only one who likes her. She seems to have attracted quite a following."

"I thought she was Will's girl."

"She would like to be, and I blame him for what has happened to some extent. If he was more forthcoming and had made some sort of declaration, this would never have happened."

The Prof frowned, "You can't make a bloke fall in love."

"You're right, though in Marie's case with Will it's not for want of trying." Jac looked around and lowered her voice. "Anyway, to cut a long story short, Marie is one of those girls who seems to be in love with love, or the idea of it."

"A romantic."

"Exactly, and because Will seems reluctant to be involved romantically, the silly little tart went and fell for somebody else."

The Prof scratched his head, "Hardly our problem. She's a single girl in a city full of men in uniform. Good luck to her I say, if Will doesn't recognize a good thing when he sees it, he deserves to lose her."

Jac nodded, "Couldn't agree more if she had chosen a decent fellow. As it is she fell for the biggest cad in town, and now she's in trouble."

The Prof slapped his forehead and shut his eyes, "Oh no, the poor girl, what a mess."

Jac shook her head, "No, not that sort of trouble. She hasn't got a bun in the oven. This is worse."

"Worse? How could it be?"

Jac stopped walking, took Smith's hand and turned him toward her, "Look, I have come to you because I know you can get things done, and keep your mouth shut. The fact is that this romance, if you can call it that, went way beyond dreamy looks and a bit of snogging."

"I take it that it involved rumpy pumpy?"

"Oh yes, the swine talked her drawers off."

Smith sucked his teeth, "So? Her and thousands of other respectable young ladies. The war seems to have 'loosened stays,' so to speak. So I expect he's now buggered off with some trollop and she's heartbroken. She'll get over it."

"She would, if she hadn't done something unbelievably stupid."

"Try me, I'm a soldier, I deal with unbelievable stupidity all the time," Smith laughed, trying to lighten Jac's mood.

She shook her head, "This takes the biscuit. It would seem that the rumpy pumpy turned her head. Our little friend obviously found it all very exciting and agreeable, and wrote several very indiscreet letters to Lover Boy."

"How indiscreet?"

"Downright graphic. The lass is a fine expressive writer."

They had turned about again and reached the back of Number Two hangar. The Prof sat down on an upturned ammunition box. He groaned and looked up at Jac, "Let me guess the rest. Now this bastard is demanding money to give the letters back otherwise he will make them public?"

She sat down next to him, "You're no fool, that's why they call you

Prof. That means her reputation will be ruined, she will be dismissed by the Red Cross and like as not sent home in disgrace."

"What a bloody pickle! We can't let him get away with it. Who is he?"

"He's the original handsome, dashing cavalry officer. His name is Buley. He's the son of an earl and a thoroughly nasty piece of work. He can charm the birds out of the trees when he wants to, but is an utter brute under the gloss. He's not above hitting a woman—in fact is on record as saying that women are like any good mount and respond to firm handling. He owes money all over town, and I suppose this is why he's doing this." Jac suddenly stopped, "Why are you smiling?"

"Is he sporting a sling at the moment? Playing it for all he's worth as the wounded hero?"

"He is. What do you know about that?"

"He fell and broke his arm in a punch-up with one of my blokes at a pub nearby."

"Really? That's wonderful. I knew I had come to the right place."

The Prof grinned, "So what do you want me to do? Beat the living daylights out of him? It sounds like he deserves it."

Jac laid her hand on his arm, "That's terribly sweet of you to offer, Prof, but this situation is far too delicate. What I want you to do is help me raise five hundred pounds."

"Blimey! Are we just giving in to him?"

Jac shook her head, "Of course not—nice to hear you say 'we.' Can I take it you are onboard?"

"Of course."

"We need to get the letters back, then we will get the money back."

The Prof looked at her in the thin light from the flare path, "You know, blackmail is a two-edged weapon. If he carries out his threat, his reputation will be in tatters as well."

"Oh, come off it, Prof. You're a socialist. You know the rich always get away with it unless somebody is determined to stop them. He will sell the letters to some sleazy journalist and get paid that way, then just deny any knowledge of how they became public, then revel in his new reputation as a thoroughbred stud. It will all be forgotten as far as he is concerned in a few weeks, but poor Marie's life will be ruined."

Smith snorted, "Yes, I suppose you're right. Do you have a plan?"

"I do. At the moment the only people who know about this mess are yourself, the two girls, me and Joe Thorpe. If you can keep it that way it would help."

The Prof stood and pulled Jac to her feet, "Leave it to me." He regarded her for a moment. "Why have you got involved?"

"Because Marie and Vicky are my friends. I need no other reason."

Smith nodded, "I understand. Now come along and you can watch how a crack unit is dealing with the Zeppelin threat."

She proved to know a great deal about the watcher system and the Ingram signals. The men of the unit, not used to women in their male world, nevertheless made no remark about her presence or her knowledge, especially of the weapons in use by all the combatants. They knew and had pride in the fact they took part in an unusual operation. Mrs. Jacquieline Courroyer worked for Colonel Penrose, and that was good enough for them. They knew better than to ask even if they were curious about her exact position in the general scheme of things.

The first airplane fluttered like a moth from the darkness and settled on the grass. The Prof and Dizzy knew at once it had to be one of the Avros from the ripping sound of the engine as the pilot used the "blip switch" to cut the engine in and out. The biplane waddled back to the hangar with mechanics guiding it by holding onto each wingtip.

Ned Robson dismounted and walked over to where the Prof, Dizzy, and Jac waited for news. "Nothing to report, sir. Not a dicky bird. Didn't see a thing."

"I'm not surprised," Dizzy said. "All the listening posts have called in to say that nothing has come in over the coast."

They heard the phone ring again and turned to the office. Bowen appeared in the door, "That was Mr. Highams, sir. He's down at Sutton's Farm with engine trouble."

The Prof made a note of the time, "That's two down safe."

"Do you want me up again, sir?" Ned asked.

"No, there's no point unless one of our outposts calls in with a definite contact. Get yourself a cup of tea and stand by."

Over the next hour, most of the remaining aircraft found their way back with the exception of the two machines carrying the Frenchmen, Simpson, and Moore. Smith looked at his watch and frowned. "They're cutting it a bit fine. The Frenchies are okay for another hour, but even with the extra tank we fitted to the boss's B.E.2, they can only have another half- hour in the air."

Twenty minutes later an audible sigh of relief went up from the group at the front of the hangars. As the time ticked on, the personnel of the unit had gradually gathered around the Prof to wait anxiously for the first faint drone of an approaching airplane. For once Sergeant Major Cole had not chased the mechanics back to work. Now they could hear a B.E.2 approaching from the river. A minute later it flitted overhead and landed safely. By the time Simpson had taxied back to the hangar, the Voisin had appeared overhead and followed him safely to the ground.

Simpson taxied into the pool of light in front of the hangars and shut down. He clambered to the ground, lifting his stiff leg over the edge of the cockpit with his hand under his knee.

"Any luck, sir?" Smith asked.

Simpson pulled off his helmet and puffed out his cheeks, "Well, you might call it luck. We exchanged shots with Fritz over Chelmsford, but then we lost him."

"Really, sir? That's a shocker. The listening posts haven't reported a Zep coming in all night."

Simpson rubbed his eyes, "Wasn't a Zep we found. It was a bloody aeroplane. I know they have tried the odd raid on the coast with night bombers, but I bet this is the first time one has been that far inland. He sheered off pretty sharpish when Moore dusted his tail with a burst."

"Did you see the type, sir?" Dizzy asked.

"No, all I can say is that it was big. I just got a glimpse as it flashed past on the reciprocal course. The first I knew he was there was when a couple of tracers flew between our wings. We steamed round after him but he was gone in the dark. Are there any reports of bombs falling?"

Smith shook his head, "No, sir. Not a thing."

"That's odd. I wonder what he was doing." A disturbance in the group gathered round the B.E.2 made Simpson pause. It parted to allow Calmette and Duchenois through.

"It is true!" Calmette announced. "We also fired on this *boche*. I think he will not feel welcome in England."

"I should think not," Smith agreed. "Where were you when you saw him?"

"I think somewhere north of the River Blackwater. He came out of the night making a track opposite us but at the same height. Duchenois was fast and got away a few shots, but then the boche was gone—poof!"

Simpson called to Bowen, "Get on the blower and find out if there are any reports of a machine coming down. You never know, he was engaged twice, a lucky shot might have punctured his radiator or a fuel tank."

"What worries me is what he was up to. Perhaps it is connected with the Zeppelins? Could it be some sort of recce?" Dizzy suggested. That idea provoked a noisy discussion between the gathered pilots and gunners. Jac, meanwhile, had been prowling around the B.E.2 and the Voisin. Anything mechanical intrigued her, airplanes in particular. She reached up and touched the rudder of the French machine. As she did she noticed a small hole in the fabric. She looked further and found another hole where a wooden rib gave the rudder its shape.

"Hello," she said to herself. *"What's this?"* She took a penknife from her purse and opened it. She carefully dug a bullet from the woodwork and held it up between her fingers and examined it for a moment, before walking over to the B.E.2 parked nearby and joining Sergeant Major Cole. The crews still stood on the other side of the machine discussing the implications of the contact with the German airplane.

"Any damage, Sergeant Major?" Jac asked.

"Yes, ma'am. Nothing serious. There's a bullet lodged in the exhaust manifold, but no real damage done." He pointed. Jac could see where the missile had stuck where two branches of the exhaust came together in the collector box above the engine. She reached up. "Careful, ma'am, it's still hot."

Jac opened her knife again and poked at the bullet. It fell out and bounced off the cowling. She caught it neatly and held it up for Cole to see. "What do you make of that?"

Cole took it from her and held it up to the light, "Oh!"

"Are you thinking what I'm thinking?" Jac asked, a slight smile on her face.

"Yes, ma'am. Shall I tell them, or will you?"

Jac winked, "Leave it to me." She walked around the tail and approached the men still deep in conversation. "Excuse me gentlemen."

Simpson looked up, "Ah, good evening Mrs. Courroyer. I did not expect to find you here."

She smiled graciously, "Ah, Major Simpson, I am the female equivalent of the Scarlet Pimpernel. They seek her here, and all that."

"Goodness, where are my manners?" Simpson turned to the Frenchmen. "Gentlemen, allow me to introduce Madame Courroyer. A valued colleague." The two Frenchmen snapped their heels together and saluted. The look of surprise on their faces turning to delight when Jac greeted them in fluent French. After a brief exchange of pleasantries, she turned back to Simpson.

"Major Simpson, could you tell the difference between a British .303 bullet and its German equivalent?" She dropped the bullet she had dug out of the tail of the Voisin into his palm.

"Probably not, but Lieutenant Long can." The armorer stepped forward and Simpson passed him the bullet. He held it up to the light.

"Aye, that's one of ours right enough," Long spoke with a marked accent that most took for Canadian.

Jac held up the round retrieved from the B.E.2, "Am I right in thinking that a French Hotchkiss fires a round with a distinctive copper jacket?"

"Aye it does, a French slug is easy to recognize." Long looked at her with surprise and growing respect.

"Well, I just dug the British .303 round out of the tail of the French machine, and the copper-jacketed French bullet out of the manifold on Major Simpson's B.E.2. I leave you to draw your own conclusions gentlemen, but please don't shoot the messenger."

Prof Smith later described it as one of those silences you could cut up with a knife and sell off in slices. Somewhere in the distance an owl hooted, the pinging sound of the exhaust on the B.E.2 cooling could be heard quite distinctly.

Duchenois spoke first, *"Mon Dieu!"*

"Bloody hell!" Moore spoke quietly, his face pale, as he realized that in the darkness the French and British airmen had taken each other's airplane for a German intruder, and reacted by opening fire.

"Oh, for Christ's sake!" Simpson threw his helmet on the ground. He stood there shaking his head. "What a shower we are!" His voice sounded resigned rather than angry, then to everybody's surprise he started to laugh. It was as if he had given permission. There was uproar. Duchenois stepped forward and embraced Moore then kissed him noisily on both cheeks provoking more hilarity.

Calmette held up his hands, "Gentlemen, stillness if you please! We have had a lucky escape. But the Boche will not be so fortunate with marksmen with the skill of Sergeant Moore and my Duchenois. To have shot each other, in the dark, at such speed was magnificent shooting. Next time it will be the German, not each other." He pointed to the mess hut, "Come—cognac to celebrate!" The airmen fell in behind him as he stumped off toward the mess leaving Simpson, Smith, and Jac standing on the tarmac.

Simpson scratched his head, "I'm not sure we should be celebrating. We achieved bugger all," he paused and looked at Jac. "Begging your pardon, Mrs. Courroyer."

She smiled, "Don't worry, I hear worse every day, but I agree with Capitaine Calmette, you should be celebrating a lucky escape."

"Oh, I don't know. The chances of a bullet finding us in those circumstances were pretty remote, even if one or two did hit the aeroplanes."

Jac shook her head, "I wasn't thinking about the bullets, sir. It's the fact that in all the thousands of cubic miles of air above East Anglia, you very nearly managed to crash headlong into each other. Same height, opposite direction, with only yards between you. Pretty bloody close, don't you think?"

Simpson looked at Smith and back to Jac, "Hell's teeth! You're absolutely right. I think I need that drink after all."

CHAPTER 17

The North Atlantic Ocean

Matty Ellerkamm lowered her binoculars and pointed to the horizon, "Look, the enemy coast!"

Will gave her a sideways look, "Really? Have I missed something Miss Ellerkamm? I was not aware that the United States had declared war on the Shetland Isles." He stood beside her on the promenade deck of the SS *Margarethe*, pride of the Danish Hansen Shipping Line. At ten thousand tons she was a fraction of the size of the *Olympic*, the White Star liner on which he had sailed for England in 1914, but she maintained the same high standard of service. The Danish flag painted to cover most of her sides added to the sense of security her passengers enjoyed, even if it spoiled her smart lines. The party from the German American Alliance had to sail on a neutral ship. All German merchant shipping had been captured or interned in the naval blockade enforced by the Royal Navy. *Margarethe* sailed under a cloudless blue sky on an aquamarine sea. From inside the ship's luxurious saloon, a passenger might convince themselves they sailed in the tropics, but as soon as they stepped on deck the chill wind reminded them this was the North Atlantic in early summer.

Matty turned and smiled, her big blue eyes sparkling, "Oh, don't be so pompous, Will, you know what I mean," she squeezed his arm. "And it's *Matty*, okay?"

Will found it hard to resist her. There was something just so damn wholesome about the girl. That was Mr. Becker's description as he watched her playing deck quoits, but Will had to agree. She stood nearly as tall as Will, and the way she pinned her thick blond hair up in the latest fashion, added to her presence. Her wide mouth always seemed ready to smile and when she did she revealed perfect white teeth. He had to admit that while she had what Mr. Kaltenbach described breathlessly as an athletic build, nobody could accuse her of having a boyish figure. The outfits she sported in the evening made sure nobody entertained that idea. Matty Ellerkamm had made herself very popular with the gentlemen in the party. The wives may have resented the way their husband's gaze strayed toward the plunging décolletage of her gowns, but they said nothing because she was their leader, and they were in awe of her energy and her ability to organize their journey.

Will did his best to sound disapproving, but his grin gave him away, "You know what I mean . . . *Matty.* We are neutrals, on a neutral ship, in neutral waters."

"*You,* might be neutral, Will, but my loyalty lies with the Fatherland."

"Matty, whatever you say, you are an American citizen," Will studied her for a moment, the afternoon sun caught her hair in a way he found charming, and the pout she now affected was irresistible. He thought how true his remark was: only America could have produced a beauty like her.

"Oh, you are so, so . . ."

"Neutral?" Will suggested.

She threw her head back and roared with laughter, "Yes, neutral." She raised her binoculars again and peered at the rugged shoreline of the island of Unst, the northernmost point of the British Isles. She took the glasses away from her eyes, then adjusted the focus and peered through them again. She grabbed his arm, "Will, just over the end of the island, what is that?" She pushed the binoculars into his hand and pointed. She still had the strap around her neck so Will had to lean close to use the glasses, so close their heads touched. He did not complain.

"Excellent field glasses, Matty."

"Yes, German of course, never mind that, what is it?" Her voice whined with frustration and excitement.

"That is a Short seaplane. A machine used by the British Royal Naval Air Service. I believe it is known as a '225 because of the horsepower of the engine . . ." he paused, ". . . and it is coming this way." He handed the binoculars back.

Matty still clutched his arm, "Ohmigod! It's coming to attack us." She seized him around the waist and held him tight.

"No," he tried to keep the laughter out of his voice. "As I just said, we're a neutral ship, in international waters. As far as I know, the British have never attacked a neutral ship."

"They've boarded them," she did not sound reassured and her panic had infected other members of their party who had been enjoying the fine weather on the upper deck. From the corner of his eye Will saw Mr. Schoeffer pushing his wife behind a ventilator while Mr. Kaltenbach edged toward a lifeboat. Other passengers, mostly Scandinavian or Americans, had now stood up and crowded the rail, pointing at the approaching machine. The hum of its engine filled the air. What had been a speck in the sky a minute before expanded into a seaplane with an enormous wingspan. Massive pontoon floats dangled underneath.

"Why! It looks like a dragonfly on skis," an American passenger remarked to his wife.

When it reached a point half a mile from the ship, the seaplane suddenly banked right and climbed, revealing the bright red, white, and blue cockades under the wings. Will knew the pilot made the maneuver to display the national markings to the ship's captain. The naval aviators leveled off and flew across the bow of the *Margarethe,* a light flashed from the rear cockpit, and Will heard the clatter of a signal lamp replying from the bridge above. The passengers swiveled as one to watch the airplane rush down the port side. They had turned a full circle by the time it reappeared low on the starboard side, flying parallel and overtaking the ship. The two crewmen waved, and the passengers waved back as people do on vessels passing at sea. The Short dipped its wings in salute and sheered off, and within a minute was a diminishing dot on the horizon.

"You can come out now, Mrs. Schoeffer," Nils, the old steward, paused in collecting glasses to put his head around the ventilator. "The wicked Britisher has gone now." He winked at Will, his sing-song Danish accent making it harder for Will to suppress a grin.

"What was that all about?" Matty had lost her good humor. She realized she still held Will tight around the waist, let go, and stepped back a pace.

"That was your first sight of the 'enemy,' Matty," Will said.

"I suppose he has gone back to fetch a battleship to sink us," she glared at the island behind which the airplane had disappeared.

Will sighed, "No, I do not imagine that is the case for one moment. He just came out to make sure we are who we say we are." He knew exactly what the procedure was for a neutral ship in those dangerous waters, but thought better than to explain that they sailed around the northern route past the British Isles on the advice of the Admiralty. He was not going to tell her that just before the ship sailed from New York, a messenger from Gaunt's office would have boarded the ship and given the captain a sealed envelope, containing the response code he should give to positively identify his ship when challenged by ships or aircraft of the Royal Navy.

Matty gave him the benefit of her pout again, then the smile. She put her arm through his, "Come, Mr. Turner, you can escort me to my cabin door. I have to get ready for dinner at the captain's table. If we are to end up in a lifeboat tonight I intend to look suitably dramatic."

For once, Captain Axel Dalgaard did match Will's idea of how a sailor should look. Broad in the shoulders with a rolling gait, he had a full gray beard cut square so that it appeared his chin sported a shovel. He never looked comfortable in his role as host to the first-class passengers at the top table in the dining room. He always insisted another officer join him. Tonight Peter Nielsen, the second engineer, received the benefit of Matty Ellerkamm's charm. He seemed dazzled and despite his perfect English found himself tongue-tied.

Captain Dalgaard had no such problem. "So, Miss Ellerkamm, you are taking your party into occupied Denmark?"

She smiled sweetly, "I understand it is many years since the people of South Jutland elected to join the German nation." The rest of her party fell silent and turned to their part of the table.

Dalgaard snorted, "Elected at the point of a Prussian bayonet," he looked around at the rest of her group. "Has nobody told you that Tønder and the surrounding country were part of Denmark until 'sixty-four?" He used the Danish name for the town. The blank looks confirmed his suspicion. "I thought not."

"I understand that the people of that area are historically German and asked to be taken into the German Union," Matty replied, her smile fixed.

"Some spoke German, it's true, but neither they nor the Danes had any choice. The war was over in days. It takes somebody like the British to resist German militarism," he stuck a piece of steak in his mouth and chewed fiercely, making his beard jerk up and down. Will thought the old sailor magnificent. No doubt the owners of the line considered the main part of the captain's job was to entertain and charm the passengers. Axel Dalgaard considered his task to ensure the safety of his vessel and everybody on it, and damn anything else. He had all the tact of a naval broadside.

Peter Nielsen found his voice, "Well, Miss Ellerkamm, I am sure you will receive a good welcome from the Danish people in the area. We Danes pride ourselves on our hospitality."

"Oh, I am sure we will, if the welcome we have received onboard your beautiful ship is anything to go by. She is quite magnificent." Will watched her and marvelled. The woman had no shame. She aimed her comment at the captain with the subtlest flutter of her eyelashes, and like any man made of flesh and blood, he melted.

"Thank you, Miss Ellerkamm, we do our best."

She reached out and put her hand on his, "And your best really is *the* best. I have traveled with the Hamburg Amerika Line and while they are quite good, their ships do not match the *Margerethe* for comfort and speed." Will thought she might have just overdone it with her praise, but she leveled it off neatly. "What speed have we averaged, Captain?"

Dalgaard beamed, "Thanks to young Peter here, and his colleagues in the machine room, twenty-point-two knots," he looked around the table. "Please do not tell this outside, ladies and gentlemen, because you will get me into trouble, but if the owners would allow me the extra coal, *Margerethe* could take the Blue Riband for fastest Atlantic crossing."

Peter Nielsen caught Will's eye and winked. He had taken Will on a tour of the engine room where he had marveled at the triple expansion engines and the sophistication of the steering gear, the gleaming paint-work and the glittering brass. She was a beautiful ship, but the compound steam engines with their pounding pistons would never propel her at the speeds being achieved by the turbine-powered ships coming into service when war broke out.

Matty had used her charm to great effect and steered the conversation to the captain's travels in the merchant service. With a little prompting he was soon entertaining his guests with tales of the sea and the faraway places he had seen. For most of the party from the German American Alliance, this was their first journey overseas. They listened intently.

Yet again Will found himself next to Dorothy Schubert at the dinner table. She was a pretty, slim, dark-haired woman, a few years older than himself and Matty Ellerkamm. She soon revealed a wicked sense of humor.

Her husband had been the driving force in their joining the trip. John Schubert played the bombastic American German, despite the fact only his grandfather had emigrated from Germany. He felt especially proud of his name, and insisted on a direct family connection to the great composer. The captain excused himself to return to the bridge and the conversation splintered into groups around the table. John Schubert launched into his familiar refrain about the musical talent latent in his family.

Dorothy leaned close and whispered to Will, "Do you know what the family name really means, Mr. Turner?" He shook his head. "Cobbler. A 'schubert' is somebody who makes and sells shoes, I looked it up." She tried to cover it, but her New York accent often forced its way through.

"Do you come from a German family, Mrs. Schubert?"

"Nah, my people came from all over, mainly Italy. My maiden name is Bonnetti."

"Are you interested in politics?"

"Nah, but if you're wondering why I came along, when else is a girl going to get a chance of a trip, first class, to Europe? We could never afford it," she flipped a grape into the air, opened her mouth and caught it.

Will laughed, "You are refreshingly honest. Most people on this ship would die before they admitted they did not have a million in the bank."

Dorothy shrugged, "What's the point? Everybody else from the Alliance knows the krauts have paid for most of the trip," she looked around. "Hey, the band are tuning up. Let's dance."

This was the last night of the voyage. Next morning the ship would turn south for the run down the North Sea between the coasts of Norway and Scotland, to the port of Esbjerg on the west coast of Denmark. *Margarethe* sailed over a calm sea making dancing a pleasure rather than a dangerous sport. As the only single man in the group Will found himself in demand. He did not disgrace himself on the dance floor. His sister had made sure he mastered all the latest steps, and he could foxtrot and quick-step with the best. He found himself leading Dorothy Schubert around the floor more than any other lady in the group. He glanced over to her husband as she pulled him close yet again.

"Nyah, don't pay him any mind, he's too busy bending that Norwegian guy's ear. You could ravage me right here on the floor and he wouldn't notice," she pushed herself against him, making more contact below the waist than he expected.

Will coughed, "Yes, ma'am, but I daresay the crew might have something to say about that."

Her nasal laugh made the couples near them smile, "Yeah! They'd put a fire hose on us I guess."

He sat a few dances out, pleading exhaustion but just as the band tuned up for the last waltz he found his hand seized and he was dragged to his feet. Matty pushed him onto the dance floor. "You don't get away without a dance with me tonight, Will Turner. I know Dorothy is glaring daggers at me but I don't care. We are, after all, the only single people in the group."

"We are indeed, but well-chaperoned."

She pulled him close and breathed in his ear, "Yes, dammit, but just pay attention." The dance ended and they drifted back to their table. Matty addressed the group and reminded them that by this time the next day, they would be in their spiritual home, Germany. She picked up her wrap and turned to Will again. "Mr. Turner, would you escort me to my cabin door," she emphasized the "door." "I am feeling a little tipsy and would not want to fall overboard."

Will offered his arm, "I would be honored."

They stepped out on deck where he felt her pressing hard against him. She stumbled, "Whoops! I really am a little drunk. Must be the fresh air."

He steered her along the passageway to her cabin but she made it hard work, tottering from side-to-side. The couple in front of them disappeared through their door and at that precise moment Matty seemed to recover. She strode to the door of her cabin pulling Will with her. She had the key ready and quickly stepped inside. Will stood on the threshold.

"Well, Matty, it's been . . ."

She ignored him, put her head outside again and looked up and down the passageway. She grabbed his tie and yanked him into the cabin, kicking the door shut behind him. He stood for a moment, unsure.

Matty turned away, reached up to her hair and unpinned it. She turned back to Will and shook her head, making her hair cascade down over her bare shoulders. She took his hands in hers and grinned, "Well, Mr. Turner, what is it they say where you come from? Are you just going to stand there and whistle Dixie?"

◦ ▸━━◂ ◦

Per Rasmussen, the second officer, pointed at the ship crossing their course. Even at a distance of three miles it looked massive, and threatening. "That, Miss Ellerkamm, is a dreadnought of the Royal Navy with its escort. The smoke you can see on the horizon," he paused and raised his binoculars. "Is a cruiser squadron, probably out from their base at Scapa Flow."

She scowled, "My God! They are so arrogant. Do they think they own the sea?"

Rasmussen smiled, "They don't *think* they own the North Sea, they do own the North Sea."

"Well they certainly got a bloody nose two weeks ago. I think they are calling it the Battle of Jutland. How many ships did the British lose, Mr. Rasmussen?"

He shrugged, "More than the Germans, but as you can see, they have plenty left, and you will not see any German ships out here. They scampered back to the safety of their harbors." He smiled, it was obvious to Will where the young Dane's sympathies lay, but he kept out of the discussion.

Matty gave Rasmussen a brittle smile, "Thank you for the information."

He saluted, "My pleasure, ma'am."

Matty tugged Will's arm and they continued their stroll along the promenade deck "Insufferable little prig," she muttered under her breath.

Will patted her hand, "It does seem that the Danes do not have much sympathy with the German cause."

"But why should they think like that? His Highness the Kaiser has been at pains to express his friendship towards Denmark, and Holland for that matter."

Will shrugged, "They are nervous of their powerful neighbor. It must be tempting for Germany when they look at the map. If they took the Jutland peninsular they would control the entrance to the Baltic, and don't forget they did seize a big slice of Danish territory at gunpoint within living memory."

She stopped and turned to face him, "Will, just whose side are you on?"

He looked her in the eye, "Matty, I am on the side of the United States of America. As I made it clear to your Herr Von Rintelen at the consulate when you took me there before we sailed, I am neutral. I am a journalist and my job is to report what I see."

She relaxed and her grin sprang back, "Oh, don't try to sound so grand. *Modern Mechanics* isn't exactly the *New York Times*." Will frowned. "Don't start sulking on me, Will," she reached up and stroked his cheek.

He laughed, "Okay, point taken, but I do take my job seriously. I am going to ask searching questions."

"Good for you, and I'm sure that Kapitaen Friedmann will be happy to answer them, when he's not fending off Dorothy Schubert."

"What do you mean by that?"

"Oh, come off it, Will. You can't pretend you haven't noticed. She's a man eater. I am told he is an absolute dish and quite charming. You mark my words, she'll make a bee line for him. I personally think that power acts as an aphrodisiac for some women, and he is the commander of the airships at Tondern."

"But it does not work like that for you?"

Matty blushed and giggled, squeezing his hand, "No, I fall for charm and honesty. Now come on, I am starving and this will be the last meal we take aboard." Will led her toward the dining room. The word 'honesty' had struck home, and suddenly he did not feel so hungry.

Margarethe sailed on under a gathering overcast. The sea stayed calm but a layer of high cloud slipped over the sun. The ship slowed. Dorothy Schubert called up to the Captain when she saw him appear above her on the open wing of the bridge.

"Hey, Skipper! Why we crawling along?"

He looked down and smiled, "Mines, madam, drifting mines. We navigate through what is supposed to be a cleared channel, but the damn things break free of their moorings and float into the open sea."

"What happens if we hit one?"

Dalgaard made a face, then threw his hands up in the air, "Boom! And then we sink."

"Geez! Take as long you like, skipper." Dalgaard grinned and turned back to his slow scan of the ocean. It was not a mine that stopped the ship. In the early afternoon the masthead lookout spotted drifting wreckage through his telescope. As they drew closer he identified half a lifeboat, kept afloat by the buoyancy tanks but awash. He studied it and groaned, then picked up the telephone to the bridge. The engines reversed, and *Margarethe* wallowed to a dead stop in the water. The crew launched a whaler and motored over to the wreckage.

The passengers crowded the rail. Matty watched through her binoculars, "I can't really see what they are doing. They seem to be getting something into their boat. Oh!" She turned to Will, her face drained of color. "It's a body."

The whaler turned and headed toward the ship. The seaman in charge shouted through a megaphone as they neared the side. Dalgaard appeared on the bridge and bellowed down to Rasmussen. "All hands on deck, Mr. Rasmussen, and I mean everybody, stewards and cooks and non-essential engine room staff included." He addressed the passengers now gathered expectantly, "Ladies and gentlemen, please move away from the side."

Matty had not been overheard and the passengers had no idea why the ship had stopped. A buzz of conversation surrounded them. The crew spilled out of hatchways and hurried to form a line a few feet back from the rail. Two men manned a light davit as the launch bumped against the side. They engaged the electric winch and a minute later a stretcher appeared at deck level. It supported a canvas bag, laced at the top. The crew removed their caps as the two sailors swung the stretcher on board. At this point the passengers realized what had happened. A murmur went through the crowd and the men doffed their hats. Dalgaard appeared and draped a British Union flag over the stretcher, stood back and saluted. Will caught himself and resisted the now automatic urge to stand to attention. He glanced sideways to see how the members of the German American Alliance reacted. Their response was as somber as the other passengers, but Matty shocked him with her reaction. She turned into him and buried her head in his shoulder. He put his arms around her as he felt her sob.

Dalgaard faced them, "Ladies and gentlemen, we have recovered the body of a British seaman from the wreckage of a lifeboat. It is most likely he died at the naval battle fought in these waters recently. We will proceed but rendezvous with a vessel of the Royal Navy at the first opportunity. It is unlikely to cause any significant delay. I would ask you all to observe a minute's silence and offer your prayers for this poor sailor."

Will felt Matty pushing him away from the others. He put his hands on her shoulders and she looked up at him, her eyes red. "Sorry, I'm being a silly goose."

He looked at her, puzzled. He had been about to point out that the dead sailor by her reckoning was her enemy, but he bit back the words.

He pulled a handkerchief from his pocket and she took it without a word, dabbed around her eyes, then blew her nose noisily. She looked at the handkerchief, then tucked it in her sleeve. She managed a weak grin, "Sorry about that, I'll wash it for you when we get to the hotel." Matty sighed, then took his arm, "Will, I need a drink."

Two hours later *Margarethe* heaved to. A launch from HMS *Aurora*, a light cruiser, pulled alongside, and the remains transferred. The two ships lay just a hundred yards apart. The captain appeared on the armored bridge with a loud hailer.

"Thank you, Captain Dalgaard, your assistance is very much appreciated," the voice floated across the water, eerily clear.

Dalgaard raised his megaphone, "A sad duty, Captain, but an honor."

Aurora dipped her ensign in salute, foam appeared at her stern as the propellers thrashed the water and she slipped away, her captain anxious to put on speed. A stationary warship made a fat prize for a U-boat. Four hours later, *Margerethe* nosed around the island of Fano, that sheltered the new port of Esbjerg from the open sea. They had run down the coast of Jutland, as near the land as possible. Neither combatant dared place mines inside national waters as both courted neutral Denmark. Matty's binoculars revealed a landscape of salt marsh interspersed with tidy fishing villages. Brightly painted cottages clustered around harbors dotted with small fishing vessels. In the distance Will made out a landscape of low green hills, fat farming country. Esbjerg impressed him. *Margarethe* dwarfed most of the shipping in the harbor, a mixture of sail and modern steamers, but two busy tugs had her safely berthed within minutes. The wharves had none of the clutter and garbage he expected. Beyond the harbor, solid brick built commercial buildings with red-tiled roofs lined wide cobbled streets.

From the gangplank as they disembarked Will could see a short train drawn up on the quayside. The line ran right into the harbor for the convenience of passengers. Their baggage had been loaded while they attended to the briefest of landing formalities. Before the members of the German American Alliance had settled in their seats, the train jerked and started rolling.

Matty patted the seat next to her, "See, Will? German efficiency."

Will dropped into the seat, "Correction, Danish efficiency."

Matty pointed to a plaque screwed to the wall of the compartment, *Deutsche Laenderbahn.* "What does it say?"

Guy Gaunt had drummed into Will that he must not, under any circumstances, reveal that he spoke German. It gave him a huge advantage. He shrugged.

Matty looked smug, "German Territorial Railroad."

He gave a low whistle, "I stand corrected. Do you mean to say that the German Navy has laid on a special train for us? Just sixteen people?"

She squeezed his arm, "Nothing but the best for their guests." The train picked up speed. The sun had broken through again and even though it was now early evening, at that northern latitude it was still high enough to throw a golden glow over a landscape of neat farms with lush fields where fat cattle grazed. In some areas fields of rye and wheat had already taken on their dusty ripe mantle.

"A country at peace," Will said. "I wonder what the German side will look like."

The train jerked and slowed, "You won't have to wait long to find out."

He felt a sudden emptiness in his stomach. On board ship his mission had felt remote, unreal, but within minutes he knew it was about to become very real indeed. Captain Will Turner was about to go behind enemy lines. The crossing came as an anticlimax. The train slowed to walking pace then clanked to a full stop. Seconds later it moved off again. Will saw a fence topped with barbed wire extending away into the distance on either side of the track, and guessed it marked the frontier. He noted that it did not appear to be in good repair, and in some places trees leaned against it with their branches extending into the next country. Nature had no respect for man-made barriers.

They stopped again. Moments later a green-uniformed official entered the car and saluted. Matty had collected all their passports. He glanced at them, then made a quick head count. Satisfied, he clicked his heels, smiled and saluted again. "A hearty welcome in Germany, ladies and gentlemen." He disappeared through the door leaving Matty grinning smugly at her party.

"As you can see, unlike the stories you may have read in the pro-British newspapers, the natives are friendly." She dropped back in her seat as the train moved off.

Will gazed at the passing countryside. At first glance little different to the Danish side of the frontier, but revealing significant details. He had seen a scattering of motor vehicles in Denmark: cars, trucks, a motorcycle and even one of the new gasoline-powered traction engines working in a field. On the German side he saw only drab painted military trucks. In both countries horsepower of the old-fashioned kind still ruled, but whereas the Danish animals looked sleek, groomed and well-fed, their unfortunate cousins in Germany were old, tired, and thin. The army had requisitioned any decent animal.

Something was missing from the scene, something so obvious it took him ten minutes to recognize it, "Color!"

Matty turned back to him, "I beg your pardon?"

Will shrugged, "Color. There is no color in the landscape. In Denmark every house you see has a flower garden. The little town we passed before the frontier had a tidy little park with masses of blooms. Over here every inch of land is under the plough."

She frowned, "Will, these people are fighting for their existence. The British blockade means they can't import what they need, so they are beating them by growing their own. Practical and efficient." She gave him a prim little smile.

They bypassed the railroad station in Tondern. The airship base was served by its own spur line, everything from personnel to gasoline rolled in by train. John Schubert opened a window and stuck his head out, "My God! You are not going to believe this!" He ducked back inside, his thin hair scattered by the breeze. The others abandoned any pretense of reserve and crowded the windows. The airship station made a striking sight. Situated on a flat, dusty plain outside the town, it covered hundreds of acres. Three vast sheds dominated the view. Even at a distance of a mile they appeared to Will to be the biggest manmade structures he had ever seen. The lack of other buildings in the vicinity made it hard to judge their exact size. The two sheds nearest the train obviously each housed a single Zeppelin, but the third in the row dwarfed even these. He judged it had to be capable of swallowing at least two airships with room to spare.

Yet, it was not the sight of the sheds that had made Schubert so excited, he had caught a glimpse of the reception committee ready to greet them. As the train squeaked to a stop, the passengers heard the opening bars of *The Star Spangled Banner* blasted out by a military band. Matty grabbed his hand, "Come on Will, we're leading the parade," he held back for a second. "For heaven's sake, don't be shy."

Oh hell! He thought to himself. *In for a penny, in for a pound.* He followed Matty to the door where steps had been placed. Despite himself he gasped. A red carpet had been laid over the tarmac next to the tracks. A group of naval officers stood waiting to greet them while two ranks of sailors in dress uniform flanked the other side of the carpet with rifles at the present. Their brilliantly polished bayonets glistened in the sun while the breeze made the distinctive black ribbons on their caps flutter.

An officer stepped forward, clicked his heels, saluted Matty then offered his hand, "Strasser. Welcome to our airship home at Tondern." Will looked at the little man, an icy shock of recognition chilled him. Korvettankapitan Peter Strasser had made his reputation as a passionate advocate for the Zeppelin as a weapon of total war. This was a man who had dared to argue with the Kaiser for permission to unleash his bombs anywhere in England, while the old emperor dithered for fear that his airships would destroy the palaces of his royal cousins in England. This was a man demonized by the British press, built up in the minds of the civilian population as the leader of the "baby killers": the devil incarnate. This was a man who commanded the loyalty and obedience of every officer and man in the Imperial Naval Airship Service. This was also a man who wore lifts. Will tried not to stare at Strasser's glossily polished knee-high boots, laced at the front, with obvious high heels.

Strasser's eyes swept over the Americans gathered by the train. "Ladies and gentlemen, it is my great pleasure to welcome you to Tondern." They responded with muttered words of appreciation, all overawed by the strange little man before them. He wore a tight goatee beard and mustache that accentuated his sharp features. His cap sat at a jaunty angle and he moved with a curious strut, with his thumbs hooked in the pockets of his tunic. For a fleeting moment, his gaze fell on Will as they shook hands. Their eyes locked for a second before Strasser turned back to Matty. Will knew that look in an instant. He had seen it before in the eyes of Preacher Flint at home: a certainty bordering on the messianic that what he believed to be true must be the truth.

"Mr. Turner?" Will turned to see a second officer standing with his hand outstretched. "Friedmann. I can't tell you how pleased I am to meet you." Will shook his hand and smiled, Kapitaenleutnant Martin Friedmann was the light to Strasser's dark. Taller even than Will's six foot, he had acquired the slight stoop, no more than an inclination of the head, often adopted by the very tall in an attempt to make others feel comfortable in their presence. He had a lazy grin that lit up a handsome face topped by a cap jammed on over blond hair that showed a lack of regard for regulation length. His smile crinkled the skin surrounding his blue eyes. Will had seen that look before as well, but this time it reminded him of Sir Percy Scott, they were the eyes of a man used to looking into distance: a sailor's eyes.

"Captain Friedmann, I declare we have much to talk about. The Zeppelin to replace the ocean liner?"

Friedmann threw back his head and laughed, "The monoplane to replace the biplane for military service?" He clapped Will on the back, "We will bore everybody senseless at dinner tonight with our aeronautical chatter." He spoke fluent English, but with a slight accent that Will found hard to place.

"Mr. Turner, won't you introduce me to this handsome officer?" They both turned. Will fought to suppress a smile: Matty's prediction had come true within minutes of their arrival, Dorothy Schubert stood beside them, her most winsome smile in place.

"Captain Friedmann, may I present Mrs. Dorothy Schubert."

Martin Friedmann clicked his heels, bowed, then took her hand and kissed it, "Friedmann, at your service, *Gnaedige Frau.*"

"Oh my!" Dorothy simpered.

"Ah! There you are, dear," Matty stepped to Will's side. He repeated the introduction but Friedmann simply offered his hand and a warm smile.

"Miss Ellerkamm, it is a great pleasure to meet you."

Matty returned the smile and shook his hand. "Kapitaenleutnant Friedmann, I am told by your commanding officer that you served your apprenticeship on a real windjammer."

"That is correct."

Matty's eyes sparkled with mischief, "Then I am sure you have a voice used to hailing over great distance," she raised an eyebrow.

Friedmann laughed again, "Of course!" he stepped back and raised both hands. "Ladies and gentlemen! Pay attention please. We have arranged a motor bus to take you to the finest hotel in Tondern. For those of you used to the Waldorf Astoria, it may seem modest, but to us poor sailors it is the height of luxury. I hope you enjoy your stay. Anything we can do to make your visit more pleasurable, please just ask." He stepped to one side and made a sweeping gesture toward the bus that stood waiting beyond the guard of honor.

Dorothy Schubert touched Matty's arm, "What a tour guide! He could lead me anywhere."

"Perhaps home to tea with his wife, Dorothy. I am sure he will be delighted to show off their two little daughters." Dorothy gave her a sour look as she took her husband's arm as he marched past deep in conversation with another naval officer.

Will had stayed at the Waldorf Astoria, he was the only person in the group to have enjoyed its luxury, but he had to admit the modestly named Crown Hotel in the center of Tondern matched it for service, if not for size. It soon became clear to Will that this was a family run business, and the elderly lady with the distinguished air of a misplaced aristocrat who welcomed them, was the matriarch. This was a lady who stood for no nonsense: in fact she would not even let nonsense set foot in the door. As the only two single people in the party, Matty was allotted a room at the front of the building on the first floor, and Will found himself in a small, but comfortable room at the rear of the building on the floor above.

Strasser's attendance at the formal welcome banquet hosted by the hotel gave Will a guide to how much importance the German Navy attached to the visit from the German-American Alliance. He would have expected the Commander of Airships to be at one of the major airship bases, perhaps at Nordholz or in Berlin itself, instead he conducted proceedings at this outpost with a wit and style that surprised Will and delighted Matty and her friends.

Will managed not to choke when he joined the toasts to German American friendship, he steeled himself to drink a toast to the Kaiser and recovered in time to propose a toast to aviation at Matty's instigation.

Every officer at the base who could be spared duties that evening sat at the long table, and roared their appreciation, thumping the table and cheering. In his role of base commander, Martin Friedmann felt obliged to circulate and entertain, but as the evening wore on in a haze of champagne and strong liquor, he managed to make time for conversation with Will. Soon they found themselves surrounded by the junior officers, eager to join in.

"So, Mr. Turner, you think the biplane will soon be replaced by the monoplane for military service?" Will turned to the speaker, a balding stocky man who had introduced himself as Georg Klaas.

"Not just for military service Lieutenant, also for civil freight and passenger service."

"Please, my name is Georg," he topped Will's glass. "So you think the airplane has a future in commercial service?"

Will nodded, "I do. I think one day the airplane will challenge the railroad."

Martin Friedmann gave a low whistle, *"Gott in Himmel!* Will, you are a true visionary, but for myself I do not think the airplane will ever have the weight-carrying ability to be able to handle more than two or three passengers or a sack of mail. To be economic an aircraft must be able to carry twenty or more passengers and tons of freight. For that you need an airship."

Will felt a tightness across his forehead: he had already drunk too much, but the exhilaration he felt helped keep his thinking clear. "I agree that the Zeppelin seems to offer more potential at the moment, but there must always be a big question about safety. You must agree there have been some disastrous fires caused by hydrogen gas."

Martin made a slight inclination of his head, "That is sadly true, but I have a solution."

Will felt a sudden emptiness in his stomach, his heart hammered, he waited for the airship captain's next words, but he just stood smiling: Will heard himself saying, "Is there some way of shielding the gas bags with the spent gases from the exhausts?" He regretted it instantly, expecting furtive looks, a sudden suspicious silence. Instead, Martin slapped him on the shoulder and laughed while the others shook their heads and rolled their eyes.

"Oh dear, Will. If only it were possible. Every armchair expert in Germany has put that idea forward, and on the surface it has some appeal, but the reality is that the engines could not produce anywhere near enough inert gas."

Will felt a rush of relief and buoyed by confidence made another suggestion, "How about taking compressed nitrogen in cylinders to pump into a second chamber surrounding the gas envelope?" The airship officers looked at each other and then back to Martin; the idea had some merit.

"That is a new one, I have to say," he scratched his chin. "But I think weight would be a problem again. I hope you do not mind me saying, but these ideas are, how you say, patches? No, my solution is very simple – we replace our hydrogen gas with helium gas."

"Helium?"

"Yes. It is completely safe. It will not burn and it generates enough lift." Martin paused and picked up the bottle on the table in front of them. He refilled everybody's glass, "but there is a problem. It is very, very expensive and difficult to produce in quantity. I regret that we will continue to fly with hydrogen."

Will relaxed, hoping his relief did not show. The prospect of having to deal with Zeppelins that had no Achilles heel was too horrible to contemplate. He was about to reply when the sound of a glass being tapped caught the attention of the guests. Strasser stood and waved a slip of paper.

"Ladies and gentlemen, I have good news. Our tree frog . . ." the German officers thumped the table and Strasser smiled indulgently ". . . I should explain—our weather forecasting officer—predicts a fine day tomorrow. I invite you all to a short voyage on our training airship, *Viktoria.*" An audible gasp filled the room, followed by a stunned silence and then a babble of excited chatter.

Will turned to Martin Friedmann, "So we get to ride on hydrogen as well!"

Martin passed Will a cigar from the box on the table and struck a match. He winked, "Make the most of this, Will. It's strictly no smoking tomorrow."

❖ ◆━━◆ ❖

Will kicked off his shoes and flopped down on his bed. The party had broken up after midnight when the German officers had departed the hotel in a flurry of heel clicking, bowing and noisy declarations of friendship. He shut his eyes tight and breathed deep, running the events of the day through his mind. He had drunk far too much, but somehow managed not to do or say anything that might dent his cover. Too much booze usually dulled his senses, but tonight he recognized that it also made him more aware of his feelings, and that gave him cause for real concern. He liked these men, he could not deny it; they were friendly, enthusiastic and welcoming. Strasser struck him as what his aunt would describe as a "cold fish," but of the others he could only say they seemed no different from the men he socialized with in squadrons, and latterly on ships, in the British service.

His sleepy reverie was interrupted by a rattle against the window. He sat up, puzzled, there had been no prospect of rain. He moved to the window and peered out. His room overlooked a yard at the rear of the hotel, something moved below. He pushed up the sash to see and had to jerk his head back as the top of a ladder swayed past his face. He grabbed it and pulled it against the sill.

"Matty! What the hell do you think you're doing?" He spoke in an urgent whisper.

"What do you think I'm doing, you nitwit? I'm coming up." Matty arrived at his level and flung her arms around his neck. "Well, aren't you going to invite me in?"

"For God's sake, what about your reputation?"

She already had one knee on the window ledge, "I'll only lose that if they catch us, and they'll only catch us if you leave me here dangling." She pushed herself through the window forcing him to catch her. He staggered back and collapsed on the bed with her on top of him.

"Matty Ellerkamm, you are drunk."

She pushed herself up by her elbows on his chest and breathed in his face, "Yes, are you going to be a pompous prig and disapprove?"

He laughed in the face of the inevitable, "No, it was just a statement of fact, not disapproval."

"Good."

"Your face is flushed."

"That happens when I get excited."

"Oh, why are you excited?"

"Because I'm going on a Zeppelin ride tomorrow," she sat up and tugged at his tie, moving her knees astride him. "And when I get excited, I get kinda . . ."

"Kinda what?"

"Kinda more excited."

CHAPTER 18

The Skies above Essex, England

Prof Smith glanced over the side of his bathtub cockpit and tried to gauge the height of the F.E.2, as they swept over the boundary of their field. They were high, at least five hundred feet. On a hot day with a tired engine they had sometimes found leaves in the undercarriage when they staggered into the air, barely missing the hedge, but today two hundred and fifty horsepower of brand new Rolls Royce engine thrust the Prof and Dizzy Lipman into a clear summer sky. For once they flew in daylight, and today they knew where to find their enemy, and what machine he flew.

The crew of the German two-seater that had crossed the coast only ten minutes before had no way of knowing they had presented themselves as a perfect practice target. McGuigan located them ten miles out to sea with the sound detector. Bert Hickman identified their machine as either an Albatros or Rumpler two-seater, and accurately computed their height and course, while Chalky White transmitted the information straight to Simpson's office.

Jacquieline Courroyer stood beside the Vauxhall open tourer she had driven to the field, while Major Ernie Simpson leaned on the hood to steady his binoculars. "My word, that new Rolls Royce gives the old F.E.2 some get up and go!" He handed the glasses to Jac.

"It got up and went. I can hardly see them. The Frenchmen are nearly keeping up though," she paused while she refocused. "I count another four aeroplanes behind them."

Simpson nodded, "I've never seen this collection of misfits and reprobates move so fast. I have to admit I'm quite pleased with them."

"But you will never tell them that?"

Simpson shook his head and laughed, "Never, but I might tell them I'm almost satisfied if they bring this bird down."

Jac's eyes narrowed and her lips compressed in a thin smile, "Fritz is going to wish he never got out of bed this morning." She would have been surprised to know that the pilot of the new Rumpler biplane really was a Fritz, Leutnant Fritz Werther, and at that moment he felt very satisfied with his mission. The weather had cooperated for once and he felt confident that Paul Salzbrunn, his observer, would take advantage of the clear air to make some excellent photographs of the River Blackwater. Their orders stated that they must concentrate on the waterways to the north of London. Werther guessed that the Zeppelin navigators kept mistaking any large body of water for the River Thames, and wandered off course as a result, but it was not his concern, he just followed orders:

Their's not to make reply,
Their's not to reason why,
Their's but to do and die

The words from Tennyson's poem sprang into his mind, and he smiled. They had studied the poem in English class at high school. He had loved the rhythm of the words and the tale of heroism they told. Not that there was any question of death today. They flew the latest model of a Rumpler two-seater powered by the ever reliable, and now even more powerful, Mercedes engine. He had a synchronized machine gun to fire forward through the propeller, even though he had to lean far out of the cockpit to sight it round the massive lump of the engine and its exhaust blocking his view. Salzbrunn had a second parabellum machine gun mounted on a free-swinging mount to deal with anything that managed to drag itself up to their altitude and attack from the rear.

They had flung four token bombs at a warship off the coast, a gesture to mislead the British as to the true nature of their business. Relieved of the weight the Rumpler had powered up to nearly five thousand meters as they crossed the coast. Werther felt secure, safe in the knowledge that on previous visits to England he had encountered no serious opposition: a couple of distant specks had revealed themselves as defending scout aircraft, but they had possessed neither the speed nor the height to trouble him.

The steady roar of the big Mercedes surrounded him, caressed him. He felt as if it embraced him with its power while he sat safe and secure in his spacious cockpit, surrounded by control levers and instruments so solid and well-crafted, they would not look out of place on a railroad locomotive. He could feel a gentle tremor through the control column and the rudder pedals: a combination of engine vibration and the slipstream pressing on the control surfaces. It made the machine feel alive. He leaned to one side and looked ahead; the propeller showed as a shimmering disc, the high sunlight picking out a wavering line where it caught the edge of each blade as it turned at a steady twenty revolutions each second. Fritz pulled up the fur collar of his leather coat and reached for the rubber tube attached to the oxygen bottle fixed behind his seat. He sucked and breathed in. It tasted foul, contaminated by oil and rubber, but it cleared his head. At five thousand meters the air felt brittle and thin.

He turned in his seat. Only the top of Paul's head was visible as he crouched down attending to the camera fixed in the cockpit floor. To the south, London lay invisible, cloaked under a thin haze of smoke and dust that the sun's glare turned into a blinding wall, but the East of England stretched ahead and away to his right as if laid out for their convenience on a vast map that he hung suspended above, seated in splendor and comfort courtesy of Herr Rumpler and the Mercedes Engine company.

Yes, Fritz felt very safe. So safe that when a blast of steam from the engine followed a bang that he felt as much as heard, he thought for a split second the radiator had burst. He did not connect it with the glimpse of an ugly, black-painted machine flashing past on the opposite course. Salzbrunn reacted faster. He snatched at the cocking handle on his gun even as he sprang to his feet, and heaved it round. The maniacal chatter of the parabellum as he opened fire on the black F.E.2 now curving in behind them, jolted Werther into action. He threw the Rumpler into a turn and opened the throttle wide. For a few seconds the Mercedes responded, but Werther felt it fade as the F.E.2 made another pass. Salzbrunn struggled to bring his gun to bear on the British airplane, against the centrifugal force pushing him down into his cockpit. Another volley of shots from the gunner in the front cockpit of the F.E.2 rattled through the fuselage and wings.

Werther cursed and pushed hard on the stick. If he could duck under the Englishmen he might be able to outpace them in a shallow dive. Maybe nurse the overheating engine as far as the German occupied Belgian coast. A shove on the rudder sent the Rumpler sliding beneath the F.E.2. Werther twisted and turned his head, seeking even a shred of cloud to duck behind. The clear sky so useful a minute before now left him naked and exposed.

He ducked as a bullet screamed off the cylinder block. The ricochet audible above the clatter of the failing engine and the roar of the wind. Where the hell did that come from? He slammed the stick over, gripping it in both hands. Another strange pusher biplane floated past. A huge, ungainly machine painted dark brown, the muted colors relieved by the bright cockades under the wings, the colors reversed from the British blue white and red. Good Grief! A Frenchman.

He had no time to wonder why. Werther flew by instinct: any notion of reaching home gone. He engaged in a fight for his life, and by God, he would make it a fight. He watched the falling rev counter needle from the corner of his eye. The stink of hot metal and oil as the overheating Mercedes ground itself to death filled the air. The fighter in him took in every detail of the sky. He plotted his next move as cool as a chess master. The F.E.2 had slipped behind them, but Salzbrunn had the measure of him, firing short bursts over the tail. The Frenchman had tried to cut them off from below but had underestimated the speed of their dive and now lagged far behind.

Everything seemed to be happening in slow motion. Werther saw a B.E.2 clawing its way up towards them. He pushed harder on the stick and leaned out of the cockpit to sight his gun. The propeller still turned in the slipstream and he wondered if the synchronizing gear would work, then laughed out loud as he squeezed the firing lever. What difference did it make if he shot his propeller off? His new tormentor slipped into the ring of his sight, then dived away as the gun thundered. He saw clear air before him, a patchwork of fields and woodland. He snatched a glance behind. The F.E.2 clung on, the flash from the gun in the front cockpit visible even in bright sunlight. He heard the snap of bullets passing close by, and kicked the rudder bar to twitch the tail from side-to-side.

They dived steeper than he had ever dared before, but the speed had stabilized. He gritted his teeth and pushed harder against the stick, his arms trembling with effort. The propeller, windmilling against the drag of the dead engine, acted as a giant air brake, allowing him to stand the Rumpler on its nose. If he could steepen the angle, the British machine would overshoot, giving Salzbrunn a clear shot. He could worry about tearing the wings off when it came time to pull out of the dive.

Salzbrunn's gun roared again, then fell silent, "That's the lot! We're out of ammunition," the observer leaned against the back of Werther's seat and screamed in his ear.

"Hold on tight." He held the rudder pressure and forced the control column over: and prayed. The Rumpler pirouetted and reversed direction. The fields so distant a minute before now took shape in his windscreen, but the pursuing Britisher had disappeared. He shut his eyes and eased the pressure on the stick. The note of the wind screaming in the wires changed instantly. He kept his eyes shut, hearing the pitch drop down the register, waiting for the shattering crunch that would tell him the wings had folded and he would die seconds later. It never came. He might live. Werther opened his eyes. The fields reeled past a hundred meters below. Good fields, rich with new crop, just like the fields of his family farm near Hannover. He might see them again one day, if he acted fast.

A bootful of opposite rudder with the stick held in the far corner of the cockpit sent the Rumpler plunging into a sideslip. The wind blasted his cheek and he blinked furiously as a draught found its way under his goggles, making his eyes stream. A line of trees swam into view. He straightened the controls then pulled back on the stick and hurdled over them; a wide meadow stretched ahead. He let the Rumpler settle. Too high and too slow. He gave the stick a nudge forward: "control speed with the stick, your height with throttle," the voice of Granny Schulz, his instructor, whispered in his ear. He leaned over the edge of the cockpit, scanning from the horizon to the grass beneath. Satisfied they now skimmed the ground, he pulled the stick back to his stomach to stall the wings, kicking off the remaining drift. The tailskid rasped in the long grass as the wheels rumbled beneath them.

"God in heaven, Fritz! You'll never make a better landing than that. That was perfect," Paul slapped him on the shoulder as they bumped and rolled to a stop. "Now, out! *Raus!*" Fritz unbuckled his safety belt and tried to stand, his legs made of jelly. "Come on, man. The Englishmen are coming in and I don't think they are about to invite us to tea." Paul grabbed him and bundled him over the edge of the cockpit. "Stand away!" He drew a short-barrelled semi-automatic from his pocket and aimed it into the front cockpit. He fired twice then jumped down; the stench of raw gasoline filled the air. "Quick, a match."

Fritz tore off his gloves and fumbled in his pocket, spilling his pipe and tobacco on the ground. They both ducked as the F.E.2 roared overhead, then threw themselves flat as a volley of bullets smacked into the ground next to them.

"Bastards!" Fritz shook his fist at the British machine as it curved around. Paul snatched the matches from him.

"Give them here, they're trying to stop us firing our machine, they could have killed us up there if they wanted." He struck a match, thrust it back in the open box and threw it into the cockpit. "Now run!" The Rumpler exploded with a dull *whuuump*. They felt the heat on their backs through their heavy flying clothes as they stumbled towards the field gate. They turned and looked back. Flames leaped high, sending the black smoke above twisting and roiling into the blue sky, a majestic and appalling sight. They could see the F.E.2 landing beyond the blazing Rumpler, its shape distorted by waves of heat.

"Shouldn't we make a run for it?" Fritz gasped, fighting for breath. "Hide up until nightfall and then steal a boat?"

Paul nudged him and pointed over his shoulder, "The game is up, my friend." A policeman stood leaning against his bicycle in the road beyond the gate, his dark blue uniform buttoned to the neck despite the early summer heat. A huge walrus mustache gave him a serious aspect, but he beamed at them from under his helmet.

"You're nicked, sunshine," he grinned. The German fliers raised their hands in surrender. "I don't know why you be doin' that, I ain't got a gun."

"I do have a pistol, Constable," Paul replied in perfect English, keeping his hands raised.

"Then you better be giving it to me, then. But I'd be obliged if you would make it safe for me."

Paul took the gun from his pocket, "I fired my last two shots into the petrol tank, it is safe," he jerked back the toggle then pointed the Luger at the ground and pressed the trigger to prove it was empty before passing it to the policeman, holding the barrel.

"Thank you, sir. We wouldn't be wanting any accidents would we now."

Paul turned to his pilot, "Fritz, lower your hands, you look ridiculous," he pointed behind them. "Ah, it looks like the victors have arrived."

Dizzy Lipman and Prof Smith came striding across the field. "Do either of you two speak English?" Prof demanded. The Germans snapped to attention, Smith had stripped off his flying coat revealing his captain's rank badges, and they were junior lieutenants. Enemy or not, he was still the senior officer.

"Yes, sir," Fritz replied. "We both do."

The Prof stood with his hands on his hips, leaning forward, "I suppose you think that was clever?"

"Sir?"

"That dive with the crafty turn, followed by the sideslip to the ground and the tidy landing."

"Doing my job, sir."

"Well, we thought it was bloody clever. We could hardly get a shot near you, and if you hadn't gained that much ground on us we could have stopped you firing your machine. We could have shot you on the ground when we saw what you were doing, you know."

"Yes, sir," Paul answered. "But we relied on you feeling it wasn't quite cricket to kill defenseless men."

Dizzy stroked his chin, "Hmmm, Oxford or Cambridge?"

"Oxford, sir."

Smith allowed himself a smile, "Lucky for you we play cricket. Anyway, you did your best, there's no shame in being captured after putting up a fight like that."

"Thank you, sir."

"Now stand easy." Smith turned to the policeman. "Constable, have you got a lock up at the police station?"

"Yes, sir, but it's four miles away in Witham."

Smith pointed to a car chugging down the lane toward them, "Whose is that?"

"Doctor White's, sir."

"Commandeer that, and take them there," an escort will be sent from our field within the hour." He turned back to Werther and Salzbrunn, "Do you give your parole until tomorrow morning?"

The two young fliers looked at each other, Fritz shrugged, "Of course, sir." He had agreed not to attempt to escape and given his word of honor.

"Good, then we can entertain you in our mess tonight if you care to join us."

"Thank you, sir."

The policeman saluted Smith then turned to his captives, "You two come with me," they both came back to attention, saluted then followed the country copper to the car the local doctor had eagerly put at the disposal of the Royal Flying Corps.

Dizzy watched them climb into the back of the car and frowned, "Seem like nice boys, as my maiden aunt would say."

The Prof grunted, "Maybe, but I'm glad we'll have them safely banged up for the rest of the war. They flew bloody well and would have been a real nuisance over the Front." They walked over to the smoldering remains of what had once been the Rumpler biplane, approaching it warily. The unused ammunition in the fixed gun had exploded in the fire like a dozen Chinese firecrackers, and an odd round still spat angrily. The fire had burned out, the combustible wood and fabric quickly reduced to ash leaving a smoldering tangle of wires, some twisted steel tubing around the cockpit area and the charred lump of the engine the only recognizable parts of an airplane.

Dizzy knelt down, "Hullo! What's this? Looks like somebody's pipe and baccy."

"Must belong to one of those lads. You can re-unite them later." The Prof prodded a lump of blackened metal lying next to the observer's machine gun. He leaned forward to examine it, "Now this is interesting!" He touched it cautiously and found it cool enough to tug from the surrounding debris. "What do you make of that?"

Dizzy rolled the object over with his foot, "It's a camera, and a pretty jazzy one at that. It looks to me as if this was fitted in the cockpit floor. "I'll put money on it that this was the real reason for their little jaunt."

The Prof nodded, "Map making for the Zeppelins, I'll be bound. Well, let's see about getting a guard on this until we can get some men here to haul away anything useful." A crowd of locals had gathered at a respectful distance and Dizzy had noted two army uniforms among them. He called the two young soldiers over.

"Home on leave, chaps?"

The older of the two carried a corporal's two stripes on his sleeve. They both stood at attention. "Yes, sir."

"Well, I'm sorry to have to ask you to put in some duty, but it would be awfully decent of you to stand guard over this wreckage until we can get our lorry out here with some mechanics to take it away."

"Oh, yes please, sir," they answered together. Dizzy had the odd ability to make a direct order sound as if he were asking an enlisted man to do him a personal favor: unconventional but effective. He dug in his pocket for some coins, "Here's five bob for your trouble." The corporal began to protest but Dizzy silenced him with a casual wave, "No, take it. You will be on duty when you should be on leave and I'm damned if I can be bothered to sort out the paperwork to get you the extra pay you deserve."

"Thank you, sir," they could hardly believe their luck. "We'll make sure no souvenir hunters pinch anything."

"Good, we'll have you relieved in an hour or so. Now we have to push off. Thank you both." With that, Dizzy followed the Prof who already stood behind the F.E.2 waiting to swing the propeller to start.

Dizzy shut his eyes as the gap between the bus they were overtaking and the approaching truck narrowed. He opened them to see the open road ahead again and the danger behind. He sat beside Jacquieline Courreyor in the Vauxhall tourer that belonged to her boss, Colonel Frank Penrose. Despite the fine weather, they had the canvas canopy raised to cover the car. The Prof sat behind them. They had left the flying field as soon as they landed, intent on a mission of an entirely different, and personal nature.

"This is a very fast car, Mrs. Courreyor."

"Yes, it's really sporting don't you think, super to drive," she replied airily patting him on the knee, oblivious to his heavy hint. "And it's Jac, to my friends." She shifted down the gears again and accelerated hard. "So tell me how you nailed those Hun bastards."

Dizzy shrugged, "It was easy for once. The silly ass had no idea we had something that could climb to their height in the time available, but the old bus with the Roller went splendidly. I've always thought that any German machine with one of their big water-cooled engines, must have a terrible blind spot directly in front and below. When we saw him ahead, all I had to do was line us up and let the Prof pot him."

"Pity you couldn't have put a bullet or two through each of them."

"My word, Jac, you are in a bloodthirsty mood," Prof Smith lounged in the backseat smoking one of his skinny hand-rolled cigarettes. "I would have done so, but the engine that prevents the pilot of a Rumpler from seeing ahead also protects him. Even so, I rattled off a whole drum before we sheered off to avoid colliding head on. It only needed one shot to do the damage, and it seems I hit their radiator. Once that had gone they stood no chance of getting home."

"Couldn't you have machine-gunned them on the way down?"

Chris Davey

Dizzy frowned, "We tried, but they had a stonking great gun too. I had no intention of getting killed over a machine that we had in the bag anyway."

"Why not kill them once they were helpless on the ground?"

The Prof roared with laughter, "There's this inconvenient little thing called the Geneva Convention that covers that sort of thing."

Jac shrugged, "Doesn't always bother them."

"That's as may be," the Prof sounded serious again. "But they are more use to us alive than dead."

"So have you got any useful information out of them? When are they being interrogated? I would love to have a word with them."

"I dare say you would, but I suspect that awkward old Convention might cover your methods as well." The Prof flicked the end of his cigarette over the side of the car. "But I expect the lads in the mess tonight will get as much information out of them by filling them with cheap whiskey, as you would by pulling out their toenails."

"I would never do that! And what do you mean by 'in the mess tonight'?" She turned in her seat to look at the prof .

Dizzy grabbed the steering wheel and jerked it over to avoid a cyclist, "For heaven's sake, old girl! Watch where you're going."

Jac wrested the wheel back from him and directed her attention to the road, "Whoops! Sorry about that."

The Prof shook his head, "Don't worry about us: it's the poor bloke on the bike you need to apologize to. Anyway, where were we? Oh yes, the mess tonight. It's a tradition in France that when we bring a Hun down alive and well on our side, we entertain him in the mess that night. They do the same for us."

"My God fathers! That's all very nice and gentlemanly, I must say," Jac's voice rose indignantly. "Very cozy."

The Prof leaned forward, "And very effective. What's the first thing that happens when young men drink too much in like company?"

246 –

Jac glanced sideways at Dizzy who sat grinning, "They start talking too much, I suppose."

"And what do they usually talk about?"

"In my experience, how clever they are," she had started to smile. "Alright, they start boasting."

"Indeed they do. If the boys play it right tonight we will get all the information we need, and send our new chums off into captivity thinking what splendid fellows we are."

"On second thoughts that sounds like a good wheeze, thoroughly underhand."

The Prof leaned back, "I thought you would approve. Now, talking of underhand, do we have a plan for this evening?"

Dizzy pulled a brown envelope from his tunic pocket, "Five hundred smackers to buy the letters back."

Jac took her hand off the wheel and squeezed his arm, "I can't tell you how grateful we girls are. By getting the dosh all from one source it keeps the rumors down. Pardon me for me being so rude, but how on earth did you do it?"

Dizzy shrugged modestly, "I lied. I told Gramps that I had been drinking, wenching and gambling, and now owed my bookie five hundred quid, and could he help me out with a loan."

"What! And he gave it to you?"

"As a gift, with a huge smile and warmest congratulations."

"I don't believe it! You're pulling my leg."

"Not at all. You see brother David and I have been a disappointment to him. Grandfather was, and quite frankly still is, the most appalling old rake. He drank, gambled and, pardon me for being so direct, rogered his way around the Empire. Then, probably to enrage the Victorian stuffed shirts still further, he compounded his various misdeeds by falling in love for the first time in his life at the age of fifty, with a beautiful Polish Jewess, whom he promptly married."

Jac sighed, "Ah, what a lovely, romantic story. He gave up everything for love. I expect he was ostracized by polite society."

"Ha! He couldn't give a tuppeny-damn for polite society; but polite society took the decision to ignore the fact my grandmother is Jewish for the simple reason they were all too busy sucking up to him."

A slow smile spread across Jac's face, "This is sounding very familiar. I never made the connection. Is your Grandpa the famous, or should I say infamous, 'Sir Jasper' about whom various indelicate ditties have been composed?"

"The very same. Colonel Sir Jasper Lipman, VC, DSO, and friend of Her Majesty Queen Victoria and her ne'er do well son, King Edward the Seventh. One of the richest men in the country, with many members of polite society in hock to him."

"But how could you and your brother possibly be a disappointment to him?"

"We're too earnest, too well-behaved. David is a qualified doctor, now in the Medical Corps. I got a first at Cambridge, and my biggest misdemeanor was a five-bob fine from the magistrates for riding my bike without lights. The only thing I did to redeem myself in Gramps' eyes was to win a boxing blue." Jac glanced at him. His delicate features gave no clue to his bouts as a lightweight amateur boxer. The thought crossed her mind that if he had been born a woman he would have been a beauty.

"I heard rumors about that. You must have been good, there's not a mark on you."

Dizzy laughed, "Yes, though I say it myself, I was pretty handy. The old boy came to every one of my matches, roaring me on with his drunken chums. He confessed that when I won the army championship he won over two thousand guineas backing me. He said the five hundred quid was a token of his appreciation."

They had reached Marble Arch and now set off down Park Lane. The early evening sun still had power. It slanted through the trees at the edge of Hyde Park and cast a golden glow on the elaborate stonework of the buildings lining the roadway on their left. Wartime economies had done nothing to mute the exuberant flowerbeds lining their route. It was a classic, beautiful summer's evening in London. The Prof sat up and looked around as they arrived at Hyde Park Corner. He touched his finger to his cap in salute as they rolled past Number One London, the Duke of Wellington's old residence.

"Where the hell is everybody? Why aren't they out taking the air?"

"Buggered off to their country retreats I expect," Jac replied. "Cowardly bastards are scared of the Zeps."

Dizzy shrugged, "There might be some truth in that, but most people in this part of town would be in the country by now anyway. I expect it will be busier outside The Royal Albert Hall with tonight's concert though. Methinks that's why Buley has chosen it as a meeting place. He probably thinks the Prof is going to tear his head off rather than tamely hand over the cash."

The Prof leaned back in his seat, extended his arms, linked his fingers and stretched, "I would like to, but if we are going to get the letters and your money back, we'll have to be more subtle."

Dizzy laughed, "If we do recover my money then I will be paying for dinner. If we don't then we will have to have a whip round."

"I suppose that's one good thing about tonight, at least you chaps will have the evening off," Jac said. "I'm surprised your boss allowed it."

"It really is very unlikely that the Zeps will try a raid tonight, or for at least another month or so," Dizzy explained. "It's just too light at this time of year. I doubt if there are two hours of real darkness at altitude even as far south as London around midsummer day. The time taken to pass over the picket boats, get to London, and then back over the coast out of range would be just too long. We would see them either coming or going."

The Prof nodded, "There are still two machines on standby, but everybody else is stood down. Most people are entertaining our new

German friends, apart from Calmette and Duchenois who will be meeting us at the Savoy after we complete our little business."

Jac pulled up outside the house in Knightsbridge where Vicky and Marie waited at the top of the steps. The Prof jumped down and opened the door for them. He touched Marie on the arm as she made to step into the car.

"Don't you worry, m'dear. We'll sort out your little problem." He pinched her cheek and gave her a wink.

She smiled, tight-lipped, "I don't know how to thank you all."

"Just cheer up, that's all we ask."

This was not the Marie they had come to know. Her pale face accentuated the dark rings under her eyes. She looked frightened, her eyes darting around as she nodded at Dizzy and Jac in the front seat.

Jac leaned back and squeezed her hand, "Darling, the only people who know what this is about are Joe Thorpe and those of us in this car. We all keep secrets by profession. In a few minutes we'll have those damn letters back, and we'll be on our way to a party," she winked. "Just you see." She thrust the car into gear and peeled away from the curb. Minutes later they pulled up opposite the alpine flight of stone steps leading to the south entrance of The Albert Hall. None of them had eyes for the grand old building—they had seen the three army officers loitering on the lower steps. The Prof and Dizzy recognized Buley and his usual companion, a plump young officer with a moon face called Peters and universally known as "Porky." The other looked barely old enough to be in uniform.

The Prof stepped down, making the car bounce on its springs. He marched across the road followed by Dizzy who had to lengthen his stride to keep up. Buley stepped forward, his sneer already in place. "Captain James Smith, I believe."

"It's customary to salute a superior officer," the Prof barked. Buley visibly jumped, collected himself, and made a lazy salute.

"How very regimental," he said.

"Yes. I am," the Prof stated, his eyes firmly holding Buley's. "Do you have the letters?"

"And businesslike." Buley said, and turned to the men with him, "With none of the pleasantries you associate with a gentleman."

"Neither of us are gentlemen, and there is nothing pleasant about this business. The letters. . ." The Prof extended a hand.

Buley raised an eyebrow. "The consideration. . ." He extended his hand.

The Prof spoke without turning, "Lieutenant Lipman, show him the cash." Dizzy glanced around, the few late-arriving concert-goers showed no interest in the group of army officers. He pulled the envelope from his pocket.

"Do you want to count it?"

"Of course."

"Then please give the letters to Mrs. Courroyer to take to Miss Julien for her inspection." Jac now stood next to them both, glaring at Buley and his friends. Only Buley could meet her gaze, the others shifted their feet and studied the surrounding architecture.

"Don't you trust me?" Buley affected an innocent expression.

"Of course not," Dizzy said, his voice matter-of-fact.

Buley pulled a packet of letters tied with green ribbon from his pocket. He passed them to Jac who snatched them from his hand and stalked across to the car. She stood with her back to them, deliberately concealing Marie, but Buley made a show of leaning past the Prof to waggle his fingers in a parody of greeting.

"Don't push your luck, Buley," the Prof growled.

"Oh, what's the plan then, chaps? Are you going to give me a good thrashing, Smith? Bit of a problem, you being my senior officer and all that."

"Goodness no, Lieutenant! You don't have to worry about me," The Prof suddenly smiled. "It's him you should steer clear of." He jerked his thumb at Dizzy who grinned. Buley looked puzzled for a moment. Dizzy had a build he might have expected of a ballet dancer. Slim and dark with delicate features and soft brown eyes: a girl's face without the mustache. Peters leaned close and whispered in Buley's ear. For a moment he looked uncomfortable, as Dizzy winked, then cracked his knuckles.

Jac strode back to them, "Okay. All present and correct. She looked at Dizzy who handed the envelope to Peters, who made a show of counting the enormous white five-pound notes, each as big as a handkerchief. At last he nodded.

Buley raised his hand, "Step aside. Must dash." He pushed past the Prof as a green Daimler slipped into the curb behind them. He trotted to the car and stepped back to let his friends jump into the passenger compartment. He swung in after them and then leaned out of the window. "Can't delay. Wouldn't want to find ourselves waylaid by some ruffian," he tapped on the glass separating him from the uniformed chauffeur. "Toodle pip." He waved an ironic farewell. They saw him collapse into his seat roaring with laughter as the Daimler swung in a complete circle.

"Bugger!" the Prof swore, as he watched the car turn the corner into Exhibition Road.

Jac frowned, "So was that your plan? To have him waylaid by some ruffian?" Didn't it occur to you he might use a motor to get away?"

The Prof shrugged and pointed. On the far side of the street a thick set man strained over the starting handle of a small open car. "They were meant to follow him."

"Then smack him over the head with a lead filled sock at an opportune moment, and take the money back?"

"Something like that. I prefer a simple plan."

Jac shook her head, "James, you of all people should know that a plan never survives contact with the enemy," she linked her arm through his. "Come on, cheer up, it's Dizzy's money after all, and he will be so rich one day it will seem like pocket change. Isn't that right?"

Dizzy shrugged and smiled, "Actually, I think that may be the best way of spending five hundred quid I will ever find. Worth every penny in my opinion."

They paused by the car for a moment. Dizzy made to step into the front seat but Jac stopped him, opened the back door and motioned him to climb in next to Marie. He hesitated, she was looking at him, tears welling in her eyes. She clutched the letters to her breast. Dizzy took off his cap and sat down next to her. He took her hand.

"Miss Julien, please think nothing of it, I will only be embarrassed if you make a fuss." Marie lost what composure she had left. She fell into his arms sobbing. Dizzy sat there not knowing what to do with his hands. A true English gentleman, he was at a loss and settled for patting her on the back.

"There, there, my dear," his eyes met Vicky's. She just grinned at his discomfort. He pushed Marie away gently and took her chin in his hand to make her look at him. "Look, it's over, finished. Job done. We'll take these damn letters and burn them, and nobody will ever say a word about them again."

"But, Mr. Lipman, all that money. I can never hope to repay you," she collapsed sobbing again, falling against him once more.

"Yes, you can. You can promise me that you will never, ever, do anything so foolish again."

She sat up, "You can be sure of that!" She looked at him again. "If there is anything, and I mean *anything* I can do to repay my debt to you, you must say."

Prof Smith shot a glance at Jac whose face betrayed a struggle not to laugh out loud. Dizzy, the gentleman as ever, refused to misconstrue Marie's innocent remark and just smiled. He whipped a handkerchief from his sleeve and handed it to her.

"Miss Julien, there is something you can do."

"What is it?" she asked, breathless.

"You can compose yourself, and become once more the gay little thing who was such good fun at Will's leaving party at the Ritz. We are going to the Savoy for dinner where you will meet some real gentlemen, including two dashing Frenchmen who will no doubt sweep you off your feet."

A smile broke through, "Oh no! No more gentlemen for me. I thought that pig was a real English gentleman. From now on I am going to behave myself."

Vicky giggled, "That will be the day!"

Jac glanced over her shoulder and grinned at Marie as she pulled off from the curbside, "My dear, Buley is still classed as a gentleman, because of his family. However he belongs to a sub-species known as the cad, or bounder. In future, I suggest you ask me to carry out a thorough investigation of their reputation before you allow yourself to be introduced." She let out the clutch and soon had them bowling through the heart of London. The evening shadows had at last lengthened. As she swung off the Strand into the short street leading to the forecourt of the hotel, Vicky gave an alarmed yelp.

"What's the matter?" Jac called back.

"You're on the wrong side of the road. We should be on the left, even I know that."

The Prof raised his hand, "Take note, Vicky my dear, if you feel homesick and want to drive on the right, this is the only place in the whole of the British Isles where you not only can do it, you *must* do it."

"Why-ever is that?"

The three English people in the car looked at each other, as Jac pulled on the handbrake, each hoping another might have a rational explanation. Marie giggled at last, "It must be one of those famous English eccentricities I keep hearing about."

"Us?" The Prof raised an eyebrow.

"Eccentric?" Jac appeared puzzled.

"Surely not!" Dizzy tried to sound indignant.

"Surely am," Marie took his hand and stepped down. She held on to his fingers, stood on tiptoe and kissed him. He blushed, but held out his arms for the two American girls to take one each.

The Prof held out his arm, "Mrs. Courroyer?"

"Captain Smith," they linked arms and followed the younger trio through the foyer into a blaze of light, music and laughter. In no more than twenty-five years the Savoy had gained a reputation for impeccable service, innovation, and a stunning dance band. It was a magnet for young men and women. Jac had known the Savoy for years, and had seen how the war added a madness to the already frenetic atmosphere.

Marie stopped on the threshold, "My Lawd! This place is jumping."

The Prof took her arm, "Before we do anything else, we have a little job to do." The under manager had appeared at their side and greeted the Prof as an old friend. He led them past the tables and through the swing doors into the hallowed ground of the kitchens. They stopped in front of a range. A chef opened the door to the furnace within without a word, or a glance at the pretty girl clutching a packet of letters. She tossed them into the flames. The chef slammed the door shut, made a slight bow, and returned to his work.

Marie looked at the Prof, "Job done."

He nodded, "Come on, let's join the others." The under manager led them to the table where they found Vicky and Jac already in deep conversation with the two Frenchmen, both resplendent in their best uniforms: black high-collared tunics with a white cravat. The two Frenchmen jumped to their feet. Calmette, the older man, embraced Marie then kissed her on both cheeks like an affectionate uncle. "Ah, the beautiful Mademoiselle Julien. We 'ave heard so much about you."

"All good, I hope," Calmette had no idea how much Marie hoped that was true.

"But of course!" He indicated his companion with a sweeping gesture. "May I introduce Jean Duchenois, aviateur and scourge of the skies."

Duchenois bowed, took Marie's hand and kissed it. He straightened, still holding her hand and gazed into her eyes, *"Mon Dieu!* They said you were beautiful, but I had no idea . . ."* his voice trailed away.

Marie gazed back, captivated by the young pilot's black, soulful eyes. She gulped and heard herself saying, "Charmed, I am sure."

Dizzy turned to Jac, "Good Lord, if I tried a line like that, I would probably get a slap round the chops," he whispered.

Jac leaned close, "Dizzy, if you tried a line like that, you would deserve a slap round the chops. Only a Frenchman could get away with it."

Vicky turned to the Prof who had sat down next to her, "Oh no, not again!" she groaned. Marie and Jean Duchenois stood gazing at each other, oblivious to those around them.

Henri Calmette shrugged his Gallic shrug and laughed, "Waiter! Champagne." The evening roared on in the way any self-respecting young officer would have hoped. The food was magnificent, the drink flowed, the women looked stunning, the conversation was as witty as only champagne-fueled conversation could be. By midnight, Dizzy sprawled in his seat, exhausted by dancing and laughter. His tunic was undone and his face glowed. Calmette called for still more champagne.

"I say, chaps, are we still celebrating?"

Jac, who barely touched alcohol, looked over his shoulder at a couple who had just entered the ballroom and stood talking to a waiter. "Do you know, Dizzy my dear, we just might be."

The woman moved toward them, trailed by a young officer who sported a gold rimmed monocle and smoked a cigarette in a long tortoiseshell holder. Dizzy tried to sit up and focus. The woman had an ethereal air about her. She could have been a model for Aubrey Beardsley. Her face had a sculpted beauty: high cheekbones, the tiny turned-up nose the French called retroussé, and porcelain skin. She wore a deep blue gown that shimmered in the light of the chandeliers.

"Jacquieline, how wonderful to see you," the goddess spoke in a low husky voice. Jac stood and they greeted with continental kisses on each cheek. "Is this the wonderful young man you told me about? Our modern day knight in shining armor?" Jac smiled and nodded, while Dizzy started to struggle to his feet. "No, don't get up dear boy, chivalry is exhausting." Before he could move, the dazzling creature had draped herself over his lap with her arm behind his neck. The buzz of conversation at their table hushed.

"Er, I don't think we've been introduced," Dizzy stammered.

She leaned close and whispered in his ear, "Oh, no need to be so formal darling. Anyway I have a little something for you." Dizzy stared in disbelief as the young officer with her produced the envelope he had handed over to Buley just a few hours before. "I think this is yours." She kissed him full on the lips and unwound herself, trailing her fingers through his hair as he sat, open mouthed in shock. "Must dash, darlings." She blew them a kiss and with a languorous wave disappeared into the crowd with her companion at her heels.

Dizzy sat for a moment with his jaw open staring at the envelope. "It's my five hundred quid!"

Jac took it from him and quickly counted, "Not quite my dear, Eleanor has taken her ten percent commission, but I was sure you wouldn't begrudge her fifty pounds for her trouble."

"Her trouble? I don't understand," Dizzy looked from her to the Prof, and the two Frenchmen.

Calmette grinned and winked, "I do not think she finds it trouble." The Prof just smiled.

Jac patted him on the cheek, "You are so sweet, Dizzy. You really don't understand do you?"

He frowned, "No I'm sorry, I don't. What has that gorgeous girl got to do with Buley?"

Jac raised her eyes to the ceiling then took his hand, "Dizzy, you must have noticed that a certain type of gal, often from a very good family, has found the war a wonderful liberating experience. She has the excuse to be in London doing some token war work, getting her picture in the papers bandaging a nice tidy injury, and all that sort of rot."

"Well yes, I know it irritates the hell out of the real nurses."

"These gals couldn't care less about that. They have the pick of the handsome young officers, a constantly changing round of young officers what with leave and casualties, and they have a high old time, and live very well on the proceeds."

"What do you mean by proceeds?"

Jac sat back and looked at him, a slight smile on her lips, "Dizzy, these are often wealthy young men like yourself."

"Ohmigod! You're not suggesting that she's a . . . "

"Tart? Yes. A very high-class tart though."

"What! A professional woman?" his voice rose.

Jac patted his hand soothingly, "Oh no, I wouldn't go that far . . . more of an enthusiastic amateur in the finest English tradition. She would never charge in the obvious way, but these young officers can be very generous when it comes to gifts you know."

"But Buley, the pig, how?"

Jac laughed out loud, "Men! You are hopeless. Eleanor has had Buley wrapped round her little finger for months. He would do anything for her. He gave her the money. She told him she needed five hundred pounds to settle an embarrassing debt, and he wanted to play the gentleman. The man is pathetic."

Dizzy blew out his cheeks as he looked around the table at his friends who smiled sympathetically. "Phew! I really am an innocent abroad."

The Prof nodded, "You are, old chum," he turned to Jac. "So that was your plan. It beat mine into a cocked hat. I suppose that's what you meant by 'subtle.' "

She grinned, "Yes, allow me to look smug."

"Be as smug as you like."

Dizzy sat for a moment looking at his money fondly, "Now we really are celebrating." He looked up, "Waiter! More champagne please."

CHAPTER 19

German Imperial Naval Airship Division, North Germany

Oberleutnant zur See, Jochen Wolff, held a sausage above his plate, "Now you see, Fraulein Ellerkamm, imagine this *wurst* is our airship."

Her eyes sparkled, "Without the bend in the middle."

He laughed, "Indeed we hope so." He had fallen under her spell. "And without the mustard of course."

"Of course."

"Now the engines are mounted here and here. It is important to understand that our beautiful Zeppelin does not rely on the lift of the gas alone to fly, the engines thrust us through the air, and at the same time give us what we airship men like to call dynamic lift. The pressure of the air passing under our hull helps to keep us up."

Matty nodded, "So just as some fish will sink to the bottom if they stop swimming, the airship will tend to sink to the ground without the power of the engines?"

Wolff looked at her with new respect, "A splendid example, Fraulein Ellerkamm!"

"Please, Jochen, you must call me Matty," she gave him her full-power smile. They sat together in the dining room of the Crown Hotel. Wolff had been sent by the base commander to join their guests at breakfast before the promised flight. Like all the officers they had met so far, he spoke near perfect English. With his immaculate uniform, slim build, and slicked back dark hair with perfect center parting, Will could imagine him as the maître d' of an expensive restaurant. Martin Friedmann could not have chosen a better tour guide.

"But the Zeppelin can still hover at altitude with the engines stopped, I believe," Will said.

Wolff warmed to his theme, "Yes, it is one of the safety features of airship flight. However, it is done by dropping ballast to achieve a balance, and then we have to vent precious gas to come down again. A skilful captain will make perfect buoyancy near the ground, and then use his engines to take him to cruising altitude, reducing speed to come down and so saving gas and ballast."

Matty poured more coffee into Wolff's cup, "But I recall from my science class at high school that the gas expands as you go higher. Does that cause a problem?"

Wolff nodded his thanks, "Only because we then have to vent gas and lose it, and then we have to make the balance calculations again."

"Surely you have to make rapid readjustment when you drop your bombs? Your craft must shoot up into the air when it is relieved of that much weight." Will said.

Wolff winced, "You are correct, Will, but it is something I personally do not like to think about, even though it is my duty. I look forward to the balance problem when we drop the mail on London when we overfly on our luxury passenger service to New York."

Matty frowned, "Will, stop playing devil's advocate."

He nodded, "Telling off accepted, Matty." He turned to Wolff with a smile, "So you are another reluctant military man, Jochen?"

Wolff lowered his voice, "I am a reservist as are most of my comrades: sailors first, soldiers second. It is my duty to serve my country, but one day this will be over, and soon, God willing, and then we can show the world just what the Zeppelin can really do."

"I think everybody I have spoken to here believes the airship is the future of long-distance travel. You almost have me convinced."

Wolff's face brightened, "Good! After today's little tour we will make a new disciple of you, Will. I expect you to write great things about us for your magazine." He pushed his chair back, "Ladies and gentlemen, if you are finished, we must now make our way to the field. Your aerial carriage awaits!" A ripple of applause ran around the dining room. The guests from the German American Alliance followed Wolff outside to a bus waiting on the forecourt. Sentries presented arms as the bus rolled through the gates of the airship station ten minutes later without stopping. They turned on to a dusty track running beside the perimeter fence. The three massive sheds proved every bit as imposing as the glimpse they had seen the previous day promised. They stood on the far side of the field that was in itself the largest flying ground Will had seen. The flat plain and surrounding countryside gave no scale to the airship hangars, but the people and vehicles gathered before them gave an indication of their size as the bus trundled along the track towards them.

Matty's party fell silent. They stepped from the bus gazing awestruck at the spectacle before them, their eyes lifted trying to take in the height of the double hangar. Nothing had prepared their imagination for the sheer size of this cathedral to aviation. None had seen a man-made structure so breathtaking.

Wolff ushered them into a circle, "Ladies and gentlemen, you see before you our biggest hangar, known as 'TOSKA.' Beyond you can see the single hangars, 'TOBIAS' and 'TONI.' "

Dorothy Schubert raised her hand, "Excuse me, sir. How many Zeppelins do you get in each shed?"

Wolff smiled, "Two here in TOSKA, just one each in TOBIAS and TONI."

Dorothy's eyes opened wide, "Do you mean the Zeppelins are as big as these sheds? That's impossible!"

Wolff laughed, "Permit me," he turned and waved to a group of men standing at the corner of the hangar. "Open the doors!" An electric motor whined. Nothing happened for a few seconds and then, with a grating screech the doors began to slide apart on steel tracks. They watched in astonishment as the morning sun flooded the interior of the hangar, revealing the contents as if a stage curtain had been slowly drawn open. Will smiled, it was arranged as a piece of pure theater for their benefit.

The second the doors stopped rolling, they heard a trumpet fanfare, followed by the thump of a military band. The airship *Viktoria* edged forward. As she nosed out of the shed into the sunlight, Will saw that she floated above an electric dolly, controlled by a sailor walking beside it, that ran on the triple track extending out on to the tarmac where they stood. The dolly drew her forward, while two long lines of marching men held ropes suspended from the sides and the control gondola to control any sideways movement. The band led the procession.

Georg Klaas, touched Will on the elbow, "How do you like our little show, Will?"

Will turned and shook Klaas's outstretched hand, "Magnificent, Georg. Barnum and Bailey could not have done it better."

Klaas looked puzzled for a moment, then slapped Will on the back, "Oh yes! The circus people. My thoughts exactly." He touched Will's arm and indicated for him to step away from the group, now standing with mouths open in astonishment as they craned their heads back to try to take in the size of the Zeppelin. "Kapitan Friedmann has asked that you join us in the control gondola. The rest of your party will be seated in the car amidships. I hope that it is permissible with you?"

Will glanced up at the gondola now above their heads, "Georg, it will be an honor. I am sure Matty can manage without me for the day."

Klaas coughed, "But not for the night!" he winked and laughed. Will turned to him, eyes open wide with surprise. "Don't worry, Will, your secret is safe with the navy. Even though we are all jealous as hell."

"But how?"

Klaas chuckled, "This place is worse than a Bavarian village for gossip. But a piece of advice, move the damn ladder before daybreak."

Will passed his hand over his face, "Oh my, that was indiscreet."

Klaas briskly changed the subject, "So what do you think of dear little *Viktoria*?" he waved a hand to indicate the airship now floating above them.

Will laughed, "Little?" They stood beneath the control gondola near the bow. The gentle curve of the hull made it impossible to see the entire length of the ship.

Klaas nodded, "Yes, she is only about one hundred fifty-meters long, not even five hundred of your American feet."

"But that makes her longer than most ocean liners."

"Yes, but the new ships will be over two hundred meters, so we class her as a small training vessel. That white band around her nose warns other ships to give us plenty of room in case a new helmsman cannot tell his port from his starboard." Klaas looked thoughtful for a moment, then laughed, "or the navigator can't tell 'his arse from his elbow,' as the British say."

Will pointed along the belly of the ship, "Is this why she has only three engines?" Two pod-like structures extended to the side and below nearer the tail, beyond the second gondola. Each pod carried a huge two-bladed propeller mounted on the rear to act as a pusher.

Klaas shook his head, "No, we have four new Maybach engines. This prop here," he pointed to the propeller attached to the rear of the control gondola above their heads, "is driven by two engines in series in a separate engine room behind this bulkhead."

"Is that unusual?"

"Yes, but no two Zeppelins ever seem to be the same, we are always experimenting with new ideas. Kapitan Friedmann's idea is that we should let the military pay for all the experiments, and then when the fleet is handed over to the merchant service when this war is finished, all the investment will have been made."

The bulk of the airship hung between them and the sun putting them in shade, but the air still felt oppressively warm. "We are lucky to have such still conditions," Will said.

Klaas sucked his teeth, "Yes, but I am a little concerned about visibility, and this heat could make some storms later."

"Still, your local knowledge will help I am sure," Will said.

Klaas shook his head, "I wish I could claim that, but I have only been transferred two weeks ago to Tondern. Before that I served in Belgium."

"Ah, promotion?"

Klaas smiled, "Not exactly, my old Kapitan arranged for my transfer."

Will picked up on the tone in Klaas's voice, "Oh, did you not get along?"

"You could say that. I am an old sea dog and I suppose I can be less than diplomatic."

"I would rather go flying with an old sea dog than with a smooth-tongued diplomat. I am sure you will navigate us safely on our trip."

"Oh yes, in fact we will probably be in sight of the station for most of our little *rundfahrt*. I plan a simple tour over the town, and then down the coast to see if we can spot a battleship to amuse our passengers." He pointed at the gondola mounted halfway down the length of the airship. The passengers sat in what looked like a smooth aluminium boat hull suspended from the belly of the Zeppelin, glazed panels rose up and out from what would have been the sides if it had been a boat, to join with the body of the airship and enclose them. They rode in comfort in a long aluminium and glass capsule looking out as if from a glass house. A door in the side gave access. "They will have a perfect view. It is usually used for training navigators, but we have stripped out the tables and fitted chairs and settees. We have even added a little steward's station for serving refreshments. You might say we are practicing for peace," he indicated a long table that had been set up near the aft gondola. "Come, we will issue you with a pair of these stylish shoes," he lifted his foot to show that he wore short boots with soles made of a close-woven rope material. "Guaranteed not to make sparks."

They joined the rest of the party at the table. Each passenger sat in turn in a chair where a quartermaster fitted them with a pair of the safety shoes in exchange for their own footwear, and a signature in a ledger. The Alliance party laughed and joked among themselves and with the quartermaster, and another helper who made a show of looking away as he fitted the ladies into their boots.

"Ah, Bruno I knew I could rely on you to be a gentleman!" Klaas greeted the big man as he knelt at Dorothy Schubert's feet.

He looked up with a grin, "The sawbones said I had to be careful, sir. The sight of all these pretty ankles might be too much for a man with my poor health." Dorothy reacted as Will expected, with a giggle as Bruno gave her a big wink. He stood and raised her to her feet. "Enjoy your ride, madam."

She patted his cheek, "I'm sure I will."

Bruno wore civilian clothes: his jacket hung over the back of the chair; he had his shirtsleeves rolled to the elbow revealing heavy-muscled forearms. He had a barrel chest and a thick neck. Bright blue eyes twinkled from a square, tanned face over a big handlebar mustache. He cropped his gray hair short.

Klaas introduced him, "Will, I would like you to meet the only real pilot on the field, Feldwebel Bruno Loewe, holder of the Iron Cross, First Class."

He took Will's hand in a bone-crushing grip, "Very pleased to meet you, sir. I have to say it is just plain Bruno Loewe these days" He spoke good, but heavily accented English.

Klaas laughed, "You will always be the Drill Sergeant to us, Bruno."

"Feldwebel? I thought that is an army rank," Will said.

"It is, sir. I do not know about the American Army, but the British have their company sergeant major as the same rank. I am like a turkey among seagulls on this base. A flightless bird who lives on land," he said with a grin.

"You are grounded? I am sorry to hear that."

Bruno shrugged, "For now—but I think I have good luck to be here. I flew two-seaters in France. An Englander pilot put a bullet through my lung, and I was made prisoner. But I have no complaints, the British doctors saved my life and arranged for me to be repatriated under an exchange. I spent a few weeks in a Swiss hospital and now here I am back home, nearly good like new. A lucky man."

"I should say you are! Is there no chance to get back to flying?"

"*Es tut mir leid,* not a hope. They say even if I was fit, I am too old, and I cannot serve under the terms of the prisoner exchange, so they sent me home with an honorable discharge and an Iron Cross. Better than many poor bastards who just get a wooden cross."

Klaas smiled, "Well, the army's loss is the navy's gain. We couldn't do without you."

"Thank you, sir."

Klaas turned to Will, "Bruno is not a man to sit around on his backside. He volunteered to work here as a welfare officer for our young sailors, making sure they stay out of trouble."

Bruno threw back his head and roared with laughter, "And that is a big job as you would think, Mr. Turner." He ushered Will into the chair and fitted him with his safety shoes. Will signed the ledger, they shook hands again and Klaas led the way to the gondola. Bruno watched him walk away, his bright smile replaced by a thoughtful frown. Alone now he sat down and spun the ledger towards him. He studied Will's signature for a long moment, and then pulled his wallet from the jacket hanging on the chair back. Anybody watching would have thought it strange but he seemed reluctant to open it. At last he pulled a folded slip of faded paper from the wallet. He studied it for a moment then held it against the ledger.

"Damn!" he spoke under his breath.

Will followed Klaas up a short ladder fitted to the side of the gondola. He had expected the Zeppelin to be controlled much like a ship, but he was surprised at how similar it seemed to be—with the engine telegraphs and big ships' wheels to control rudders and elevators. Klaas gave him a quick tour; a few paces covered the length of the gondola. A ladder disappeared through a hatch in the roof at the rear of the car. Klaas jerked his thumb toward it. "That goes up to the catwalk that runs above the keel of the ship. I will take you on a tour later, but we are anxious to get underway as soon as possible, so for now . . ."

"Shut up and stay out of the way?" Will grinned.

Klaas squeezed his arm, "You are a good guest," he pointed to a seat fixed to the bulkhead next to the ladder. Will sat down and watched the flight crew making the airship ready to fly. Martin Friedmann had not boarded yet, but he heard his voice. He realized the captain stood directly below the window next to where Will sat, talking to another officer. Will's command of German was good enough not only to understand what the discussion was about, but also to catch the inference that this was more than a discussion, it was a full-blown argument couched in the strained polite language used when somebody argues against the views of a superior. It took a second for Will to recognize the other voice. It was Strasser.

The issue was simple. The captain wanted to cut the trip short because all his instincts told him that thunderstorms, a Zeppelin captain's nightmare, could erupt at any time. Strasser was adamant that they must not lose face and the journey should be extended, not cut short.

Inevitably, Strasser won. Will heard a strained, *"Jawohl"* and a click of the heels as Martin saluted. Seconds later he sprang up the steps, a broad smile on his handsome face, unaware that at least one person on board had overheard his misgivings.

"Gentlemen, are we ready to fly?" Shouts of "Ready" and "All correct" came from the crewmen standing to their controls. Martin turned to the engineer standing by the engine telegraphs, "Start the engines." Will heard a loud hiss from behind the bulkhead followed by the cough of big gasoline engines coming to life. They steadied to a rumble, transmitted through the deck beneath his feet. The engineer watched a bank of indicators above his head. He held up his clenched right fist and flicked up a finger as each of the needles jumped on the dial.

"Eins, Zwei, Drei," he paused for a second. *"Vier! All engines running."*

Martin nodded to Georg Klaas, "Cast off, navigator." Klaas saluted, leaned from the open side window and shouted an order. Nothing happened for several seconds, then Will saw his perspective of the people waving below the gondola had changed, they grew smaller. Instead of the roar, the rush of wind and clatter of an airplane taking off, with all the vibration and sensations of speed that created, the Zeppelin's ascent was so smooth the only immediate indication of flight came with the expanding view around them. The people below became white blobs, their bodies foreshortened so only their upturned faces showed. The hangars, so huge and intimidating from the ground diminished as they took their place in a gentle landscape of green fields and marsh where the land nudged against the North Sea, now visible as a glittering line beneath a misty horizon. It was hard to discern where the sea ended and the sky began. The summer sun, already high, had still not burned away the overnight mist. Will stood and squinted into a milky white sky.

Martin gave his orders, only raising his voice to be heard over the rumble of the engines. Most of his instructions he gave with a nod or a movement of his hand, his crew so practiced they moved like the members of a concert orchestra, each absorbed in his own part, but watching Martin Friedmann, their conductor, as he held them together in harmony. He stood behind the helmsman, feet apart, then turned with his hands held out with the palms turned upwards.

"Gentlemen," he raised his hands, "let's fly." The engineer pushed the four engine-room telegraphs to 'full ahead.' The elevator man spun his big wheel, then yanked on a toggle above his head to release water ballast from the nose. Will watched it trail away, the fine spray dissolving like smoke. The deck tilted beneath their feet. Will staggered for a moment and grabbed the edge of the chart table for balance. His stomach fell, for all the world he felt as if he stood in one of the Otis company's new high-speed elevators, as *Viktoria* raised her nose and climbed into the bright summer sky. Martin smiled, "Have you ever climbed like this in an airplane, Will?"

"Never. We must be making over a thousand feet a minute."

"Yes, nearly five hundred meters. We have a very light load. We weighed off with less than full volume of hydrogen gas and still we climb like a bird. Excuse me," Martin turned to the helmsman. "Bring her round to two hundred degrees." The horizon moved past the windows revealing a new view of the coast. The land now disappeared into the glowing murk on their left while a long line of sandy beaches stretched below. Martin leaned close again, the drone of the engines at full power making it harder to be heard. "South by southwest, more or less. Klaas and I have decided that we will head down the coast first and then return to show our guests the town from the air. There may be some rough weather coming up from the south and best to go there before it arrives, then move away."

Will pointed forward; the helmsman had stopped the turn. "The flight is so smooth it feels as if we stand still and the world moves around us."

Martin laughed, "If we do our job well, that is what the passengers think. And if my experience of passengers in First Class on an ocean liner holds true, they think the world turns around them anyway."

Will smiled and nodded, "I know just what you mean."

Georg touched his arm, and pointed upwards, "Are you ready for a tour of the ship?"

"You bet!" He followed the navigator up the short ladder through the hatch. Georg reached down to help him up on to his feet on the catwalk. Will looked around as he stood, now inside the hull of the ship and gasped. "Good God almighty, Georg, what a piece of work!" The skin of the Zeppelin allowed a soft light to fill the interior. In many places sunbeams speared through the skin where gaps showed where the outer fabric panels joined. It was as if he stood inside an old barn on a bright summer's day. The roar of the engines was now muted to a drone, allowing conversation at normal levels. Ducking down and looking along the catwalk, a thin lattice of aluminium rails filled in with flat panels of plywood to make a footway, he could see almost to the end of the ship, nearly five hundred feet away. As they moved along they ducked under the gasbags that hung suspended within the vast latticework rings that formed the circular shape of the Zeppelin.

Georg prodded one of the bags, it gave to his touch, "There is surprisingly little leakage. Spring-loaded valves operate to vent gas if the internal pressure goes too high, but we can also vent gas from the control car." He led the way further aft to a platform surrounding a rectangular bay. He leaned on the safety rail and pointed down to a flat panel split along the length of the airship. Will could just make out the ground passing beneath through the gap between the panels.

"This is where the ship had its sub-cloud car while on active service."

"Sub-cloud car?"

Georg nodded, "Yes, it is a little one-man vehicle lowered by a wire from a winch that would stand here. It looks like a very long bomb complete with tail flights to keep it steady, about three meters long. There is a little cockpit and a windscreen for the man inside, and a telephone link to the control car."

"What is it used for?"

Georg grinned and shook his head, "It is one of those ideas that perhaps sounded good over a long dinner. In theory the ship is supposed to hover concealed above or in the clouds. The car is lowered beneath the clouds and the rider then directs the bombing by telephone, while the ship stays hidden from searchlights and guns."

"And in practice? It sounds frightening for the man given the job."

"Not as bad as it sounds. I tried it and it was an interesting experience. It is quite a popular duty with some men because they are allowed to smoke, but in practice it adds much weight and drag. That winch and cable on their own weigh over a ton, and the drag! Well let me tell you what happened to Petersen's sailmaker when he tried it on L32. They lowered it over the East of England and had their man down to less than five hundred meters off the ground while they motored along two thousand meters above. Nobody realized the drag had started to pull the ship down and suddenly poor old Pops Schneider, the sailmaker, looked ahead through a cloud of pipe smoke and saw the roof of an English public house coming straight towards him in the moonlight."

"Goodness! What happened?"

"He yelled on the telephone for them to pull him up, but he still knocked a chimney pot clean off. He nearly had it in his lap. He told me the people coming from the pub all looked up and all he could do was wave and shout a cheery, *Guten Abend* as he sailed off into the night."

"That is a terrific story to tell his grandchildren."

"Yes, and the best part is that it was true. A few weeks later we read in the English *Times* newspaper that some villagers in Norfolk had sworn on oath that they had seen a terrible flying monster that had knocked the chimney pot from their pub. They thought it was the devil, not making any connection with our ships. Poor old Pops will never live it down." Georg pointed towards the tail, "Come."

They paused above a hatch. Georg knelt and opened it, "Hello, everybody! Is Oberleutnant Wollf looking after you?" Will knelt and waved to Matty, seated at the front of the passenger gondola revealed under the hatch.

She waved back, "We could not have better service, thank you." Her people sat drinking coffee from bone china cups served by a white-coated mess steward, as they lounged in armchairs admiring the view through the picture windows. Wollf glanced up, he stood next to Dorothy Schubert with a map spread on the low table in front of her.

"Are we on course, Mr. Navigator?" Wollf asked with a smile.

Georg waved his hand, "You would never know if we are not." He winked at Dorothy, "Don't believe a word he tells you, Frau Schubert, especially if he tells you that you can see Berlin below."

She patted Wollf's hand, "I would go anywhere with Jochen," she smiled up at him.

Georg laughed, "Enjoy the rest of the trip, my friends." He closed the hatch and they scrambled to their feet. Georg blew out his cheeks, "*Mein Gott!* That woman is . . . is . . . how do you say in English?"

"A flirt."

"Yes, a flirt! I do not understand why her husband does not say something. He is either patient, or an idiot."

"I think he is so busy giving everybody the benefit of his opinion, he never notices."

Georg nodded, "I think you are correct." He pointed toward the tail, "Come, this is the interesting part." They moved along the catwalk, the noise of the rear engines growing. He pointed to two cylindrical tanks mounted along the axis of the keel at head height on either side of the cat-walk. "Benzin in gravity tanks, we are not carrying much today for this short flight," he pointed to four tanks lying along the keel beneath the cat-walk. These are our slips tanks, the long-range reserve. If it is needed, it has to be pumped into each service tank using those levers." Long-han-dled pumps stood fixed to the framework supporting the gravity tanks.

Will reached out and touched a pump handle. "Good exercise."

"It warms you on a cold night." He beckoned Will forward and pointed. A door-sized section of fabric was missing from the hull. A short length of companionway led to it. Georg motioned him forward. The din of the motors now throbbed in his ears. An icy wind slapped his face as he stepped forward and looked out, then recoiled.

"Whoa!"

Georg laughed, "Quite a surprise first time you see it, don't you think?"

Will recovered himself, then laughed with him, "Good Lord! And your people use that?"

"Of course, it is quite safe." The open section in the hull gave access to the starboard, rear engine gondola, little more than an egg shaped shell the size of a large automobile. This was supported on struts fixed to the internal framework, but Will had been surprised by the means of reach-ing it. A single ladder, laid flat, with just two wires on each side at waist height to act as handrails, stretched across a gap over ten-feet wide. Three thousand feet of thin, empty air lay between the ladder and the North Sea. Georg tapped his head, "It is all in the mind."

"Then you won't *mind* if I don't use it."

Georg threw back his head and roared with laughter, "A good play on English words. No, you are sensible. Oh! Excuse me." An engineer had stuck his head out of the hatch in the side of the gondola and beckoned to Georg. He handed his cap to Will and casually stepped on to the ladder and strolled across. He bent down to enable the engineer to cup his hand around his ear and shout a message. Georg nodded, stood up and walked back. "Thank you, Will," he took his cap back and settled it on his head. "They have a magneto, *kaput,* but these new Maybachs have two, so it is not a big problem. Perhaps losing fifty revolutions at the propeller. Come, or we will miss coffee in the control car. This is the real stuff, not that filth made from acorns."

They made their way back along the catwalk to the bow of the ship. Will followed Georg through the hatch back into the control car. As he stepped from the ladder the radio operator looked up from his desk.

"Herr Turner, there is a message for you."

"For me?"

"Yes, please don't go away when we land, an officer from the Army Field Security Service wishes to speak with you."

CHAPTER 20

Estuary of The River Thames, England

Windy Gale opened the throttle and pushed the stick forward. His B.E.2 wobbled up on its wheels. He picked a tree in the distance and pinned it between two struts in his line of vision by deft pressure on the rudder pedals, to keep his run straight. He held the stick steady, resisting the temptation to pull back too soon and rush his machine. The ride smoothed as the wings took the weight, another bump as his wheels touched again, and he sailed into the air. He checked his oil pressure and settled into the climb. The village passed beneath his wings and he looked over the side to wave back to his friends sitting in the beer garden of the Black Swan, enjoying the warm evening.

It was Midsummer's Day, Saturday the twenty-fourth of June; ten o'clock in the evening and still light enough to read a newspaper. He smiled at the thought of Will Turner, the American, who could never quite believe how long the daylight lasted in the English summer. You had to look at a globe to appreciate just how far north England lay compared to most of the Continental United States, giving long lingering days in summer, and long brutal nights in winter. He wondered what Turner would be up to now on his leave. Probably sitting on the veranda of the old plantation house sipping a mint julep. Windy had traveled to the American South before the war, and enjoyed two weeks of the best shootin' and fishin' of his life. He planned to return. For now he concentrated on the task in hand.

Chris Davey

It seemed inconceivable that the Germans might try a raid at this time of the year. With a speed of only sixty miles an hour, a Zeppelin could not make a run inland, and escape before the half-light of the northern dawn silhouetted it against the sky. But Windy had argued that if he were a German planner, he would try something just because it did seem inconceivable. Perhaps not an attempt to bomb London, the big prize, but why not a quick dash across the North Sea to hit one of the ports during the two or three hours of near darkness? The weather would help this evening, with a light westerly wind at altitude to aid an escape. He had argued his case to such good effect Simpson had authorized him to make a patrol to the east. Windy had been delighted, he was supposed to be duty officer so he could not join the party at The Black Swan anyway. There would be plenty of time to stroll to the pub tomorrow, his day off.

He soon reached the observation post near Maldon. The regular rotation of staff had brought McGuigan and his team back to that position, and Windy knew he could rely on them. The fields below had slipped into the purple twilight of dusk, but enough light remained at two thousand feet to cast a glow over his instrument board. He held his signaling lamp over the side and beamed his recognition letter down to the men below. Seconds later the flickering Morse reply flashed back, "Nothing to report." Windy turned away, perhaps a tour up the coast towards Felixstowe might be rewarding. As he banked, he caught the flash of light on the wings of a turning airplane. The rays from the sinking sun, just visible at height but long since out of sight on the ground, illuminated a biplane. Windy smiled to himself. He recognized young Ned Robson's favorite Avro 504. Ned claimed to be up testing a new lighting system, but in reality he flew for the joy of it, and was always looking for trouble. Ned made it no secret that he wanted to be the first man to bring a Zeppelin down. He appeared to be heading north up the coast, so Windy could see no point in doubling up in that sector.

He turned south toward the Thames Estuary. It shone silver between the dark mass of Essex below, and the county of Kent on the far side. He flew on a roving commission, no orders constrained where he might search. German seaplanes had made several incursions in recent weeks, dropping bombs on Margate, Chatham, and Dover, doing little damage but creating a nuisance that had the press demanding action from the RFC. This might be his lucky day, or night. He angled towards London to cross the river at a narrow point to be able to glide to either side if his engine failed. Windy could swim, but even in high summer the Thames Estuary would be cold and besides, he was wearing his best trousers. He crossed the river below Tilbury, then followed the Kent coast towards the North Foreland, the tip of land that jutted out into the English Channel. The white finger of a searchlight sprang up from Chatham, then waved around in the hope of finding him. He flew in near darkness now. A few seconds later a shell burst two hundred yards to his left, leaving the imprint of its flash dancing on the retina of his eye. A second shell exploded half a mile to his right.

"Bloody matelots!" Windy swore at the naval gunners but held his course. They fired blind at an unknown airplane and they had no way of knowing what nationality it was. He could hardly blame them for taking a pot shot or two. He cut the corner over the oddly named Isle of Thanet, that part of Kent that appeared to be as solidly connected to the rest of the country as any other, but still claimed to be an island. He glanced at his altimeter. The dim bulb showed the needle at two thousand feet. Windy pushed the throttle forward and climbed as he approached the Port of Dover. If a Hun airplane did make the mistake of calling while he flew overhead, he wanted to have the advantage of height.

He made out the distinctive shape of the breakwater protecting Dover harbor as he wheeled over the town. He knew the landing ground next to Dover Castle and contemplated dropping down to see if he could land and cadge a cup of tea, but dismissed the idea as it came into his head.

Although he could make out some detail on the ground in the odd gleam of this summer night, the thought of damaging his airplane made him cautious. It was not the thought of Simpson's thunderous lecture, but the look of icy reproof he knew he would see in the eyes of the mechanics and riggers if he bent a wingtip or broke a wheel. There were certain people that an English gentleman tried to earn respect from. This modern age had added mechanic to the old list of cricket captain, butler and gamekeeper. Windy aspired to be known as a gentleman who knew his stuff.

A flash of light caught his eye, far off to the left, out over the sea towards France. He looked again; perhaps a warship had caught a German raider briefly in a searchlight. He saw it again: dim but now persistent, a wavering, flickering gleam. Windy pushed his goggles up and stared. Lightning maybe, far over France where the summer heat gave birth to the thunderstorms that wandered up across the south of England. No, this was continuous, sometimes flaring to light the horizon, then fading to a glow, but constant.

Realisation dawned, "My sainted aunt!" Windy spoke out loud. "Artillery."

❋ ✦━━✦ ❋

David Highams regarded Windy with one eyebrow cocked, it made him look like a suspicious schoolteacher presented with a note for absence.

"The Somme must be over eighty miles from Dover. Are you saying you could see gun flashes from there?"

"As I live and breath old boy. Last night, from four thousand feet they lit up the sky." Windy reached over the breakfast table and selected a slice of toast.

Jankowski sipped his coffee and regarded Windy over the rim of the cup, "Bloody oath, sport, what kind of a barrage lights up the sky like that?"

"The heaviest in the unfortunate history of mankind," Dick Thomas looked up from the sheet of paper he held in his one hand. "It kicked off yesterday according to these orders from HQ."

"So this is it, then," Ned Robson looked around the table. "The big push has started."

Dick nodded, "It certainly appears that way."

"And we're stuck here in this backwater chasing shadows while the biggest battle in history is fought in France," Ned gripped the edge of the table.

The Prof lowered his newspaper and looked at him, "You don't like it here?" he smiled. "After all the trouble we've taken to make it comfortable?" He shook his head and sighed, "The youth of today."

Ned relaxed and sat back with an embarrassed grin, "You know what I mean."

"I take it you mean you would prefer to be over there in the thick of the action, dodging shells and strafing the Hun?"

"Yes."

The Prof shook his head, "Forget it. We're all supposed to be on Home Establishment. It's the luck of the draw where you happen to be when the action kicks off. In fact, we are all stretching it by being here with this crowd, because strictly speaking we should not be anywhere near combat. You could just as easily be instructing, or touring schools recruiting more cannon fodder."

Ned waved the butter knife above his plate, "Yes, but it's all going to be over now, in a matter of a few weeks." His comrades greeted this with snorts of derision and loud laughter.

"Ned, I know you were still at school but surely you remember that back in 'Fourteen, it was all going to be over by Christmas?" Windy spoke gently.

Ned looked around the table, a deep frown on his face. He looked younger than ever, "Come on, chaps, you heard, 'the biggest barrage in history.' The German line will never be able to withstand that."

Stan Jackson sawed at a piece of bacon, "Don't you believe it, mate. I saw what they've done close-up when I went over with Colonel Brett. It'll take more than a few whiz-bangs to winkle the bastards out of those bunkers."

Louis Calmette had followed the discussion with interest, "Ned, *mon brave,* your spirit, this is a good thing, but my waters tell me you 'ave much time to earn that Victoria Cross. Be patient, there are plenty boches for all."

Dick Thomas held up the sheet of orders for all to see, "If this prediction from HQ is correct, there will be enough boches to keep even you happy, Ned. They think that the German Navy will be tasked to make raids on the east coast and up the Thames as far as London using Zeps by night, seaplanes night and day, whatever, to try to draw RFC squadrons away from the big push." He slid his chair back and stood, "It might get lively chaps, make sure your aeroplanes are in tip-top condition. We don't want to be caught with our trousers down."

The Prof joined Dizzy inspecting their favorite F.E.2 after breakfast. "Do you think HQ are right?"

Dizzy looked up at the sky, "Do you know what I would do if I ran the German military?"

"Go on."

"I would attack the ports and shipping. We've got thousands of men camped behind most of the Channel ports and up to Harwich waiting to reinforce the men already in France. They have no protection, no trenches dug because HQ see no danger. In fact their tents are all lined up nice and neat to make it easier to bomb and strafe them."

The Prof nodded, "I see your point."

"And as for the shipping! Imagine the carnage if they managed to bomb a transport ship loaded with troops for the crossing. You could drown thousands for the cost of one bomb. Destroy a complete battalion that might otherwise be pouring over the top to attack your line a few days later." Dizzy tugged on a bracing wire, "It grieves me to agree with HQ on anything, but on this occasion they could be barking up the right tree. If the Hun does pull something like this, we would have to pull squadrons back to deal with it.

The Prof nodded, "Better pull our trousers up then."

That evening found Dizzy and The Prof airborne and dashing for the east coast. The sun, still well above the horizon, lit a column of smoke rising above Harwich that told its own story. The Prof trained his field glasses on the sky above the port.

He stood and leaned back to speak with Dizzy. Having the din of the engine behind made it just possible to communicate by yelling over the roar of the wind. "How does it feel to be always right?"

"I wish I wasn't."

The Prof pointed ahead, "Two small aeroplanes, one big bugger I don't recognize, we'll go after that." A second F.E.2 flown by the Australians, Jankowski and Jackson trailed behind. Ned Robson's Avro 504 could be seen as a speck above and behind them. He had recently fitted a Lewis gun to the center section of his top wing to fire straight ahead over the propeller, and had high hopes of success.

The smoke poured from the superstructure of a small troopship aground on the muddy banks of the River Stour outside the harbor entrance. Dizzy's projected disaster looked to have come to pass. Even from two thousand feet they could see men struggling in the thick, brown water. Small boats swarmed around the stricken vessel. The dirty smudges of anti-aircraft shells drifted in the air while glowing green balls of light curled up slowly from ships in the harbor. Their one pound "pom pom" automatic cannon fired a low velocity round that seemed to make the tracers hang in the air.

Dizzy recognized the two seaplanes as Friedrichshafen two-seaters, he wondered if they had hit the ship as their bomb load could only be small.

The third machine seemed the likely culprit. He made rapid calculations as they drew closer. It was bigger than the two seaplanes, and had the strangest configuration of any airplane he had seen. A twin-engined biplane, the fuselage sat on the upper wing, with the engines mounted on the lower wing driving conventional tractor propellers. That was the only conventional thing about it. The tail unit carried two vertical stabilizers, clearly designed to take advantage of the slipstream generated by the propellers to increase control at low speed. The makers had painted it a drab dark green, relieved by white squares on the wings and tail surfaces framing the sinister black Maltese cross national markings.

Dizzy opened the throttle wide and pushed the nose down for speed, intent on driving the enemy away from the stricken troopship. As they closed, the Prof opened fire at long range on the nearest seaplane. No point in trying for surprise. He wanted them rattled. He wanted them to run. From behind and below, Stan and Basil Jankowski saw the bombs falling from all three enemy machines as they jettisoned their remaining loads to explode harmlessly in the estuary and fields. Stan did not blame them for a moment. Eighty miles from home across a hostile sea, their best chance was to run for it. They had struck a heavy blow. There would be iron crosses all round, if they made it.

Stan saw the seaplane at their level turn towards them. "You're a plucky bastard, I'll give you that," he roared at the enemy plane as it tried to circle behind him. Jankowski's Lewis gun stuttered. Stan ducked as the German observer returned their fire. He heard a metallic clang but ignored it as he rolled into the turn to follow the Friedrichsafen. Jankowski fired again, but the big seaplane had reversed direction and dived. For all its size the German airplane danced around the sky like a fighting scout. Jankowski snatched the empty ammunition drum from his gun and slammed a replacement on the breech. He turned to shout to Stan, then looked above his head and pointed. His lips moved in a silent curse. Stan twisted in his seat and groaned. Two bullets had pierced their fuel tank fitted under the top wing. Gasoline disappeared behind in a fine mist. Even as he watched, the mist disappeared as the last of the fuel gushed out. Ten seconds later the engine stopped.

Stan slowed the F.E.2 to its best glide speed and turned back towards the land. At fifty miles an hour, with a silent engine, they could converse easily. "Baz, mate, don't light a gasper, there's a good bloke."

Above and now over the coast, Dizzy tried to work out how to deal with the twin-engined machine. It too had dropped its bomb load and was now diving for the sea, but their Rolls Royce-powered F.E.2 had gained ground. The Prof cursed the German designer. The big advantage of this unusual layout came from the ability of the gunner in the front position, unhindered by a wing above, to fire back over the pilot's head in the cockpit behind, and add the weight of his fire to that of the observer in the rear gun position behind the pilot. It made it two against one, unless they could get below and attack from the usual blind spot under the tail. But the pilot was too old a hand to fall for that. He dived for the surface of the sea, but Dizzy had no intention of giving up. He followed him down and maneuvered to take up a position exactly behind. They now flew so low their wheels skimmed the surface at what felt like break-neck speed. The two machines matched each other for pace, but Dizzy saw they had a tiny advantage. For the first time the odd design of the German bomber betrayed it. It stood too tall. The pilot sat far above his wheels, making it hard to judge his height above the water. Dizzy let the F.E.2 sink lower until he knew the tires must be brushing the waves. The gunner in the rear cockpit disappeared, masked by the tail.

At long range, the Prof opened fire again. Short bursts. Each aimed with care. The tail of the German machine twitched to one side, and an answering burst tore between their wings. This pilot was good. He swung his machine to get the F.E.2 back into his gunner's field of fire. He lost a little ground, but he knew the British machine must give up the chase soon, or run out of fuel over the sea. All he had to do was keep low and keep going.

Dizzy and the Prof knew that, so their surprise when the German machine suddenly climbed made them hesitate. "Never look a gift horse in the mouth," Dizzy mouthed to the Prof when he looked back in amazement. The bomber had climbed above them, putting them under its tail. The perfect position. Dizzy hauled back on the stick as the Prof took aim. They both saw the black rectangle appear under the fuselage. Dizzy reacted fast, his hands and feet moving before his brain confirmed his suspicion, but it was too late. The flash told him that a machine gun had been mounted above a hatch in the floor of the fuselage to cover the blind spot. They had fallen for it.

The Prof pressed the trigger of his gun even as he felt a light blow high on his chest to the left of his neck, and another below his knee. Not even as heavy as a punch, no more than a tap. But he felt himself falling into the cockpit. He could not hold his head up and held on to his gun as he slid to the floor.

Dizzy flung the F.E.2 round half a turn and headed for the shore. He saw the Prof's gun spraying bullets into the sky then stopping. He settled the biplane on course for the land, loosened his seatbelt and leaned forward. He could not reach his friend, but could see him lying on the floor. Dizzy pressed the throttle hard forward and raced for the shore. He knew exactly where to go.

High above, Ned Robson looked down in dismay. He had watched the first F.E. turn and glide away with its propeller stopped, then Dizzy and the Prof wheel away from the big German machine and head for land. He did not stop to question why. He did not even consider that he too was now ten miles out to sea in a flimsy, rotary-engined Avro. All he saw was three German machines fleeing the scene of their crime unscathed. And all he considered was that he had the advantage of height and a full magazine. He pushed the stick forward.

CHAPTER 21

North Sea Coast, Germany

Will forced himself to smile as Georg poured coffee into his cup from a metal thermos container. He glanced quickly around the control car, hoping he did not look furtive. Nobody's attitude had changed. The crew attended to their tasks while Georg pointed out landmarks below. Will's stomach tied itself in knots. Obviously his hosts had no idea of the significance of the message, but he had no doubt. "Air security service" could only mean one thing. He had been betrayed, or he had betrayed himself. Suspicion rattled through his head. Matty? Could he have said something? Had she gone through his clothes and found his cigar case not what it appeared to be? Would she betray him? It would be naïve to deny that possibility. She was committed to the German cause, even though she seemed to have a thing for him. He had two choices: make a run for it when they landed, or try to bluff his way out of trouble.

"Will? Will?" Martin had turned to him.

Will blinked, "Excuse me, I was enjoying this coffee. It took me back in my mind to home."

"Yes, it is excellent. Usually we make do with that *ersatz* rubbish, but for our very important visitors, only the best. Now, another treat for our important guest, would you care to take the helm?"

"Of course!" The helmsman stepped to one side and gestured at the wheel with a smile. Will stepped forward and grasped the spokes. He had to continue as if nothing had happened.

Martin stood next to him, hands behind his back, "Have you ever steered a boat?"

"Oh, yes, many times."

"The principle is much the same. Do not try to chase the helm. You will over correct and end up steering a zig-zag course," he pointed to a brass indicator that moved over a graduated scale set into the bulkhead below the glass panel. "This shows the position of the rudder. At the moment you see it is straight ahead."

Will planted his feet apart and fixed his eyes on an island off the coast directly in front of them. The island started to drift to the side and he added a quarter turn of the wheel to starboard. Nothing happened, but he resisted the temptation to spin the wheel further. A few seconds later the nose of *Viktoria* swung ponderously back on course.

"Excellent!" Martin slapped him on the back. "Now, bring us round on to a new heading. We need to steer zero-three-zero, a little east of north." Will spun the wheel to port, and held it steady. "Again, just as in a ship, you must anticipate the turn, about twenty degrees will do it." Will nodded, the view ahead changed as the clouds paraded past the windows as the Zeppelin turned. As the compass in the binnacle passed the fifty-degree mark, he spun the wheel back to dead ahead. Martin watched the compass as the natural stability of the airship overcame the inertia of the turn. "Zero-three-two, fantastic!"

Will moved the wheel a fraction to capture the heading exactly, "Beginner's luck, I expect." He indicated forward with a nod. "The weather ahead looks to be changing. Coming up a cloud, as we say at home."

Martin frowned, "Yes, we will hold this course for just a few minutes, and then steer toward Tondern." The clouds that had formed a bright amorphous mass over the land, had coalesced into classic summer cumulous cloud, their sides bulging with light, now etched against a deep blue sky. Martin leaned forward and tried to look as far upwards as possible, his view masked by the nose of the ship. He pointed, "I don't like the look of that." A towering cloud had formed inland, south of their path, and seemed to be growing even as they watched. Tell-tale streamers trailed from its flat summit where it met the high altitude winds far above them. "Bring her round past north to three-five-zero degrees. We must stay well clear of that monster." Will spun the wheel again and settled the airship on her new course.

Martin nodded his satisfaction, "You are a natural, Will. Now I know our man on the elevator wants to show you his controls and how we handle the ballast." Will followed Martin from station to station in the control car and gave the impression of eager interest as the operators explained the controls, while his mind reeled with the danger of his situation.

Tondern appeared below with the airship station spread out on the edge of town. Martin walked to the side of the gondola and held a brief discussion with Georg. They both looked at the vast thunder cloud boiling up behind the airship, and nodded in agreement.

Martin beckoned to Will, "Thunderstorms are the biggest danger to the ship, as you probably guessed. We are going to circle north of town while we lose altitude, then come in fast and try to get the ship back inside TOSKA before any high winds strike. In this way our passengers have the full tour, but perhaps a little short, and we keep them safe. We may need all hands on the lines when we come in. Are you ready to help?"

"Of course!" Will's breath came tight in his throat. This might be his chance. In the confusion of landing, with people rushing in all directions to grab the mooring lines and subdue the airship, he might be able to slip away and head for the frontier.

"Good! As we come in, you will see maybe hundreds of people, many of them are civilian workers eager to help, but we do not have enough experienced men to control them. Bruno Loewe will divide them into two teams. He will take the starboard team, you take the port. What you have to do is make sure you have about the same number of people on each mooring line. Have too many on one line, and if the ship rises you have people dangling in the air and all kind of problems."

"I only have a few words of German."

"Not a problem, they are good Germans, just shout and push them into place, they like being told what to do."

Georg hooted with laughter, "Try telling my wife that!" Will laughed with him, while he calculated how this might help or hinder the plan forming in his head.

Martin nodded to the engineer. The engines slowed, their drone dropping to a steady throb. The elevator man reached up and pulled on the toggle that released water from the rear ballast tank, then spun his control wheel. The deck tilted as the nose dropped and *Viktoria* started back to earth, but Will noticed him tapping a gauge, a frown on his face.

"Kapitan, we have a problem. I have just tried to release another hundred liters from the rear tank, but the valve is stuck."

"Damn!" Martin turned to the electric telegraph and picked up the mouthpiece. He spoke quickly then turned to Will. "One of the machinists in the rear engine gondola is attending to it."

"Can I help?"

"No, thank you. I am sure Frankhanel will manage."

As the airship sank towards the ground they passed from bright sunlight to shadow. The sea still glittered but an eerie gloom had settled over the land. Tondern lay beneath, its streets spread out like a map. Will made a mental note of the position of the railroad in relation to the town.

The first indication of trouble came as they began to circle to the north. The deck trembled beneath their feet and then jerked sideways and dropped sharply making him grab the nearest support. Martin strode to the helm.

"We're losing height fast, sir!" the elevator man had his eyes glued to the altimeter above his head.

"She's not answering, sir," the petty officer at the helm sounded tense.

Martin checked the rudder indicator, "She's hard over, a gust has just shifted us sideways. Look she's coming round now."

"Yes, sir, she . . . *Gott in Himmel!*"

Martin looked up. A black wall of cloud confronted him, conjured up so fast by the advancing storm they had not seen it as it swelled out of sight behind.

"Hard a starboard. Hold ballast. Elevator full down. Engines full ahead." He rattled off his orders, his experience almost saving them from the updraft he knew lurked just inside that towering wall. It seized them. Will felt his knees bend as the floor of the control car rose sharply. The nose tilted up as they plunged into darkness. Their ears popped as *Viktoria* shot up. A tumult of noise made it hard to think: the windows rattled and shook, the engines bellowed, the metal structure groaned and squealed, but through it all, Will could hear voices.

The helmsman, "Coming through two-seven-zero, Kapitan."

The elevator man, "Two thousand meters, two thousand five, steady on three thousand meters, Kapitan," he sounded triumphant.

Georg Klaas on the telephone, "Have you freed that valve yet?"

And above them all, calm, confident, Captain Martin Friedmann, "Steady as you go on the helm, Bosun. Stand by for the down draft, elevators."

A dull roar penetrated the surrounding din. A curtain had fallen around the ship. They looked out from the control car as if standing behind a waterfall. It took Will a second to realize that sheets of torrential rain and hail fell on the Zeppelin, but the bulk of the hull above meant the control car stayed in an area of relatively calm air. The weight of water arrested their ascent, just as the smart about-turn took them out of the cloud. The storm spat the airship from its flank into a gleaming light.

"Up elevator. Release forward ballast. Engines to emergency power," Martin knew what was coming. "Hold on everybody." Every updraft has its downdraft as sure as night follows day. As they had been overtaken by the storm the downdraft had given them not much more than a boisterous shove as it burst against the ground and exploded outwards from the center of the storm cell, before they were sucked into the cloud. Now at nine thousand feet, it waited to smash them back to the ground.

It struck like a hammer. Will's feet left the floor, weightless for a second, as the Zeppelin plunged. All he could do was hang on and watch in admiration, overtaken by sensation, fear suspended, as the crew fought to control the ship. He watched as the ground expanded: remote on first sight, but growing solid by the second.

"Descent slowing," the elevator man called. Then, "Altitude stable, My Kapitan."

"Keel angle thirty degrees and increasing," Georg Klaas sounded matter-of-fact, even though the bow had risen at an alarming angle.

"Elevators to neutral. Engines to cruise power. Maintain this heading," Martin ordered. Georg turned to him, his eyebrows raised. "How far are we from the frontier, navigator?"

"About fifteen kilometers, Kapitan, but we are just about to cross the coast."

"We may have to overfly Danish territory to avoid this storm line, gentlemen," he turned to the radio operator. "Metzing, when you judge it safe to wind out your antenna again, send a signal to base requesting the Danish authorities permission to overfly as a vessel in distress. But not before we are clear of this cloud, that copper wire is the best lightning conductor we have."

"Yes, sir."

Georg consulted his instruments again, "Keel angle still increasing. It's that damn valve. We need to dump ballast from the rear tank."

"Elevators half-down. Rear engines to full power. Forward engines half-ahead. That should do the trick and bring us on to an even keel."

"Sir! We are losing power on the starboard rear engine." They heard alarm in the engineer's voice.

"It's those damned magnetos," Georg cursed.

"Full ahead on the forward engines. Elevators full down," Martin still sounded calm.

"Sir! The port rear engine is failing!" The engineer sounded desperate. Nobody spoke for an instant, then Will leaped for the ladder leading into the hull.

"Leave it to me, I'll get the damn things running." He flung the hatch open and launched himself on to the catwalk. Half-sliding, half-running, he slithered down the catwalk, now starting to resemble the longest ladder he had ever used as the stern of *Viktoria* sank. The din of the coupled engines driving the thrashing propeller behind the control gondola faded as he reached the amidships section. He reached the open hatch beside the starboard engine. He paused for a second then stretched out across the ladder, now at an awkward angle. He forced himself to look down. It was the most bizarre sight he had ever witnessed. The tail of the airship was now only a hundred feet above the water, while he clung to a ladder a hundred feet above that, because of the perilous angle the ship had now assumed. The howling engines in the forward car could not hold them for long. The Zeppelin was sliding tail first into the shallow water a mile north of the frontier.

He hauled himself across and stuck his head and shoulders into the gondola. The two mechanics crouched beside their stricken engine. "What's the problem?"

"We think the second magneto failed, sir."

"Try the priming lever." The two mechanics glanced at each other, then one reached up and jerked the small lever that pumped fuel into the carburetor to aid starting.

The mechanic looked up in amazement, "It's empty, no fuel."

"How do you restart?"

"The new compressed air starter, sir."

"Right, I know the problem. Watch for my signal." Will pushed himself back on his elbows, and hauled himself back inside the ship. Clinging to the frame that supported the gravity tank he reached for the valve to open the inlet pipe, grabbed for the pump handle, and tugged for all he was worth. Halfway through the stroke he felt resistance. He pulled harder. The glorious sound of fuel gushing up from the slip tanks reached his ears. He pumped furiously, sweat streaming down his face. At last he judged that enough fuel had flowed into the tank to cover the outlet pipe to the engine.

He leaned from the hatch, the first mechanic knelt on the edge of the gondola waiting for him; Will made a winding gesture with his finger. He heard a loud hiss, a puff of smoke jetted from the exhaust, the engine heaved over once more then spun into glorious life with a lusty roar. The propeller jerked and then disappeared in a blur.

The mechanic reached out for the flimsy handrail and hauled himself out of the gondola and over the tilted ladder, he cupped his hand around Will's ear, "I'll help you pump for the port engine too, sir." he had recognized the problem as soon as he felt the lack of resistance on the primer. Together they rushed across the companionway and opened the valve for the port tank and heaved together on the pump handle. A mechanic scrambled from the port gondola and joined them.

Will shouted in his ear, "Give us one more minute, then try for a start." They could already feel the airship levelling beneath their feet, they no longer had to hold on to the frame for support. The same sequence of hiss, cough and roar reached their ears. The most wonderful music they could hope to hear. The port engine chimed in with its twin in glorious harmony.

Will knelt on the edge of the hatch, then glanced down. He stood up.

The drop below had lost its power to turn his knees to water. Martin had leveled the airship by allowing the nose to drop, he stood no more than thirty feet above the water off the Danish island of Fano. *Viktoria* had been saved inches from disaster, and now hovered just above the water. All he needed to do was take one step forward, a short drop into the sea, and he could swim ashore in neutral Denmark. He leaned forward.

"Will!" Georg's voice sounded urgent in his ear. He turned, Georg stood with Jochen Wolff on the companionway. "*Mein Gott!* You are a genius, Will!" He pumped his hand. "But, how do you say? We are not out of the forest yet. We need to free off this damn valve on the ballast tank, while these men pump more fuel into the service tanks. We need an extra pair of hands." Will took one more look at the water below, then followed the Zeppelin crewmen into the heart of the ship.

The builders had bolted the tank to the keel in the stern of the ship to allow the hatch for filling to be accessed from the catwalk, but the valve could only be reached by swinging down to stand on the keel. Georg and Will crouched by the valve, operated by cables and bell cranks.

Will yanked on the operating arm, "What in tarnation has happened here? It's stuck fast."

Georg stood and shouted up to Wolff, "Get me a hammer, a big hammer, we are going to have to knock it off."

"Whoa! Hold on, if we do that we will dump all the ballast and we will be in worse shape than when we started."

"Damn, you are correct, Will. What do you suggest?" Before he could reply, Frankhanel, the machinist from the starboard gondola, appeared above their heads on the catwalk. He dragged a long length of hose and a small hand-operated fire fighting pump with him.

"Sir, I had a plan but the engines failed before I could try it."

"Shoot," Will clambered back on the catwalk.

"Excuse me, sir?"

"Sorry, I mean explain your plan."

"We put this in the filling hatch so the end is under the water, then fix the other end to the fire pump to suck water out. As soon as it is running, we take the pump off and let the water siphon."

Wolff frowned, "I could pee faster than that."

"Yes, sir, but I have fifty meters of hose here, we can cut it in lengths and use them all. It will be slow, but we can also control the flow by pinching off the ends of the hose as we go."

Will and the two officers looked at each other for a second, then Georg slapped the young sailor on the back, "Frankhanel, you will be putting up your petty officer's badge after this. Start cutting that hose!" Within five minutes, a thin stream of water trailed from the hull as *Viktoria* slowly mounted into the heavy, moist sky. Will followed Georg and Jochen Wolff back along the catwalk leaving the ballast control in the care of Frankhanel and the second machinist from the port engine. They paused at the hatch above the passenger gondola.

"How are our passengers, Wolff?" Georg's concern showed in his voice.

"Oh, fine. I told them the ride in the storm is normal, and I think they almost believe me," he winked, saluted, and dropped through the hatch.

Georg shrugged, "His problem, but he knows how to deal with it. He worked on a big transatlantic liner where he learned to soothe rich passengers." They carried on to the forward control gondola, as Will stepped off the ladder the crew greeted him with cheers and a round of applause.

"What was wrong, Will? How did you get the motors running?" Martin asked as the noise subsided.

"I just happened to notice the feed pipe from the gravity tanks was closer to the front than the back by a few inches. Georg had mentioned that we were not carrying that much fuel for this short trip. I guessed that when the tail of the ship sank, the fuel ran to the back of the tank and uncovered the outlet, so the gas stopped flowing. I just pumped up extra fuel from the slip tanks, enough to bring the level over the outlet again, and away the engines went."

"You make it sound simple, but it takes a cool head to solve a problem when disaster is seconds away."

Will shrugged modestly, "Ah well, it is often experience. I once got a truck stuck halfway up a steep hill for the same reason," he pointed forward. "Speaking of problems, are we under control now?" The storm cell had now passed over the field and drifted over the marshland between the airship station and the coast, where the base of the cloud sat on a bulging skirt of rain, silver in the weak sunlight squeezing through the sodden sky.

Martin scanned ahead, "We are under control, thanks to you and Frankhanel with his clever emergency ballast control."

"You have some excellent men."

"The best, all hand-picked volunteers. Now it is my job to get them all, and our passengers, safely back on the ground." He turned to the helmsman, "Bring her on to one-two-five. We will cut behind the storm, let down quickly, and have her in the shed before the next squall line hits."

Will stood back and watched as her dedicated crew brought the elegant ship back to earth. He reflected on how disappointed the writers for the British press would have been if they could witness this crew in action. Nobody barked orders, nobody goosestepped, and he could not see a trace of a Prussian dueling scar. He knew that the stereotypical German officer did exist, Strasser seemed to fit the mold of a cold-eyed fanatic. Unless he could find a way to sneak away, he suspected he might find himself in an uncomfortable interview with just that type of officer.

The airship station expanded in their view as they brought her sliding smoothly towards the field. *Viktoria* had taken a slight nose-down attitude, with the engines throttled back and the ballast now adjusted. From two thousand feet it looked as if the ground swarmed with ants, at two hundred feet individuals could be recognized among the hundreds of people waiting to rush the airship into the safety of her shed.

Martin beckoned Will to stand with him behind the helmsman, "If we have the balance correct, we will level off a few meters above the ground. We drop a grounding line first to discharge static electricity, then the handling lines. Our people then haul us to the ground. We will dump forward ballast to bring us almost level, and when we are close to the ground, we will dump you to finally make us straight."

"Will my weight make that much difference?"

"Oh yes, when we are this finely balanced, eighty kilos makes a difference," Martin squeezed his shoulder. "But, Will, don't get excited and jump too early. We are dropping a rope ladder for you to climb down." He pointed to a gaggle of civilians, Will could now make out women in the crowd as well as men, standing in a group to the left of the landing point, marked with a white cross. "Those are your people, Will. Do not let too many on one rope, and if we are lifted by a gust, for God's sake yell at them to let go!" he offered his hand. "Break your neck and legs!" Will grinned, German sportsmen knew it was bad luck to wish anybody good luck.

He stepped to the door and looked out. They had cleared the buildings on the edge of the field and now drifted across the scrubby grass at little more than fifty feet. Georg knelt in the doorway and pulled a pin. A rope ladder tumbled towards the ground. Will leaned out and stepped on the first rung, anticipating the swing. He clambered down. Despite his perilous position, under the airship and under suspicion, he felt a surge of elation and let out a yell and waved his cap in the air as he swung through the air like a circus trapeze artist. He timed his drop, and stepped off as the ladder touched. He hit the ground running and dashed toward his team, now standing gazing up at the ship. They accepted his instructions without question, he had dropped from the control car and that was as much authority as they needed. Lines snaked from above and he quickly divided his group into three teams, with shoves and shouts of encouragement, one each for the lines they had appropriated. Brawny ground workers in the distinctive bib and brace coveralls favored by German laborers, mixed with smartly dressed staff from the administration offices, and women who he guessed might be volunteers from the surrounding farms, judging by their sturdy build and plain clothes. He had to smile, despite the rush of the job in hand, they all still wore their fancy hats.

They subdued *Viktoria* amid shouts and laughter. People slid across the ground, hanging on for dear life as they dragged her to a full stop. The women shrieked as ballast gushed from the bow and soaked the men. The airship now hung level in the still air. Will looked around gasping for breath. A petty officer shouted an order and the handlers began to drag on the lines. Foot by foot they brought her down until some abandoned their lines and took hold of the rails running under the gondolas. The band had formed up again, and to the tune, *Look what has come from the skies,* they set out to drag the ship into her shed. Will marched at the head of his team, the last man on the line. He could see into the hangar. A canvas curtain, over ten-feet high, stretched across the full width behind another Zeppelin already safely moored inside. He could see his way out. Duck under that curtain, assess who might be beyond it, then slip out the back way. They passed from light to the shade of the hangar. An officer walked backwards between the band and the leading teams, giving hand signals to bring the Zeppelin safely through the doors. Sailors heaved trestles in place under the gondolas to support the weight if the airship sank and scurried to secure the lines to rings sunk into the concrete floor. Shouts from above made him look up. A gangway wide enough for one man to walk ran high in the roof of the hangar. A team, hidden by the hull, attached bridles to lifting points on the back of the ship to suspend her from the roof. *Viktoria* hung in a balance so delicate that the weight of one man working on an engine would make her move gently down on the trestles.

Chris Davey

A collective sigh whispered around the hangar, followed by loud applause as Martin Friedmann appeared at the open window of the gondola and announced, "Ladies and Gentlemen, we are safe home!"

Will looked behind him, the curtain hung only a few feet away. He guessed it concealed some sensitive area from the eyes of the public who strangely, seemed to have access to the sheds. He calculated that the emergency docking of the Zeppelin was an "all hands on deck" situation, and there should be nobody working behind the screen. All he had to do was slip away, something that appeared to be harder by the second. His rope handling team crowded around, eager to shake his hand.

"Hey! Will! It *is* you!" Will stared at the man in the field gray uniform of the German army who now stood grinning in front of him, hands on hips. Recognition dawned, he knew two Germans from his time at university before his adventures took him to England. Only one had flaming red hair.

"Johnny? Johnny Behncke? "Good Lord, what are you doing here?" Will's heart sank to his boots. At any other time meeting an old friend was a pleasure, but Johannes Behncke's appearance at this precise moment was the last thing he needed. He saw his chance to escape slipping away.

"I'm on official business, but you and your friends are big news in Germany. I saw your name and put two and two together. Did you get my message?" He pumped Will's hand in greeting.

"Message? I don't think so. Did you leave it at the hotel?

"Ha! Always the clown, Will. No, I have some clout now you know," he grinned and pointed to his army rank badges. "I had the people here send a message to the ship. I did not want to miss you if your party are traveling on today."

Will still had hold of Behncke's hand, but now he took him in a bear hug, "Johnny, you old son of a gun, it is good to see you." Relief flooded through him. He held Behncke by the shoulders. "But what are you doing? I never saw you as some kind of cop."

Behncke's eyebrows shot up, they had always reminded Will of hairy red caterpillars, "Policeman? Why do you think that? I'm a pilot like you." he grinned and pointed to the pilot's badge on his left breast.

"But the radio operator said you were an officer in the Army Field Security Service."

Behncke laughed, "Maybe his English is quite good, but not good enough. *Sicherheit* means safety as well as security. English is such a subtle language, as you always told me back at MIT. No, I have this fantastic feather bed of a job while I am out of the line. I am the Army *Flying* Field *Safety* Officer. If more than one of our machines crashes on a field, then I fly out to investigate and make recommendations. I have a hot new ship for my personal use, an office back at base, and a hot new secretary to type up my reports," he winked and nudged Will in the ribs.

Will laughed, "You always did have an eye for the ladies."

"And talking of that, how is your beautiful sister? You know I am still in love with her."

"You only met her once when she came up to visit me," Will said.

"That was enough to fall in love."

"I will let her know," Will smiled and put his arm round Behncke's neck. "Have you met our hosts?"

"Not yet, I will visit Kapitan Friedmann when the report is done and tell him what I think he needs to do here. Do you know there have been six airplane crashes here in the last three months? All this space, you would think it would be easy, but there are holes in the ground you could lose an elephant in. Of course these guys don't care, their gasbags never touch the surface." Behncke spoke English with a marked American accent gained from his two years studying mechanical engineering at Massachusetts Institute of Technology.

Will looked around, a crowd had gathered about them, mostly enlisted men from the *Viktoria* and the other ships on the station. The men from *Viktoria* were pointing Will out to their friends, Frankhanel stood to the front. He saluted Behncke.

"Sir, have you heard that Herr Turner saved our ship?"

Will groaned, "Oh no, I never, I just helped out some."

Behncke stood back and looked at Will wide-eyed, "My God, Will! You are a hero. You always were full of surprises," he turned to the sailors. "Come on, men, there's only one way for Mr. Turner to leave the shed." Seconds later Will looked down on the crowd from the shoulders of the sailors bearing him out of the hangar in triumph. The people had formed two lines. The sailors carried him behind the band as they marched out into the sunlight through the applauding crowds.

Will twisted around and waved to Behncke, "Join us for dinner tonight!"

"My pleasure!"

They carried him to the door of the bus where Matty and the rest of the party waited for him. It was a relief to slump down in the backseat with her, all his strength had drained away with the tension. He put his head back and closed his eyes

"How much trouble were we in, Will?" Matty prodded his arm.

He turned his head and opened his eyes, "What did Wolff say?"

"That it was normal and the captain had just brushed the edge of the storm to give us a roller coaster ride."

"Then that is what happened," he smiled and closed his eyes again.

"Don't damn well patronize me!" Matty whispered fierce in his ear. "What did they mean about you saving the ship?"

Will sat up, shocked by her language, "Exaggeration, I just re-started the rear engines. I am an engineer, it is what I do."

She gazed at him, her blue eyes bigger than ever with tears in the corners. She took his hand, "Good Lord, William Turner, you are some kind of guy."

He coughed, "Don't be silly, I just did my job. The important thing is, did you enjoy the ride?"

Her face brightened, "I did, and I think the others did too, though one or two looked a tad green around the gills when we tilted up like that. Dorothy squealed and clung on to the steward, though I think that was just another excuse to grab a man."

Will put on a frown, "Now, now, Matty, do not be wicked. Show some charity."

"Oh, I like being wicked."

"I had noticed."

"Anyway, it was thrilling, the most exciting experience I have ever had," she paused and gave him a sideways look from under her long lashes. "And you know what happens when I get excited."

CHAPTER 22

Military Hospital, Colchester Garrison, England

S ergeant Major Cole took another turn on the nut. "How does that feel, sir?"

"Spot on, Sergeant Major. Who's bright idea was this?" The Prof asked.

"Bowen and myself, sir."

Captain Winstanley, the senior orthopaedic surgeon at the military hospital in the garrison town of Colchester watched over Coles' shoulder. The German bullet had hit Smith just below the knee, breaking the bone and leaving ragged entry and exit wounds. A treatment for the shattered bone would be to plaster the leg to the thigh, but that would make treatment of the wound difficult. Cole and Bowen had applied themselves to the problem, and devised two padded clamps, one to fit above the knee, the other around the ankle, connected by three long threaded bolts to make a frame supporting the lower limb. Cole explained how they adapted the studs used to clamp the cylinders of a rotary engine to the crankcase to make the long bolts.

Winstanley ran his fingers over the finely machined bolts and smiled. At heart, like all orthopaedic surgeons, he was a craftsman. "Let me have the drawings for this, Sergeant Major, I'm going to make sure you and your colleague get full credit."

"Thank you, sir."

Winstanley smiled at the Prof and extended his hand, "Good luck, Smith. Those wounds are healing nicely. We'll have you out of here in no time."

The Prof grimaced, "Thanks, Doc, you're going to need all the beds you can lay hands on when the big push starts. I'm off as soon as I can be."

Winstanley laughed, "You're right, but it's not me you have to convince, here comes Sister Crowley. I'm off before she puts me on a charge for malingering." He left the ward quietly muttering, "brilliant workmanship."

Julia Crowley pushed Dizzy to one side and leaned over the bed. A strand of jet black hair had escaped from her cap; the Prof reached up and pushed it back, "Good morning, Julia, you're looking as beautiful as ever."

"Don't try to sweet talk me, Jim Smith. Here, open your gob." She thrust a thermometer under his tongue and stood back, arms folded, trying to scowl and failing. With her porcelain skin, smiling blue eyes and black hair she did not need to speak before most people guessed at her nationality, but her voice gave it away instantly. Julia Crowley was as Irish as a pint of Guinness. Dizzy allowed himself an approving glance. In his own words, she was a peach, an absolute stunner, even their famously severe commanding officer, Major Ernie Simpson, had fallen under her spell.

"Tell me, Sister Crowley, is it true you're stepping out with the old man?" Dizzy asked her with an innocent look, knowing full well it was true.

"Tell me, Lieutenant Lipman, is it any of your bloody business if I am?" She replied with a sweet smile as she took the thermometer from Smith's mouth.

"Oh, yes. Because if you're not, I'm available," he said, twitching his eyebrows up and down.

Her roar of laughter made the men in the other beds look up. "Away with you. You're a mere boy. I'm nearly old enough to be your mother."

Dizzy laughed, "Well, maybe my big sister. Anyway, we can't thank you enough for what you did."

"Ah, it was nothing, just doing our job, but you caused quite a stir landing on the parade ground like that."

The instant Dizzy had seen the Prof collapse in the front cockpit he knew he had to get him medical help. Everybody in the squadron knew that Julia Crowley had been promoted to senior nursing sister, at the military hospital attached to Colchester Barracks. She and Simpson made no secret of their relationship, and he always left her contact details in the squadron office when visiting. As Dizzy had told the others on his return to the field, having a friend in the medical business made his decision easy. He had put the nose down and flown hell-for-leather to nearby Colchester after the Prof was hit, where he had quickly located the hospital within the military complex by the red crosses painted on the roof. He had slammed the F.E.2 on to the empty parade ground. The attitude of the irate senior officer who had scuttled from his office had changed instantly when he saw the blood-spattered cockpit and the Prof unconscious, but with his hand still clutching the pistol grip of his gun. He had mustered enough men in seconds to extract him from the cockpit and rush him into the hospital on a stretcher. He had then taken the protesting Dizzy into his office and poured him a large brandy. Now, two days later, Dizzy had returned with Cole and the improvised leg brace.

Julia glanced at the thermometer, then leaned over and raised the edge of the dressing on Smith's shoulder. She pulled him forward to examine the exit wound.

"Ow!" the Prof complained. "That hurts."

"Oh, stop whining, you big baby," she chided.

The Prof shook his head and looked at his comrades, "See what I mean? You get no sympathy in this place."

"Ah, you know right enough the only place you'll find sympathy in here, is between 'sycophant' and 'syphilis' in the big dictionary on me desk." She rearranged the dressing carefully and patted the Prof on his shaven head. "Go on with you, you'll do. We'll have you out of here in a few days. You must have some of the Irish in you because you're a lucky feller and no mistake. That bullet went straight through you without even hitting your collarbone. An inch to the left and it would have killed you for sure."

"A miss is as good as a mile, Julia m'dear," he patted her hand, then looked at her seriously. "I don't suppose there's any word of young Ned Robson being admitted to any of the hospitals in this area?"

Julia shook her head, her face sad, "Sorry, Jim. I tried every hospital for miles around, including the navy hospital, seein' as he was last seen heading out to sea, but there's not a sign of him."

Dizzy nodded, "We've been in touch with all the seaplane stations, including the RNAS at Dunkerque, we've alerted the Harwich Patrol, even the controller of the fishing fleet. He's disappeared without a trace."

The Prof leaned back, "Damn. I'm afraid he's had it, lads." He seemed smaller.

"There might still be a chance he was picked up by a merchant vessel without radio, or even by the Germans." Dizzy suggested.

The Prof shook his head, "No, we have to face it. We all know what he was like. For a bright lad he had a very poor grasp of tactics. If he saw an enemy aircraft, he attacked it, simple as that. If he just went headlong at those three, he was up against four gunners. You can bet they would have grouped together in a tight formation, and we learned how good they are. Even if he did use his head and attacked the big green bastard from underneath, he would have fallen for it the same way we did."

"Major Simpson has already sent the 'Missing in Action' letter to his family," Cole said.

The Prof sighed, "In some ways worse for them than knowing he's dead. They'll hold out hope for months, even years," he looked at Dizzy.

"Pack his kit, but make sure you go through it first, especially any letters, to make sure there's nothing in there to embarrass his family." Dizzy's raised eyebrows showed his surprise. The Prof smiled sadly, "You know, it would be nice to think he did have time to get up to some mischief in his short life. Such a waste."

Julia nodded, "It was, it was. He was a fine-looking young feller. He would have made some lucky girl proud."

"Well, he did us proud, that's for certain," Dizzy said. "Let's hope we can live up to his example, and bag that Zep on his behalf."

Smith sat up, "Abso–bloody–lutely. I'm with you there. But you won't do it standing around here. Go on, off you go. I'll be out of here in a day or two. Don't let 'em slack, Sergeant Major."

Cole grinned and saluted, "Don't you worry, Mr. Smith, sir. I'll keep the young gentlemen on their toes."

Julia walked with Dizzy and Cole to the marbled entrance hall of the hospital. "You realize the Prof's flying days are probably over?"

Dizzy stopped and took her hand so she faced him. "Are you serious?"

She nodded, "He'll be lucky to be walking without a stick inside a year, so he'll have the devil of a job standing in the cockpit, and his shoulder will be too stiff to work a gun," she studied Dizzy's face. "Do you want me to break the news?"

He frowned, "No, leave it to me next time we visit." They walked slowly to the door. Dizzy stopped and turned, his face brightened, "Will we be seeing you at the guest night?"

She winked, "Wild horses wouldn't keep me away. Take care, Dizzy, and you too John, I know you keep volunteering to fly with these maniacs."

The Sergeant Major smiled and touched his cap with the end of his cane, "Somebody has to keep an eye on them."

She laughed, "Just make sure you do."

Dizzy climbed into the driver's seat of the Crossley tender they had used to drive to Colchester. Cole dumped his toolbox in the back and swung the starting handle. The engine rattled into life and he joined Dizzy in the narrow cab.

"That's a bloody shame about young Mr. Robson, sir."

"And Captain Smith. I tell you, at this rate the Hun is going to whittle us down to nothing, Sergeant Major."

"Time we evened the score, sir."

Dizzy nodded, "I know we can't win every time."

The grizzled old NCO struck a match and sucked the flame into the bowl of his pipe, "But it would be nice to draw a few." He flicked the spent match over the side.

CHAPTER 23

The Crown Hotel, Tondern, North Germany

Dinner turned into a wild party, the American guests in high spirits after the excitement of their flight, the Zeppelin men relieved after their escape from disaster. Johnny Behncke had not changed from his days at MIT: hard-drinking, piano-playing and flirting outrageously with the women. Will escaped to his room long after midnight. He heard a soft tap at his door. Dorothy Schubert, a little drunk but very determined, fell into his arms. He caught her under the elbows and stood her upright, still on the threshold of his room.

"Mrs. Schubert! Whatever are you doing?"

She fluttered her lashes, grinned, and in a low and slightly slurred voice announced, "You, as soon as you let me in." He stood his ground, praying for rescue, in peril for the second time that day.

"Ah, Dorothy, there you are my dear. I've been looking all over for you." His prayer had been answered; Matty approached holding a clipboard. "I'm afraid your husband is a little the worse for drink, but before you put him to bed, can I put you down for a tour of the lacemaking industry here in Tondern tomorrow?" Dorothy glared at her. "I'll take that for a yes." Matty put a tick against her list. "Now come along my dear, I know how easy it is to get lost in these old hotels, you have come up one flight of stairs too many. Come along." Matty took her arm and steered her firmly back down the corridor, turning to give Will a broad wink. He sighed, turned out the light and left the door unlocked. When Matty joined him ten minutes later he could only laugh.

"You know, if looks could kill, Dorothy Schubert just blew your head off."

"It's a risk worth taking," she replied, slipping under the covers.

It seemed only seconds later when Will jolted awake, but from the soft light in the room he knew hours had passed. For a few moments he lay still, mustering his thoughts, finding his place. Something had woken him. He remembered and flung out his arm to find the bed next to him empty, but still warm. A breeze caressed his face like a recent fond memory. He opened his eyes; the open window framed the twilight dawn. He sat up and shook his head. Matty would surely make a better agent than him on any day. She had slipped out of his room without making a sound, and she had the nerve of the Devil. No ladder stood against the windowsill, she had left the same way she came in, through the door.

Will lay back, wide awake, and groaned out loud. He had to admit that even Simpson's chocolate Labrador would make a better agent than him. So far he had made a complete balls of the job. He had achieved nothing. He had not even checked to see if there was a gas-shielding system in place on *Viktoria*. He never expected there to be, but he still should have photographed the engine exhausts with the sophisticated miniature camera concealed within his cigar case to prove it. He had also forgotten to make any notes regarding the layout of the airship station. That would have been easy to disguise as he was supposed to be a technical journalist.

Perhaps worst of all, he now faced a personal dilemma. He had met his enemy face to face and found not only did he like him, but he admired him for his skill. It was no use saying that in other circumstances these men would be his friends, Martin Friedmann, Georg and Jochen already were his friends, a bond forged in the heat of dire emergency. To cap it all, he had to admit he had enjoyed the reunion with Johnny Behncke.

"Oh pull yourself together, man," he muttered to himself out loud. "You are a British officer. You have taken the King's shilling and you have a job to do." He rolled out of bed and took his wallet from his jacket. He looked at the picture of his sister inside. She looked back at him with a half-smile, captured perfectly by the photographer at home. He wondered how she would feel if she knew about his feelings. The previous year she had nearly been killed by a torpedo fired into the ship carrying her and Marie to England; for her the war was something personal. Whatever would she say if she knew that the way in which the war had become personal for him was to sleep with the enemy, literally.

He sat back on the bed. It sounded awful in those terms. The fact he had become intimately involved with a girl whom he had no plans to marry would be enough to send his mother and Cordelia through the roof. They might cut him some slack on the moral issue because of the war, but they would feel exactly the same way about Matty's involvement with the German cause. But somehow he could not bring himself to condemn her. Perhaps if both his parents were German immigrants, as hers were, he might feel and act the same way. He knew he was making excuses for her, and he guessed why; he was falling in love. It was not just her looks, and her open, honest passion: he sensed a generosity of spirit, and something else, a boldness, that he found irresistible. He had to control himself. Now more than ever he needed some discipline. She would despise him if she knew who he really was, so there could be no future for them. He hated the fact that he was deceiving her every minute of the day, but it had to be done.

He closed the wallet and thought of the smashed shop he and Ernie Simpson had encountered on their drive to the War Office all those weeks ago. He recalled the shattered farms and frightened refugees he had witnessed during those first weeks of war and above all, he thought of the row after row of plain wooden crosses, standing sentinel in the fields behind the lines in France.

He was an intelligent young man, not taken in by propaganda. He knew the British, French and Tzarist Russia took much responsibility for the war; the imperial ambitions of these countries had helped create the friction with Germany, but his own argument to Matty in their often-heated discussions stood any test: Germany had invaded Belgium and France. Without German military ambition, there would be no conflict. The German officer corps had clamored for war, and the Kaiser had been unable, or more likely unwilling, to stop them. Now Europe reaped what that ambition had sowed. The French would not stop fighting until the last German soldier had been killed or driven off their sacred soil, and the British were too honorable and too stubborn to give up the fight. Whether he liked it or not, he was part of that tradition. Yes, the Zeppelin men he had met were fine fellows, but he wondered if at any time in history had such fine fellows ever served such a rotten cause and such an arrogant leader as Kaiser Wilhem.

Will walked to the window and took a deep breath. He could just see the tops of the airship hangars over the roofs of the town. He had to get into those sheds. Get in, take the pictures, get out and get home. That was his duty. That was his job: and Will Turner had never shirked either. He narrowed his eyes: the growing light sharpened the edges of TOSKA. He had a half-formed plan, and Johnny Behncke would be the unwitting means of putting it into play. During the party Johnny had boasted about his "hot new ship" and invited Will out to the field in the morning to see it. He planned to leave for his Berlin base "as soon as his hangover allows." Will remembered that Johnny had a reputation as the man who could drink them all under the table, and still be first down to breakfast. He washed, shaved and dressed quickly, pulling on an old sweater and his boots. He patted the pocket of his jacket, to check he had his cigar case, then hurried down to the dining room.

"Ah! Good morning, Will. Still the iron man I see. You almost beat me." Johnny had just sat down. His black riding boots shone and his field gray uniform fitted like a glove. As always, Will thought, he looked immaculate and none the worse for wear.

"I would have to be quicker to beat you," Will shook his hand. "So, does the offer to see your new airplane stand?"

Johnny nodded, "Of course. My car will be here in ten minutes. Time enough for breakfast." They wolfed down eggs, black bread and a pot of coffee. Precisely ten minutes later a uniformed driver marched in and saluted. On the way to the field, seated in the backseat of the open Mercedes, Will prompted Johnny about his experiences in France. Away from company the young German spoke with candor about his experience, speaking of the elation and terror that came with combat, and his horror at his second victory flying an Eindekker, when his French victim fell in flames.

"My God, Will, it was awful. I flew through the smoke and I could feel the heat and I swear I could smell those poor guys burning," he shrugged. "Maybe that is my imagination or my conscience, but I can tell you that when I got back and my comrades were toasting my victory, I got away as quick as I could and made my way to the nearest church to find a priest to hear my confession." He turned to Will with a half-smile, "I bet you did not expect to hear that."

Will nodded, "Knowing you, I am not surprised. You might be a damn fine pilot, but you make a lousy assassin."

Johnny's face lit up, "Thanks, Will, I take that as a compliment." The car rolled up to the gate. A sentry raised the barrier; they moved forward then stopped outside a small gatehouse. An officer stepped out to greet them. He recognized Will and saluted with a smile as he handed him a register to sign. Johnny laughed as they pulled away. "It looks as if you have made a name for yourself with the big balloon boys."

"Aw, any fool can start an engine."

Johnny laughed, "Any fool can start an engine, but it takes a crazy fool to do it hanging fifty meters above the ocean," he paused, then turned to Will, his face serious. "My friend, when America declares war on Germany, what will you do?"

"You make it sound inevitable."

"It is. The British blockade is killing us. The only way to break it is with unrestricted submarine warfare. When the naval chiefs get their way, the United States will have no choice but to declare war on us, mark my words."

"Then I will have to do my duty as an American citizen," he shrugged. To his surprise, Johnny smiled and slapped him on the back.

"Of course you will," he pointed to the single shed known as TONI. "Look, they have my bird out of her nest."

Will gave a low whistle. He hoped it sounded like admiration, but his feelings ranged from envy to a mental, *Oh hell!* His heart sank. With one glance he knew the German designers had jumped far ahead of the Allies. This looked like the machine that he and Tom Armstrong would dearly love to build. It screamed speed, just standing on the tarmac. The smooth, round section fuselage tapered to a long vertical stabilizer. The airplane looked predatory, reminding Will of a shark. As they drew to a stop beside it, he saw the twin machine guns were mounted on either side of the engine block in order to fire through the propeller. He had no doubt he was looking at a killing machine. Will knew those guns: stripped Maxims with a perforated jacket around the barrels, and a rate of fire that ripped the sky apart.

Johnny jumped from the car and strode over to his airplane, he stroked the fuselage and turned to Will with a grin, "What do you think?"

"She is a beauty, Johnny, and no mistake." He meant it. Standing close he could see that the fuselage of the airplane had been constructed

like a racing skiff. He and Henry Walker had used the same technique on the airplane they had built. They had carefully steamed strips of wood to shape and formed them over a light frame. The German designer had used the same method, creating a strong, light and smooth "semi-monocoque" structure. The biplane wings looked conventional enough, but braced with the minimum of speed-sapping struts and wires. A sleek cowling shrouded most of the Mercedes engine into the line of the nose, with a streamlined spinner covering the propeller boss and curving seamlessly into the lines of the airplane as a whole. And then there were those damned guns: two of them.

Will was shaken, but was not about to show it. He laughed and pointed to the playing card emblem emblazoned just behind the cockpit. "The Ace of Hearts. I would expect nothing less."

Johnny grinned as he shrugged into his leather coat, held by one of the mechanics attending the machine. "But of course! I have a reputation to maintain." He beckoned Will to follow, "Come, we will check her over." Johnny leaned into his cockpit and checked that the magneto switch was in the off position, then strolled around the airplane, checking wires, waggling the control surfaces and moving the propeller to inspect for damage. Will recognized a professional aviator from the obvious care Johnny put into his pre-flight inspection.

"So what is it called? Or is that a secret?" Will asked.

"Not at all, it's called an *Albatros* because that is the company that makes it, but I think it's a lousy name. It should be the *Hawk* or *Eagle,* don't you think?"

Will nodded, "Absolutely, it looks superb, the latest thing; I am surprised I am allowed to see it."

Despite the fact they spoke in English, Johnny drew Will away from the mechanics. "I'm not going to give you any—what was it Freddie used to say back at MIT?—'Bullshit.' "

Will chuckled, "Yes, I think he invented that expression."

"Well, no bullshit. My bosses *want* you to see this machine, and report back to the American people what clever guys we Germans are, and how it's pointless to go to war with us because we have superior weapons."

Will looked around, then leaned close to Johnny's ear, and whispered, "Johnny, that really *is* bullshit." Johnny exploded with laughter and vaulted into the cockpit, then pulled on his flying helmet. Will reached up to shake his hand. Johnny held it.

"Will, if it does come to war with America, and you end up at the front. Keep an eye out for the old 'Ace of Hearts,' and aim to miss."

Will grinned, "You have my word." He stepped away from the Albatros as the mechanics turned the propeller to prime the engine for starting, but Johnny held up his hand to make them pause.

"Hey, Will, how will I know it is your airplane so that I can aim to miss too?"

"Do not worry about that, my friend, I will be such a crack pilot you will never get your sights on me long enough."

The roar of the engine drowned Johnny's laughter; he warmed it for a few minutes then throttled down, he turned and smiled, "*Aufwiedersehen*, old friend, *Hals und Beinbruch!*" He waved the chocks away. The Albatros bumped across the scrubby grass with a mechanic running at each wing tip. They dragged the airplane to face into a faint breeze that barely stirred the windsock, and stepped away. Johnny opened the throttle wide and within seconds the tail came up. A moment later the wheels left the ground and the Albatros climbed away. Will held his hand over his eyes to shield them from the low morning sun to watch Johnny take a wide sweep over the town, and then come roaring back over the field. He smiled, guessing what would happen next. The biplane dropped lower and lower, until the wheels skimmed the grass. Will stood waving until, like the mechanics around him, instinct made him duck. With a twitch of the stick, Johnny hurdled over them, the blast from his propeller snatching the cap from the head of one of the mechanics.

Will straightened up while they roared their approval and joined him waving at the fast-disappearing airplane.

"What a pilot!" the petty officer in charge of the team spoke with admiration in careful, slow English. "You know he is what the British call an 'Ace,' sir?"

"I did not know that. What does that mean exactly?"

"He has destroyed five enemy machines."

"My goodness! Whoever would have thought my friend could do that." Will meant it. He looked back at the hangar and could see no sign of a truck or car. "Do you have any transport to take me back to the guard room?"

"I am sorry, sir, we do not. But I can telephone for a car."

"No, that is not a problem," Will said quickly, then regretted answering in haste. He smiled, "To tell you the truth, we had a bit of a party last night, and I have a thick head. The walk will do me good."

The sailor smiled, relieved to be rid of the responsibility of looking after their guest. "I understand, sir. I hope, as the English sailors say, you 'kept your end up.' "

"Oh, yes, I did that," Will said with a smile. "Good day to you." The young German saluted and joined his comrades walking back to the open doors of TONI. Will fought down the urge to sprint toward the giant double hangar, TOSKA. It loomed in front of him, casting an enormous shadow as he strolled, hands in pockets across the deserted tarmac. He glanced at his watch: still only 5:30 on a Sunday morning. Even the hard-working Germans appeared to observe the Sabbath. The doors of TOSKA stood shut. The party that helped Johnny launch his journey to Berlin had been the only men he had seen on the field apart from the guard at the gate.

Incredible. Could the mighty German war machine really have such poor security? He had heard stories of British agents operating from Switzerland returning with information from the heart of Germany. Perhaps it was true. He glanced over his shoulder to see that the group of men responsible for handling the airplane had disappeared inside the hangar, no doubt enjoying the real coffee that Martin Friedmann prided himself on supplying to his men. He quickened his pace and made a sharp turn into the space between the two hangars. Or could it be that the naval airmen simply had no great secrets to conceal? The technology he had seen so far held no mystery. He had witnessed nothing that he had not seen at British naval air stations. The construction methods used in the Zeppelins, while impressive, were straightforward, the techniques for fly-ing them well known to the small band of British and French airship men who used small, non-rigid ships, to patrol the Channel and Atlantic Western Approaches. With these thoughts in mind, Will convinced him-self that if challenged he could argue that his cover job as a journalist made him professionally curious. But it began to appear unlikely that he would be observed—the hangars looked to be deserted.

He moved along the wall of TOSKA. Windows pierced the corrugated iron sheets at regular intervals. Will contemplated trying to scramble up to see into the hangar, but the lower edge of the window frames stood ten feet from the ground. He looked for something to use as a ladder but found nothing. He moved on to a small door and tried the handle. It would not budge. He moved on again. He had nearly reached the end of the giant shed when a gap between two panels caught his eye. He tugged at the exposed edge; to his surprise, it moved easily. His nose twitched at a familiar odor, and he smiled.

"Lazy buggers," he muttered. He guessed that the men working at the rear of the hangar had created their own unofficial exit to slip outside to relieve themselves, to save a long walk to inconvenient latrines. Will eased inside and stopped, standing quite still while his eyes adjusted. The rising sun poured into the vast space through the windows and numerous gaps in the structure. TOSKA's builders had no time for finesse. He now saw that he had entered the hangar well behind the canvas curtain that had shielded this part of the shed from view when they had dragged *Viktoria* inside. He glanced around. Benches, stacks of timber, and machine tools lined the walls. A skeletal structure mounted on a massive wheeled trolley took up much of the space in the middle of the floor. He guessed at a sub assembly for some part of a Zeppelin's massive tail section, but it held no interest. He had to see beyond the curtain. There was no going back now. If a guard caught him it meant trouble, and no amount of bluff would dig him out. He moved forward, holding his breath.

The curtain had been tied back where the walkway passed into the main part of the hangar, making a door. He stopped and peered around the edge of the canvas. *Viktoria* hung suspended next to a larger ship. A curious smell filled his nostrils: a mixture of gasoline and hydrogen gas, he guessed. He peered into the distant recesses of the hangar, still nothing or nobody stirred beyond the vast, looming bulk of the two ships. He gauged the light as he pulled his cigar case from his pocket and pressed the catch that allowed the bellows of the concealed camera to slide out. A long exposure would do it, with the camera steadied on one of the trestles conveniently placed beneath the ships. Holding his breath, every fiber of his body alive for the slightest sound or movement, Will crept beneath *Viktoria* and aimed his camera at one of the rear engines he had so recently coaxed back to life; the exhaust pipes no more than stubs to direct the spent gases away from the flanks of the ship: no ducts, no extra pipes, no secret system.

He forced himself to make a total of six exposures from different angles. Satisfied that he had what he needed he started to turn away, letting out the breath he had been holding almost since he slipped from behind the curtain. The slamming of a door made his breath catch again. He stopped, standing rigid. The best concealment was to remain absolutely still; he had learned that fighting with the Contemptibles in the retreat from Mons. He saw movement in the shadows beyond the noses of the two airships. Five hundred feet away two men strolled across the end of the hangar carrying buckets. They disappeared as quickly as they had come, slamming through a second door, their voices and laughter echoing in the vastness of the shed.

Will allowed himself to breathe again. Fighting down the urge to run he strode to the curtain, folding the camera and slipping it back into his pocket. He stepped through the gap and started down the edge of the workshop, keeping to the shadows. He had covered only twenty paces when he glanced at a drawing board between two benches. Curiosity momentarily overcame his urge to get out. He studied the blueprint, his brow furrowed. His gaze picked out a scale, and his eyebrows shot up. He turned, slowly, abandoning the security of the shadows, and walked into the middle of the shed. He stopped in front of the wheels of the giant trolley supporting the structure he had ignored on his way in. The wheels stood taller than him. He raised his eyes, craning his neck back.

"Oh—my—God!" Will took his camera out again.

CHAPTER 24

The Flying Field, Abbots Roding

Sergeant Major Cole pushed the prof's wheelchair around the end of the wing and jabbed his thumb at the *Le Prieur* rockets. "What do you think, sir?"

Prof Smith squinted at the installation. Close inspection revealed nothing more than large fireworks, with wooden sticks slotted into steel tubes fixed to the wing struts of the B.E.2 and angled up from the line of flight. The pilot fired them with an electric switch instead of lighting a paper fuse, the only concession to sophistication. Morphine dulled the pain from his wounds, but the drug did nothing to impair his intellect. "I think, John, that I am bloody glad I'm not going to be up there when young Jackson lets fly with this lot," he shook his head. "I'm not happy with this idea, not happy at all."

"He did volunteer."

"Yes, but the boy is an idiot. A brave idiot, but an idiot nonetheless."

Cole pointed, "Here comes our heroic idiot now." Stan Jackson and Basil Jankowski appeared from the map room. Jackson casually swung his helmet by the strap.

The Prof beckoned to him from his wheelchair, "Jacko, you don't have to do this. In my opinion those things are more likely to kill you than a Zeppelin."

"Aw, come off it, sir. It's only a demo. All I have to do is fly out over the sea a little way, find this balloon they're dragging along behind a battleship, let go me rockets and come back. I'll be home in time for lunch."

"It's the flying out over the sea bit that worries me. Bowen has trimmed down a lifejacket for you to wear." On cue the mechanic, Bowen, held up a cork lifejacket. Designed for use at sea, it covered the whole chest and back with vertical cork strips.

"Aw, strewth, sir, do I have to? I'm a championship swimmer back home you know."

"Too bloody right you have to. That's an order," Smith frowned. "There's a hell of a difference between doing the doggy paddle across Botany Bay in your swimming togs, and trying to swim five miles to shore across the North Sea wearing full flying kit." Jankowski grinned and helped Bowen strap the lifejacket over Stan's leather coat.

Stan held his arms away from his sides, "I feel like Bloody Barnacle Bill the Sailor."

The Prof winked, "You look like him, but don't forget he always made it home from the sea to have his wicked way with the vicar's daughter." Cole wheeled the Prof away from the B.E.2 as Stan carried out his inspection then strapped in, all the while grumbling about the lifejacket. Bowen swung the prop, and after a few minutes to warm the engine, Stan took off and climbed away, heading east to the sea.

His Majesty's Ship *Carysfort*, a light cruiser and part of the Harwich Force, waited for him five miles off the coast. She steamed north into a light breeze trailing a kite balloon on a thousand feet of cable, the drum for that having been jury-rigged behind the six-inch gun on her aft deck, to the amusement of her crew, and the displeasure of her chief engineer. Khaki uniforms mixed with naval blue on the open bridge.

Lechelle shaded his eyes with his hand, "Simpson, have you a never-ending supply of young madmen prepared to test the latest hare-brained idea?"

Simpson continued to search the sky for Jackson, "It would appear so, sir."

Lechelle opened his mouth to reply, then stopped and pointed at a long, low vessel thrusting its way through the gentle swell toward them. "Aha! I do believe Sir Percy has made it after all," he turned to the signal officer standing beside them. "What exactly is that? It's an odd-looking thing."

"CMB, sir. Stands for 'Coastal Motor Boat,' " the young officer replied enthusiastically. "Two-hundred-and-seventy-five horsepower Thornycroft V-12 petrol engine, one of the new wooden planing hulls, and a top speed of nearly forty knots. Fastest thing on water. It fires a single torpedo over the stern, though that one seems to have had the gear removed."

Lechelle's description of the boat as "odd" was justified. Forty-feet long, it appeared to have no deck as such, the sides of the hull merging with the top in a continual curve giving a distinct, humped appearance. At a distance and stopped it could have been mistaken for the bottom of a capsized boat, or even a submarine, but at full speed, throwing a spectacular wake with the White Ensign trailing in the wind, nobody could fail to see that this was a radical step in fast-ship design.

The inspiration came from the racing boats built before the war. Young officers argued that a fast boat with a shallow draft would be able to skim over the mine fields and attack German shipping at anchor. This idea created the design brief to Thornycrofts for a, "fast vedette skimmer," later given the more prosaic title of Coastal Motor Boat. They carried a single torpedo facing forward in a trough behind the cockpit. To launch, the compressed-air motor of the torpedo would be started and a cordite charge punched it over the stern. The boat then swerved away leaving the torpedo running on course. Much to everybody's amazement, the system worked—despite the turbulence left by the wake of the boat, the torpedo ran straight and true.

From the first lines on paper in January of that year to the following July, the Thornycroft company delivered twelve boats. Two extra vessels, with the torpedo gear removed, arrived at Harwich a week later. With no launching trough cutting into the rear deck, these boats featured a low crawlspace to a second cockpit cut near the stern where a Lewis gun gave protection. Inside the space the navy crammed two bunks, ammunition, an extra fuel tank and radio equipment. A department at the top of the War Office had a very specific job for this pair. The boat now running alongside *Carysfort* was one of these two.

In the narrow cockpit protected by a low windscreen, Admiral Sir Percy Scott, dressed in an old uniform jacket over a turtleneck sweater, with his feet in sea boots and cap set at a jaunty angle, was having "a whale of a time." He stood at the helm, a plain steel wheel.

"Do you know, Lieutenant Blake, when I first went to sea, anything that could manage much over ten knots was considered fast?" He shook his head in wonder. "You are a lucky beggar." He eased the throttle to haul the boat back to the steady pace of the cruiser, two hundred yards off her port bow.

Blake laughed. A young man with the odd combination of straw blond hair and brown eyes, he knew just how lucky he was. "If you offered me *Iron Duke* tomorrow, sir, I wouldn't take it. This is the future of naval warfare. The Dreadnought battleship is already obsolete."

Jac stuck her head through the hatch separating the open cockpit from the engine compartment at the heart of the boat. The V12 nestled low in the hull ahead of the cockpit, tended by a sailor with the rank of Leading Motor Mechanic. "That's a controversial viewpoint, Lieutenant," she held a mug in each hand. Jenkins, the mechanic, had rigged a kettle he heated on the exhaust manifold. "Here's your tea, gentlemen." Blake took the mugs then helped her through the hatch. She had to crouch to move around the engine and then stretch as she emerged.

"This, the submarine and the aeroplane, will decide naval campaigns in the twentieth century." He did not turn a hair at the appearance of a woman on his ship. Jacquieline Courroyer was one of a series of women he had welcomed aboard, but the first not picked up from a Belgian beach in the dead of night, or collected from a blacked-out Dutch fishing vessel in the middle of the North Sea. He liked her forthright manner, and the obvious delight she took in his vessel. She looked the part too, dressed in blue sweater, trousers and sea boots.

"And all three have the torpedo in common," Jac said.

Blake raised his mug in salute, "Indeed they do, Mrs. Courroyer. With speed, stealth, and a torpedo on your side, a dreadnought is just a magnificent, anachronistic, target." He had no idea his willingness to explore new ideas had marked him out at Dartmouth Naval College as a troublemaker. Wise heads at the Admiralty knew they needed trouble-makers to win a naval war in the twentieth century. Sub-Lieutenant Rodney Blake had earned the envy of his friends by being given his first ship at the age of twenty-four. Small as it was, with only two men under his command, he loved it.

Blake took the helm while Sir Percy pulled a small telescope from his pocket and snapped it open. He perched his backside on the edge of the cockpit, rested his elbow on the windscreen and focused on *Carysfort*. He followed the cable up to the kite balloon, Stan Jackson's target. The fabric showed multiple patches. He turned and looked back to land. A speck had appeared over Harwich. He focused again, the image danced in the lens but he recognized a B.E.2. He closed the telescope and pointed out the biplane to Blake and Jac. Sir Percy had been invited to join the group on the cruiser, but a desire to see how the new motorboat performed, and an uncanny instinct for trouble, prompted him to ask for Blake's services for the day. He could not say why, but he had a bad feeling about the planned demonstration.

Blake kept the boat steady, he gunned the engine from time to time to stop the spark plugs fouling, but most of the time only a low grumble came from the machinery, with an occasional hollow splutter from the exhausts, not enough noise to drown out the hum of Stan Jackson's approaching airplane. They watched intently as he curved around to approach his target from the side.

Blake gazed up, "I know how useful they are, but you won't get me up in one of those things." The gap between target and airplane closed rapidly.

"Come on, come on," Sir Percy urged. "You'll collide with the damn thing if you don't watch out." As he spoke, thin trails of smoke leaped from the B.E.2 to the balloon as if the two had been suddenly linked together with black thread. The airplane tilted on one wing and swerved away as a brilliant flash enveloped the balloon. Within seconds it reduced to tumbling fragments, falling beneath a mushroom of thick, black smoke "Good result!" Sir Percy shouted, banging his fist on the windscreen frame.

"Oh hell!" Jac shouted as she grabbed Blake's arm and pointed. The spectacle of the balloon burning had distracted them from Jackson's airplane now plummeting with a plume of thick, oily smoke trailing behind. Without a word Blake slammed his throttle open and spun the wheel. The Thornycroft bellowed as the CMB spun on its heel and surged toward the spot where he guessed the B.E.2 would hit the water.

Jac hung onto the windscreen and braced herself against the motion to keep her feet. She could see Jackson's airplane sliding sideways with flames streaming behind the starboard wings. Twenty feet above the surface the blazing airplane straightened, seconds later it slammed into the water. They watched in awe as a mighty geyser of water erupted. It hardly seemed possible that one small airplane could create such a splash, and impossible that anything could survive, but as the water subsided the B.E.2 emerged from the commotion floating tail-high. Stan had already clambered out of his cockpit. He sat astride the rear fuselage, pulling himself toward the tail like a man riding a log. The nose sank lower as Blake pulled the boat back to idling speed and approached the wreck. Stan saw them and waved, he launched himself clumsily into the water and struggled toward the boat. The lifejacket did its job, keeping most of his upper body out of the water, but making it difficult to swim.

"Hang on, lad, we'll come to you," Sir Percy bellowed. Blake skillfully maneuvered the boat across the direction of the waves to set them drifting toward the wreck. Jac had already scrambled through the hull to emerge in the rear cockpit. Leading Seaman Prentice, responsible for most of the ship handling, stood there coiling a line. He judged the distance and cast the rope. Stan grabbed it with both hands, and between them they hauled him in, dragging him over the side. He slid into the cockpit and lay on the deck at their feet in a pool of water, gasping. Blood poured from his nose.

"Aw hell, thanks for that everybody," he spat seawater. "Did you ever see such a bloody shambles?" They dragged him to a sitting position and unfastened his lifejacket.

Jac knelt down and studied the cut, "Almost every day I spend with Simpson's bold birdmen. You chaps always give value for money, a shambles guaranteed every time." She opened the first-aid box, "The sea water is making that look worse than it is. I'll soon sort it out."

Five minutes later Blake steered alongside the cruiser. Stan clambered up a ladder lowered over the side, helped by brawny sailors. Sir Percy followed him up, leaving the motorboat to curve away and head back to port. As Stan stepped on deck a resounding cheer greeted him from the crew of *Carysfort*, a display of their relief at seeing him safe and appreciation for the magnificent show he had provided. The pubs of Harwich would resound with his exploit that night. The captain leaned over the wing of the bridge.

"Welcome aboard, Lieutenant. My men have some dry clothes and a tot of rum waiting for you below. We'll join you presently."

Stan pulled his uniform cap from his pocket, jammed it on his head and saluted, "Thank you, sir." Water trickled down his face.

Lechelle, Frank Penrose, Ernie Simpson and Sir Percy stepped over the coaming into the wardroom half an hour later to find Stan slumped in a leather armchair, wearing a stained, white sweater over blue trousers a size too big. A piece of cotton wool still plugged each nostril. He started to struggle to his feet, the day's adventure, the bang on his nose and the glass of rum had combined to make him feel dazed and confused.

Frank waved him back in his seat, "Sit down, Jackson, you earned the rest, now tell us what happened."

Stan shook his head ruefully, "I managed to shoot myself down. That's going to go down as a first. One of those bloody rockets—begging your pardon, sir—misfired. It plopped out of the tube, started to fall underneath me going end-over-end, then fired properly and came up from straight below and stuck in my starboard wing, just where it meets the fuselage where all the leaking oil and spilled petrol soaks into the wing root. It went on fire in seconds and all I could do was get down and pancake into the drink."

Lechelle's sandy eyebrows shot up, "My God, man, you could actually see this happen?"

"Yes, sir. Believe me, it all seemed to happen in slow motion. There was nothing I could do to avoid it. I swear the bloody thing chased me."

A trace of a smile crossed Lechelle's face, "Well, damn fine show to get yourself down in one piece. They've managed to fish your machine out as well so no great harm done."

Sir Percy perched on the edge of a table and regarded Stan for a moment, "So, Jackson, your opinion. *Le Prieur* rockets as an anti-Zep weapon?"

"*My* opinion, sir?"

Frank Penrose laughed, "Yes, Jackson, your opinion. After today's little demonstration I would hazard that you are the acknowledged expert."

Stan levered himself into a more upright position, "Well, sir, in my opinion, no. I don't think they are much good, and that's not because of what happened."

"Why do you think that?" Lechelle demanded. "The balloon went up a treat."

"Well, actually, sir, I suppose it is because of what happened. The rocket that hit me could only have traveled twenty yards at the most, so it was at full-power, but it only stuck in the fabric of my wing, it didn't even go halfway through. It set fire to the wing only because it hit the part soaked in juice. The fabric of a balloon is very thin and the head of a rocket cuts into that, but a Zeppelin has an outer skin similar to that of my wing. I don't think they will go through and set fire to the gasbags," Stan paused and sipped his rum. "And the rockets and their tubes knocked ten miles an hour off my speed, and probably a thousand feet off my height."

A mess steward appeared with drinks for the four senior officers, and topped up Stan's rum. Simpson looked into his glass, "Well, gentlemen, I am inclined to accept that. It looks like incendiary bullets are still our best chance."

Lechelle raised his glass, "A toast, gentlemen, to the first man to bag a Zep."

"I'll drink to that," Stan said with feeling.

CHAPTER 25

Tondern, North Germany

Jochen Wolff faced the group. They stood in a cobbled street of thatched, half-timbered houses. Lime trees alternated with ornate lanterns beside the roadway. Will agreed with Matty's description, it really was quite charming.

"Ladies and gentlemen, Tondern is an unusual city. It was a fine seaport until the Middle Ages, when the harbor silted up. The people needed a new trade, and they turned to lacemaking. Tondern lace is now world famous, and very popular in England, where local lacemakers exhibited at the Great Exhibition of 1851." He waited while the groan from his audience subsided. Jochen raised his hands in front of him and smiled. "They may be our enemy, but you must give the Britishers credit for good taste." He waved his hand toward one of the larger houses, "If you will follow me, Frau Jorgensen has arranged a demonstration of lacemaking where she will show her most beautiful, but difficult, art. You will then have the opportunity to purchase samples of this wonderful work."

Matty linked arms with Will, pulling him close as they strolled after the group, "He's quite something isn't he? The perfect tour guide."

"If he gets out of this war alive, I bet Thomas Cook will find him a job," Will murmured. "He is quite the charmer. Dotty Dorothy Schubert is very taken with him."

"He's not the only one she's taken with," Matty spoke out of the side of her mouth.

"Yes, thank God you showed up when you did," Will murmured.

"It's not you I'm talking about."

"What! Who?"

Matty smirked, "Honestly, you men. You love gossip as much as we do," she glanced around. Then squeezed his hand. "Tell you later."

They followed their group into the airy, wood-paneled room. Frau Jorgensen demonstrated how she drew the fine thread from a bobbin at the side of the cylindrical cushion, over which she created her designs. Craftsmanship of any kind fascinated Will, and he studied her work intently.

At the end of the demonstration they moved to a table running along the far wall of the room under the window, where examples of lace lay spread on a deep-blue cloth. "Oh my, where would you use these delightful trimmings?" Dorothy asked, holding up two matching strips of lace.

"Oh, around the legs of your drawers," Frau Jorgensen replied in English, she spoke Danish as her first language and her sing-song accent made the remark sound even more innocent. The American ladies blushed while the men tittered, not used to this matter-of-fact European attitude to undergarments.

Dorothy turned to Matty, "You should buy these, my dear, I'm sure you know somebody who will admire them." A collective sharp intake of breath sounded loud in the room.

Matty smiled sweetly, "Oh, I daresay, but _I_ will only need the one set."

Dorothy glared, her mouth working as she groped for a reply. Before she could speak, Mrs. Schoeffer jumped in, "My oh my! Aren't these precious! I must buy a set." She held up some lace-embroidered napkins. The other wives in the group chimed in. They enjoyed a gossip, but a scene would be too rude. Dorothy turned on her heel and minced to the far end of the table.

Outside in the street, Matty admired her purchases, "I just had to buy these for my drawers," she giggled and held up the strips of lace.

Will frowned, "What on earth was all *that* about?"

Matty shook with suppressed laughter; she drew him apart from the others, "Last night, as I was sneaking out of your room, I caught sight of Dorothy sneaking out from your friend Johnny's quarters."

Will gasped, "My Lawd! That leopard has not changed his spots. He did not say a word this morning."

"I should think not! Women loathe a blabbermouth, and love a discreet gentleman."

"So did she see you?"

Matty giggled, "No, that's the beauty of it. All the others think we have a little something going on between us, and the old girls love that idea, but they would never believe I'm such a shameless hussy as to spend the night with you. On the other hand, I now know just what a trollop Dorothy is, and I've just made sure she knows I know."

Will took her arm and they joined in the slow stroll along the street, "It is her husband I feel sorry for."

She squeezed his arm, "Oh, don't heed him. He has his nose so far up the backside of these naval officers he has no idea of what she is up to."

Will looked at her, trying to frown, "My mother would describe you as a regular little minx. I declare you are really enjoying your little duel with Dorothy."

Her laughter rang out, "Oh, Will, you don't know the half of it," she grabbed his hand and swung it in time to their steps. "Anyway, you can't deny you have enjoyed this visit. You came here with a bunch of preconceived ideas about Germany, and if you are honest with me, I bet you have had to change them."

He nodded; he had to admit his mission had changed some of his ideas. While the German naval airship section displayed the smartness and efficiency the world associated with the German military, it could not be described as *Prussian,* the word the British press loved to use to suggest mindless drill and formality. Will had seen little marching and foot stamping. In fact, beyond the courtesies of saluting and styles of address, there was an ease between officers and enlisted men that he did not find in the British service. Whatever else he may have expected, being able to walk in and out of an operational airship station had not been high on his list, but he had achieved it that morning.

He had eased his way out through the gap in the panels and scurried down the wide grass alleyway between the airship hangars. He had peeped around the corner, ready to duck back, and found the tarmac apron still deserted. He had straightened his jacket, put his hands in his pockets and strolled to the perimeter road and set out for the entrance to the base. Five minutes into his walk a small truck appeared. His heart beat faster when he saw four men in the back, but he relaxed when he saw they all wore working fatigues. He smiled and waved as it drew to a halt.

The driver leaned from his cab, "Good morning, Mr. Turner. The oberleutnant said you might need a ride back to the gate. I will collect you when I have dropped these men." He spoke in German, and Will decided he could afford to drop the pretense of knowing little of the language. Last night at the party, Georg and Jochen had teased him and told everybody that during the engine failure emergency, Will had shown a fluent command of German, but with a marked Bavarian accent. Relieved to tell the truth for once, he explained how from the age of five, every week, his mother had insisted he took piano lessons. His teacher, an old Bavarian lady, had tried her best, but even though he had attended until the end of high school, she had failed to make a concert pianist of him. She had, however, taught him in her own language. He had attended German language classes at MIT to polish the skill, and to enable him to read scientific papers in the original German. Matty had been delighted, the others just as pleased to find he played the piano.

The truck had deposited him at the gate, where he signed out. A second truck traveling into the town to collect civilian workers for the Hydrogen gas plant, dropped him at the hotel, in time for a second breakfast and to join the tour of the town.

Matty nudged him, "Go on, Will, admit it, you are enjoying yourself. Why don't you come on to Berlin with us?"

"My job is done, Matty. I am a technical journalist and your people at the consulate in New York only cleared me for this part of the visit. What point would there be in me coming to Berlin?"

"Will! How could you?"

He heard real hurt in her voice and knew he had blundered, "Apart of course from spending more time with you."

Her frown changed to a pout, then a grin, "That was the right answer, and just in time, buster."

Will steered her behind a tree and kissed her, "I would love to spend more time with you, but do not be fooled. These naval types are charming, but believe me, they have to watch me and control my movements. When we reach Kiel tomorrow, I will change trains for the journey to Holland while you go on to Berlin. They have already told me that I will have a 'guide' to make sure I do not get lost. What they really mean is an escort to make sure I do not stray."

Matty shrugged, "Well, can you blame them? This is a country fighting for its life."

"Not for a moment. I am sure the French or British would do just the same. And yes, I have enjoyed my journey, but it is you that has made it."

Chris Davey

Matty giggled, "Oh, don't try that southern charm on me. I know that you find those damned airships more interesting."

He thought of the previous night, "Interesting, but not thrillin' like you." He kissed her again.

She responded, then drew back, "Mr. Turner, I imagine we will be meeting again in the good old USA." He made to reply but she placed her finger on his lips. "No, that is what is called a rhetorical question." She grinned, "We *will* be meeting again."

"Yes, ma'am."

By the time they sat down to a farewell dinner that evening, he could not say he enjoyed playing the part of a secret agent, but with the end of his mission in sight, and the evidence in his pocket, he could admit to finding it exciting. He cautioned himself not to drink to excess. A sense of relief had swept over him during the day. Nobody gave any indication they thought him anything but a visiting journalist to spoon-feed propaganda. Within twenty-four hours he should be safe inside neutral Holland. His situation almost seemed too good to be true. Mission accomplished, and on his way home. It *was* too good to be true.

Among the guests at the dinner he found Bruno Loewe, the former army aviator. His Iron Cross made him a celebrity and the naval aviators clearly liked and respected him. He wore a double-breasted field gray jacket with a distinctive velvet collar that Will had noticed other civilian officials wearing. During the course of the dinner Will noticed Bruno watching him. He put it down to curiosity. Late in the evening, as Will strolled down the long corridor returning from the men's room, Bruno stepped from a side door and took his arm.

"Captain Turner, please step this way."

"Yes, can I . . .." he realized in an instant he had given himself away. "I am sorry, I think you have made a mistake."

Bruno closed the door of the small office behind them, he turned to Will and smiled, "No, there is no need to say anything," he unfolded a slip

338 –

of paper and held it under a desk lamp. "Your signature and your army number?"

Will stared in disbelief, the blood pounded in his ears, he looked around, run or bluff? He took the note and read, in his own hand, *Give this man all urgent medical assistance.* Underneath he had signed his name, written it again, with his rank, in capitals, and for good measure added his service number. He looked at Bruno, "How?"

"Do you remember, last winter, a British attack and a Rumpler?" Will said nothing, but nodded. "You fired a short burst from below. We had not seen you. Your first bullet went through my back. My observer put us on the ground and you followed us down. The doctors told me that your quick help and medical knowledge saved my life, and that note helped later."

"But how did you recognize me?" Will saw no point in denials.

"They say your life flashes past when the Angel of Death knocks at your door. Maybe that is true, but I can tell you the last face you see before you pass out for several days is stuck in your memory," Bruno smiled. "You looked familiar the moment I saw you, and when you signed my record book, it was easy to compare with this."

"You kept that note all this time?"

"Yes. I had planned to find you after the war and write a letter to thank you for my life. Now I can do that personally."

Will sat down on the edge of the desk, "Damn, my luck!" he felt as if somebody had punched him in the stomach. So near yet so far.

Bruno laughed and opened a cabinet. He took out two glasses and a bottle of scotch. He poured and handed Will a glass, "To your good luck!" He raised his own glass.

"I am sorry, I do not understand."

"Your good luck. That I have found you before the army intelligence idiots get their hands on you." Bruno drank, then held up his glass to the light, "Excellent, only the finest."

"Now you really are confusing me."

Bruno's face looked hard in the dim light, "You have been betrayed, my friend. They know who you are."

"Well they would if you have told them," Will folded his arms.

Bruno shook his head, "I have not. I know in truth not how army intelligence have discovered who you are," his English sometimes slipped and he used German word order, making him sound old fashioned and curiously courteous. "It is not anybody from here, I know."

"So, what is going to happen?" Will drained his glass. He knew his fate lay in the hands of this genial, but tough ex pilot.

Bruno refilled both their glasses, "What should happen is that you will remain unaware of the trap they have waiting for you. When you arrive at Kiel, after your sad farewells to your friends, you will be taken to the barracks for questioning, instead of going on to Holland. They think it better not to make a big thing, you understand. Your friends will not know."

"And then what?"

Bruno shrugged, "Spies are not treated well."

Will eyes narrowed, "You say that *should* happen. What do you think *will* happen?"

Bruno took out his watch, "What will happen is in five minutes you will climb down the ladder that is against your window and then get into the back of the little truck waiting in the corner of the hotel yard. You will hide yourself under the canvas sheet in the back. I will take you to within five kilometers of the Danish frontier. From there you are on your own."

"Do I have time to say goodbye to a certain someone?"

Bruno tapped his watch, "Five minutes. Come." He opened the door and beckoned him through.

Will strode back to the restaurant. Matty sat chatting to Jochen Wolff and Mr. Kaltenberg. She wore the same shimmering blue gown she had showed off on the ship. She had piled her hair high and pinned it in position with a tiny, diamond clip. She wore a string of pearls at her throat with matching earrings with gold settings. His heart jumped. He moved behind her chair.

"Will," she turned to face him and gave him a dazzling smile. "I thought you had got lost." She turned back, expecting him to sit down. Instead he bent over and whispered in her ear.

"You know, my dear, I believe I have been hopelessly lost since I met you," he kissed her neck. "I really am truly sorry, *aufwiedersehen*." He left without looking back.

He took the stairs to his room two at a time, stuffed his spare clothes and belongings in his valise, slung that over his shoulder and scrambled over the window ledge. The truck stood with its engine running. Will glanced around, then dived in the back and pulled the old canvas sheet over him. The truck jerked into motion and clattered out on to the cobbled highway. A few minutes later it slowed.

"Okay, you can come out now," Bruno leaned back from the driving seat and pulled the cover back. The truck had an open cab and Will could step over from the cargo area into the passenger seat. He sat down, breathless. They had left the town behind and trundled through open country.

"Why are you doing this, Bruno? You are a patriotic German; I would expect you to turn me in."

Bruno shrugged, "A life for a life, Captain. I owe you that. Besides, you have done no harm."

Will stared at him in the dim light reflected back from the tiny headlights, "You said it myself, I am a spy."

"Yes, but a failed spy," Bruno stuck out a big hand. "The camera, Captain, and your notebook if you please." Will hesitated, then reached in his pocket, took out the cigar case and handed it to Bruno. He then opened his valise and gave him his notebook. Bruno steered with one hand and clicked the catch on the case to reveal the miniature camera. "Magnificent! It could be German."

"I still do not really understand why you are doing this, but I am grateful of course."

"Oh, it is loyalty to my comrades at the base as well. I expect the British have big competition between the army and navy?"

"Yes, they do."

"Well, the same is here. Somehow army intelligence have discovered you, and they want the credit. That is why they planned to catch you in Kiel instead of asking the naval police to arrest you here. In this way, now we have the evidence," Bruno waved the camera. "We can claim we discovered you, but somehow you gave us the slip, perhaps helped by Danish nationalists." That way the navy does not lose face, and army intelligence look like stupid fellows for not acting faster." Bruno accelerated as they rolled on to a main road. "In all ways, it is very satisfactory: the army look like fools, the navy is seen to be efficient, I get the credit for discovering you, and have the satisfaction of knowing that a very fine gentleman is safe and I have done my duty to you."

Will regarded him for a moment, then shook his head in wonder, "How on earth do you manage all this? How do you know? How come you have a navy truck for your personal use for God's sake?"

Bruno steered off the road and stopped, "I suppose you might say I arrange things for Friedmann and the others. Perhaps, most important, I smuggle all luxuries over the frontier. The navy knows this and helps, while looking the other way of course. As for knowing what is going on, well, I have twenty years service in the army, and that means twenty years worth of good friends, some in good places."

He jumped down from the truck and pulled Will's valise from the cargo bed, "This is as far as I go. The frontier is just a few kilometers ahead."

"Could I use the railroad?"

Bruno shook his head, "Not a good idea. They search the trains. There are hundreds of escaped English prisoners of war running around at any time. I wonder why we bother. They seem to walk out of our camps when they like. We should just lend them all a bicycle and have done with it. Most leave through Switzerland or Holland, but a very few must like bacon and pretty girls so they come this way." He pointed into the darkness. "Where it does not follow the river, the frontier is just an old fence, in some places a wide ditch. There are no mines. It is patroled by a few reservists, but they spend most of their time tucked away in their huts drinking schnapps and smuggled coffee. There are many holes where goods pass through, if you understand. You will have no problem."

He seized Will's hand, "I will say *aufwiedersehen,* Captain. When this war is over, come find me and we will have a real aviator's drinking party." He jumped back in the truck and jammed it into gear, "*Hals und Beinbruch!!*"

Will realized that a man in evening dress strolling toward the border might look suspicious. He changed into his comfortable jacket, thick trousers and boots. He stuffed his evening clothes under a hedge and set off. A low moon illuminated the countryside, giving enough light to make his way. He moved off the road and struck out over the fields. The ground had quickly soaked up the rain from the thunderstorm that had nearly downed the airship. He found the going easy. After an hour he slowed and began to move with more caution. He did not want to stumble into a patrol, no matter how old the soldiers in it.

He moved along a hedgerow, tripping over roots. He peered at the far side of the field, his eyes adjusting to the moonlight. He could just make out a line of poles. He held his breath and listened. Apart from the distant hoot of an owl, and the sighing of the breeze in the leaves, he heard nothing. He took a deep breath and sprinted forward, crouching low. The fence was little more than chicken wire with a single strand of barbed wire along the top. He looked along it. A footway had been worn by the boots of the patrols, but what caught his eye was the shape of a tree that grew up on the German side, and spread its branches over the wire into Denmark. Will grunted, no need to cut himself to ribbons on the barbed wire. He scuttled to the tree and shinned up the trunk. He paused to catch his breath, in the first fork, just in time to hear the clink of accouterments as two figures came into sight at the edge of the next field. The moonlight caught the silhouettes of the distinctive coal-scuttle helmet issued to the German Army.

Will froze. He had to make a quick decision. A flying leap into Denmark, or stay still and hope they passed without seeing him. If he jumped, they might still open fire. Too late, they were too close. He held his breath. They must pass right underneath him. He looked again; thank God they did not have a dog with them. The two soldiers strolled with their rifles slung over their shoulders. The glow of a cigarette lit the face of one of the men. Their conversation carried up to Will as they drew near.

"Hold on, Theo, that beer has passed straight through me." Will shut his eyes in near despair. They stopped right underneath the tree. He could reach down and tap on their helmets if he wanted.

"Rolf, it's not the beer, it's your age."

Rolf chuckled and leaned his rifle against the fence then turned back to the tree. Will could hear the sounds of a man fumbling with his fly, a familiar hissing and then a contented sigh.

"Theo, you're just jealous. Look, I can still piss over a five-bar gate." Will groaned inside. A few feet from safety and here he crouched, unwittingly trapped by two old soldiers about to have a pissing contest.

Theo laughed, "That's about the only sport we can compete in these days. Come on, we've still a way to go, and Mr. Nilssen promised to leave some more tobacco at the eighteen-kilometer drop." The soldier, Rolf's, relief was nothing compared to Will's, when he saw him shoulder his rifle and join his friend in a slow stroll along the wire. Will breathed again as they disappeared into the darkness. Without delay, he crawled forward, threw his bag over the wire, hung from the branch and dropped into Denmark, two meters from the fence. He lay still for a moment, catching his breath. At least he had not blundered onto one of the points on the frontier where the Germans and the Danes carried on an illicit trade in tobacco and booze. He staggered to his feet and stumbled forward, and sank up to his knees in thick, cold ditchwater. He thrashed across to firm ground, holding his bag high, "Welcome to bloody Denmark, Will," he cursed.

He had no plan, beyond making his way to Esbjerg where he hoped to find a British Consular office. He only carried his American passport, but a cable to London should confirm his status. He walked across the fields in the darkness, sometimes forced to angle along ditches and hedges until he found a narrow country road that appeared to head away from the frontier. He plodded along. The excitement of his escape behind him, he had time to think, and a wave of something near despair swept over him. For the second time that day, he had to tell himself to take a grip on his emotions. He had not made a complete hash of his mission. He had confirmed in his own mind that the Zeppelins did not use a gas-shielding system, even if he did not have the evidence now, and he had seen and learned much that would be of use. Most of all, he had come out in one piece, physically at least, but he felt as if his heart had been ripped out by what he saw as his betrayal of Matty's trust. While all might be fair in love and war, they made for a dangerous mix.

He came to a fork in the road. He had been walking for hours; the moon looked paler as the early summer dawn crept up on it. A haystack beckoned in a field next to the highway and he accepted the invitation, sinking into the softness. He dragged off his boots and lay back, weariness caught up and he felt himself sliding. He looked up at the moon and addressed it out loud.

"Mr. Moon, I came, I saw, I fell in love, and I was kicked out. I reckon I should stick to piloting in future." Will fell into a deep sleep.

The heat of the morning prodded him awake. His head throbbed, and he had a desperate thirst. He pulled on his boots and walked to the road. There was no one on the road in either direction, so he flipped a quarter he had in his pocket. The coin chose the right fork and he started walking. At last he saw what looked like a village ahead. Cottages, thatched and half-timbered, lined the road. He strolled into the center to find himself in a small town. The smell of fresh baked bread teased his nostrils. He was famished, and thirsty. He found the source of the aroma, a small bakery that doubled as a café. Round tables stood on the sidewalk. He stopped and looked in his wallet. To his delight he found a few Danish bank notes left over from the voyage on the *Margarethe*. He stepped into the cool interior, blinking as his eyes adjusted. A pretty, dark-haired girl stood behind a wooden counter. He felt her eyes travel down to take in his stained and muddy trousers and boots.

"*God morgen,*" she smiled.

Will smiled back, "*God morgen,*" He had exhausted his knowledge of Danish.

"Do you speak English?" The girl looked puzzled. So far he had been impressed by the way most Danes spoke at least some English, but they had been seafarers. He was in rural Denmark now. "*Kaffee? Wasser?*" He tried German. The girl laughed and waved him to a table. He pointed to a pastry on the counter and she brought it to him before disappearing into the kitchen. Seconds later she reappeared with a glass of water and a pot of coffee, before stepping back out of sight. He was enjoying his second cup when the doorbell tinkled. A tall thin man with unusually large ears, wearing a dark blue, military style uniform stepped inside.

"God morgen."

"God morgen," Will smiled, perhaps he should learn some more Danish. Their coffee and pastries were excellent.

The man sat down in front of him, *"Deutsch?"*

Will sensed trouble, he looked like a policeman, "No, American."

"Ah, we use English," he extended his hand and Will shook it. "So you are American. May I ask what you are doing here?"

"Why would you be interested?"

"Because I am a police officer, and we are interested in everything. We are interesting fellows you know."

"In that case, I am on vacation. A walking tour."

"Really? You know it is such a big coincidence, but our colleagues over the frontier have asked for us to look out for an escaped British officer who might be posing as an American, and to send him back to them."

"And do you do what your colleagues over the frontier ask?"

The waitress appeared over his shoulder with a second cup. He held up the pot, "May I?"

"Of course."

He poured then looked up and smiled, "No, never, but as a neutral country, we are obliged to intern combatants of either side if they appear on our territory."

Will pulled his passport from his pocket and flipped it open, "I am as neutral as you, an American citizen."

The policeman took it from him and studied it for a moment, "Mr. William Turner, a journalist I see." He handed it back. "Or is it Captain William Turner, of the British Royal Flying Corps, carrying Mr. Turner's passport? You won't mind coming to my office while I make enquiries?"

Will sat in the sunshine at his favorite table in front of the café surrounded by his new friends, the old men of the town. He had copies of the *Daily Mail,* and *The New York Times,* spread in front of him, a Danish/English phrasebook and dictionary at his elbow. In a mixture of Danish and English they discussed the progress of the war. Over three weeks of what he could only describe as "town arrest" had given him a working knowledge of the language.

He had spent two days in a cell at the police station. At his insistence the American consul had been summoned. They ended up in a heated discussion. Will's homegrown politeness, instilled in him from childhood, was the only thing that prevented it from blossoming into a blazing row. The consul, a Mr. Weeks, made it clear that Will was an embarrassment to the American government, and he would do nothing for him. Will's parting shot, delivered from behind the bars of his cell made him laugh when he recalled it. "Well, I would be obliged if you could tell Uncle Sam just what he can do with that last income tax demand, if this is the service I get."

The British consul had not been much help either. He told Will that he would just have to lie low until the dust settled.

"This business really is deuced inconvenient, you know," he had said, mopping his pink, bald head with a spotted handkerchief.

Will looked at him for a moment, "World wars do cause a lot of inconvenience, I guess. I am most sorry if my being incarcerated has interfered with your arrangements for tea." His acid remark had goaded the consular official into some action. He suggested to Niels Mortensen, the town policeman, that Will could offer his parole and agree not to escape, in exchange for a move to more comfortable quarters. Mortensen had readily agreed, with the proviso that Will would continue to challenge him at checkers as he had done for the two previous evenings. Will had moved into a guesthouse where he had been spoiled with superb food and delightful company in the form of the owners' two daughters, both anxious to improve their English. He enjoyed his time with them, perhaps because they reminded him so much of Matty, but he needed more to occupy him. He seethed with frustration at not being able to return to England with the information he possessed. He had committed everything to paper in his first few days. In the following days he had tidied the graveyard of the Lutheran church, weeded the garden surrounding the police station and, on the previous Saturday, played for the local soccer team and scored in the last few minutes of the match to give them victory.

Niels had been most indiscreet. The whole town knew who he was, and the people had taken to addressing him as "Captain." It caused him no problems. The town was solidly pro-British. Memories of the War of 1864 with Prussia lingered. Old Knud Pedersen had fought in that conflict, and his memories stayed fresh and bitter. At any excuse he would roll up his trouser leg to show the bayonet wound above his knee.

Knud held up the *Daily Mail* as they sat drinking coffee, "Captain, this map shows the British advancing all along the Somme front. This must be good news."

Will looked at the map, "It should be, Knud, but I am sorry to say that whatever happens, this paper calls it a big victory." Will held up a copy of *The New York Times,* now two-weeks old. "This American paper has to use whatever the British authorities give them, but they do have other sources, and they speak of terrible British casualties."

Jesper Nedergaard held up a popular Danish daily paper, "I think this may be true. This reporter has information from the Red Cross. They speak of fifty thousand British losses."

Will frowned, "Well, I do not think that can be accurate, no army could sustain that, but there will have been many men killed and wounded."

Knud sighed, "And some of these are your friends, Captain. I know how it feels." He waved to the waitress through the window, "Let's drink some cognac to honor the dead."

Niels, the policeman, arrived on his bicycle as Birgitte served the cognac, she went inside to fetch him a glass. He turned to the others, "Gentlemen, permit me. Captain Turner and I have official business," he ushered Will to a table away from the old men. "Sir, I have good news, you are to escape today."

Will gave a whoop, "At last! How?"

"You are to steal my spare bicycle and go to the railway station at Ribe. There you will catch the train for Esbjerg, where you will be met at the station."

"When do I go?"

"As soon as you can."

Will sprinted to his lodgings. The mother and her two daughters cried. He kissed all three and shook the father's hand. Niels waited for him at the café with his spare bicycle: tires pumped up and chain oiled. Niels strapped his bag to the carrier and Will swung his leg over the saddle. Birgitte, the waitress, rushed from inside with a paper bag containing his lunch. She hugged him and he hugged back. The whole town seemed to have turned out to see him off.

Will put his foot on the pedal and prepared to push off, "Hey, Niels, my friend, what do I do with the bike?"

"Take it to the police station. That's where all stolen bikes end up."

Will rang his bell and pedaled away. He waved as he went, "Thank you, everybody. I will come back one day."

CHAPTER 26

Esbjerg, Denmark

Will guessed the boy's age at about twelve. He wore short pants, a smart tweed jacket, and a matching cap that looked a size too big. He politely asked Will if he also waited for the train to Esbjerg. Will replied in halting Danish, at which the lad switched into near perfect English.

"Goodness! How did you know I spoke English?"

"Oh, I know the accent. In my father's business we have many English sailors. He is a chandler." The boy gave an emphatic nod, proud of his knowledge and his father.

"Did you learn all your English from sailors?" Will guessed his mother might not approve of some of the words picked up from that source.

"No, also we learn English at school," he offered his hand. "Eric Amstrup, at your service."

Will shook his hand, "Will Turner, likewise." While Eric explained he had been to visit his grandparents, the train wheezed into the station jetting steam into the air, the only cloud in a perfect blue sky. The boy held the door open for Will and they settled into their seats.

"Are you a sailor, Mr. Turner?"

"No, I am an aviator, and you must call me Will."

The boy's eyes opened wide, "An aviator! You mean you fly?"

"I do indeed."

Eric's formal façade fell away. He was in love with flight and bombarded Will with questions. He carried a school bag from which he pulled photographs of Allied and German airplanes clipped from newspapers. The politics of the conflict held no interest for the boy, he had his favorites and Germany built most of them. Will agreed the Rumpler looked a better airplane than the ungainly British B.E.2. The train slowed as it neared Esbjerg. Eric was desperate to show Will his prize collection of *sanke* cards. Will had seen these in stores and the hotel in Tondern: postcard-size propaganda portraits of the new German aviation heroes. He had been amused to find that Johnny Behncke had just been immortalized for the benefit of an adoring public, and he had signed a few for Will.

"How do you get these?" Will asked.

"Oh, my uncle is a smuggler. He sells drink, tobacco and coffee to the Zeppelin station at Tondern. A nice man called Bruno gets them for me and gives them to my uncle." Eric was matter of fact about his uncle's nefarious activities.

"I bet he does!" Will laughed.

"Do you know him?"

"Yes, very well, and he is a nice man." Will thumbed through the collection, and froze. He picked out one card. His hand shook slightly. "Do you have swaps of this one?"

"Oh yes, I have many of the airship crews, that is Kapitan Friedmann and his crew with the new ship."

Will's mouth felt dry. "I have swaps of a very new card, Leutnant Behncke, five victories," he pulled out one of the cards from his valise, and played his ace. "Signed. Interested?"

Eric's eyes bulged, "Yes please! This is not even in the stores in Germany. How did you get it?"

"He is a friend of mine. That's how I got it signed." They did the deal as the train clanked to a stop. A porter opened the door and Eric jumped down, clutching his prize. A tall blond man with a heavy mustache waited for him on the platform.

"Father, I would like you to meet Mr. Turner, he is an airplane pilot."

Will and Mr. Amstrup shook hands, "I hope my boy has not been annoying you, Mr. Turner."

"Not at all, sir. Not at all. He is very good company, and you must be proud of such a polite young man who speaks such good English."

"I am," he turned to his son and playfully tugged the peak of his cap over his eyes. "Are you traveling on, Mr. Turner? Can we give you a ride?"

"I am, but I am being met here I believe." Will shook hands again with them both, and the father and son strolled away, Eric chattering about his journey and the amazing Mr. Turner, the pilot.

Will sat on a bench and took the sanke card from his pocket. He hesitated to study it for a moment, worried his first impression had been too optimistic, but he had been right. The photograph, an excellent reproduction, showed most of the men he had met on *Viktoria* posed in front of the control car of a Zeppelin. They sat and stood in two lines, those in front sitting cross-legged. Will recognized Frankhanel, the machinist, in the middle with the ship's mascot, a scruffy white mongrel called Otto. The control car hovered just above them with the wheel visible through the forward windows. Martin Friedmann and Georg Klaas leaned from the side windows, facing forward, like locomotive engineers leaning from their cab. The men's expressions ranged from severe to happy to Martin Friedmanns' proud smile. It was a fine group photograph, one that would be treasured for years to come by the families of the men, but what had caught Will's eye appeared in the background. The ship was not *Viktoria,* it was the new, much bigger craft that hung next to her in TOSKA. She boasted a new engine arrangement, and the forward starboard engine projected from the hull in plain view. Even without a magnifying glass, the clutch of long exhaust pipes could be clearly seen sweeping down from the engine nacelle, where they spat the spent gases away from the ship.

Will shook his head in amazement. He held in his hand a photograph better than those he had worked for weeks to obtain, and then lost. How could they have been so careless with the sanke photographer? The answer made him think hard about the origin of his mission. Naval intelligence had passed the picture because they believed it showed nothing of interest, and they were right. A hull and an engine nacelle told the British nothing they did not know already. Could it be that it never occurred to the German Navy, that anybody would even consider a gas-shielding system, because they themselves saw the idea as a non-starter? If that was the case, he thought, what about the business of Hubert Matrett overhearing two men discussing such a system in Switzerland? Had two German intelligence officers fooled Matrett with an elaborate charade on their own initiative in the hope of planting misinformation? Or did the Matretts fabricate the whole thing for commercial gain? A polite cough interrupted his train of thought.

"Captain Turner?"

Will stood up, "Yes, are you Helge Hansen?" A stocky man with thinning blond hair, a neatly trimmed beard and a deeply tanned face offered his hand.

"At your service: Master of the steam drifter *Orion.* Follow me please." Hansen took Will's bag and threw it into the back of a Model T Ford. As they clattered toward the docks, he chatted in almost accentless English, explaining that he had often taken escaped British prisoners of war, and agents to a rendezvous point far out in the North Sea, where they transferred to Royal Naval ships, and even on one occasion to a flying boat. "That was a thing to see, Mr. Turner! I would love to ride in one of those."

He made it clear where his sympathies lay in the present conflict, "Bloody Boche, they took half my country in '64. That was before I was born, but I still have an uncle and an aunt who are forced to live in so-called, 'Greater Germany,' " he paused to spit over the side of the car. "You know the British actually pay me to do this? I would do it for nothing, but I take the money because it would be rude not to." He threw back his head and roared with laughter.

Orion lay tied up to the wharf, a handsome vessel with her straight stem, smart paintwork, and long, slender funnel decorated in Danish red and white. Hansen and his three-man crew had steam up and the ship underway in an hour to catch the evening tide. They gave Will an old sweater and sea boots to make him look more like a commercial fisherman, and instructions if a German patrol boat stopped them.

"It is really only to trade for coffee and fish, they are always polite," Hansen shrugged. "When this is all over we will all have to get along together. But we don't want you to arouse suspicion."

Will nodded, "Is there anything I can do to help work the ship?"

Hansen grinned and handed Will a telescope, "Take this, stand in the bow, and watch out for drifting mines until your eyes ache. The Germans are not supposed to mine our coast, but the damn things break free and drift up from the south."

Will took the telescope, "Trust me, I declare I did not come this far to be blown up!" The North Sea stretched away to the western horizon, reaching for the setting sun that burnished its flat surface like steel reflecting fire. He peered ahead, alert for anything that could be the horns of a contact mine breaking the surface. The hiss of the bow cutting through the water and the throb of the engine sounded like music to his ears, telling him that every minute took him nearer home. He leaned back against a winch.

"England, home and beauty?"

Will jumped, he had not heard Hansen join him in the bow. He turned with a smile, "You read my thoughts, Captain."

Hansen handed him a mug of coffee, "That is what I have heard Englishmen say. They are very anxious to be home by this stage in their journey. We carried a young sergeant last month who had escaped from a camp near Hanover. He had been captured at Mons in 1914, nearly two years a prisoner. He was looking forward to seeing his family again."

"I bet he was," Will sipped his coffee. "How long before we rendezvous?"

"In the morning. By the time it is dark, we should be past any mines, but if you would be so good as to stay lookout until then, we would be grateful. Then you can get your head down for a few hours."

Will shaded his eyes against the glare of the setting sun and swept the horizon, "It looks peaceful enough, but fishing sounds like a dangerous game, even for a neutral."

Hansen nodded, "Yes, quite dangerous, but *very* profitable. You see while it is difficult for British and Germans to fish, that has given time for the stocks to build up. We dip our nets and come up with tons of profit, and then I get a fine catch like you," he laughed and clapped Will on the shoulder. "Give me another couple of years like this and I will buy the German High Seas Fleet, sell it for scrap and end the war for you. After the big battle a few weeks ago most of their ships are only fit for the knacker's yard anyway."

"Really?" Will's eyebrows shot up. "I thought the Royal Navy got the worst of that engagement."

Hansen shook his head, "It is true that more British ships sank, but I watched the Boche limping back to port with their tails between their legs. They had taken a pounding and no mistake. *Seydlitz* barely made it home, she was listing so bad and well down at the bow." Hansen drained the remains of his coffee and cast the dregs over the side. "The big damage was done to the spirit of the German Navy. Their propaganda people dressed it up like a victory, but I tell you that the scuttlebutt in the bars is of mutiny. There are Bolshevik agitators at work, you mark my words."

Will stared at the Dane, "Mutiny? In the German Navy? That is incredible."

"We live in unusual times, Mr. Turner. The old order will be changed forever after this war. The British blockade is biting hard, and meanwhile that old fool Kaiser Wilhelm struts and puffs and lives in luxury. His people know that, and they are not happy." Hansen shrugged, "Another hard winter, more reverses at the front, and who knows what might happen."

Will rolled into his bunk with Hansen's words in his head. The thought of men like Martin Friedmann and Georg Klaas doing anything other than fighting to the death seemed inconceivable, but much of what the captain had said made sense. It was one thing for the officer class to swear undying allegiance to the kaiser, but they had to carry the people with them. He recalled a conversation with his cousin, Rupert, during the big retreat two years ago. Rupert had told him that mutiny was never far below the surface in a beaten army. He lay with his arms behind his head, wondering what the situation on the Western Front really was. Tomorrow his questions would be answered, and he could return to his real job. Aviator.

He slept as *Orion* chugged through the night under a brilliant star lit sky. A change in the rhythm of the engine pulled him wide awake. Frederik, a partner in the ship and first mate, brought him coffee and showed how they had the luxury of hot water, piped straight from the boiler for shaving. As he toweled his face dry Will glanced from the porthole. A thin early light showed the ship drifting, surrounded by a thick mist. He stepped on deck, glad of his sweater. Hansen beckoned him into the wheelhouse.

"Good morning, Captain Turner."

"Good Morning, Captain Hansen. Have we arrived at our rendezvous?"

"If my friend from Harwich navigates as well as Frederik, then yes." He reached for a chord hanging above the wheel and tugged. The ship's whistle split the damp air with two short blasts, and one long. They listened, not speaking. Seconds later a noise that to Will sounded much like a motor horn, honked from somewhere in the surrounding mist. Hansen laughed. "Not bad, not bad at all. We've been in and out of this mist since dawn, but Frederik is a genius with the stars. He only needs half a sight and he will tell you where you are within a mile."

Will stepped out on deck and listened, turning his head to try to calculate where the other vessel lay. His ears picked up a low rumble, a big gasoline engine at idle, and for a moment his hopes rose that perhaps a naval floatplane might creep out of the mist. A long, low shape materialized from a bank of fog a hundred yards off their bow. "Good Lawd! How did that get here?"

Hansen leaned out of the wheelhouse, "Same way as us, just a hell of a lot faster." The Coastal Motor Boat sidled toward them describing a wide arc to come alongside. Hansen hailed the officer at the helm, "Good Morning, Skipper. Did you have a good voyage?"

Blake laughed, "Very pleasant, Captain Hansen. How's the fishing?" He wore a battered and oil stained cap and grubby coveralls over his uniform.

"I fished an army officer out of Germany for you." Hansen appeared at Will's side holding his valise. "Have a good journey, Captain Turner. Get back to the front and give those bastards some hell for me."

Will shook his hand, "Consider it done, Captain." The motorboat had edged in to the hull of the fishing vessel, presenting the stern where he could see a second cockpit with a Lewis gun on a high-angle mounting. A sailor lounged against the gun while a second grappled the boat against the fenders on *Orion's* side. Will stepped across, the gunner leaned forward to grab his arm and steady him.

"'Ello sailor! Want a good time?"

Will's jaw dropped as he saw who held his arm, "Jac! What the hell are you doing here?"

She grinned as he pumped her hand, then leaned forward and kissed her cheek, "I can see you've been on the Continent too long, picking up their fancy ways."

"Damn right I have been there too long," he paused. She too wore dark blue coveralls and sea boots, but he could see she also wore a khaki shirt and tie underneath, and a soft peaked cap with an unusual badge. "Jac, have you just joined up?"

She shook her head, "No, I joined up nearly two years ago. Hadn't anybody told you I'm a 'FANY'?" She stopped and burst into laughter at the look on his face. "First-Aid Nursing Yeomanry, you ninny. It's my cover in case I get captured. We pitch the gun over the side and claim this is a rescue boat, and I'm the medic, and just hope to God nobody recognizes me." She broke off to wave to the crew of the *Orion* as they slipped away from her side. "So, tell me how you got away."

Prentice, the leading hand, disappeared through the hatch to make his way forward to prepare a cold breakfast, giving Will room to sit down in the cramped cockpit. Will gave Jac a brief account of his adventures from the time he had scrambled out of his hotel window. She nodded approvingly when he told her how he had crossed the frontier, and laughed out loud at his story about the two old soldiers and their weak bladders. The boat slid through the mist just maintaining steerage way; the engine a subdued rumble, the swish of the water under the stern sounding louder. Jac unlocked the ammunition drum from the Lewis, turned it over and checked the load, then examined the bolt and cam. Satisfied, she clipped the drum back in place and locked it, then swung the gun from side to side and up and down to make sure she had a full field of fire. Will watched her with a half-smile. "Very professional. I would say you enjoy that."

"Yes, and what I can do with it given half a chance."

"Do you think you might get a chance?"

Jac adjusted the rear sight, then turned to him, "I might. This fog is burning off fast. Prentice admits he's a lousy shot, and we often see German seaplanes out here."

"Where exactly is 'out here'?"

"A bit under two hundred miles from Harwich. You have been sailing southwest all night."

"You mean you have already sailed two hundred miles in this?"

Jac pointed forward, "We had a lift. This little beauty fits in the davits on anything bigger than a destroyer." As Will peered into the murk, a gray wall of mist solidified, took shape as the side of a warship, then dissolved into vapor again. "We are not alone. That's why Blake has us creeping along."

Prentice appeared with tea and the inevitable bully beef sandwiches before ducking back through the hatch. Will turned to Jac. "Now, for heaven's sake, tell me what has been happening while I have been away. It has been over two months and God knows how many miles since I left."

Jac spoke fast, all the while checking around the boat as the mist thinned. She told him how Simpson, Moore and the two Frenchmen had nearly shot each other down. She told him about the success in forcing down the German reconnaissance airplane, and the disaster over Harwich in the fight with the German bombers.

"What do you mean, Ned is 'lost'?" Will asked.

She looked at him, her lips compressed, "We held out hope that he might have been rescued, but two weeks ago floating wreckage washed up on the Norfolk coast. It was Ned's plane, the poor little sod must have been shot down. If he had been rescued by a British or neutral ship we would have known at once. If a German ship had picked him up we would have been informed by now through the Red Cross. Say what you like about the bastards, but Brother Hun does play the game when it comes to prisoners, and efficiently at that."

Will sat silent, then passed his hand over his face, "Any more bad news?"

"Plenty. The Prof is hobbling around on a crutch. He was badly wounded in the same fight. They say he will never fly again. Jankowski is in hospital. He smashed up landing on the wrong field in the dark and hit the side of a barn, but he should live."

"Oh, good grief!"

"And not forgetting Stan Jackson," the ghost of a smile came over Jac's face as she spoke.

"How could I ever forget the Wild Colonial Boy? What has he done now?"

"Shot himself down in the sea testing *Le Prieur* rockets. We fished him out with this. He's okay, but he did it in style in front of all the top army and navy brass."

Will shook his head slowly, "And on top of all this, we still have not downed a Zep?"

Jac nodded, "On top of this, we *still* haven't downed a Zep," she repeated. She picked up a sandwich and bit into it, "Oh!" She spoke through a mouthful of bread, "your merry men did manage something constructive, if you can call it that. Bill Ives and Stan Jackson piled Matrett's brainchild, the *Destroyer,* into a big stack of sh—" she checked herself, "farmyard manure."

Will brightened, "Really? That is topping news. How did they manage that?"

Jac grinned, "Let's just say it was a joint effort. You will be delighted to hear that Matrett is still arguing with the War Office about funding the repairs. It's a shame you lost those photographs; that would have driven the final nail in the coffin of that idea. When your report arrived from Denmark about your escape, you could have heard the groan from our office on the next floor. Though nobody is blaming you," she added quickly.

Will reached into his bag and took out the precious *Sanke* card. "I might have lost all the photographs I took, but the German Imperial Navy kindly gave me a better one."

Jac took the card from him and stared, her lips moved for a moment before the words came out, "You can see the bloody exhaust as plain as day; there is no ducting system, it proves it. This blows Matrett's case out of the water – but how? What is this? A snap of their outing to the seaside?"

Will smiled and took the card back, "They are made for propaganda. You can buy them all over Germany from newsstands and in hotel lobbies."

Jac hooked her thumbs in the belt of her coveralls and fixed him with her stare, "But Will, do you realize what this means? The German Navy could not care less if we see the damn engines. They have never even considered a gas shielding system and don't imagine we ever have either. This means that young Matrett's story about overhearing that conversation is probably a load of rubbish."

"That thought crossed my mind as well," Will sipped his tea. "And another thought that crosses my mind, is that one of our agents in Switzerland could have crossed the frontier, stopped at the first railroad station, bought that card, and posted it back to Uncle Frank's office, saving a whole heap of time when I could have been working on Zeppelin defenses, and saving me from making a damn fool of myself in the process."

"Now what do you mean by that?"

"Oh come off it, Jac. I must be give up to be the worst agent in the history of British intelligence."

Jac shrugged, "Why? You came back with a most useful photograph, and from what I hear you have some other valuable information."

"That is as may be, but I am not going to get by with that," he paused. "Jac, I gave myself away."

"Why do you say that?"

Something about the way she spoke made him wonder if she teased him, and his voice showed his irritation, "Well, number one, I gave in to pressure and wore my uniform home in Tallahassee."

It was Jac's turn to be surprised, "That wasn't the wisest thing to do, but it did not give you away."

"Well, if that was not stupid enough, I made a fool of myself over the very woman leading that damn party of German sympathizers. The goddam sympathizer in chief!"

"And you think you might have talked in your sleep?"

"Jac!" It came out as if he were about to deny his actions, but he realized how foolish that would sound. She obviously knew what had gone on by the smirk on her face.

"No, that was not it either," Jac said. "That was the most damnable piece of luck running into the very German pilot whose life you saved, though The Prof says that aviation is a very small world. Still, as it turned out, it worked to your advantage, he saved your skin because you did not give yourself away—you were betrayed." She stopped and pointed, "The fog is clearing."

Will stood up and stared in near disbelief, the motorboat had run clear of the fog bank and he could now see why Blake motored with such caution. They had been running between two columns of ships. On either side he could see two light cruisers, but as he looked back, he saw the tripod mast of a battleship above the fog bank. Seconds later the bow thrust through the mist as if pushing through a curtain, the barrels of the mighty guns in the two forward turrets sniffing the clear air.

Jac waved her hat, "Doesn't it make you proud to be British?"

"It makes me damn glad I am on the same side," he sat down. "Has all this been laid on for me?

"Don't flatter yourself. This is a coat trailing exercise to see if we can coax the buggers out for another scrap. We just came along for the ride, but it was well timed."

Will looked at her. "Now what do you mean, I was betrayed?"

"Just that. We heard that German intelligence had been alerted to who you were. We have worked hard to find out the who and why, and we do know the information originated from Switzerland, but that's as far as we have got." She frowned, lifted her cap and set it back on her head at an angle. "What you have just told me has me thinking the unthinkable."

"What is that?"

"That a man, knighted by His Majesty, could be a traitor."

Will's pulled his head back and stared at her, "You mean Matrett could have ratted on me? That is one hell of an accusation. I know they hate me, but to betray a British agent is treason of the worst kind. By God, if you proved it he could swing."

She nodded, "Yes, that's a happy thought. Just think about it for a moment. He has 'previous' as a copper would say. Remember he scuppered your synchronizing gear for his own gain."

"That is correct."

"They stand to lose a fortune on the *Destroyer*. He has been heard ranting about you in his club, saying you are just a jumped-up Johnny Foreigner. He is always boasting about his connections, and we know he does a lot of business in Switzerland."

"That is all true, but it is a big step to give information to the enemy."

Jac stroked her chin, "He didn't: or at least not in his own mind or in any way I could prove. Here's my theory: Somehow he did get wind of you joining the German American Alliance Group. You visited the German Consulate in New York, and the Germans did mention you in a newspaper article about the Alliance visit. Word got back to him that an American journalist called Will Turner was in the party, and it would have been easy to discover you were absent on leave, and put two and two together. Then all he had to do was entertain some Swiss businessman to dinner, and come out with some line about the stupid British

Government not believing his theory, and paying a neutral American to go snooping on their behalf. The Swiss bloke, knowing on which side his bread is buttered, slips a warning to his German contact, and you are in the—"

"Precisely. I still think it sounds far fetched."

Jac smiled, "That's what I like about you—you always prefer to think the best of people."

"It is not that. I just cannot imagine Matrett taking such a risk."

"But can't you see? There was no risk; if anything ever came back to him, he could just pass it off as a drunken remark to a trusted friend. The man is too damn clever for us to pin anything on him, for now at least." She caressed the butt of the Lewis gun, "Perhaps he might meet with an accident—a fatal accident."

"Jacquieline!" Will frowned.

She just smiled and changed the subject, "Anyway, you should not be so hard on yourself. Matty said you were very convincing," she had been looking ahead as she spoke, eyes narrowed. "Look out! It's a bloody Hun!" She snatched back the cocking lever on the Lewis and swung the gun around in one movement.

Will lunged and jammed his fingers between the trigger and the back of the guard, stopping the gun from firing, "Whoa Tex!! It's one of ours." A big biplane bore down on them, pontoon floats dangled from long wings, Will recognized a Short 225 instantly.

Jac watched it approach, "Are you sure?" She sounded disappointed.

"Of course I am sure."

Jac craned her head back as the floatplane roared over their heads, its colorful British cockades clear under its wings. She grinned sheepishly, "Whoops!"

Will sat down again and shook his head in wonder, "My! You are bad off to shoot a German," he stopped and looked at Jac hard. "What did you just say?"

"Whoops."

"No, before that. Before you made to open fire." Will stiffened in his seat.

"I said, you should not be too hard on yourself, Matty said you were very convincing." Will just sat and stared. Jac leaned against the bulkhead and smiled. At last she spoke, "You still haven't worked it out, have you?"

"No, I have not. I seem to be missing something here," his voice, slow and precise as ever, now sounded low, as he tried to contain himself.

Jac stuck her hands in the pockets of her coveralls, she looked at the deck under her feet for a moment, then looked him in the eye. "Some might say you are naïve. I prefer to think you are just one of nature's gentlemen who cannot believe women can be so devious, even in a good cause."

"Are you saying what I think you are saying?"

Jac raised her eyes to the sky for a moment, exasperated, "Yes. Matty Ellerkamm is no more a German sympathizer than you or I. She's one of my girls, sent along to look after you." Will sat glaring at her. Jac continued, "Don't look at me like that. What's got your goat? The fact you didn't work it out? Or that I did not think you could look after yourself?"

"Well, I mean. I mean that is just not fair . . ."

"Oh, give over, Will. You're just suffering from male pride." She pulled a pack of cigarettes from her pocket, plucked one out, bent low behind the windscreen and lit it, giving Will time to think.

"But how the hell was I supposed to guess?"

Jac stood up, took a long drag, then exhaled, "That's just the point, you were not supposed to guess."

"But her name?"

"Her granddad was Dutch."

"But the German American Alliance. How did she get to where she was in the organization?"

"A year's hard work. Good agents don't just appear in the right place, you know." Jac watched him, her eyes narrowed against the smoke from her cigarette.

"But she was so damn convincing, she took *everybody* in." The tension drained from Will's voice as he spoke.

"So she should, it's her job. Matty is an up-and-coming actress. Or at least she was, before the Hun torpedoed the British merchantman her brother was serving on as an apprentice deck officer. I can tell you before you ask why: same as me, same as your sister. Revenge, pure and simple."

Will slumped back in his seat, "Well, that answers a question that had been at the back of my mind. And I can tell you that her guard did slip once."

"What's that? How did she slip up?"

"Not a million miles from here, on the way to Denmark on the *Margarethe,* we picked up the body of a British seaman in the remains of a life boat. She really broke bad; she was deeply upset. It seemed peculiar to me that she would be so out of sorts about the death of a British sailor, when she had been talking about us as the enemy only minutes before. I put it down to her being confronted by the reality instead of the propaganda, but bless her, she really was moved, and for good reason."

Jac leaned forward and patted his arm, "Now you see she's not a bad person, and you can give yourself credit for sensing that, and stop feeling guilty about falling in love." Will frowned but Jac just winked and laughed, "You are quite predictable, you men. Now can I explain why I sent her to keep an eye on you, so you won't think I am such a bad old bat?"

Will leaned back and laughed, "Alright. Explain away."

Jac flicked her cigarette butt over the side, "We know enough about how the wily Hun operates to know that amongst the party from the Alliance, there would be a full-fledged intelligence officer. They had to be suspicious of you, and they had somebody planted to keep an eye on you." She paused. "Any guesses?"

"Nary a clue."

"Well, did anybody try to get close to you? Dare I say, 'intimate'?"

He had been sitting shaking his head, but he stopped and looked at her, eyes wide. "Good God! That floozy Dorothy Schubert!! No. . . impossible, she was Italian, she came from New York," he stopped and shook his head again, "No, dammit, she was just too dumb."

"Yes, she's a bloody good actress as well. She also had everybody fooled. We've had her number for the past year. Matty had to stop her getting her hooks in you."

Will slumped, "Oh."

Jac threw back her head and laughed, "Men!! Now you're thinking the only reason Matty slept with you was out of duty."

He shrugged, "Well, the thought did cross my mind."

Jac patted his head, "Trust me, duty was the excuse she used to salve her conscience. She wanted you, Sunshine, and she made up her mind the minute she met you. Believe me, the woman is crazy about you."

"Hold on, you talk as if you have spoken to her recently. She must be in some danger if she is still in Germany."

Jac shook her head, "The party left Rotterdam in neutral Holland last week. I met her there. Their ship docked in New York yesterday. Matty is auditioning for the Ziegfeld Follies even as we speak."

"So her career as an agent is finished?"

"In Germany, yes. It is too risky to send anybody more than once, but I have no doubt she will be able to get up to plenty of mischief at home. She is a great friend of Mrs. Gaunt and the captain. Need I say more?"

Will laughed, "No." he was about to speak again when Blake hailed them from the forward cockpit.

"Hold on everybody. I'm opening up." The easy fluid motion of the boat hardened as the stern dug in with the thrust of two hundred and sev-

enty five horsepower hurling the boat on to the step. The fleet, now clearly visible as the mist dissolved under the heat of the sun, fell behind as
they skimmed across the surface at thirty knots. Jac joined Will on the
bench seat, sitting with their backs against the bulkhead sheltered from
the wind now whipping the White Ensign out behind. They watched as
the cruisers and battleships dwindled until only their upper works showed
above the horizon, each marked by a smudge of smoke.

"How long to Harwich?" Will asked.

"About five hours at this speed. Home in time for tea," Jac stretched
her long legs and rested her heels on the edge of the cockpit. "The chaps
will be awfully bucked to have you back. The war is not going well and
they need a boost. We all do."

Will nodded, "I kinda guessed that. The British papers I saw trum-
peted big victories on the Somme, but the ones from neutral Europe and
the States spoke of big casualties. One Danish paper even claimed that we
suffered fifty thousand on the first day, though I realize that is not possible."

Jac looked at him, then turned away, "Fifty-seven."

"What?"

"Fifty-seven thousand, with nearly half of those killed," Jac lit another cigarette. "Uncle George Brett had it exactly right. Our barrage hardly
dented the Hun fortifications, and it didn't breach all the wire. The crafty
buggers just sheltered deep in their hidey holes until the barrage lifted,
then poured out to man their machine guns. Our men were cut down in
their thousands as they went over the top. Whole battalions wiped out in
a few minutes."

The color drained from Will's face, "So the attack just stalled?"

Jac shook her head, "That's the wonder of it. The battle is still going
on. We have made some gains: a few yards here, a ruined village there, but
every foot seems to cost a hundred lives." She watched the smoke from her

cigarette whipping away in the breeze. "It's a balls-up, Will. A lethal balls-up. If Haig had any decency, he would shoot himself."

"How has George Brett taken it?"

"Badly. He threatened to resign, but your Aunt Constance talked him out of it. We need experienced soldiers who can think more than ever. They have shifted him sideways and attached him as a liaison officer to the ANZAC Corps. He is sailing for Australia this week. Haig wants him as far away as possible."

"I can see why he would not want George around. The old boy is a born troublemaker. He will do well with the Australians and the Kiwis," Will pulled a sweater from his valise, rolled it up and put it behind his back. "On a more personal level, how are my girls doing in London?"

Jac coughed, "Ah, yes. There's something I need to tell you." She told him the story about Marie's indiscretion, and how his friends had dealt with the aftermath, in matter-of-fact tones. She did not try to soften the details or spare his feelings. She concluded by telling him about her new romance with Jean Duchenois. "I think in aviation terms, you might call it a full-throttle affair, with all that means."

Will blew out his cheeks, "Well, I am hardly in a position to judge her, now am I?"

"Some might," Jac said with a half-smile. "In fact some do. She does seem to live a busy romantic life. She is gaining a reputation in London as a bit of a . . . "

Will shrugged, "Trollop? Floozy? So she likes men. She is an adult and she is far enough from home for it not to matter. She is also honest, kind, brave and loyal. Frankly, I do not give a damn what people think of her. I prefer to think of her as a good sport and I am proud to call her my friend."

Jac laughed, "That makes you very unusual. Most chaps would be very disapproving."

"Ha! Most chaps are full of . . . well, let us just say they can be hypocrites. They might look down their nose at the Maries of this world in what passes for 'respectable' company, but I declare they would rather spend their last night before going back to the trenches in the arms of a good sport, than sipping tea with a respectable young lady."

Jac grinned, "Good for you, I know you're right." Though I suspect Marie would rather call you 'lover' than friend."

"Ah, well, she has her dashing Frenchman now, and it sounds serious. I just hope to God he manages to stay alive. I would hate for her to lose him."

"You really are not jealous?"

"As I said, I am not in a position to be."

She patted him on the shoulder, "But you are in a good position to enjoy the journey. I'm going up front to spell Blake at the helm. He trusts me not to turn us over while he has his sandwiches."

Will settled back and despite the noise, and rough ride, he dozed. Jac nudged him awake and thrust a bundle into his hands. It was his working uniform. He squeezed into the space inside the hull and managed to change by lying flat. An hour later a dark line on the horizon took shape as the low hills behind Harwich. Will squeezed through into the front cockpit and stood behind Blake at the helm, and watched as he throttled back to bring his craft sliding through the shipping to its berth.

Will shook hands with Blake and climbed a short ladder to stand on the wooden pier. A voice sounded loud behind him, "Mind your back, sir. Coming through." He stepped aside as two sailors pushed a cart loaded with anchor chain on to the quayside. The cart stalled at the slight incline. The bearded sailor turned to his mate, "Come on Ginger, you idle bleeder. Put yer fucking back into it!!" Will smiled. He was home.

CHAPTER 27

The War Office, London

A dmiral Sir Percy Scott peered over the top of his spectacles, "Oh, for goodness sake, Bloomfield, you're obsessed with invasion."

Bloomfield, an artillery officer, had waxed his mustache so the ends came to a sharp point. They twitched as he spoke, "Well I should think I am! We hardly want the bally Hun traipsing ashore unopposed, just when he feels like it."

Sir Percy raised his eyes to the ceiling and leaned back, "Look, first the enemy has to break our lines and capture the Channel Ports. Then he has to assemble an invasion fleet. Then he has to defeat the entire Royal Navy, something he singularly failed to do at Jutland, so that he can get his invaders over without them being chewed to bits. I think that might take him a week or two. I imagine that would allow time to get the guns back in position to repel the invasion, don't you think?"

"Yes, but it will take weeks to arrange, the paperwork alone. . ."

Sir Percy glared, "No. It will take you five minutes to issue the orders. I accept that the guns you have capable of firing at high angles are not very mobile, but if you are short of transport, we will arrange extra help. We need those guns pulled back to positions in and around London, not spread in penny packets up the east coast, and we need them here by the end of this week, before the Zeps appear in force as the nights draw in. Please set this in motion now, there's a good chap."

Bloomfield swallowed, "Yes, sir."

Sir Percy glanced up again from his papers, "You can sort out the bureaucracy once we have moved them. If there is any come back, pass it to me."

"I will give the orders immediately," Bloomfield said, mollified. He gathered his papers and left the room.

"Thought you were an enthusiast for aeroplanes, Sir Percy," Lechelle said as the door closed.

"I am, but don't forget we have potted a Zep with artillery, and so have the French," the Admiral turned to Will, sitting with the Prof at the other end of the table in the War Office conference room. "Do you chaps approve of the changes to our spotting-and-tracking system?"

Will spoke for them, "Yes, sir. Giving code names for each reported Zep should make it easier to keep track of them. Giving them girl's names is a nice touch. With the other detail changes, I think we have a sophisticated system."

Sir Percy took off his spectacles and polished them, "Sophisticated, or complicated?"

"A bit of both, sir," the Prof said. "But we do have the men capable of making it work."

"Good. Do that. Bag us a Zep." Will and the Prof stood to leave. The Prof collected his crutches and saluted awkwardly. Sir Percy eyed him for a moment. "Smith, we need to discuss your future. You will be hearing from us soon."

Lechelle looked up from his papers, "Bloody good show you put up, Turner. Excellent work. That bally postcard was a stroke of genius—it finally put paid to Matrett's gas-shield nonsense. A picture is worth a thousand words and it convinced the committee."

"Thank you, sir."

"Yes, but bear in mind it has cost Sir Norman a tidy sum. He'll have your guts for garters given half a chance. Watch your back, laddie, watch your back."

Will saluted, "Thanks for the warning, sir."

A staff car drove Will and the Prof to Liverpool Street Station. Will had spent his first night back in England in London at his uncle's club off Baker Street, where the Prof had surprised him by arriving for breakfast, before joining him for a short meeting with Admiral Sir Percy Scott and Colonel Lechelle. Smith had fleshed out the brief details Will had been given by Jacquieline Courroyer. With time to spare before boarding their train to Chipping Ongar, they found a table in the station buffet.

"Park yourself there, Jim," Will helped the Prof into a chair. "I will get the teas." Will turned away, but as he did the Prof caught his arm and pointed to the door. A small knot of Tommies, laden with kit and with their rifles slung stood looking into the crowded dining room. They shifted their feet and stood uncertainly in the doorway. Will knew by the stains on their uniforms and kit, and the dull sheen of their boots that these men had come straight from the trenches, doing their best to clean up on the journey.

A hush fell over the room as the civilian crowd noticed them. They preferred their war at a distance. The Prof half-raised himself from his seat, "Oi! You lads, over here," he beckoned them in and turned to Will. "Four extra teas, and anything you can get in the way of sandwiches and buns." The men only hesitated for a second. Not used to sitting with officers, but hungry and tired, they piled in to the room. They paused, ready to salute but Smith whipped his cap off and waved his hand to prevent them. "Sit," he ordered, his peremptory manner softened by a smile. "Captain Turner is getting the refreshments from the counter." They sank into the empty seats with a scraping of chairs and a chorus of thanks. Will returned with a tray laden with tea and sandwiches. A waitress followed, bringing a selection of cake and pastries. Their eyes opened wide at the treat that had appeared in front of them.

"Blimey, sir," the senior man in the group, a red-haired lance corporal barely out of his teens, looked at Will in open admiration. "You must have pulled rank to get this lot."

Will passed the teas, "No, I did not, Corporal. It was easier than that. I told the manager you would shoot him if he did not sell me the best he had."

The four young soldiers laughed, but one shook his head slowly, "To be truthful, sir, a couple of times I have felt like shooting some of these stuck up . . ." he stopped, conscious of the difference in rank.

"Bastards?" The soldiers nodded. The Prof continued, *"It's Tommy this, an' Tommy that, an Tommy, go away; But it's thank you, Mister Atkins when the band begins to play."* The Prof quoted Kipling's famous, and bitter poem;* the one piece of verse that every British soldier knew. Will understood, even as an officer he had experienced the same chirpy bonhomie from civilians eager to congratulate him, but unwilling to hear anything bad about the war firsthand. He guessed it must be ten times worse for a soldier from the ranks. He imagined the view of the suited businessmen in the buffet: "Good chaps, but you would not want to sit next to one on a train in case he told you uncomfortable truths, or smelled of the trenches."

The Prof probed gently. These men were fresh from the line: survivors of the Somme. Plucked to safety to train new drafts after a period of leave, and feeling guilty about their mates left behind. Reticent at first, they gradually opened up. They would not have spoken to an officer from a regular unit in the way they now did, but these RFC men in their strange, high-collared uniform, seemed different. They would not even try to tell their loved ones of the horrors they had witnessed. They did not have the words, and they wanted to spare them, but the battered, shaven

---

* *Rudyard Kipling wrote his poem "Tommy" in 1892 in protest at the treatment of off duty soldiers by civilians. "Tommy Atkins" is said to come from an army form the Duke of Wellington was asked to approve. He filled it in using the name of a private soldier on sentry duty nearby and the name stuck as a nickname for all British soldiers.*

headed captain and the sandy haired young officer with the scarred forehead and broken nose, both wore the ribbons of the 1914 Star and the Military Cross. They might understand. Some of the experiences these haunted young men told would live with Will for the rest of his life.

"I looked back and shouted for C Company to come on. They all lay face down in a perfect line. Then I saw they were dead. The whole bloody lot of them."

"We made a hundred yards in four hours. Twenty of us left out of two hundred, and they told us we did well . . . well?"

"The captain sent me to look for Major Hopgood. I found him: or what was left of him, in three different places."

They ran out of steam as Will and the Prof listened. Eventually the lance corporal fell silent, and then he seemed to notice Smith's crutches for the first time, "Did you cop that over the Front, sir?"

The Prof laughed, making the soldiers straighten up and smile, "Believe it or not, over bloody Harwich, and it was a Hun machine gunner who got me as well. The buggers get everywhere." He looked at the empty plates then glanced at his watch. "Well, lads, our train will be off soon," he pointed his finger at each in turn. "Now, don't go feeling bad about your mates. It's the luck of the draw: where the shell lands, or who gets detailed for home. You will all have plenty of chances to get yourselves killed before this is over."

The men slung their packs and rifles and followed Will and the Prof, now moving with ease on his crutches. Will stopped outside the door, "Hey! What the dickens is going on here?" A mob of civilians had collected around the ticket barrier for one of the platforms, angry voices rose over the usual clamor of a railroad station; a policeman, helmet awry, tried to push the crowd away from the gate. In the middle of the melee, they could see familiar uniforms, one khaki and the rest gray green.

The young lance corporal assessed the situation in a second, "It's the alleyman,* prisoners, this lot are givin' 'em an 'ard time. We're not bleed-

---

* *Slang term used by British soldiers referring to Germans. A corruption of the French "Allemand."*

in' well standing for that!" The four tommies barged into the crowd, unslinging their rifles and holding them at chest height to push the angry mob apart. Will and the Prof followed. The German Prisoners of War had edged back to the barrier and stood in a frightened semicircle while two policemen and an older private soldier tried to restore order.

"What the hell is going on here?" the Prof's bellow silenced the crowd for a second.

"They're Huns, bloody baby killers," a big man in a stained suit, with a day's beard growth on his ugly face, confronted the Prof, who knew instantly this was the ringleader.

"They're German Prisoners of War under our protection, and don't you forget it," the Prof said. To emphasize the point, he poked the man in the belly with the end of his crutch. "Now sod off down to the recruiting office if you want to fight the enemy."

"Ain't it always the same, toffs telling us what to do," a second man, even bigger than the first pushed his face into Will's. "'Ere, you're one of them Flying Corps. Wot you doin' about them Zeps? Fat lot of good you are, poncin' around in your fancy uniforms. . ." his voice rose an octave on the last words as Will grabbed the man's belt buckle and lifted and twisted, tightening the material in the front of his trousers.

"You look like a big healthy fellow. Why are you not in the army?" Will's voice sounded mild, but the extra twist he applied felt anything but.

"Flat feet," the man gasped, tears appearing in his eyes as the pressure on his balls increased.

"Flat feet?" The contempt in the voice of the young soldier standing beside Will could have scorched concrete. The crowd fell back, the angry voices now sullen murmurs.

The Police Sergeant in charge seized his chance, "Right, anymore nonsense from you lot and you're nicked. Now clear off!" The four soldiers, the Prof and Will stood either side of the gate, forming an impromptu guard of honor between the crowd and the prisoners. The grateful Germans trooped through, shaking hands with the British soldiers who greeted them as old friends, making sure the civilians heard them.

"Good old Fritz. Enjoy your stay."

"Need some fags, mate? There you go, take the lot."

The Prof recognized the rank badges on the last man through the gate, "Sorry about that, Sergeant, some of our people need to learn some manners."

He lit a cigarette and passed it to the German Noncom who replied in perfect English, "Oh, don't worry, sir. I know how excitable these cockneys can be. I was a wine waiter at The Ritz before the war. Thank you for sorting them out."

The Prof looked at him in surprise, "Our pleasure. I hope you get your job back when this is all over."

The sergeant saluted, "So do I, sir."

They watched the Germans shepherded aboard the train by the old soldier. Will turned to the police sergeant, "How was that allowed to happen?"

The copper blew out his cheeks, "Came out of the blue, sir. The prisoners were as good as gold, glad to be out of it if you ask me. That old sweat with them is supposed to be their guard, but I think he's only along to make sure they got on the right train. They came off a lorry in the yard outside and by the time they got halfway to their platform, we had a near riot on our hands. If you ask me, it's those bloody Zeps. They've got people well and truly rattled." Will and the Prof exchanged a look. The policeman touched the peak of his helmet, the back of his hand facing toward them in the official police salute, "Well, must be off, gentlemen. Thanks for your help. We'd have been well buggered if you hadn't been here."

They found their train and settled in the dusty seats. Will rubbed the scar on his forehead as he looked over the roofs of the city as the train gathered speed. "They have people well and truly rattled," he repeated the policeman's words.

"I can't really blame them," The Prof replied. "What would calm them down is to see a Zep come down in full view."

"I fancy I might try to do that, and soon."

"I wish I could join you, but Simpson won't let me near a machine."

Will frowned, "Jim, I hope you will not be offended, but at the moment you would be a liability in an airplane. To be frank with you, about as much use as a chocolate sunshade, as Stan Jackson would say."

The Prof smiled, "That's right, break it to me gently."

Will sat back, "Well, I do not believe it is going to be in Simpson's hands anyway. You heard what Sir Percy said. They have a job for you. I would not be surprised if you find yourself sporting a major's crowns on your shoulders, lording it over us from your own staff car."

"It won't be the same."

"No, it will be better, and safer, and God knows you have earned it."

"When somebody brings down a Zep. Then I'll feel as if I earned it."

The mess greeted Will's return with cheers and good-natured "ragging." Only Simpson, the Prof and Dizzy Lipman knew where he had been during his long absence, the others assumed a long and well-deserved leave with a surfeit of wine and women. They had heard him sing and hoped he left that out.

He could not wait to get into the air. As the evening faded, he stood in front of the Voisin, hands on hips, studying the nose. "Well, Henri, they told me she looked like some damn great insect, but now you have stuck a big stinger in the nose we will have to call her the 'mosquito.' " Will had felt equal surprise and pleasure at finding Calmette at the field. The Frenchman had examined Will for his pilot's certificate at Hendon just before war broke out. They were old friends. The surprise that Calmette promised a few weeks before had finally arrived packed in a long wooden crate: a 37mm cannon to replace the Hotchkiss machine gun. The concept was similar to Matrett's Destroyer, the difference being that the Voisin flew surprisingly well for such an ungainly bird. French engineers had fitted similar weapons to airplanes even before the war, and had high hopes of success against a Zeppelin.

Calmette grinned and pointed to the cockpit, the single, long bathtub affair common to pusher airplanes, "To horse, *mon brave!* Let us go sting an airship." They clambered aboard using a ladder steadied by two mechanics.

Will bent over the breech of the gun then turned to Calmette, "Henri, this really *is* a cannon. It fires single shots."

Calmette leaned forward and showed Will how to open the breech and load the long, fat shells from the rack screwed to the side of the cockpit. "To be honest, my friend, I am not convinced myself. If we hit an airship with one shell, it might start the flames, but I think we need several hits. All will depend on how fast you can load and fire." They strapped in and took off, the Voisin bouncing and rocking across the grass on its giant baby carriage wheels. Will enjoyed the experience of playing passenger for once. He had complete confidence in Calmette who some said could see in the dark. In reality, it was a combination of good eyesight, experience and a flair for navigation that made the Frenchman a formidable night pilot.

Will sat in the front seat of the pusher airplane with the breech of the cannon between his knees. He could swing the gun a few degrees either side or elevate and depress the muzzle, but essentially the only way to bring it to bear was for the pilot to aim the whole machine.

He looked over the side to see the darker mass of Chelmsford against the background of fields passing beneath. A pale light still lingered in the western sky, but at ground level, the night had caught up. He wondered for a few moments why the town showed up so well, before he remembered that farmers in this part of England grew mainly cereal crops. The golden fields of wheat cradled the settlements below in a soft glow harvested from the light of a huge yellow moon still low on the horizon.

The Voisin forged a climbing path on a stairway through the night sky. Calmette held his course eastward. As Maldon appeared ahead, both men gazed in awe at the scene before them. Beyond the town, the estuary of the River Blackwater opened to the North Sea, drawing the harvest moon to the land along the glittering path of its reflection on the surface of the water. Will twisted in his seat and looked back at Calmette who smiled and raised his thumb. They both knew they might pay for privileges like these with their life one day, but they accepted the risk.

Calmette pointed to his left, to the north. Will nodded. This would be where they would find the Zeppelins if they came, groping their way inland over the coast of East Anglia before turning south for the big prize: London, heart of the British Empire, the seat of everything the paranoid Kaiser despised, envied and admired about his British enemies.

The Voisin droned on and upward. At Harwich, they reached fourteen thousand feet. Calmette eased the throttle to relax the straining Renault engine behind them as he leveled out. The mechanics had mounted the gun barrel through a slot cut beneath the windscreen, and shrouded it with a leather apron to stop the wind blasting into the cockpit. Will looked through the glass to sight the weapon, sitting in a bubble of calm air created by the windscreen and the shape of the nacelle. He felt a tap on his shoulder and a cup appeared. Henri Calmette had taken his hands and feet from the controls and opened a flask of hot coffee. The big airplane motored along with no guidance from the pilot. Will turned, raised his cup and mouthed "cheers." The coffee tasted rich and strong, boosted by a measure of cognac. The Frenchman cracked a bar of Cadbury's excellent chocolate and passed half to Will. He sat back and sipped his coffee, then smiled to himself. The cheese board and port might appear soon, Calmette knew how to make the most of any situation.

The airplane sagged as Calmette cut the power to reduce the noise level, he leaned forward and shouted, "Tonight we trip the light fantastic! It is fabulous, but too light for les Zeps?"

Will leaned back, "It works for them as well as against them. They will be able to see to navigate. If they are as bold as I think they are, they will come." They sounded as if they spoke down a long tunnel, the thin air distorting their voices. Henri opened the throttle again and nudged the controls to follow the coast, easy to see as even at that height, the surf washing the beaches reflected enough light to be visible.

They both saw it together, to their left and well inland. Will guessed at the famous Kelvedon searchlight, a wavering white finger that abruptly poked into the sky. But, as on many previous occasions, the beam steadied, its target caught as if balanced on top of the shaft of light, a tiny, silver pencil, a Zeppelin in-bound to London.

"*Avant!*" Henri roared as he hauled the Voisin round in a steep turn.

Will twisted in his seat and leaned back to yell above the tumult of engine and slipstream, "Try to cut them off at the pass. He is headed for London. Cut the angle and we should catch him there." He flung his arm out and pointed. Henri nodded his head and banked sharply. The Zeppelin hovered well to the west, its course for London almost due south. Will and Henri could fly southwest and cut the corner to intercept. The searchlight still held the airship, but the angle of the beam now tilted from vertical to forty-five degrees as the German craft slipped away.

"Come on, come on," Will urged another light to take it up. "Damn!" He swore as the beam abruptly dropped away then showed as a silver disc. A few drifts of cloud wandered over the fields and villages of Essex and Hertfordshire and the captain had taken advantage of the cover they afforded. The Voisin roared on, Henri coaxing every last revolution from the engine as they dashed for the city, signposted by the familiar curves of the Thames reflecting the silver moonlight. Will leaned forward and studied the ground. His eyes had adjusted to the thin light and he could make out enough detail to tell him they must be near their field. A few minutes more and they would be above the expensive suburbs of Romford. He twisted and turned in his seat, peering into the sky. Unless a searchlight found its target, their best chance of picking up the Zeppelin at a distance would be as a disturbance against the carpet of stars, perhaps a lighter shadow.

Inquisitive searchlights sprang up, probing the sky. They prayed that they would not be held in a beam, destroying their night vision. An explosion blossomed like an orange flower in the sky as the gunners below loosed off a speculative round. Henri circled, their target had to be close.

"There!" They both saw it together, no more than two miles away, a Zeppelin trapped in the beams of two searchlights, still over the northern suburbs. Henri heaved the wheel over and added a boot full of rudder to drag their machine out of the turn and straighten on course. He held it despite the pyrotechnic display erupting below the airship as every gun of every caliber opened fire. Heavy artillery shells bloomed, tracer rounds from the ubiquitous one pounder "pom poms" mounted slowly into the sky like glowing green balls, and the shells from the vicious "75s," supplied by the French, snapped and flashed. They all fell short: a hazard to Will and Henri, no more than a discouragement to the Zeppelin.

As they watched, a silver veil spread below the ship as she dumped water ballast. Henri slapped Will on the shoulder and stabbed his finger down. A line of flashes appeared on the ground, lingering at some points as incendiaries burned amidst the high explosive dumped by the airship. They could not judge if the deadly cargo had burst in open fields, or among the tidy streets at the edge of the city. They could now see the length of the ship, and make out the black Maltese crosses on her flanks. She had tilted her nose up and started to turn away. Henri pulled the throttle lever hard against the stop to squeeze every ounce of effort from the engine. Will hunched over the cannon and sighted. He held his fire, the range still too great for effective shooting.

"*Mon Dieu!*" Henri cursed. The airship mounted into the sky as if plucked to safety by an invisible hand. They could not hope to climb as fast. The Voisin had reached fifteen thousand feet and they clawed for more. The Zeppelin had made its turn, corkscrewing up into the higher atmosphere and now fleeing to the northeast.

Will unbuckled his seatbelt and turned to kneel on his seat. Henri leaned forward. They held a high-altitude counsel of war. "We still have the legs of him," Will shouted, cupping his hand around the earpiece of Henri's leather flying helmet. "We could maybe pull ahead and see if he comes down some over the coast."

Henri nodded vigorously, "*Bien sur!* We go ahead a few kilometers, then turn back and attack as he comes at us. You have time for maybe two or three shots." Will slid back into his seat and checked the cannon yet again. They could still see the airship, now above them as they outpaced it for level speed. A succession of searchlights held it, but its altitude made it less distinct. The coast appeared again; Will stood and looked back over the top wing. The Zeppelin held its course, unaware of their presence. Flight at extreme altitude was hell for the airship crews, Will had heard about the agonies of frostbite, the perils of hypoxia as the men's lungs tried to squeeze life from the thin air, and the foul taste of the oxygen they sucked from bottles through rubber tubes as a substitute. He was feeling light-headed himself, it must be worse three thousand feet above where every movement took reserves of willpower, but the ship demanded constant physical effort to fly. Perhaps their plan might work; the Zep might descend.

Henri pointed above his head at the torpedo-shaped fuel tank under the top wing. He drew the edge of his hand across his throat. Will nodded; they had been at full throttle for nearly an hour, the powerful Renault engine guzzling gasoline as its reward. They must make their move. Will settled in his seat and strapped in as Henri wheeled around. They could see the Zeppelin above and growing clearer by the second as they closed head on. She still soared way above them. Will pushed the breech down to elevate the gun, as Henri hauled back on the stick. They had not come this far to give up now. The Voisin sat up like a begging dog, teetering on the edge of the stall. The bulk of the Zeppelin filled the sights as Will squeezed the trigger. For a second he could not be sure what happened. Blinded, deafened and choking he clutched the gun as the Voisin pitched forward and plummeted earthward.

The biplane steadied, and Will heard the reassuring roar of the engine. He coughed foul fumes from his lungs and pushed up his goggles and blinked. All he could see was the image of a bright light on the retina of his eyes. The flash of the gun had robbed him of his night vision, while the automatic shell ejector had opened the breech inches in front of his nose and poured cordite smoke down his throat. The recoil of the cannon had lashed back through the mounting into the frame of the airplane, pushing it back just enough to tip it over the edge into a stall.

"Did we get him?" Will shouted.

Henri banked into a turn back toward the sea. Just in time to observe a remarkable sight. For a second the silhouette of the Zeppelin appeared against the face of the moon before disappearing into the darkness, as if fate had conspired the conjunction of angles as an insult. He shook his head, *"Non."*

CHAPTER 28

Knightsbridge, London

Jacquieline Courroyer tapped her notebook with her pencil and looked across the tea table at Will, "If I needed any more proof that Matrett gave you away, then this is it." She had joined Will and Dizzy Lipman at the girl's Knightsbridge apartment for tea on a muggy, drizzly late summer Saturday afternoon.

Will poured more tea into her cup, "What do you mean?"

"Oh, give over. Somehow, every man and his dog seems to know you went behind enemy lines. The only people who should have known are professionally tight-lipped, they did not put it around, but Vicky heard it from a radio operator at the Admiralty."

Will's sister frowned, "Yes, Will, at least you could have told yourself. You know I would not blab."

"Neither would I," Marie said as she passed him another slice of Dundee cake.

"Of course you would not, Marie, my dear. You are well known to be the soul of discretion," he grinned as she blushed, then shrugged.

Jac snapped the notebook shut and thrust it back in her bag, then struggled to close it.

Dizzy grinned, "You know, there are more compact automatics on the market."

She glared, "I am perfectly happy with the Colt, thank you." The latch clicked shut and she gave Dizzy a prim smile. "Now, where were we? Oh yes—Matrett. He put it around, I have no doubt, Will."

"But why? What good could it do him?" Vicky asked.

"I know the answer to that," Dizzy took a sip of his tea before continuing. "It puts Will in danger if he is ever captured. He will be in the German records as a spy, and they will shoot him."

Marie's eyes opened wide, "Oh no! Then you can never go overseas again, Will."

"I might not have the choice."

Jac nodded, "That's true, but there is a simple solution. We just feed the information to the right people that Will used a false name. That's reasonable enough, German intelligence would expect an agent to have a false identity, not use his real name, and there must be at least a dozen William Turners in the British Air Services, it's a common name."

"But an uncommonly nice man," Marie moved closer to him on the sofa.

He looked sideways at her and smiled, "You are most kind, my dear, but I do not think Jean would appreciate you sitting so close. I have it on good authority that you two are stepping out together."

She giggled and snuggled even closer, "We might be."

"Honestly, child, you are the most outrageous flirt," Will sighed. "You really must behave with a little more understanding when he is with you. I declare he is worried enough about me as it is, he must think he stole my girl and I am about to challenge him to a duel. The poor guy salutes me at every opportunity and stands to attention whenever I speak to him. I wish he would relax."

Marie sat up, "I shall tell him there has never been anything between us," she put her nose in the air.

"You do that, love," Jac smiled. "And if you can carry off a porky* like that, we'll make an agent out of you."

Vicky jumped in to save her brother's blushes, "So, you have met the baby killers face-to-face. What are they like?"

Rhyming slang, pork pie = a lie.

"Well, they do not have horns and cloven feet, and they would be appalled if they really knew about the civilian casualties. They honestly believe they only hit military or commercial targets."

"Oh come off it!" Jac frowned.

"I can only speak as I find, Jac," Will shrugged. "Klaas told me that Friedmann would sooner dump his bombs over open country than risk hitting a residential area."

"Then he is the exception to the rule," Vicky spat the words.

"Perhaps, there have been enough casualties to show that others might be less particular, but I doubt any of them set out to bomb civilians."

Jac looked at him, "You almost sound as if you like them."

Will met her eyes, "I will not deny that I have great respect for them. They are brave men doing what they see as their duty, just as we do. In better circumstances, I expect we would be friends. They face an awful choice when we do finally start shooting them down, burning alive or jumping to certain death, but still they come. I do not underestimate them for a moment," his voice dropped lower. "But I would be obliged if you do not underestimate me. Do not think for a moment I will not do my duty. If there was a way we could bring the Zeps down without setting them on fire, then we would do it, but there is not, and we will burn them."

Dizzy nodded, "It's every airman's worse fear, going down in a flamer. The Zep crews know it's the only way they will die. We don't take any pleasure in it."

"But when will that be? How much longer will they get away with it?" Jac asked.

Will laughed, lifting the mood, "You are sounding like a *Daily Mail* editorial," he put his cup back in the saucer. "I think now we have dispensed with the bombs and rockets on the B.E.2s, so they can climb, we shall see a result soon. Of course, if we could convince the brass hats that it is safe to fly a rotary engine machine at night, we might get there sooner still."

"What is the difference?" Marie asked. Underneath the flippant exterior, she possessed a sharp enquiring mind, only revealed to those close to her.

"Controlling a rotary is far more difficult than a stationary engine like a Rolls Royce or a Beardmore. On those, you just push the throttle lever forward to increase power. On the rotary you have to control the fuel and air supply with two separate levers," Will knew better than to patronize her.

"You mean in the carburetor?" Marie asked.

"Exactly. Fail to reduce the fuel supply on take-off and you can stop the engine by getting the mixture too rich. If you have the height, it will clear if you pull the fuel control back, but usually you will not, and down you go."

"So why do you want to fly a rotary machine? It sounds dangerous to me."

Dizzy jumped in, impressed, "Because they perform better. They are lighter and they don't seem to lose power with altitude in the same way as a Beardmore. Will has a theory that the centrifugal effect of the spinning cylinders acts in some way to supercharge them, to force more air into the cylinders and compensate for the thin air at altitude."

Will held up his hand, "Just a theory, but I would love to get my hands on a couple of the new Sopwith one-and-a-half strutters, take the Vickers gun off that we cannot use with incendiary bullets anyway, to save weight, and go after the Zeps with just the observer's Lewis. I reckon we could persuade them up to seventeen thousand, easy, and they do over a hundred miles per hour."

Jac smiled at his enthusiasm, "So how about Tom Sopwith's new scout. The one they reckon looks like the one-and-a-half strutter's pup. Would that do the job?"

"Jacquieline, if you can get us one of those, I will be your slave for life," Will grinned. "But I declare it will remain just a dream." He stood and walked to the window and looked up at the greasy gray sky. "They say it might clear during the evening. We should be making our way home."

Dizzy stood and put his cap on, "Thanks for the tea, ladies. I wish we could stay for the evening, but duty calls. What are your plans?"

"Henri has managed to get five tickets to see *Chu Chin Chow* at His Majesty's Theatre," Vicky looked smug. "He and Jean are taking us three."

Jac laughed, "Yes, Vicky, Henri and me are going to be the three biggest gooseberries ever as far as Marie and Jean are concerned."

"I am impressed! Why, I believe that show only opened two nights ago. No wonder Henri and Jean were keen to swap duty turns with us," Will picked up his raincoat and slung it over his shoulder. "You have fun, girls. Y'all earned it."

Dizzy drove the Crossley tender through rain-slicked streets. They had volunteered to drive to Hendon aerodrome to pick up spares; a slight detour from the accepted route had taken them to Knightsbridge for tea on the way home. The evening light had the dull gleaming edge caused by strong sunlight arriving feeble and tired after forcing its way through thousands of feet of cloud.

Will stuck his head out of the side window and peered up at the leaden sky, "It might be lifting; we can always give it a try." They arrived back at the field where they each prepared a B.E.2c for flight. They had settled on a gun mounting that fixed the Lewis gun to fire almost vertically above the airplane, into the belly of a Zeppelin, placing the breech and ammunition drum in easy reach for re loading. They loaded the drums with a deadly mixture of incendiary and explosive bullets. The cumbersome biplanes had their forward cockpits faired over to reduce drag, and the useless bomb racks had been removed. Instructions to do the same had been passed to the fields that surrounded them, where the three flights of Number 39 Squadron, the new Home Defense unit, had been based. "A" Flight lived a few miles south at North Weald, while "B" and "C" flights were at Sutton's Farm and Hainault respectively. Will had met two of the B Flight pilots for lunch the previous day: Lieutenants Leefe Robinson and Sowrey. He came away impressed. "Keen as mustard" as the Prof would say. He had made a mental note to introduce his sister to Leefe Robinson. The young pilot, with his trim little mustache and wavy dark hair had matinee-idol looks, and a diffident charm guaranteed to impress her. He worried about her, concerned that the bitterness she felt toward the Germans might be eating her up. A little romance, some light-hearted dates with a handsome young man on her arm, would do her good, remind her life was worth living for something other than revenge.

The clouds thinned as the evening wore on, giving a brief, spectacular show as the sun squeezed between the shredded purple stratus cloud and the horizon, before sliding out of sight. Dizzy cast the dregs from his mug into the grass in front of the hangar, "I'll take the first shift, Will." A mechanic boosted him into the cockpit and within minutes, his machine was no more than a shadow flitting above the trees.

Will and the Prof watched him go, "Expect some mist later, Will. After all this rain it's bound to come up." They both turned as Sergeant Moore, called from the office.

"It looks like a big raid is brewing, gentlemen. The navy has picked up signals from at least six Zeps, and one has already crossed the coast up near Wells in Norfolk."

Will glanced at his watch, the luminous hands showed a little before ten. "We already have Stan Jackson and Bill Ives up, and a couple of the new boys. You know what I am going to do?"

The Prof nodded, "Put the kettle on and keep your powder dry."

"Exactly. We are going to end up with everybody back on the ground just when it gets interesting. Let us see how things develop." They joined Simpson in the map room where he pushed wooden model Zeppelins over a map of East Anglia, London and the Home Counties as confirmed reports came in. As the evening wore on, it became obvious they witnessed the biggest effort so far by the German Naval and army airships to mount a coordinated attack. Nobody raised their voices as the watching posts confirmed a succession of airships crossing the coast, but the looks they exchanged spoke volumes. They soon realized that some of the Zeppelins had turned north away from London, as reports came in of bombs falling in the Midland Counties. When a picket boat reported an airship off Foulness, much farther south than its companions, shortly before eleven, Will shrugged on his flying coat.

"That is the one to watch," he pointed to the new wooden counter on the map. "He is on course."

Simpson nodded, "Very likely, but hold on for a bit. If he is coming this way, we might even be able to see him, or at least hear. It will be a good hour before he arrives. Let's keep you in reserve." Will checked the patrol lines of the other defending airplanes and made notes to use courses and heights designed to avoid a collision. He took off half an hour later and settled into the climb. Reports suggested his target followed an erratic course, trying to avoid the London defenses. The moment he left the ground, he could only rely on the efforts of the men operating the Ingram signaling system for guidance. He flew through a beautiful, clear sky, but the remains of the cloud drifting over London, and the ground mist conjured up in the folds and hollows of the farmland, made it difficult to see the ground signals. Will steered for the heart of the city. That was the target. That was where he must meet the raider if they were both to be successful.

The wind battered his head as he leaned over the side of the cockpit, out of the shelter of the windscreen, to check his course. He sniffed the air, fresh and clean, washed by the rain. He reached the Thames over Limehouse, where the River Lea joined from the north, and banked to his right in a steep turn, enjoying the sensation of looking down the wing at Limehouse Basin as it pirouetted around his wingtip. His engine pulled hard and willing as he followed the Thames to the west. Glancing down he saw lights blinking out, but the Palace of Westminster, better known as the Houses of Parliament, stood out beside the river with St. Stephen's Tower and the famous clock with the bell known as Big Ben prominent. He smiled to himself remembering Barrie's *Peter Pan* and the scene with the children flying over London. He knew nobody would mistake him for Peter; the war had already stamped itself on his face.

A hunter's instinct guided him. In reality, the German flyers resolutely refused to match the newspaper stereotype. They did not follow a rigid rulebook, their orders gave them free reign to fly their craft in the way they chose, and they chose to use every trick they knew to confound and avoid the British defenders. Will guessed that an airship commander would soon realize that all the defenses were arranged to meet attacks from the east and north. Before long, somebody would try to loop around the city and attack from the northwest. This might be the night.

Freed from the drag of bombs and rockets, the B.E.2 settled into an easy cruise climb. As he passed over Hyde Park, a black patch in the now almost darkened city, the pointer on the altimeter showed five thousand feet. He leaned over the side and pushed up his goggles. His sister and Marie lived down there. He frowned and cursed, the only clear cluster of lights shone bright from the West End, theatre land, and he remembered their date for the evening.

"Turn the goddam lights out!" he bellowed in frustration into the night. If a Zeppelin did make it this far, that would be where the bombs would be aimed. He hunched lower into the collar of his coat and flexed his fingers around the control column. "Come on, my beauty," he urged his machine on.

❧ ⊷══⊶ ❧

Far below his sister peered into the sky as she left the theatre, "Can I hear an airplane, Henri?" she asked. A high-pitched drone was just audible above the laughter and chatter around them in The Haymarket.

Calmette glanced up into the sky as he lit his pipe. He flicked the match away and puffed hard, "A B.E.2, I think," he frowned and turned to Jean Duchenois. "What do you think, does the Boche come tonight?"

Duchenois peered into the night sky. Marie had her arm around his waist, holding him fast, "You will not leave us, please."

Calmette laughed, "No, my little cabbage, we will not leave you to chase Zeppelins, for the reason we 'ave nothing to chase them with. The good Sergeant Major Cole has our engine in pieces, and there are no other machines for us to fly."

Jac looked around to see other faces turning skyward. She could sense a mood in the crowd. She heard the word "Zep" again in the murmur around them. A cabbie lounging against his taxi saw the French aviators' uniforms and winked, "They'll be on their way tonight and no mistake."

Jac glared at him, "They might be, but don't you go spreading rumors."

He stood up straight and looked down his nose at her. "Who are you to say what I can do?"

Calmette laughed and tapped the old man on the shoulder with his cane, "That is a question you really do not want to find the answer to, my friend."

Vicky linked her arm in Jac's, "Well, Mrs. Courroyer, as you are the only British person in this party, what is the correct thing to do? Head for an underground railroad station for shelter? Go home and hide in the cellar?"

Jac laughed and linked arms with Calmette so they formed a threesome across the sidewalk, "Good God no! We stiffen our upper lips, and proceed to supper as planned. We're not going to let the bloody Kaiser spoil a night out on the town."

❧ ⊷═──═⊶ ❧

Will leveled off at twelve thousand feet after making a dash to the southeast. Searchlights had trapped a Zeppelin. Flashes showed near the river, bombs exploding at Gravesend. He bent the throttle hard against the stop and traded height for speed, but the airship disappeared into cloud. Will almost wept with frustration. How could something so big be so damned elusive? He searched for twenty minutes, convinced this was the ship tracked in over Foulness. At one point, for no conscious reason, he banked hard to the right, and seconds later a shadow flitted past in the opposite direction. Will shuddered—so much sky, so little room, the shadow was another defender, probably a man as frustrated as himself.

The weak red light on the dashboard showed the hands of the clock pointing at two in the morning. This patrol had lasted for over two hours already, time to go home, but a swing to the north would avoid the risk of crossing one of the patrol lines. The B.E.2. started to descend but he maintained a trickle of power to avoid shock cooling the engine.* Will peered ahead where a reddish glow had appeared over the northern suburbs. He pushed his right foot forward to slew the nose to one side and leaned out to get a better view. Will took a deep breath as he slammed the throttle forward again. "At bloody last!"

$$\ast \ \ast\!\!-\!\!\ast\!\!-\!\!\ast \ \ast$$

Vicky pulled her coat tight and pushed open the door to let them out on the roof. Jac and Henri followed her through. She held the door and yelled back down the stairs, "Come on you two, you will miss the show." She heard a giggle and heard a low masculine voice, followed by a shriek of laughter and the sound of footsteps running up the stairs. Marie dashed through followed by a sheepish-looking Jean.

Jac made a clucking noise and shook her head, "I don't know, whatever would your mother say?"

Marie smirked, "Nothing, providing you do not tell her."

Jac turned away and raised her binoculars, "My lips are sealed."

---

* *If a pilot abruptly cuts the power with an air cooled engine it can cool too fast as the airplane glides down, sometimes causing serious damage.*

They had enjoyed an excellent supper. Marie and Jean lost in each other's eyes, while Henri entertained Vicki and Jac. The two young women had both voiced the same thought as they adjourned to the ladies room: Jean Duchenois was every young girl's idea of the romantic hero, but short, balding, ugly Henri Calmette with his big walrus mustache was a man who could charm the birds from the trees. They both adored him.

Vicki had nudged Jac, "Too old for me, but he is just divine. You better have him."

"Are you saying I'm old?"

"Oh no! I mean, well, no, well . . ."

Jac had roared with laughter and squeezed her hard, "Of course I'm older. And as an old boiler, I appreciate not having the competition." They had left the restaurant in high spirits but the atmosphere outside changed their mood. The streets had come alive at the time they should have been closing down for the night. The rumors had spread, and now seemed concrete; to the north they could hear the boom of guns. People poured onto the streets. Everybody sensed this was the big raid London expected, and should have dreaded, but instead of taking cover, they made for open ground to gain a better view. Henri had commandeered a cab and they dashed back to Knightsbridge through milling crowds. Now they took advantage of the best seats in the house for the second time that night. From their vantage point, they could see straight over Hyde Park and away to the north, where the action seemed to be taking place.

Jac swung the binoculars high as they all heard the drone of a high-flying airplane. "B.E.2 again?"

Henri cocked his head on one side, "*Oui,* but two machines," he pointed directly overhead. "This is the second machine; there is another a few miles ahead." His last words were drowned by the monstrous crack of the anti-aircraft battery in Hyde Park opening fire. Even at a mile distant, the sound slapped them in the face, taking their breath away.

Jean shook his fist, "Idiots, army gunners, zey fire at shadows, there is nothing there, you fools." The guns fell silent after a second salvo, leaving their ears ringing. Henri passed around a half-pint bottle of cognac, finesse forgotten in the excitement. A distant crump rolled across the rooftops.

Marie's eyes looked huge in the half-light, "Bombs?"

Henri nodded, "Yes, I think so, but far away, perhaps in zis place Tottenham?" He divided the syllables up making Jac smile. Seconds later the sky lit up.

"There it is!" Vicky screamed as they all saw the airship materialize from the cloaking dark as first one, then two more searchlights splashed against her hull.

"The famous silver cigar," Jac breathed, as she focused the binoculars. "Go to it boys." They watched as the sky around the ship shimmered with the flash of exploding ordnance, seconds later a continuous roll of gunfire reached their ears.

"They've got her ranged," Jac spoke matter-of-factly. "I can't see this one getting away," she paused. "Oh," she spoke quietly. A dull orange glow blossomed under the airship near the stern. In seconds, the entire hull lit up like a Chinese lantern.

✣ ✦━━✦ ✣

Will heaved the stick over and pushed hard against the rudder, "Bloody hellfire!" he yelled out loud as he swerved away from the blazing wreck still charging toward him. He twisted back on to an even keel as he pulled round level with the ship on the same course. Incredibly, it still moved forward, but as he watched, aghast, the nose dropped. He could still see the shape of the hull, but in seconds, it had turned into a blazing skeleton, a monstrous flaming pyre that lit up the ground for miles around. As he

watched, something flew off and up, spinning like a Catherine wheel, a propeller from one of the engines still running flat out.

"Oh my good God!" The heat from the blaze scorched his face as he muttered a heartfelt prayer. "Poor bastards." As he watched, a sudden fear gripped him, he hung over the side and watched as the ship fell, a man made comet leaving a trail of burning debris. He breathed a sigh of relief; the airship plunged toward open fields, and not on to packed streets. As he watched, appalled but unable to drag his eyes away, the ship crashed to the ground, sending a column of fire twisting and boiling into the sky. He took a deep breath and looked around. Clear in the light from the burning wreck, he saw a B.E.2 like his own circling half a mile away like a moth drawn to the flame. "Well done, young fellow, whoever you are." He had no doubt the other airplane had finally achieved what they strived for. The gun barrage had been impressive, but he had seen the shells bursting well away from the airship as he approached. The RFC had finally vindicated the faith placed in it.

⁑ ⊷——⊷ ⁑

Jac slowly lowered her binoculars. Nobody had said a word. The spectacle had been too shocking. Even though the Zeppelin had fallen miles to the north, the sky had lit up as if a new, bloody red sun had risen over the city, but what had made the hair stand up on their necks had been the noise. As the ship had fallen, taking its crew to a horrible death, a low moaning sound had reached them from the park and the surrounding streets. The sound had grown to an animal howl as a million voices roared in a release of relief and triumph.

The two Frenchmen crossed themselves, Vicky and Marie clutched each other. Jac stood looking over the rooftops as the glow faded. She turned to the others, her face grim, "Well, what do you think of *that?*"

Vicky took a deep breath, "I really do not know what to think. I have just watched a whole bunch of Germans die. I thought I would be pleased, but it was just horrible."

Jac nodded, and put her arms round them both, "It *is* horrible," she indicated the stairs with a jerk of her head. "Come on gentlemen, I think we all need a drink."

CHAPTER 29

Cuffley, Hertfordshire, England

Will nudged a length of charred timber with his foot, a weak flame licked along the edge as it rolled over. "This is not a Zeppelin."

Simpson looked over the field. It resembled a vast smoldering garbage tip, covered in a tangle of twisted wire with lumps of machinery standing out like islands in a sea of black corruption. He lifted his cap and wiped his brow, "What is it then?"

"It is a Schutte-Lanz airship. See here, the frame is all made of wood. The Zeppelin company uses aluminum."

Simpson replaced his cap, "Good grief. They build the skeleton of the thing with wood, cover it with a flammable fabric, treat that with dope to make sure it burns even better, then fill the thing with explosive gas, petrol and bombs." He glanced at a black tarpaulin in the corner of the field, "Poor sods didn't stand a chance." He turned to Will again, "as far as the press and public are concerned, it's a Zep. They won't be interested in details."

Will, Simpson, and the Prof had followed their three-ton truck to the site of the wreck. The airship had fallen in a field on a ridge above the village of Cuffley in the County of Hertfordshire, not far from the *The Plough* public house. They had battled past endless lines of people filling the surrounding roads, using every mode of transport: cars, hired motor buses, horse-drawn carts, motorcycles, bicycles and many just plodding through the damp, misty morning, ignoring the light rain, all desperate to see the downed airship. The police had cleared a path for them where they could, but it had still taken an hour to cover the last five miles. They had work to do. Sergeant Major Cole and his team dragged pieces of wreckage aside as they looked for anything that might give them information about the airships.

Simpson noticed two young RFC lieutenants standing by the black tarpaulin. He walked over to them, "Hey there! You two. What's your interest in all this?"

They turned, stood to attention and saluted. The shorter man spoke, "I shot it down, sir." Will stifled a laugh, Simpson had just had the wind knocked from his sails, but for once, he dropped his guard. A broad smile spread over his face. He stepped forward and seized the young man's hand and shook it.

"The devil you did! Well done, laddie, well done! You must be Leefe-Robinson."

"Yes, sir, 39 Squadron. This is Lieutenant Sowrey," Will and the Prof joined in the congratulations. A silent crowd had gathered on the other side of the fence. Will realized they were staring at the tarpaulin and not at them.

Leefe-Robinson noticed them too. He glanced down. A claw-like hand stuck out from under the black canvas, charred and twisted like a chicken's foot. A thick, sweet stench filled the air. He squatted down and tugged the canvas to cover the grisly evidence, then stood and faced the crowd.

"For goodness sake, you people. Show some respect," the men in the crowd hesitantly removed their hats, and a few crossed themselves. He turned back to Simpson, "Sorry about that, sir."

Simpson shook his head, "Don't worry, I understand." The bodies of the airship crew had been recovered from the wreck and placed together under the sheet. He glanced across the field, "Come on, let's see if we can get coffee in the pub." They trudged across the field and through the gate. A policeman glanced at their uniforms and let them through. The saloon bar had been turned into a temporary command post where the local coroner sat with the chairman of the Parish Council and the vicar from the church. They looked up as the RFC men walked in. The coroner looked relieved; he was not enjoying the sudden attention or the enormity of the task that had literally dropped on him from above.

"Ah, good morning, sir, I wonder if you could spare us a few moments."

Simpson dropped his cap and gloves on the table, "Certainly, if the publican can arrange refreshments for my men."

The landlord, immaculate in waistcoat and bow tie, leaned over the bar, "Consider it done. Coffee for you gentlemen and tea for the men outside?"

"Thank you," Simpson sat opposite the coroner and motioned for the others to arrange themselves around the long table. "What do you need from us?"

"Well, I will have to hold an inquest, so I will need to get a statement from the pilot responsible. I imagine that will be very hard to obtain from the War Office."

Simpson smiled, "It probably would be. I would suggest it would be easier to get a verbal statement from him face to face."

"Oh, how would I arrange that?"

Simpson jerked his thumb toward Leefe-Robinson, collecting a tray with their coffee from the bar, "Ask him yourself. This is the pilot who shot down your Zeppelin."

Will later described it to Vicky as the perfect "stunned silence." The three local worthies sat with their mouths open for a moment, before leaping to their feet to surround the young flyer. He placed the tray on the table just in time. They slapped his back, shook his hand and, to his acute embarrassment, the landlord's wife rushed from behind the bar, kissed him hard on the cheek and ruffled his hair. Simpson called for calm and soon Leefe-Robinson began to tell his story.

He had been up for over two hours patrolling across the Thames. Like Will, he had chased the Zeppelin that had appeared over Gravesend, but he had also lost it. He had spent less time looking, mindful of the fact he was poaching on another pilot's patch. Will realized that it was likely that it had been Leefe-Robinson whom he swerved to avoid. He had spotted the glow to the north before Will, and had been a few miles ahead. They had both seen the airship caught in the first searchlight, and for once Leefe-Robinson found himself higher than his target. He had traded height for speed and, with the ship still approaching London, he had soon come up on it. He had dived underneath and emptied a drum of ammunition along the hull with no visible result. He had reloaded and tried again, but once more without success. He reloaded yet again, thankful his gun worked so well, and this time decided to concentrate his fire on one spot near the tail. He emptied the drum and even before his gun stopped chattering, he saw a red glow from inside the ship. Seconds later, he had to dive away as explosions ripped through the airship and it started to fall on top of him. In his excitement, he fired off his Very pistol, but it was only when he returned to his field, he found he had shot away part of his own center section as well.

Will and the Prof listened with quiet satisfaction. They had always had confidence that if the searchlights found a Zeppelin at a height the second-rate airplanes they had to use could reach, a simple Lewis gun loaded with incendiary and explosive ammunition would prove lethal. Having confidence and proof were two very different things. William Leefe-Robinson had provided that proof.

By the time he had finished, the pub had filled to bursting point with officials and members of the local community anxious to congratulate their new hero. He began to look uncomfortable. Simpson rescued him by announcing that he had to return to his unit to be ready for another night's work. A dispatch rider arrived as Simpson and Will stood outside the pub doorway while the Prof and Sowrey tried to clear a path. He hesitated for a moment then marched up to Simpson and saluted.

"Excuse me, sir. Are you the senior officer present?"

Simpson glanced around, "I believe I am."

"This is a message for a Lieutenant Leefe-Robinson; could you sign for it and give it to him?"

"Of course," Simpson signed the rider's book and took the sealed slip. As the motorcycle roared into life and bumped away, Simpson raised the thin envelope to the sky and peered through the paper.

"Can you read it, sir?" Will asked, just as curious.

"We really should not read another officer's personal correspondence."

"Of course not. What does it say?" Will laughed.

Simpson shook his head and winked. As Leefe-Robinson clambered into the Crossley tender he had used to reach the site, Simpson passed the slip to him, then stood back and returned his salute. They stood and watched as the little pick-up truck bounced on to the road and chugged away.

He turned to the others, "I don't think there's much danger of young William going on patrol tonight, unless it's down to the Ritz."

"Why is that?" The Prof asked.

"Because they've given him the Victoria Cross."

⸎ ⊷⊶ ⸎

They found a stranger in the mess when they returned to Abbots Roding, an officer on attachment to the Sopwith Company as a ferry pilot. Jackson and Ives had been entertaining him well.

"I'm Tompkins, old boy," he hung on to Will's hand to steady himself. "I musht shay, your chaps have been awfully nice to me, awfully, awfully nice." He spoke with the deliberate care of the very drunk. His eyes were glazed and his big nose had begun to glow.

"I should think so too, we are known for our hospitality," he glared at Ives who shrugged his shoulders and raised his hands in a gesture worthy of Henri Calmette. Will turned back to Tompkins, "How did you get here, I did not see another airplane on the field?"

Tompkins tried to focus, "Airplane? Oh, you mean an *aer-o-plane*. You must be one of those American Johnnies. Here, have a cigar," he pulled a case from his pocket and opened it. Will took a cigar and rolled it between his fingers. Tompkins leaned back against the bar and started to slide sideways before Stan Jackson caught him and propped him up. He wagged a finger at Will, "You won't have. Truth to shay, I made a bit of a balls. Set off back from Martlesham Heath after the gun trials this morning even though the weather was a bit *iffy*. One of the chaps up there marked this field on my map in case the clag closed in, and suggested I head this way in case I needed a bolt hole."

Will lit his cigar and eyed Tompkins, "Lucky you did."

"I should say so! The cloud was closing in, but everything seemed okay, when. . ." he paused for dramatic effect, ". . . bugger me backwards, the bloody engine started to conk out! For all the world as if it was running out of fuel, though that's impossible because I told the chaps up there to fill her up."

Will frowned, "Of course, they would hardly have half-filled the tank. By the way, this chap who marked our field, did you catch his name? We should thank him."

Tompkins thought for a moment, "Yesh. He was a corporal. His name was Bo' something."

"Bowen?"

"Yesh, that's the feller. Smart chap. Him and an Irish air mechanic. Very helpful the both of them."

"I bet they were."

"Anyway, there I was with a spluttering engine, and out of the blue a big ole F.E.2 popped up with the observer waving his arms and pointing at your field. So down I came. . . whoops a daisy! Plonk! Pancaked in, I'm afraid. Not much damage, but your sergeant major . . . 'nother splendid chap by the way . . . has her in the hangar. Says she'll have to stay here for a few days while he gets the parts. 'Fraid old Tompkins is going back to Farnborough on the choo-choo. All arranged by your Sergeant Moore . . . 'nother splendid chap by the way."

The ghost of a smile crossed Will's face, "We specialize in splendid chaps. What type of *aer-o-plane* is she, anyway?"

"One of the new Sopwith Scouts. The one everybody is calling the Pup."

Will beamed, "*Really!*"

Tompkins looked into his empty glass, "Yesh. Old Tommy Sopwith isn't going to be very pleased with me. There's only a handful been built. Still on test."

"Oh don't worry about that, old boy," Ives put his arm round him and topped up his glass. "A report is already on its way to Mr. Sopwith saying what a marvelous job you did of saving his aeroplane from serious damage."

"What? Already?"

"It will be with him before you get back. Our splendid Sergeant Moore is typing it as we speak."

Tompkins looked around blearily, "Oh, that's t'riffic, really t'riffic. Here, have a cigar."

Will took Jackson by the arm and walked him away from the bar, "Typing it as we speak?"

Jackson shrugged, "Typed it before he arrived."

Will shook his head, "This has the boss's stamp all over it. How did he get the idea to shanghai a brand new scout? You all seem very confident his plan would work."

"That nice Mrs. Courroyer popped in last night after you took off, and Bowen and McGuigan left very early this morning for Martlesham Heath."

Will puffed a smoke ring at the ceiling, "Even so, it was still a long shot, and damn risky at that."

Jackson sipped his whiskey, "Not really, skipper. They calculated how much fuel he would need to get this far. It's direct on course back to Farnborough, and even if he had run out early or later, he would have come down somewhere nearby. That's partly why Bill and I were up in the F.E.2. If he came down in a farmer's field, we were to find him and drop a message back here for our fellers to go collect him. As it was it worked a treat and we led him in here."

"How much damage did he do landing?"

"Bust his undercarriage and it will need a new prop, but the Technical Sergeant Major will have it ready in a day or two. It will need testing thoroughly, before he will release it to service."

Will nodded thoughtfully, "Of course. We will do it democratically and draw names from a hat," he glanced at their visitor, propped up by Ives at the bar. "Now you have got him plastered, we might could sober him up."

The following day, in the light of a lingering evening, Will stood admiring the trim little Sopwith Pup. Everything about her looked right—the proportion of the biplane wings to the length of the fuselage, the characteristic Sopwith vertical stabilizer and rudder shaped like a single quotation mark, her perky nose-up stance on the big disc wheels, they all promised that at last the British aircraft industry had produced the machine the pilots had demanded for the last year. A mechanic bent under the wing with brush and paint pot putting the finishing touches to the wheel discs, now a bright crimson to match the vertical stabilizer, or "tail-fin" as his British comrades called it. All the machines under Simpson's command sported the distinctive markings.

"Do you think anybody will notice the new paint job when we hand it back, Sergeant Major?"

Cole smiled and touched the side of his nose with a greasy finger, "Might be a while before we are certain it is safe to fly, sir."

Will nodded and took his arm, leading him out of earshot of the mechanics, "I can see how that might be, John. Is there any chance we could lose that Vickers gun and put a Lewis on the center section to fire over the propeller? You know we cannot use incendiary or explosive rounds in the Vickers, but this machine could catch any Zeppelin. I hear on the grapevine it climbs like a homesick angel."

Cole shook his head, "I am sorry sir, that would really be pushing our luck."

Will sighed, "A pity, but you are right of course," he pointed to a B.E.2 standing in front of the hangar. "She will do, after all, she has proved herself." After thorough checks on his machine, Will joined the other pilots on duty that night in the map room. All the chat surrounded Leefe-Robinson's feat.

Bill Ives held up the front page of the *Daily Mail*, "It's bloody amazing, for once they seem to have the facts straight. This chap who wrote most of the story must be a local man. He saw the whole thing, and it ties in pretty well with what you told us, skipper. Apart from the part about witnesses seeing the crew roasting in the flames as if they were writhing in the fires of hell, I would say it tells what happened."

Will took the paper and scanned the front page, "Yes, they have it straight enough. Now who wants to earn themselves a VC?" he glanced around the room at the grinning faces. "Well, crash yourselves a Zep tonight and I will put you down for one."

To their surprise, the German airships had made no appearance by midnight. The conditions appeared perfect for a raid.

"Maybe we've scared them off?" Stan Jackson hazarded.

Bill Ives grunted, "Fat chance. They'll be hellbent on revenge," he glanced at the luminous hands of his watch in the gloom. The lights stayed off to save the pilot's night vision. "Mind you, they better show up soon, it's still getting light before six." He sank into a chair and like the others, started to doze. The shrill ring of the telephone jerked them all to wakefulness.

Will grabbed the receiver, "Yes? Where?" He scribbled notes then slammed the phone down. "We are on, fellers. Two ships reported coming in over Bacton, another just south of Wells." He gave rapid orders, sending his men to patrol various sectors in well-rehearsed patterns. Will stayed on the ground, in reserve to follow up confirmed sightings. As had often been the case, no clear pattern emerged. Reports came in of bombs falling near a village in Norfolk, and then to their amazement, near the town of Guildford well to the south of London.

"Where the hell did he come from?" Will glared at the map. "No sense in me chasing down there now. Somebody else can have that one." The telephone shrilled again, and the Prof snatched it up.

"Enfield? I'll be damned! Very well, Captain Turner will be up in five minutes," Will crashed through the door before he put the phone down. As he ran to his B.E.2, he waved his finger in a circular motion above his head. The mechanics needed no urging. He leaped into his seat. While the mechanic at the propeller went through the starting routine, Will strapped in and made his cockpit checks. Two minutes later, he roared into the air, wincing at the thought of the demands he put on the cold engine. He patted the side of the cockpit and apologized, but he had no choice. The town of Enfield lay no more than fifteen miles to the west, on the Great Cambridge Road leading into London. The River Lea ran parallel to the highway, a perfect signpost to the city itself.

A curtain of searchlights groped around the sky ahead, alerted by the shower of small bombs that had cascaded in and around the town. "Damn!" Will cursed aloud through gritted teeth. The best height he could hope to make by the time he reached the river would be five thousand feet. As he passed over the town, the cockpit blazed with brilliant light. He squeezed his eyes shut but had to open them as he felt the blast of an explosion nearby.

"Not me you idiots!" He waved a fist in helpless rage at the searchlight team and gunners who had caught, and then shelled him in their excitement. He shoved the nose down and jammed the stick over, corkscrewing out of the beam. The searchlight had destroyed his night vision, and he had lost a thousand precious feet. His sight came back slowly. He steered south by his compass, peering over the side in the hope of finding a prominent landmark. The searchlights left him alone, but looking up and forward over the city, he could see they had not found the Zeppelin either. Half an hour into his flight he had achieved eight thousand feet, the height that Leefe-Robinson had caught the hapless SL11 army airship over Cuffley, but tonight only British defenders buzzed over the city. After two hours of fruitless searching, he slapped the side of his cockpit in frustration as he remembered what the town of Enfield was best known for; the ordnance factory where they made the famous Lee Enfield rifles. The Zeppelin had bombed its target and probably turned away from the city. He steered for home, following the railroad tracks and rivers that guided him back to Abbots Roding.

Cold and tired he settled into a glide. The gooseneck flares flickered ahead through his windscreen. He throttled back and applied the controls for a gentle sideslip, more to improve his view than to lose height. The big RAF* motor popped and muttered in the exhausts as it idled. For all that, his sortie had proved a waste of time, at least no bombs had fallen on London, and he had a good landing set-up. The flares neither rose up in

---

* At this point these were the initials of the Royal Aircraft Factory.
The Royal Air Force came into being on the 1st. April 1918.

his vision nor dropped down: a perfect glide path. He flexed his fingers on the control column and started to pull it back as he kicked off the slip. The red flare soaring into the air took a second to register as he concentrated hard on his night landing. His hand jammed the throttle wide at just the moment his wheels touched, an instant's hesitation as he saw the second B.E.2 across his path, then he shut the throttle with a decisive jerk and flicked the magneto off. His right foot had already kicked full rudder.

He almost missed. But his port wingtip caught the rudder of Bill Ives machine, and held it. His airplane lurched left, throwing him against the cockpit side. A moment later the undercarriage collapsed, it had given of its best, but enough was enough. He sat for a moment, then switched off the gas, threw off his safety belt and stepped out of the cockpit. He did not have to jump down. His airplane lay flat on its belly.

"Who the hell left that there?" He stood with hands on hips as the mechanics and Bill Ives rushed up to him.

"Oh, hell's bells, skipper. That was my fault. I pancaked in from twenty feet and bust my undercarriage. We were trying to push it out of the way when you showed up. We had a Very pistol loaded, but the first flare was a dud." Corporal Bowen held up the offending cartridge.

Will shrugged, "Oh well, nobody can be blamed for that. But I would be obliged if we could clear these machines before anybody else piles in."

"That's not likely, skipper," Bill said. "Dizzy came back after an hour with a dud engine. David Highams' fuel tank split and he's back. The Frenchmen have landed at Hainault, Stan is down in a field in Suffolk with Major Simpson in the F.E.2, and Windy force-landed on the beach at Aldeburgh. At least he found a Zep, but they shot lumps out of his machine and he was lucky to get down."

Will did a quick calculation, "Just a cotton picking minute! That means we have a total serviceable strength of zero airplanes."

Bowen nodded, "'Fraid so, sir. We need to get these machines back to the hangars quick to get to work on them."

Will shook his head in disgust, "I declare that is the most rotten luck. What are the odds of that happening?"

The Prof came lurching out of the darkness, leaning heavily on his stick, "Long, but at least nobody got killed." Together the mechanics and pilots set about raising the stranded machines on to makeshift undercarriages and dragged them into the pool of light in front of the hangars.

Will looked up, "I declare it is coming up light already. We will not see any more of Fritz tonight." A scattering of mares' tails, high cirrus cloud, caught the rays from the sun still well below the horizon. They could make out faces and the silhouettes of the other squadron buildings. "I think everybody has earned a few hours rest before we sort this mess out. The pilots and mechanics needed no urging and disappeared into the gloom. Will turned to the Prof and Cole, and had just opened his mouth to speak when they heard the telephone in the squadron office. They all turned. Telephones in the small hours of the morning rarely bring good news. The door flew open and Sergeant Moore stood there, hatless with his tunic undone. He had the receiver still in his hand.

"I don't Adam and Eve* it! Mc Guigan has just reported a Zeppelin coming in over Maldon."

"What?" Will ran to the door, "He must mean going out, surely!"

Moore handed him the phone, "Ask him yourself, sir. He's positive."

"McGuigan, what is going on there? Are you sure he is not heading up the coast?"

"No, sir," Will heard a hard certainty in the Irishman's voice that persuaded him. "He's coming in as sure as I stand here. The sound locater has tracked him coming in from the sea for the last ten minutes. Here, listen." Through the crackle of static, Will heard the unmistakable hum of heavy aeroplane engines, faint but clear over the phone line, as McGuigan held the mouthpiece in the air.

"Jesus!" Will exclaimed.

"Joseph and Mary," McGuigan turned the curse into a blessing.

* Rhyming slang: "believe it."

"Thanks, Mac, good work," Will dropped any military formality in his excitement. He threw the phone at Moore and launched himself down the steps. "Quick, get my machine ready."

The Prof grabbed his arm, "Hold up, what machine? You just crashed yours remember, and everything else is u/s."

Will skidded to a stop and stared around, breathing fast, "I know, I will take a car down to North Weald and . . ." he stopped, and pointed. "No! The Pup. I will take that." The Prof and Cole looked at each other. "It is ready to go, is it not Sergeant Major? The gun is loaded?"

Cole detected an edge in Will's voice. He smiled, "I do believe it is ready for a test flight, and the weather could not be better. The gun is loaded with ball ammunition." They wasted no time. Moore and Cole dragged the little scout from the hangar and jammed chocks under the wheels. Moore helped Will strap in while Cole and the Prof filled a giant brass syringe with gasoline.

Will checked the switches off, closed the air and fuel fine-adjustment levers with his left hand, then pumped up pressure in the fuel tank with the brass-handled pump by his right elbow. "Switches off, fuel on, ready to prime!" The Prof held down the exhaust valves while Cole squirted fuel into each cylinder.

"Switches off?" Cole called. Urgent or not, the correct procedure had to be followed, propellers bite. Will confirmed the ignition as off and the Prof spun the propeller to move the mixture around the cylinders. Moore put his weight on the tail to hold it down.

"Set?"

Will opened the air lever by a third of its travel and checked the fuel fine adjustment lever was closed, "Set!"

"Contact!"

Will dragged the control column back into his stomach, "Contact!" The Prof heaved the propeller round. Smoke belched from around the cowling as he stepped back. The propeller jerked then disappeared in a blur, before slowing as the priming gas burned up. Will eased the fuel lever open, and the engine burst into full-throated life. He bore down on his own impatience, grinding his teeth as he fiddled the two levers until he had the engine idling at 800 rpm. Each movement had to be matched. Too much fuel, or too little and he would strangle or starve the engine. One other advantage of the rotary he had forgotten to mention to the girls: they warmed up fast.

Will checked the windsock. He could just make it out in the semi-darkness. What little breeze it revealed sighed across the field toward him. He pulled down his goggles and crossed his hands in front of his face to wave the chocks away. "Let her go boys!" Cole tugged on the chord that whipped the wooden blocks from in front of the wheels, Moore sprang clear of the tail as Will juggled the engine controls to give full revolutions. The Pup shot forward.

"Don't break this one!" Cole's warning was lost in the roar as the le Rhône engine dragged the little airplane away. It swung left as Will raised the tail.

"Whoa!" He shoved his right foot against the rudder bar to correct as the Pup skittered across the field.

His ground crew watched him disappear, the light fabric covering the wings making the Pup visible against the background as it floated, moth like, into the crisp dawn air. "Gyroscopic precession initiated by the spinning engine and propeller makes it swerve like that," Cole sucked his teeth.

The Prof smiled, "Really? And there's me thinking it's his big feet. Come on, let's get a brew going, this could be a long morning."

Will handled the engine controls without thinking, easing the fuel supply to prevent a rich cut as the engine revs rose. He sat back and reveled in this new machine, "Oh what a beauty!" he stroked the side of the cockpit. She was everything he hoped, and more. The controls felt alive, positive, but at the same time responded to the lightest pressure of hand or foot. The little airplane seemed to fly itself, eager to please, a true pilot's machine. He glanced over the side of his cockpit and gasped. He checked the altimeter, perhaps the gloom of the earth still shrouded by night made it look further away. No, he really was passing four thousand feet, in just a few minutes. This was an incredible performance. The little Sopwith Pup boasted a mere 80 hp, yet it climbed faster than many machines with twice the power.

As he climbed, he flew into the morning. The sun appeared above the horizon ahead, turning the tops of the clouds that still obscured much of the ground into soft shades of purple and cream. Leaning back, he could see the vast dome of the sky fading from a deep blue where a few stars still glinted, through pale lemon to an exquisite pink where the sun caressed the icy cirrus clouds flirting with the stratosphere. The light also sparkled off the sight of the Vickers heavy machine gun mounted in front of his face. It brought him back to reality. He had a job to do.

He checked the altimeter again. The Pup had whisked him to nine thousand feet in minutes. The Zeppelin must be ahead, he trusted McGuigan's judgment. Surely it must be some navigation error that would have been revealed by the daylight. They must have turned back to sea by now, but he could catch them with this little thoroughbred, even if it did mean flying out over the water. He pulled up his coat collar. The air at this height chilled despite the bright sunlight. He glanced down; Maldon lay below to his right, still in darkness. He could see for miles over the sea, the clouds only clung to the land. He quartered the sky, raising his gloved hand to peer between the fingers against the glare of the rising sun. Nothing.

He made a wide circle over the town, not even thinking about flying, the Pup seemingly responding to his thoughts. He made quick calculations. If the Zep had turned away to sea again a minute after passing over their watching station, it would still be only fifteen miles away. He should be able to see it, but it simply was not out there. It could only be over the land: but why? He frowned behind his goggles. It would be suicidal to be over land, in broad daylight. It made no sense, but many things in this war made no sense. He turned away from the sea and turned south. He would search inland. Five minutes later, he turned west, held that course for another ten minutes, and then turned northeast, still holding his altitude. His head swiveled all around and up into the sky. He rolled the Pup from side to side and nudged the nose to and fro to search the blind spots. Still no sign. Could McGuigan have been mistaken? Will shook his head angrily. It was a ridiculous notion, it was impossible that a trained man, and one of their best, could mistake a Zeppelin for anything else. No, it was here, lurking in the shadows. He reached the end of his beat, and stuck his head over the side to pick up a landmark as he rolled into a climbing turn to the right. He looked down and back through a break in the clouds for a significant feature: a road, a river, a familiar wood. Instead, he saw the stern of a Zeppelin still exposed as it slipped into the clouds, like the tail of a fish sliding into the reeds.

His hands and feet had the Pup racking round before his brain had registered what he saw. No wonder he had not seen it, the Zeppelin was way below him, probably only at three thousand feet, taking advantage of the cloud cover to work inland. He forced the nose down, juggling the controls to stop the engine over-revving. The slipstream scraped a rising note from the wires that rose to a howl at the top of the scale as the speed increased. It felt as if the huge propeller acted as a brake, the Pup standing on it as he hurtled down, but under perfect control. Will eased out of the dive before he dropped into the cloud. It would be too easy to unwittingly ram the Zeppelin in the glowing murk inside. Instead, he skimmed above the cloudbank trying to judge where the airship might emerge. He reached around the windscreen and cocked his gun and, as he did, he stared in wonder at the sight before him. For a few moments, he did not connect it with the Zeppelin. The flat surface of the cloud had started to heave up and then roll in on itself, creating the impression that he flew between two horizontal whirlpools. The effect seemed unreal, but not as unreal as the man standing five hundred feet in front of his airplane with his hand outstretched, pointing toward him.

The bullet ricocheting off his engine cowling was real enough though. Will reacted so fast the next round punched through thin air. The Pup disappeared. The gunner in the upper hull position of the Zeppelin threw up his hands in disgust at the agility of the British fighter airplane as it flicked out of sight. The airship cruised through the cloud tops, most of the hull submerged in the gray mist, the turbulence its bulk caused in the air creating the bizarre phenomenon Will had just witnessed. He had come up on it at just the moment its back broke the surface of the cloud top.

Will made swift adjustments to the engine controls to ease back to idle speed, placed the stick and rudder as near to central as he could judge, and checked his fuel pressure. *Trust your machine*, his own mantra came to him as he dropped through the cloud. The safety belt cut into him suggesting he hung upside down, but he resisted the urge to try to right the machine. His world had shrunk to the white mist that surrounded him, stealing any visual cues. The flick roll into the cloud had left him disorientated, but he knew the little Sopwith, like any airplane, wanted to fly and given time would find its way back to level flight if left to its own devices. England reappeared abrupt as a light being switched on, but at an angle above his head. He popped from the cloud into bright sunlight. The Pup glided almost inverted, nose down.

"Find the horizon and roll for it," his own advice in his head again, and easier said than done. He found it under the nose and at a sharp angle. He pushed the stick over, the Pup rolled neatly upright without drama. A quick adjustment of the engine levers coaxed the engine back to life, quickly winding up to its joyful shout as Will scrambled into a climb. The

Zeppelin would surely burst from the cloud striving for height now the crew knew they had been found. To his total astonishment, the nose thrust out of the clouds at his own level. He gasped as it slid into the clear air a half a mile ahead. No matter that he had flown in an airship, and stood beneath them on the ground, seen as another craft in the air the Zeppelin looked massive, impossible: longer than a battleship, it floated effortlessly through the ragged clouds, the rising sun drenching its bulbous flanks in a soft rosy glow: it looked beautiful. He opened fire.

Will ignored the gunsight; the hull of the airship filled the sky before him as he bore down it. Tracers arced from the gun position behind the giant tail fin, but Will pushed in enough rudder to make the Pup skid sideways, confusing the gunner, the tracers streaking away behind the little biplane. Will knew he could not miss. He approached from the rear quarter, at a shallow angle to bring his single Vickers gun to bear. He aimed at the widest point of the hull where he guessed he would be in a narrow corridor of air where the gunners in the gondolas could not elevate their weapons far enough, and the man perched on the Zeppelin's back could not reach him from above. The Sopwith Kauper interrupter gear slowed Will's rate of fire so each detonation in the breech sounded like the deliberate blow of a hammer on an anvil. He held the firing lever, knowing that the long burst stitching along the flank of the airship would probably have no effect at all. The conventional solid bullets had been loaded to test the gun feed, not to set a Zeppelin on fire, but he reasoned that each bullet would rip through the gasbags and out the other side, if he made enough holes perhaps he might effectively sink the Zeppelin as the gas seeped out.

He swerved at the last second. Glancing back as he wheeled away, he caught a glimpse of faces in the control gondola, before the next cloudbank swallowed him. Again he throttled back, but this time the primitive *inclinometer* fitted to his instrument board, not much more than a spirit level, helped him keep the wings level as he shuffled cautiously around a blind turn. He shot out from the cloud with his hand on the firing lever. The Zeppelin had gone.

"What the hell?" Will's head spun all around, searching desperately. Losing a Zeppelin at night was understandable, losing something that big in daylight smacked of carelessness. It took him several seconds to realize that he had become disorientated in the cloud, flying back the way he came. He spun the Pup around in its own length, but he could still see no sign of the airship. He rushed through the cloud canyons, now brilliant in the rising sun, swerving around the solid banks of mist, dashing headlong through wispy tatters trailing across his path. A movement caught his eye, a black F.E.2 biplane a thousand feet above approaching from the north.

He throttled back and sank below the clouds into clear air, in and out of sunlight. He reasoned that he must have caught up with the airship by now. Flying the Pup, he did not need to cling to every inch of altitude, he could climb as he needed. His best chance would be to spot his target from below as it slipped in and out of the cloud. He looked down to check his position, and swore. The German airship was below him again, now less distinct against the ground, moving slowly above the fields and hedgerows, casting a giant long shadow as the morning sun lit the land at last.

He throttled back, the implication of the shadow now obvious, the ship had sunk to the ground, even as he watched he saw it stop, and slowly swing before toppling half on to its side, as if weary after its long flight. Will shook his head in disgust at his failure to realize it had been descending from the moment it came in over the coast. No wonder he had trouble in keeping track, he had assumed it would be climbing for an altitude no British airplane could reach. He sized up the field where the Zeppelin lay like a beached whale. The surface appeared to be blackened stubble, left after the wheat had been harvested the week before, perfect, better than his home field. He side-slipped into wind, and dropped the Pup neatly to the ground, blipping the engine on the cut-out switch to keep it alive. He had imagined that one day he might send a Zeppelin crew to a fiery death; he had not expected to receive their surrender. Will switched off and hopped to the ground, stripping off his coat and flying helmet and tossing them into the cockpit. He glanced back and saw the F.E.2, now clearly visible as the machine flown by Stan Jackson and Simpson, gliding in behind him. They must have repaired whatever had forced them down during the night, and seen the airship on their way back to the field. He turned and set off toward the grounded Zeppelin at a trot, hampered by his thick flying boots.

The crumpled nose of the Zeppelin rested against a tree a hundred feet from a farmhouse, the hull stretched across a hedgerow into the adjoining field. He could see people moving away from the ship, a second group running from the farmhouse and a few figures under the hull. He broke into a run; the men under the ship must be trying to set it on fire. He wanted the ship intact. As he approached the main group a single figure, a tall man with thick blond hair under his cap, moved to cut him off, his arm outstretched.

"Halt! Stay there!" The German officer held a Mauser pistol. Will stopped and stared, then slowly raised his hands.

"Martin?"

Friedmann held the pistol steady, its long barrel aimed at Will's chest. "Well, well: it's *Captain* Turner. I am not surprised, but I admit I am disappointed. I assumed you were a gentleman, and that your sudden departure from Tondern was for personal reasons."

Will shrugged, "It was. I personally wanted to stop you killing my people."

"But a spy, Will, that is no occupation for a man of your skills," Friedmann sounded genuinely hurt.

"I am not making excuses, but I took no pleasure in deceiving you. It was a job that had to be done."

Friedmann nodded, his face grim, "Well, now I have a job I have to do. I am firing my ship and there is nothing you can do about it. Stay where you are and keep your hands up." He moved the muzzle to one side, "and your friends can do the same. Stand still gentlemen and also raise your hands please."

Jackson and Simpson had caught up but slowed to a walk as they came up to Will. Stan raised his hands but Simpson leaned forward with his hands on his knees. "Get stuffed, I'm too knackered," his breath came in gasps. He straightened and looked at Will and Stan. "I don't suppose either of you thought to bring a gun?" They shook their heads. "No, me neither."

Friedmann allowed himself a smile, "How very British, but it makes no difference now: look." The small group of men under the ship could be seen running as flames blossomed under the hull. Will expected an inferno of burning gas and fuel, but instead the flames ran up the sides of the ship, the fabric covering burning away and falling in great flakes to reveal the twisted frame beneath. Smoke rose into the air but the end of the Zeppelin was marked more by a tidy bonfire than an explosive con-flagration.

The separate groups gathered around Friedmann and the three British officers. The people Will had seen coming from the farmhouse were obviously the farmer, his wife and their three children. The youngest in his mother's arms while the next oldest clung to the hand of one of the German sailors; her parents too shocked by their rude awakening to comment.

Friedmann turned to the farmer, "Sir, I must apologize for having my crew drag you from your beds, but I was afraid that you might be trapped in your house by the fire when we burned our ship. As you can see, it has done no harm."

The countryman stared at the RFC officers, "Shouldn't you be doing something about this? Arrest 'em or something?"

Will pointed to the field gate where the village constable had appeared, bumping over the stubble on his bike as he wobbled toward them. "I think that is a job for the civil power." Several of the German crew stared when they heard his voice.

"Will? What are you doing here?" Georg Klaas stepped forward.

Friedmann turned to his navigating officer, "Yes, Klaas, meet the *real* Mr. Turner. The one you met was an imposter."

Klaas shrugged, "All is fair in love and war," he clicked his heels and saluted.

Friedmann turned to the farmer, "Sir, we have no choice, we surrender ourselves and what is left of our ship to you. It is your land we have come down on, and I think it is correct. At least I know who you are," he frowned at Will as he spoke, then turned his pistol so he held it by the barrel and offered it to the farmer. "I have no sword to offer, I hope this will do."

The Essex man looked at Friedmann in surprise, his mouth open. Will spoke, "Captain, I do not think it is a good idea to hand a loaded pistol to a civilian."

Friedmann laughed, "Loaded? Who said it is loaded?" He snapped the breech open to reveal the empty chamber and magazine. "Really, Will, I thought you knew me better than that. Don't you think that carrying a loaded pistol in the control car might be rather dangerous?"

"Damn!" Will shook his head in disgust. "You sure had me fooled."

Friedmann smiled as the delighted farmer took the Mauser as his souvenir, "Touché, Captain Turner."

CHAPTER 30

The Black Swan Hotel, Essex, England

Will stood with his cousin, Kate Penrose, outside in the yard of the country hotel. A chill November wind whipped around them carrying spots of rain, stinging their faces. Kate put her arm through Will's and huddled closer to him. She looked up, "Thanks for a lovely evening, Will."

He looked back at the door of The Black Swan. Loud laughter came from inside where the rest of the party struggled into coats and hats. "Yes, they put on a good spread for a country hotel."

"Well, so they should, the amount of custom you chaps have put their way over the last few months."

He laughed, "Yes, but I am sure the new squadron at our field will carry on the grand tradition set by our boys. Besides, we had a lot to celebrate tonight."

Simpson had arranged an informal dinner party for his men and all those local people who had helped them through the summer months. He had considered a more formal occasion at a London hotel, but with Ives, Jackson, and the recovering Jankowski hopping around on crutches, he knew the evening was likely to turn into an hilarious and drunken party. He also agreed with the the Prof, who had pointed out that country people like Constable Mick Horne and Ted, the railroad crossing keeper, would not feel comfortable in the Ritz or Savoy.

Kate nodded, "You can say that again. The Prof getting his wings *and* his own squadron, Major Simpson promoted to Staff Officer, and you managing to get out of another scrape," she poked him in the chest with her finger.

Will pushed a wayward curl away from her forehead, then pointed to the door as Bill Ives and Stan Jackson staggered out with their arms around each other, "And not forgetting that Bill and Stan have finally finished checking bullets."

Jacquieline Courroyer joined them, "That beats anything as far as they are concerned." She fumbled in her bag for a cigarette; Will lit it for her.

"So did you get to the bottom of why Martin Friedmann turned back?" Will asked. She had travelled to the prisoner of war camp where he had joined other captured German naval officers, to interview him and Georg Klaas.

"Yes, it was much as you suspected. Friedmann would not go into detail but his navigator, Klaas told me everything. His actual words were, 'What difference does it make now?' " Jac drew on her cigarette, "this was their second mission since they had worked up the new crew and moved down to Belgium. They had come in over the Suffolk coast where they had a set to with one of our machines. That was Windy Gale we think. They shook him off and headed inland where they bombed Enfield and then headed north to attack Coventry."

"That would explain why I could not find them."

"Exactly. They then set off for home; but somewhere over the coast, they were picked up by a searchlight and heavily archied. They took some near misses and splinters, wrecked one engine and damaged another, and punctured most of their gasbags. An hour from dawn they were battling a headwind with two engines out of action, losing height and still only thirty miles out to sea. Friedmann had to make a decision. Klaas calculated that they would come down in the middle of the North Sea, no matter what they threw overboard, where they would either all drown because they carry no lifesaving equipment, or at best be rescued by a British ship and taken prisoner anyway. Friedmann made the decision to save his crew."

"That sounds typical of the man."

Jac nodded, "Yes, that was what Klaas said."

"He still took a chance though," Will said. "If it had been somebody armed with the usual mix of ammunition, instead of me, they might have burned anyway."

"They planned to crash-land near the coast in darkness; the ship was sinking all the while. They were surprised to make it as far they did. Friedmann wanted to get past the coastal defenses to give them a chance to get down in open country and fire the ship. They certainly did not plan on flying in near full daylight."

"His plan worked, though I nearly wrecked it. I honestly wondered if it were some super ship filled with helium gas or such."

Jac shook her head, "The holes you punched in it made little difference, the gas was leaking out so fast. That's why it hardly burned on the ground."

Will scratched his chin, "You have to admit; he is a decent man."

Jac shrugged, "For a Hun, I suppose he is, and a good captain. I'm not certain he thinks you are a decent chap though."

"He will get over it. At least he survived, unlike the others we have roasted since then."

"Yes, he did say that his wife sends you her best regards and thanks you for bringing him down alive."

Will laughed, "Good, that makes up for being considered a bounder," he inclined his head toward the pub. "Are you girls all set with rooms for tonight?"

"Yes, I'm sharing with Sister Crowley, though I don't doubt she and Ernie Simpson will be sharing a last nightcap in the saloon bar, and you are sharing with Vicky I believe, Kate?"

Kate coughed, "And Marie has a room all to herself. All on her lonesome of course."

"Of *course!*" Jac nudged Kate in the ribs and gave her a knowing smile. Kate looked up at Will, her face a mix of curiosity and concern.

"Do you mind that Marie and Jean have become so close?"

Will squeezed her hand, "No, I really do not. Though I am concerned for her because he is in a dangerous occupation. I fear this will all end in tears. And I cannot say I am delighted at the prospect of her and Vicky heading off to France."

Jac snorted, "Young love, Will. Where he goes, she is bound to follow."

Through the window Will could see Marie and Jean in deep conversation with Vicky and Henri Calmette, "Yes, I accept that, but where Marie goes, my sister goes as well. Like the three musketeers."

"Yes, but this new American Ambulance Corps sounds like a smashing idea. I wish I could join," Kate sounded envious.

"Well, if there is trouble to be found, my sister will find it."

Jac took a last drag on her cigarette, dropped it and ground it out with her heel. "Don't worry about your cousin's love life, Kate. He's got his glamorous American actress waiting for him. She's a smasher."

Kate giggled and tried to pinch him through his heavy greatcoat, "All the girls are jealous, Will. Have you heard from Matty recently?"

He looked down his nose at her and smiled, "Well, if it is any of your business, I get about a letter every week."

Kate snapped her fingers, "Damn." She was about to probe more but Dizzy joined them.

He looked down the road toward the railroad crossing, "Any sign of the transport back to the field, Will?"

"It will be here directly."

Jac touched his arm, "Before you go dashing off. Why were you in such a stew when you got back from the War Office yesterday? Is it a big military secret?"

"No," Will grunted. "I have the same problem as dear old Uncle George Brett. I did one useful job on my mission, and saw something that is of great importance, but now nobody will believe me. They even suggested I was hung over. So it is up to me to shout it from the rooftops in the hope somebody will take notice, or at least will not be too surprised when it shows up."

They fell silent and looked at him, "Well?" Dizzy demanded.

"It was the biggest damn airplane I ever saw. When I was in the Zeppelin hangar, I found it, or parts of it anyway. I believe what I saw was a model, or a full size mock-up. They have no factory there to build it. I think it was just somewhere with enough space for the engineers to lay out their plans, but the blueprints in there leave me in no doubt the Zeppelin company are building a giant machine. They call it a *Reiseflug*."

"So why won't they believe you at the War Office?" Jac asked.

"I think because it is just so big, they do not believe it can be done."

"How big is big?" Dizzy said.

"I paced out the chalk marks on the floor. I estimate a wingspan over one hundred feet."

Dizzy jerked his head back in surprise, "Good grief! And the power?"

"Four Mercedes in tandem pairs from what I saw on the blueprints. Along with an enclosed cabin more like the bridge of an oceanliner, and gun positions in the nose, and above and below the fuselage."

Dizzy shook his head in wonder, "That is going to be a formidable machine. It will be the dickens of a job to find in the dark. Big as you say it is, it will be a fraction of the size of a Zep, twice as fast and will probably carry as many bombs."

"Oh well, if this frightful thing turns up and rains death and destruction down on us, perhaps they will promote you to Brigadier General and send you to Australia like George Brett," Jac smiled.

"Yes, they probably will, because I declare I will run around shouting, 'I told you so.' The good news is that I doubt they will be able to build many," he grinned, "'sides, we plan to end it before they can get into production. Ain't that right, Dizzy?"

Dizzy laughed, "Yes. On our own if we have to," he pointed to the door of the pub. "Hold up chaps, here comes the law."

Mick Horne, the policeman, strolled across to them. He wore a tweed jacket and bow tie, his usual cheerful face now beaming with the effects of several pints of good English ale. He winked at the ladies, "Evenin' all," he looked up at the sky where the ragged clouds tumbled along driven by the impatient west wind. "Looks like we're safe from the Zeps tonight."

Will looked up, a full moon ducked in and out of the gaps, "Yes, this wind would blow them back to Russia, and there is rain coming in later. We can sleep easy tonight."

Mick followed Will's gaze, then he turned to him, "But they will be back?"

"Oh yes, despite the losses. Strasser will not give up. That man is a fanatic," he looked up again, he could see stars between the clouds. "But we will be waiting for him."

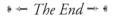 *The End*

HISTORICAL NOTE

From September 1916, the situation for the German Naval and Army airship fleets changed dramatically. Up until that point, they had attacked almost without hindrance in the face of a weak and disorganized defense. By the beginning of 1917 they had lost four more ships shot down in flames by aircraft, and a fifth, L33 commanded by Captain Böcker was forced to crash land in Essex after being hit by anti-aircraft fire. His was the only crew to survive. After setting fire to the wreck, they were arrested by the local constabulary.

Undeterred, Peter Strasser set about the construction of a new generation of super Zeppelin, dubbed the "Height Climbers." Despite their remarkable performance these new ships had little success and suffered more losses. Will Turner's words proved prophetic. In early August 1918, Strasser personally led a large force of Zeppelins across the North Sea in the brand new L70. He mistimed the approach and the fleet was seen in the late-evening light. Major Egbert Cadbury and Captain Robert Leckie were indeed waiting for him in a DH4 biplane, a type later to gain fame as the original Airmail carrier. L70, like so many of her predecessors, was shot down in flames, ending the life and career of the man who had, almost single-handed, driven the concept of aerial bombardment from airships.

Never again would the German Imperial Navy mount a serious attack on England, though Zeppelins continued to be used with the High Seas Fleet for scouting. However, even keeping them hundreds of miles from the British coast did not save them. Audacious attacks by flying boats, and fighter aircraft launched from lighters towed behind fast naval destroyers, burned them in the air and in their sheds.

Conceived as the original terror weapon, designed to strike fear into the British people, they failed on all counts, causing relatively few casualties and doing little damage in return for the resources committed to them. In fact, some historians argue that they worked against the German war effort by alerting the British to the dangers of aerial attack, and forcing them to organize an effective defense that was already in place when the far more dangerous threat from the conventional bomber force appeared in 1917. The machine that Will Turner saw in the shed at Tondern was a Zeppelin *Staaken* R-Type giant bomber, fortunately never built in large numbers, but successful in its raids on England along with the ubiquitous "Gotha" twin-engine bomber.

Most of the characters in the book are fictitious, with the notable exception of William Leefe-Robinson V.C., Guy Gaunt (sometimes suggested as the real model for the fictional James Bond), Peter Strasser and his nemesis, Admiral Sir Percy Scott, an officer never really given the credit he deserved for his part in defeating the Zeppelin menace. Sir Percy, an expert in naval gunnery, came out of retirement to reorganize the British defenses. His first problem was to stop the ridiculous inter-service rivalry between the army and navy that hampered all attempts to mount an effective response. With the energy of a man half his age, he slashed through red tape, deployed resources effectively and perhaps most important recognized that a machine gun-equipped airplane was the most effective way of destroying an airship.

For those interested in the Zeppelin campaign, I thoroughly recommend: *The Zeppelin in Combat* by Douglas H. Robinson, published by Schiffer, and *The Air Defence of Britain 1914–1918* by Christopher Cole and E. F. Cheesman, published by Putnam.

About the Author

Chris Davey has been involved with aviation all his life. His first flight was in a Royal Air Force de Havilland Chipmunk as a young Air Cadet with the British Air Training Corps. It was while a member of this organization that he was selected to join the International Air Cadet Exchange and traveled to the U.S. as part of the British contingent as guests of the United States Air Force and the Civil Air Patrol. This visit established friendships that continue to this day, and a connection with the U.S. that ultimately led to the Will Turner aviation fiction series being published by Lucky Press, LLC of Ohio.

Chris is an active member of the de Havilland Moth Club, helping to organize their events in the UK, and also of the Cambridge Flying Group, a unique organization still training pilots using the Tiger Moth biplane. He has been an EAA member since 1994. Having established a successful business, Chris found himself in the fortunate position of being able to start training toward his PPL on the Tiger Moth. With a first solo finally in sight, he went for his medical confident he was in good shape, only to find he had a serious heart defect requiring immediate life-saving surgery. Now fully recovered and with his medical at last issued, Chris has the perfect answer for those who argue that flying is dangerous: it saved his life.

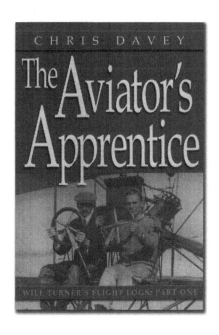

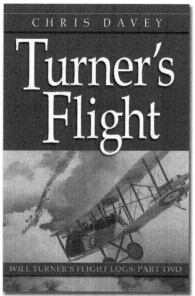

Also by Chris Davey . . .

The Aviator's Apprentice

"Will Turner is in his early twenties and desperate to fly in Chris Davey's *The Aviator's Apprentice*. The century is young and aviation is just beginning. Will is in Florida, hoping to make a name as a pilot and aviation engineer. When Europe is plunged into World War I, he is commissioned in the Royal Flying Corps where his ability and bravery are tested to the limit.

"*The Aviator's Apprentice* is a tightly woven and highly recommended novel that incorporates historical as well as fictional characters in an authentically backgrounded and detailed adventure story set in the early years of aviation." –Midwest Book Review

Turner's Flight

By the autumn of 1915 the airmen of the Royal Flying Corps are struggling to perform their task in support of the men in the trenches, against the threat of the deadly new Fokker eindekker monoplanes. Increasingly well organised, the German Air Service is inflicting terrible casualties in what becomes known as the Fokker Scourge.

Against this background Will Turner, Anglo-American pioneer aviator, arrives at a demoralised squadron to take command of "A" Flight, with a brief to find a solution to the losses. As well as fighting battles in the air, he finds himself in conflict on the ground with his harsh, and increasingly erratic commanding officer, while facing treachery from an unexpected source.

For More Information on
THE WILL TURNER FLIGHT LOGS AVIATION SERIES
visit

www.TurnerLogs.com

Articles, such as "The Rotary Revolution"
Facts about "The Aviators"
Photos, drawings and information on "The Aeroplanes"

Excerpts from:
The Aviator's Apprentice
Turner's Flight
Turner's Defense

Also, a character list and author updates